Nemoville
and Other French Scientific Romances

also translated and introduced by Brian Stableford:

Anonymous: Sâr Dubnotal vs. Jack the Ripper; *Anthologies*: News from the Moon; The Germans on Venus; The Supreme Progress; The World Above the World; Nemoville; *Henri Allorge*: The Great Cataclysm; *Cyprien Bérard*: The Vampire Lord Ruthwen; *Richard Bessière*: The Gardens of the Apocalypse; *Albert Bleunard*: Ever Smaller; *Félix Bodin*: The Novel of the Future; *Alphonse Brown*: City of Glass; *André Caroff*: The Terror of Madame Atomos; *Félicien Champsaur*: The Human Arrow; *Charles Derennes*: The People of the Pole; *Alfred Driou*: The Adventures of a Parisian Aeronaut; *Renée Dunan*: Baal; *Henri Duvernois*: The Man Who Found Himself; *Achille Eyraud*: Voyage to Venus; *Henri Falk*: The Age of Lead; *Paul Féval*: Anne of the Isles; The Black Coats ('Salem Street; The Invisible Weapon; The Parisian Jungle; The Companions of the Treasure; Heart of Steel; The Cadet Gang; The Sword-Swallower); John Devil; Knightshade; Revenants; Vampire City; The Vampire Countess; The Wandering Jew's Daughter; *Paul Féval, fils*: Felifax, the Tiger-Man; *Octave Joncquel & Théo Varlet*: The Martian Epic; *Gustave Kahn*: The Tale of Gold and Silence; *Jean de La Hire*: The Nyctalope vs. Lucifer; The Nyctalope on Mars; Enter the Nyctalope; *Lamothe-Langon*: The Virgin Vampire; *Gabriel de Lautrec*: The Vengeance of the Oval Portrait; *Georges Le Faure & Henri de Graffigny*: The Extraordinary Adventures of a Russian Scientist Across the Solar System (2 vols.); *Gustave Le Rouge*: The Vampires of Mars; *Jules Lermina*: Panic in Paris; Mysteryville; The Secret of Zippelius; *José Moselli*: Illa's End; *Marie Nizet*: Captain Vampire; *Henri de Parville*: An Inhabitant of the Planet Mars; *Gaston de Pawlowski*: Journey to the Land of the 4th Dimension; *Georges Pellerin*: The World in 2000 Years; *P.-A. Ponson du Terrail*: The Vampire and the Devil's Son; *Maurice Renard*: The Blue Peril; Doctor Lerne; The Doctored Man; A Man Among the Microbes; The Master of Light; *Jean Richepin*: The Wing; *Albert Robida*: The Clock of the Centuries; The Adventures of Saturnin Farandoul; Chalet in the Sky; *J.-H. Rosny Aîné*: The Givreuse Enigma; The Mysterious Force; The Navigators of Space; Vamireh; The World of the Variants; The Young Vampire; *Marcel Rouff*: Journey to the Inverted World; *Han Ryner*: The Superhumans; *Jacques Spitz:* The Eye of Purgatory; *Kurt Steiner*: Ortog; *C.-F. Tiphaigne de la Roche*: Amilec; *Théo Varlet*: The Xenobiotic Invasion; *Paul Vibert*: The Mysterious Fluid; *Villiers de l'Isle-Adam*: The Scaffold; The Vampire Soul; *Philippe Ward & S. Miller*: The Song of Montségur.

Nemoville
and Other French Scientific Romances

translated, annotated and introduced by
Brian Stableford

A Black Coat Press Book

Visit our website at www.blackcoatpress.com

ISBN 978-1-61227-070-8. First Printing. January 2012. Published by Black Coat Press, an imprint of Hollywood Comics.com, LLC, P.O. Box 17270, Encino, CA 91416.

Table of Contents

Introduction

This is the fifth anthology of stories relevant to the early development of French speculative fiction that I have assembled for Black Coat Press, following *News from the Moon* (2007), *The Germans on Venus* (2009) *The Supreme Progress* (2011) and *The World Above the World* (2011).[1] It continues the work of filling out a representative cross-section of the works done in that genre in the 19th and early 20th century.

The first story included, "Voyages dans le microcosme, par un Disciple Moderne de Pythagore," here translated as "Voyages in the Microcosm, by a Modern Disciple of Pythagoras," appeared in the collection *Poliergie, ou mélange de littérature et poésie* [Polyergy: Medley of Literature and Poetry] (1757). It is a very marginal precursor of the French genre of *roman scientifique* (scientific fiction or scientific romance), and really belongs to an earlier genre, being one of numerous satirical *contes philosophiques* inspired by Voltaire. It extrapolates the use of changes of scale pioneered in the latter's *Micromégas* (1752) in an interesting fashion. There is a weak sense in which it is the ancestral text of modern microcosmic romances, but it still cleaves to the mystical neo-Platonic notion of the microcosm/macrocosm dichotomy, in which the former term (human being) is supposedly reflected in the entire universe (the "Great Man"), and it is actually more interesting as a pioneering venture in the exploration of the "inner space" of the human psyche than as a mere exercise in viewpoint shrinkage. Its Swiss author, Emerich de Vattel (1714-1767), produced several other exercises in a similarly lively and eccentric vein, including an early exploration of the hypo-

---

[1] Respectively ISBN 9781932983890, 9781934543566, 9781935558828 and 9781612270029.

thetical world-view of ants and a tongue-in-cheek prospectus for an "elixir de livres" [elixir of books].

Alfred Bonnardot's "Archeopolis" was reprinted in his collection *Fantaisies multicolores* [Multicolored Fantasies] (1859), but most of the stories in that collection were first published in a periodical called the *Abeille impériale* between 1855 and 1857, and the dating of "Archeopolis" strongly suggests that it was written in 1857. That predates the boom in the popularization of science that took place in France in the 1860s, and which gave rise to a corollary boom in fiction, occasioning the first popularization of the term *roman scientifique* (primarily in connection with the early work of Jules Verne). "Archeopolis" might not have been sufficiently widely read to serve as a significant inspiration to very many writers in the nascent genre, but it certainly laid down an important template in its early pages, which describe Paris in ruins being picked over by future antiquarians. Indeed, that image became something of a key fascination for French writers, recurring in Alfred Franklin's *Les Ruines de Paris en 4875* (1875), a translation of which I hope to include in the next anthology in this series; Edmond Haraucourt's *Traversée de Paris* (1904), which I intend to include in an imminent collection of translations of Haraucourt's generic work; and Henri Allorge's *Le Grand Cataclysme* (1922)[2], to name but a few.

As might be inferred from the story, Alfred Bonnardot (1808-1884) was a notable antiquarian himself, at least in the realm of books; he wrote the first significant text-book on the repair and restoration of old books, which remained standard for many years—one of two books of his to be translated into English in the 19th century, the other offering an extended tongue-in-cheek character sketch of a Parisian bibliophile. His fiction is almost all humorous, with a certain satirical bite, and "Archeopolis" is no exception, save for its remarkable imaginative range. Although Paris has not yet fallen into ruins, the

---

[2] translated in a Black Coat Press edition as *The Great Cataclysm,* ISBN 9781612270265.

latter part of the story contains some remarkable prophetic hints in its brief but telling analysis of the reasons for its fall, as a result of the social decadence of the early 21st century.

"Archeopolis" and the third story in the collection, *La Commune en l'an 2073: au bout du fossé!*, here translated as "All the Way:[3] The Commune in 2073," published under the signature R. de Maricourt in 1874, both illustrate the difficulty that early authors of futuristic fiction had, in that the only available literary license that they had readily available for exploring possible futures was to embed the relevant image in a visionary dream. That stratagem carries the obvious penalty of giving the conclusion of the story an inevitably bathetic effect, but even if the let-down itself could be excused, it is very often the case that the dreamer wakes up just at the point when the story is reaching its most interesting phase, building a crescendo of complication that the formula relieves the author from the responsibility of thinking through.

Bonnardot had, in fact, done what he had set out to do once he had explained the ruination of Paris and reached his climactic joke about the potential misunderstandings of archaeology, but Maricourt's story gives every indication of having been envisaged as a more extensive work, with which the author lost patience and from whose further development he simply chickened out. Had he not done so, the story might be now far better known, as one of the earliest to feature a humanoid automaton—what was later to become known as a robot. Like Bonnardot, Maricourt provides some very striking futuristic imagery, especially in the context of his description of a grotesquely overpopulated Paris in which the streets have been reduced to mere gutters because the houses are so densely packed, and all travel is necessarily by air. Although he scrupulous acknowledge the fact that he had borrowed one of his

---

[3] "All the way" is, admittedly, a rather anodyne translation of *au bout du fossé*, whose French use is mostly confined to the cautionary aphorism *au bout du fosse, la culbute* [roughly, "at the end of the ditch, the ignominious fall"].

key images from a skit in the English *Cornhill Magazine*, his elaborate development of what was simply a passing mention in the *Cornhill* piece, of the extremes to which a society devoted to the principle of equality might have to go, is both amusing and scathing.

"R. de Maricourt" was one of the versions of his name used as a signature by Comte René du Mesnil de Maricourt (1829-1893), who was already well-known in 1874 as an unusually versatile writer, having made his debut as a novelist with *Lucie, épisode de l'histoire* (1860). *Marcien, ou le Magicien d'Antioche* (1866) similarly treats an episode of ancient history not far removed from the raw material of the Golden Legend from a sternly realist viewpoint, but the novel that immediately preceded his skeptical reaction to the Paris Commune of 1871 was *Une femme à bord* (1873), a contemporary romance set in Brittany and dedicated to Flaubert. In later life, Maricourt acquired a certain reputation as a scholar of the occult, although even contemporary reviewers observed that *Souvenirs d'un magnétiseur* (1884) was a work of fiction lightly disguised as a memoir. Like Bonnardot—with whom he was almost certainly acquainted—Maricourt was actually more interested in archeology, and published serious nonfiction in that field.

In 1889, when Louis Figuier took over the editorship of the popular science magazine *La Science Illustrée*, he soon began running feuilletons as a regular feature under the rubric of *roman scientifique*, beginning with a short story by Jules Verne and continuing with reprinted works by such authors as Louis Boussenard, Albert Robida and "Charles Epheyre" (Charles Richet), as well as original works by authors who had previously published in the field, such as Alphonse Brown and Albert Bleunard. The first piece of fiction he published—Joseph Montet's "Le Triomphe de la science," one of several stories of the period poking fun at early attempts by the food industry to develop cheap substitutes for standard natural products—did not appear under that heading, being labeled as a *fantaisie humoristique* [humorous fantasy], but all the rest did.

At the end of 1889, Figuier published the first original work in his series—the first of three serials by the popular Vernian writer Alphonse Brown. "Les insectes révélateurs," here translated as "The Tell-tale Insects," was the shortest of the three serials, and something of a departure from the normal pattern of Brown's work, attempting to combine a blatant exercise in the popularization of science (entomology in this instance) with a story-arc borrowed from Edgar Allan Poe—a powerful influence on French imaginative fiction in the latter half of the 19th century. The resultant hybrid is not entirely successful, but it is an interesting literary experiment. The longest of Brown's serials for *La Science Illustrée* is available in a Black Coat Press translation as *City of Glass* (2011)[4], and that volume contains an extensive introduction to the author and his work, which there is no point in repeating here. I hope to translate the remaining item for the next anthology in this series.

Not long after Figuier began running feuilletons as a regular feature of *La Science Illustrée*, the other leading magazine of the same sort, *La Science Française*, followed suit. The editor of *La Science Française*, Émile Gautier, published one story of his own in *La Science Illustrée*, "Le *Désiré*" [the name of a hypothetical submarine], but he does not appear to have anything of that sort for his own magazine. The most striking thing about the fiction published in the latter periodical, however, is how very different it was from that published by Figuier. With the exception of Gautier's story, Figuier seems to have scrupulously avoided fiction dealing with future wars, although it was a popular theme of futuristic fiction at the time, but Gautier seemed to have a strong prejudice in favor of that kind of material, publishing, among other items, an

---

[4] ISBN 9781612270234.

exceedingly long serial by "Captain Danrit," the jingoistic doyen of French future war fiction.[5]

The other two long serials Gautier used were both reprints signed Pierre Ferréol, a signature also used, sometimes in abbreviated form, on popular science articles. In 1896, however, Gautier seems to have felt that a change of policy was in order—perhaps because reader reaction to the Danrit serial, which had stretched over two years, had been negative—and switched to short fiction, beginning with "Scrupule professionnel," bearing the signature Claude Manceau, here translated as "A Professional Scruple," a melodramatic *conte cruel* revisiting a macabre theme that had seen several previous literary treatments, most notably Villiers de l'Isle-Adam's "Le Secret de l'Échafaud" (1883)[6]. Something odd then happened, when that story was followed by a serial entitled "Conte bleu" [a designation applied to all kinds of fanciful tales, from fairy tales to anecdotal tall tales], bearing the signature G. Bethuys. The end of the third episode of the story—a sarcastic but earnest account of two military men visiting an industrialist who claims to have solved "the social problem," although his son, who has ambitions to be an alchemist, denies the claim vehemently—carries the usual "*suite*" [to be continued], but no continuation actually appeared, the next issue of the magazine beginning a new story bearing the same signature, "Cataclysme," here translated as "Cataclysm," without explanation.

It is possible, given its content, that it was "Cataclysme"—a *conte bleu* if ever there was one—had actually been intended to appear under the former title but that the wrong manuscript had somehow ended up with the printer. Whatever the reason for the confusion, however, "Cata-

---

[5] For more about Captain Danrit, see the introduction to his novel, *Undersea Odyssey*, published by Black Coat Press, ISBN 9781935558811.

[6] tr. as "The Secret of the Scaffold" in the Black Coat Press collection *The Scaffold*, ISBN 9781932983012.

clysme," was the last piece of fiction published in *La Science Française*, which stuck rigorously to non-fiction thereafter; Figuier, who also began to give preference to shorter stories, eventually followed suit, although not until the early years of the 20th century. A search for further information about Claude Manceau via Google Books grants snippet access to an interview in the aeronautical periodical *Technique*, which reveals that Claude Manceau, G. Bethuys and Pierre Ferréol were all among the numerous pseudonyms employed by the interviewee. In combination with information provided by the catalogue of the Bibliothèque Nationale, which lists G. Bethuys as a pseudonym of *Technique*'s editor, George-Frédéric Espitallier, this permits the conclusion that Espitallier was the author of both the *Science Française* stories, as well as the earlier reprinted serials. Espitallier, who had risen to the military rank of Lieutenant Colonel while in service, was a prolific writer on military technology from 1892 onwards, under his own and other names (one of his books being credited to both Bethuys and Manceau). Whether he ever completed the ill-fated serial begun as "Conte bleu"—which was shaping up to be the most interesting of the three Bethuys stories in *Science Française*—I do not know, although he did publish a book under the Bethuys name entitled *L'Homme en nickel* in 1897, which might be a novel.

Soon after Gautier stopped publishing pseudonymous short stories, a batch of them appeared in *La Science Illustrée*, under the signature "C. Paulon." Two of the three, "Un message de la planète Mars" (1897) and "Le Laboratoire bleu" (1898) are translated here as "A Message from the Planet Mars" and "The Blue Laboratory." The third and longest of the stories bearing the Paulon signature, *Les Mines d'or de Bas-Meudon* was subsequently reprinted in book form in 1903 under the signature Paul Combes, which was presumably "C. Paulon's" real name. Paul Combes (1856-1909) was a relatively well-known writer at that time, having published both poetry and fiction, but it is possible that C. Paulon was the pseudonym of his similarly named son, who published several books on geology in the early years of the 20th century. The elder Combes was not uninterested in science, however—the younger one could not possibly have been the author of *Le Secret du gouffre, aventures d'un chasseur d'insectes* (1888)—so the three *Science Illustrée* stories could have been an experimental venture on his part. Paul Combes *fils*' memoir of his father, *Paul Combes, sa vie, son oeuvre* (1910), presumably clarifies any possible bibliographical confusion, but I have not had the opportunity to consult it.

The two pairs of stories by Espitallier and Combes reproduced here are of no great literary merit, but they are interesting as a batch, in providing an illustration of the various ways in which writers of the period were attempting to solve the problem of constructing a *roman scientifique*. Although the handicap suffered by Bonnardot and Maricourt, of being virtually compelled to write off fantastic material as the substance of dreams, no longer afflicts them—although all that separates the Bethuys item from the dream formula is its blithe refusal to let his protagonist wake up—it remains manifest that they have not yet found any substitute for the other device that Bonnardot, Maricourt and Alphonse Brown had all felt obliged to use: that of embedding material within expository lectures, either delivered directly to the reader or pontificated by a character in the story.

In this respect, the Paulon couplet illustrates two horns of a dilemma on which many would-be users of fiction in the popularization of science found themselves painfully stuck; the first item is a relatively anodyne conversation-piece, which merely voices its central idea as a hypothetical possibility, while the second is a frank melodrama, which, in using scientific speculation as a source of melodramatic threat, makes the vocation of science seem literally insane. "The Blue Laboratory" was not the first *roman scientifique* to obtain its plot by means of the transfiguration of a classic *conte bleu* (Charles Perrault's "Barbe-Bleue" [Bluebeard]), and was certainly not the last, but it provides an excellent illustration of the perils of a method that tacitly represents science as a species of magic, whose plot value is entirely in the custody of maleficent sorcerers.

There is an interesting contrast between the entire tradition of French stories about the possibility of interplanetary communication leading up to "Un message de la planète Mars" and the English tradition that was founded almost immediately after the publication of that story when H. G. Wells' *The War of the Worlds* began serialization in an English periodical. The French tradition had been primarily inspired by Camille Flammarion, who hosted the salon in which Charles Cros introduced his proposal for interplanetary communication by optical means (described in some detail in the introduction to the four stories by Cros translated in *The Supreme Progress* (q.v.), and illustrated by one of the stories), which was subsequently repopularized in the 1890s, as fictionalized in several items translated in *The Mysterious Fluid* by Paul Vibert.[7] Paulon's story illustrates the innocent enthusiasm with which the theme was routinely treated in France, blithely unaware of the fact that the innocence was about to suffer a rude and fatal shock—for innocence can never be regained, even if commitment survives, as the French imaginative commitment to the possibility of fruitful and harmonious communication did.

The publication of Wells' scientific romances in France had a marked impact on the way many French writers thought about the possibilities of the *roman scientifique*, not simply because of their popularity but because of the manner of their publication. In England the first appearances of the works in question were scattered over a number of different publications, mostly belonging to a new generation of "middlebrow" publications aimed at a wide audience. Although there was some degree of variety in the appearance of Wells' French translations—Figuier published a couple of short stories in *La Science Illustrée*—the core of that body of work appeared in a

---

[7] Translated in the eponymous Black Coat Press collection, ISBN 9781612270203.

single venue, in a remarkable continuous series. The periodical that exposed Wells' generic work to the French public was the conspicuously upmarket periodical the *Mercure de France*, the unofficial organ of the Symbolist Movement. Between late 1898, when Henri Davray's translation of *The Time Machine* began serialization there, and early 1901, when his translation of *The Island of Doctor Moreau* concluded, there was hardly an issue of the magazine that did not carry a Wells translation, short stories filling in the gaps between the serials (the translation of *The War of the Worlds* appeared in 1899-1900). The magazine never gave such sustained prominence to a single author again, and the only other writers to whom it had previously given similarly prolific exposure—Remy de Gourmont and Gaston Danville—were both on its staff.

Perhaps curiously, although the press associated with the *Mercure* published several notable Wellsian scientific romances, including Charles Derennes' *Le Peuple du pôle* (1907)[8] and Maurice Renard's *Le Docteur Lerne, sous-dieu* (1908)[9], the periodical itself did not publish a great deal of speculative fiction once its brief love-affair with Wells was over, and the work it published by the two writers who became the most prominent French "Wellsians"—Renard and J.-H. Rosny aîné—was marginal, to say the least. The most significant genre works the periodical serialized, Henri Falk's *Le Maître des trois états* (1917)[10] and Marcel Rouff's *Voyage au monde à l'envers* (1920)[11], appeared long afterwards. That made no difference, however, to the impact of the *Mercure*'s introduction of Wells to the French public, which established examples

---

[8] translated in a Black Coat Press edition as *The People of the Pole,* ISBN 9781934543399.

[9] translated in a Black Coat Press edition as *Doctor Lerne*, ISBN 9781935558156.

[10] translated as "The Master of the Three States" in the Black Coat Press collection *The Age of Lead*, ISBN 9781935558422.

[11] translated in a Black Coat Press edition as *Journey to the Inverted World*, ISBN 9781612270395.

for future French writers in the genre that were not only significant in terms of their innovative content, but also their perceived prestige. It also helped to make the notion of speculative fiction sufficiently familiar to readers that the kinds of apologetic device that previous writers had been forced to use in introducing every endeavor of that kind became unnecessary.

French language fiction was not, of course, confined to France, and there is a sense in which futuristic speculation was of special interest to the inhabitants of Quebec, living in a country still under development and in highly ambiguous political situation. Much early French-Canadian speculative fiction is, in fact, rather narrowly confined by political preoccupations, but as the genre became popular it spread into lighter kinds of fiction, including juvenile fiction. Although female writers are conspicuous by their virtual absence from the early history of the *roman scientifique*, Quebec helped to make up for what France lacked when Emma-Adèle Lacerte (1870-1935) produced *Nemoville* (1917), one of several sequels to Jules Verne's accounts of the super-submarine *Nautilus* to be produced by other hands. Although it is a children's story, and thus a trifle weak-kneed in narrative terms, it does serve to illustrate the continue appeal of the fundamental Vernian dream of remote escape by means of exotic technology—a dream that had inevitably become more poignant while Canada, along with the greater part of the civilized world, was at war.

The Great War inevitably changed everything for French writers in general, and—as it turned out—for writers of *romans scientifiques* in particular. Several writers who had begun to build highly promising careers in the genre, including Renard and Rosny, found the marketplace much more hostile thereafter, as publishers began to feel, rightly or wrongly, that the technological weaponry deployed in the war had created a general hostility to technology, and that works of fiction featuring scientific advancement now could not help being bleakly pessimistic—not a good selling-point for popular fiction.

The genre did not disappear, of course, but it did indeed take a conspicuous turn toward the prolific production of *contes cruels*, melodramatic horror stories and bitterly scathing satires, none of which recommended themselves for routine recreational reading. The crucial examples provided by Wells, however, allowed some of the periodicals launched or relaunched after the war to experiment with such work, at least for a while.

One periodical that did experiment with scientific romance in an interesting fashion was *Oeuvres Libres*, which published one of Rosny's bolder ventures in the genre and a whole series of ingenious speculative comedies by André Couvreur (which I hope to translate when the works in question fall into the public domain in 2014). Another of the periodical's early venture into futuristic fiction was "En trois cent ans" (in issue No. 7, January 1922), here translated as "Three Hundred Years Hence," by the journalist and novelist Pierre Mille (1864-1941), which provides a good example, not only of the deeply jaundiced tone of much post-war futuristic fiction, but also of the marked contrast between the way in which writers of "literary fiction" tended to tackle such themes (and still do today), as opposed to the old stalwarts of *La Science Illustrée* and similar specialized outlets. The great strength of Mille's story—simply as a story, rather than a specimen of *roman scientifique*—is that it no longer feels the slightest need to employ the apologetic devices that Bonnardot, Maricourt and the *Science Illustrée* writers thought compulsory. Largely thanks to the archetypal examples provided by Wells, it had become possible to take a much more robust approach to the business of setting stories in the future, and Mille simply goes straight ahead and does it, considering his title as sufficient introduction to the notion. That method was to become standard thereafter, but it is worth remembering that it had been considered effectively impossible before.

Oeuvres Libres soon stopped dabbling in speculative fiction, as did the other upmarket periodicals that had dipped a toe in the after the end of the Great War, including the *Mer-*

cure. The most considerable fraction of the genre that remained was confined within the arena of action-adventure fiction, but that arena was itself shifted markedly in the direction of lowbrow and juvenile fiction, in parallel with American "pulp fiction." One of the most prolific writers in that sector of the field was José Moselli, who frequently dabbled in speculative technology for the purpose of hyping up the melodramatic component of his thrillers, going to a remarkable extreme in the gory futuristic extravaganza *La Fin d'Illa* (1925).[12] The introduction to the translation of the latter volume gives a broad account of the author's career and work whose detail need not be reproduced here, but pointed out that he did make a brief attempt to write *romans scientifiques* of a more dedicated stripe for the *Almanach scientifique* [Scientific Annual], an experiment in more earnest popularization briefly published as an accessory to the long-running periodical *Sciences et Voyages*. The stories included here were the first two of the three he produced for that publication, and provide an interesting example of the way in which some popular examples of *roman scientifique* had begun to mirror, probably not entirely coincidentally, the kind of speculative fiction that was beginning to appear in the American pulp magazines and would eventually obtain its own generic niche there, initially as "scientifiction" and then as "science fiction."

"Le Voyage éternel, ou Les Prospecteurs de l'infini," here translated as "The Eternal Voyage; or, The Prospectors of Space" first appeared in the 1924 edition of the annual (actually published in 1923, bearing the date of the coming new year, as almost all Christmas annuals do) but seems rather old-fashioned, especially as it borrows its hypothetical method of spaceship propulsion from *Les Aventures extraordinaires d'un*

[12] translated in a Black Coat Press edition as *Illa's End*, ISBN 9781612270319.

savant russe (1888-1894)[13] by Henry de Graffigny and Georges Le Faure. It is, however, a typical example of the manner in which pulp sf writers mocked-up melodramatic frameworks to contain speculative notions.

"Le Messager de la planète," here translated as "The Planetary Messenger," which first appeared in the 1925 issue of the *Almanach Scientifique* (published in 1924) is the more interesting of the two stories, not so much because it provides the same kind of anticipation of the methods of pulp science fiction as because it provides a kind of elegy for the French tradition that had culminated in Paulon's "Un Message de la planète Mars," addressing the same question in the same hopeful manner—but adding a tragic twist, which transcends its admitted awkwardness to achieve a certain bleak poignancy, in a fashion akin to one of the most famous and effective early pulp sf stories, Raymond Z. Gallun's "Old Faithful" (1934). "Le Messager de la planète" provides a fitting end to the anthology, not only by illustrating a kind of watershed in the unsteady evolution of French *roman scientifique*, but also by re-voicing a particular philosophical cynicism that runs through the entire tradition, echoing the narrative voice of Bonnardot and Maricourt, and perhaps even that of Vattel. It is a kind of cynicism that is subtly different from its parallels in British and American scientific romance, but is not absent even from the most vulgar pulp sf, and reflects an essential element of the speculative imagination: that thinking about what we might become inevitably encourages a dissatisfaction with what we are.

The translations of "Voyages dans le microcosme," *La Commune en l'an 2073*, "Les insects révélateurs," "Scrupule professionnel" and "Cataclysme" were all taken from version of the texts reproduced on the Bibliothèque Nationale's inva-

---

[13] translated in a Black Coat Press edition as *The Extaordinary Adventures of a Russian Scientist Across the Solar System* (2 volumes), ISBN 9781934543818 and 9781934543825.

luable website *gallica*. The translation of "Archéopolis" was taken from the version of *Fantaisies multicolores* reproduced in Google Books. The translations of the two Paulon stories were taken from versions reproduced on the *gloubik* website (the relevant volume of *La Science Illustrée* is not in the BN). The translation of "En trois cent ans" was taken from the London Library's copy of the relevant issue of *Oeuvres Libres*. The translation of *Nemoville* was made from the 2003 reprint published in Montreal by Les Éditions du Résurrectioniste. The translations of the two Moselli stories were made from versions contained on the *idesetautres* website.

Brian Stableford

Emerich de Vattel: ***Voyages in the Microcosm, by a modern disciple of Pythagoras***

(1757)

The last time that my soul left the body with which it was united, it did not pass immediately into another. Detached from its gross envelope, it was not devoid of organs; a subtle body remained to it, almost exactly as Leibniz had imagined, and I realized that it was inseparable therefrom. I then experienced the truth of the Philosophical maxim that the idea of size is purely relative: the human body appeared to me as an entire world, the marvels of which I resolved to visit. As you can imagine, Reader, the head of a Philosopher was the first of these ambulant Worlds to excite my curiosity.

Having introduced myself without difficulty into that head, I made my way to the brain by diligence. I soon found myself in the middle of a grand plaza, at which five exceedingly wide streets converged, each of which bore the name of one of the five senses. Merchandise of every sort was arriving continually by way of each of these streets: images, sensations, confused ideas, etc. A robust street-porter named Memory took responsibility for everything he could grip, and carried it into the shops. There, he carried out a triage; I saw him select one fraction of the things he had brought and distribute them in an orderly manner in clearly-labeled boxes, in much the same fashion that pharmaceuticals are arranged in an Apothecary's shop. The rest remained, pell-mell, in a confused heap, in which the majority were reduced to death and vanished over time.

Above these shops lived Reflection, a sort of Official who came to inspect the pharmaceuticals. He took some of them away into a laboratory, where a Chemist named Abstraction put them in an alembic and made Extracts of them, which were carried into the Study of Understanding. I witnessed an admirable spectacle in that Study: the principles of all the things contained in the shops of Memory, arranged in the most beautiful order, by genus and species; and these principles, like all Spirits, last much longer than the matter from which they had been extracted. They were even unalterable, when the operation was properly carried out.

A wise Minister, named Reason, considered them attentively, compared them, mixed them in different proportions in a thousand various combinations, and carefully observed what resulted therefrom. Then he wrote in his Ledgers, thus forming Metaphysics, or the primary Philosophy. It was on the discoveries that the Minister made in his operations that he based his orders, in order to send them to Will, who is charged with their execution.

He had a dangerous rival, though, in the person of a fairy named Imagination. The soul had taken this fairy into its service, to preside at its pleasures, and even for various useful tasks. She could make herself commendable with her pleasing talents, if she consented to submit to the orders of Reason, but, being excessively capricious, she accepted no regulation and often occupied herself by merely disturbing the Minister's work. She excels in Painting; with a couple of brush-strokes she can capture the image of anything that the senses bring into the public Plaza, the objects that Memory collects; she can unite them, separate them, mutilate them, combine them according to her whim and convey them to Will like Reason's orders. Often, by means of a Magic Lantern, she represents all these vain phantoms on the exterior wall of Understanding and sets free the Passions, an impetuous and turbulent soldiery, who take the enchantress's illusions for the signals and commands of the Sovereign. Sometimes she presumes to paint the essences of things and to substitute her figurations for the Extracts that the Chemist Reflection furnishes to Understanding. The soul of my Philosopher was very determined to render this enchantress more tractable; it had high hopes of her, if she could be persuaded to get along well with the Minister.

After having seen the entire Court of that little world in which I found myself, I was ambitious to discover the Queen—but she hid herself away from me; I thought that I was in the abode of one of those Oriental Monarchs who are careful to display their splendor while hiding their persons from the gaze of their people. To begin with, trusting in Descartes, I went to the pineal gland, but I did not find what I was looking for there. Then, suspecting that a few Moderns might have reasoned more accurately, I raced to the *corpus callosum*, but with no greater success. Finally, I became convinced that, being in possession of material organs, it was impossible for me to perceive a simple and spiritual being, and I made a firm resolution to inform the philosophers that, their eyes being infinitely more gross than mine presently were, it would be futile to seek the head of a Giant in order to dissect it; they would not perceive any vestige of the soul.

I began to get bored in so serious a World. My curiosity was satisfied; I promised myself more amusement in some other planet of the same species, and I planned to go there as soon as possible. An opportunity to get out of the place where I was soon presented itself. An Adversary attacked my Philosopher's doctrine; immediately, a terrible storm broke out in his head; everything there was in ferment; animal spirits rushed impetuously toward his mouth; he shouted at the top of his voice. I emerged, swimming in the torrent of his words.

Avid for knowledge, I soon recommenced my journey—but it was a question of choosing a World in which I would not see exactly the same things again. I decided on a young Coquette, in the expectation that I would never find a head less similar to that of a Philosopher.

I wanted to begin, however, by visiting the heart, which I thought much more cultivated and alive than the head. To do that, on seeing a dandy about to give her some flowers, I got ready, and entered the lady's ear along with the breath of his words.

My astonishment was great when I saw that I had reached her brain; I had assumed that such sweet words would have conducted me straight to the heart. I learned, though, that the heart is ordinarily difficult to access. A monster known as Pride guards the entrance. Besides, it is almost always surrounded by snow and ice, which render the avenues impracticable—except that, in certain seasons, vapors rising from the lowest-lying regions melt the snow and ice; even the monster is inconvenienced by the thaw, and anyone who can take advantage of the moment can enter the Plaza. The climate, however, is hardly tolerable, and no one ever stays there or very long. The Reader must content himself, if he will, with the account I have given him of good Memories, for I have lost the desire to travel in such places.

Meanwhile, I found myself in the head and resolved to visit it. The public Plaza was infinitely more tumultuous than the one in the Philosopher's head. I thought I was in the middle of the Saint-Germain Fair. Torrents of sensations of every species were filling the five streets of the senses and emptying out into the Plaza. The sensations that were the keenest and most lively were going through the windows into the store of Memory, who did not bother to arrange them—except that I noticed that she set aside those indicated to her by certain Royal Messengers.

I asked one of these people if I might be able to see the Mistress of such a remarkable Country. "Without difficulty," he replied. "One encounters her everywhere."

"Oh!" I exclaimed. "I shall finally see a soul! I suspected that it would not be as invisible as the Philosopher's."

"What soul are you talking about?" he asked. "We don't know anything about that here. A lovely and lively face is our Sovereign, the sole object of our attention and homage. Go throw herself at your feet straight away; she has a natural liking for newcomers."

I went up to the apartments and I saw a pretty little face on a throne, exactly similar to the body into which I had entered. That was the Sovereign, the principle of all that happened in this little World. Self-Esteem was her favorite, Imagination fulfilled the functions of Prime Minister and Caprice was in general command thereunder. Vanity, Folly and Frivolity, with two or three Passions, made up the Council.

Surprised by this arrangement, I asked a Courtier whether the Queen did not have a Minister named Reason.

"Ha!" he said. "He only appeared in the Court for one day; he went unheeded; his advice was obsolete; it would have spoiled the Queen's affairs. Pleasures are the occupation of our lovely Sovereign, and the conquest of hearts the great objective of her labors. That old dotard disturbed our pleasures, and with him in charge we wouldn't have conquered two hearts a year. We all ganged up on him; the Queen banished him in perpetuity. Beware of talking about him or admitting that you know him; you won't be well-received. Go into the Council Chamber; you can listen to the deliberations."

"What!" I said. "Dare a foreigner penetrate therein?"

"Oh," the Courtier replied, "no one will notice you; the Council changes so frequently that the Queen never knows all the Members; the Favorite, and those you see sitting in the first five or six places, are the only permanent ones."

I went in; Vanity was opening her mouth at that moment to warn that a proud and brilliant dandy had just been spotted, whose heart would be a significant conquest, very suitable to add to the reputation of the Princess's armies. It was resolved unanimously, by acclamation, to make the attempt. They began to deliberate as to the means, but Caprice took the floor, saying in a curt tone: "He's handsome, let's get on with it."

The Queen got up and a part of the Court followed her into the Gardens. She noticed me as she passed by, and having greeted me with a gracious smile, ordered that I be taken to see the rarities of the Palace, while awaiting her return.

The person charged with guiding me took me through a multitude of Halls, Galleries and Closets, where everything exhaled luxury and softness, but I was struck by the uniformity of the furniture; everywhere the walls were covered with mirrors instead of tapestries.

"It's necessary," my guide told me, "that our Sovereign is able to see herself everywhere; whichever way she directs her gaze, she encounters her reflection; nothing more agreeable can be offered to her. At the very most, she tolerates the Portraits that you see at intervals; those furthest away represent her past conquests, these much closer to hand advertise those she intends to make. There are people of all estates—Courtiers, Soldiers, Clergymen, Magistrates—but all fops. Intelligent people are too much alike and too modest; they don't merit our attention."

I remembered the Philosopher World, and wanted to know whether there was anything similar in this one.

"Take me to Reflection's apartment," I said to my guide. "I'm curious to see how Extracts of things are made here."

"What are you talking about?" he said. "I don't know this Reflection."

"He's the Official who puts ideas into the alembic with skillful artifice," I said, "in order to extract their quintessence."

"Ha ha!" the guide replied. "I seem to remember hearing mention of him; he performs the operations of the old world, which are only good for Pedants. We know nothing of them here. Reflection was thrown out along with Reason. Imagination suffices for everything. The Queen only requires a superficial knowledge of things; her Prime Minister makes miniature paintings of them, on which basis she makes decisions and formulates resolutions. Admit that all your Chemist's Extracts have been advantageously replaced. Let's go into the Minister's Office—you can see him at work."

I did, indeed, see scrolls of parchment, on which a delicate brush had traced figures of every kind; I thought I was looking at the hieroglyphic books of the ancient Priests of Egypt.

"There," he said. What's the point of knowing about causes and making accurate measurements? Consider the face of that Cavalier. Can one not see at a glance that he has a noble air about him, a well-proportioned figure and a well-turned leg? Besides, one can easily judge him by his physiognomy. Look at that crowd of Captives attached to a Triumphal Chariot—can all your alembic-processed ideas express with the same force the glory that stems from the conquests of two handsome eyes?

I could hardly restrain myself from laughing in that august sanctuary of the State. Fortunately, my guide saved me the trouble.

"Come in," he said. "I still have more important things to show you—let's go to the Arsenal."

"What!" I exclaimed. "There's an Arsenal here?"

"And why not?" he retorted. "Doesn't every Conqueror need one?"

He led me into a vast courtyard surrounded by buildings of the Composite order, which appeared to me to be constructed out of glazed Chinese porcelain. Military equipment was assembled n the courtyard. There were Caleches, Cabriolets and *cul-de-singe* Obligéantes with Martin's varnish,[14] extremely brisk and gallant; not many coaches, almost entirely made of glass. Further away, trophies could be seen: Presidential Bonnets, Miters, Clerical Collars, Plumes and Financier's Strong-Boxes, heaped up pell-mell, surmounted by bleeding hearts and addled brains. On one side were the workshops, where thousands of Artisans of every sort were continually occupied. Lipsticks and make-up were fabricated there, whose secret was only known to one trusted man; perfumes and marvelous waters were distilled there. The first Lady of the Bedchamber was in command of the entire Arsenal.

---

[14] This is a slightly enigmatic reference. *Cul-de-singe* [literally, monkey's bum] has several possible referents, being a slang term for a medlar and a bearskin hat; it presumably refers to the shape of the carriage here described, unusually (in the interests of wordplay) as an Obligéante [obliging]. Martin's varnish, so called because it was patented in 1744 by Simon Étienne Martin, was manufactured by adding gold or bronze powder to green varnish, giving it a metallic sheen.

We went into the principal outbuilding. There I saw an immense Hall, completely surrounded by crystal cupboards containing attire of every sort: dresses, hats, lace, ribbons, etc. A Dressing-Room adjoined the Hall, contained everything specifically concerned with matters of personal hygiene. I observed locked cupboards, which were not transparent, like those in the Hall. My guide whispered in my ear that they contained admirable remedies against natural defects and the ravages of time.

A kind of altar, known as a Dressing-Table, attracted my gaze specifically. It was consecrated to Beauty. The Lady of the Bedchamber fulfilled the functions of High Priestess here; rouge, make-up, beauty-spots, pomades, essences and perfumes, neatly arranged in boxes, jars and bottles, seemed like so many offerings devoted to the Divinity in question. Stray hairs and asymmetrical eyebrows were so many victims to be sacrificed there. All of that was carried out with extreme attention; the High Priestess seemed to meditate profoundly—and in order that all that seriousness should not spoil the Queen's charms, a young clergyman was charged with entertaining her with the day's news, or reading something to her.

The Library was next door to the Study. All the books were sorted into two categories, History and the Fine Arts. In the former, I saw all the modern Novels and all the fashionable gossip; in the second, various singular Works, of which the Reader will doubtless be interested to see a Catalogue here. These were the principal titles:

Garments of the Fair Sex, in Alphabetical Order, 50 vols., folio.

Treatise on Battlefields: 1. Going for a Walk; 2. Spectacles; 3. Balls; 4. Intimate dinners. 4 vol., quarto.

The Art of Placing a Beauty-Spot. 2 vols., octavo, with diagrams.

The Art of Putting Nature's Gifts to Work; in which is treated the conduct of the eyes, the management of the voice, especially huskiness, etc. 4 vols., duodecimo.

Correctives of Nature. 12 vols., duodecimo.

Satires of Modesty, Sentiment, Constancy, Fidelity, etc., octavo.

Recreations of the Toilette, or Initial Preparations for the Day. (This was a collection of Tales, Epigrams, Songs etc., in more than 30 vols.)

Essential Knowledge for Ladies of High Society, in Philosophy, History, Geography etc. Pamphlet of 6 pages, demi-duodecimo, by a Fashionable Savant.

After making a rapid survey of this curious Library I returned to the Dressing-Room. Flirtatious glances, amorous glances and simpers, were being exercised there before a mirror. I spent some time admiring them. The Prussian infantry could not have presented its arms and executed its drill more efficiently. Two violins and a flageolet gave the signal; all the troops arranged themselves in battle order. Coquetry was the commander-in-chief and Intrigue her major-general. It was a matter of conquering the heart of the dandy I mentioned previously. They marched off. Laughter and Games formed the advance guard.

In a trice, they surrounded the enemy; the battle-corps advanced, and, the Amorous Glances having pierced the dandy's lines, the Queen came running to enjoy her triumph. Immediately, though, the man she thought vanquished got up, hummed a little tune, turned a somersault and vanished into thin air like a wisp of vapor; either the thrusts he had received had been insufficiently penetrative, or, as the army's Surgeon-Major claimed, that species had no heart and could not be mortally wounded.

Mortified by the adventure, the Queen made plans to devote herself to more solid and more glorious conquests. Imagination had sometimes made mention of a very well-to-do Lord, nurtured with a knowledge of the finer things in life, perfectly formed for the purposes of society. "There," said the Princess, "is a conquest suitable to restore my glory."

Orders were given for the great enterprise. The Lord in question was enclosed within a Plaza, which Reason and Experience had fortified; he was besieged therein. The Queen deployed all her might and skill—but the terrain was difficult, the besieged forces vigilant and full of valor; the campaign made no progress. Discontented with her Generals, the Queen entrusted the command and direction of the siege to Love.

That malign Deity resolved to take advantage of the opportunity to avenge himself on the Princess, who had never rendered him anything but deceptive homage. He seduced Caprice, and, that traitor having opened a secret door to her Mistress's Heart, Love took possession of it.

The distressed Queen offered the Lord of the besieged Plaza a Treaty of Alliance, proposing that the two Empires be united under their common authority—but that proud enemy replied that their subjects were not fitted to live together; he advised her to decamp secretly during the night and generously promised not to harass her during her retreat.

Here, Reader, you will exempt me from describing what happened in the head in which I was lodged; my pen would not be up to the task. Everything was plunged momentarily into great confusion. Imagination was in distress; the Favorite, Self-Esteem, fell dangerously ill; Vanity was gripped by an ardent fever. The Queen broke some of her mirrors in a fit of chagrin, and got so carried away at first that she ordered the Arsenal to be set on fire.

"I no longer want these unworthy weapons," she declared, "that have served me so badly."

In spite of her fever, however, Vanity had enough presence of mind to remonstrate that the reverse was not so much due to the Arsenal itself as to its commander, who had doubtless performed her duties very badly.

The Queen kissed her tenderly for this salutary advice. The Lady of the Bedchamber was expelled in disgrace, and the greatest success as anticipated in consequence. Tranquility was gradually restored.

I took advantage of the calm, and escaped through a crack that had opened up in the Palace Dome during the tumult.

Alfred Bonnardot: *Archeopolis*
(1857)

I. The Ruins of Paris

From the summit of an isolated mountain, as arid as those which form a gray ring around Jerusalem, my gaze overlooked an immense, uneven plain strewn with ruins as far as the eyes could see. A river with muddy waters traversed that valley of desolation from east to west.

My initial surprise was son succeeded by a solemn grief; I had recognized the point of the globe where the city of my birth stood, the city that inspired so much love and so much hatred, so much admiration and so much scorn: Paris, the vast reservoir of all grandeurs and the receptacle of all turpitudes.

Suddenly, a distant and mysterious voice vibrated in the air, and harmonized with my melancholy thoughts. It sang, with a plaintive modulation, a hymn as sad as the limitless desert, like the canticle *Super flumina Babylonis*.[15] I could not reproduce the melodious notes, but I have remembered the meaning of a few verses:

"O Paris, Paris! The shadow of our splendid edifices no longer falls upon the flagstones. Nettles with stinging sap have come to turn your now-soundless streets and squares green. The specter of ruins has passed over you, and your proud columns have collapsed on the ground.

"The Seine has seen the willows of old Celtic Gaul reborn on its banks. Only the seething foam of its waves, around heaps of mossy stones, indicates the places spanned by the

[15] Palestrina's musical version of Psalm 137 [By the Waters of Babylon…] (1584)

bridges with massive piles; their debris flows away in fine dust to mingle with the Ocean sands.

"River Seine! The mirror of your waters no longer doubles, when night falls, the thousand lights of illuminated palaces, or the twin towers of the ancient cathedral. Your waves undulate amid the silence, and you resemble a desolate mother weeping all her tears over the cadaver of her child.

"What were the instrument of the divine will? Was it you, rapid messengers of human vengeance, bullets invisible in flight? You, subterranean furies of volcanoes without issues? Have the abysms of the catacombs swallowed up your high towers, vast cupolas born of their entrails?"

The voice expired in the immensity, and I slowly descended the hill. It was that of Montmartre. One could no longer see, as of old, windmills and a telegraph on its crest, waving their huge arms, to feed the capital the bread of distant news. Its bald silhouette stood out sadly against the leaden horizon to the north.

At first I did not know how to combine these anticipated catastrophes with the intimate memory of the century in which I lived, but my imagination was gradually able to reconcile the two contradictory states. I seemed to remember that I had been dead for a long time, and that I had just been reborn into the world.

Having wandered through a labyrinth of formless ruins and deserted, humpbacked roads invaded by brambles, I recognized the location of the garden of the Tuileries, where the members of the Parisian élite, with their petulant tendencies and precocious intelligence, had once met up beneath the quincunxes of chestnut trees. Near a sort of pot-hole, I found some debris of the Luxor obelisk, twice-antique plunder of the ancient cradle of the world.

Suddenly, a sound became audible, the increasing intensity of which agitated the atmosphere. I raised my eyes and perceived, floating in the air, an immense aerostat with sails, which had just dropped anchor a hundred paces away. I saw a numerous company of people get down, clad in white robes and wearing turbans of the same color. Their language was not easy to grasp; it was an entirely new sort of French, much modified in its consonance and pronunciation. They were considering me with a kind of mocking hilarity; that was, I thought I understood, because of my costume, which was very bizarre in their view.

The dragoman of the troop questioned me as to my age and homeland. Collecting all my memories, I replied that I was born in Paris during the reign of Napoléon the Great. There was an outburst of general laughter. One of the most earnest turbans in the group said to his neighbor: "Leave the poor man in peace and let's go straight on to the objective of our expedition."

They were unanimous in regarding me as a cretin or a visionary, and no one paid any further attention to me. I took advantage of that compassionate silence to watch the exotic savants at work.

"I doubt," one of them said, "that we'll be able to reap much of a harvest of bronze medallions here, for toward the end of the forty-ninth century, those Kouktman vandals"—probably the invaders of French soil—searched carefully for them, in order to found cannons."

They all launched into a thousand conjectures regarding the stone or marble debris that they encountered on their route.

"Here," said the doyen of the troop, "Are three mutilated columns, still standing, from the church of the Madeleine; here once stood the palace known as *Les Invalides*—which is to say, the infirm—which was one of the most sumptuous monuments of the right bank.[16] You can admire the vestiges of the portico that ornamented the entrance to that vast edifice."

All his colleagues applauded this ingenious explanation, with one exception, who dared to say: "There never was a portico in front of the Hôtel des Invalides. In a fragment of an

---

[16] This is a joke; as subsequently suggested, Les Invalides is on the left bank, and the ruins to which the tourist is referring are presumably those on the site of the Élysée Palace.

ancient book, for which I paid its weight in gold, there was no mention of it at all, and moreover, I read there that the immense house in question was established on the left bank of the river."

The doyen's face contracted and took on a ruddy tint. "For my part," he replied, dryly, like a man who takes offense at contradiction, "I've also read books as ancient and authentic as yours, and I dare to advance with certainty—certainty!—that on the very spot where we are now, stood the Palais des Invalides, otherwise known as the Infirm. The peristyle, gentlemen, had twelve fluted columns, three of which are still here, before your eyes."

A sort of secretary, leaning his elbow on a capital, was taking the whole discussion down in shorthand. He would have to render an exact account of it to the public of some country overseas. I drew nearer to him and read at the head of the page the date 7 July 9957.

As I was burning to know with what foreigners I was dealing, I approached the dragoman, who was smoking some aromatic plant delightedly, and I questioned him. He understood me perfectly, and replied; "Don't you recognize, by their costume alone, the inhabitants of the celebrated city of Archeopolis, situated in the part of the globe that the ancients called Central Africa?"

I stood there astounded.

"What!" he continued. "You've never heard mention of our capital, the queen of the civilized world, or the famous museum of antiquities that our worthy sovereign Matoupah IX founded some three centuries ago—the museum whose buildings alone occupy a surface of more than a hundred thousand square meters? Have you, then, always crouched down among the ruins of the Celtic deserts?

On my affirmation that all this information was new to me, he proposed to knock me into shape, to take me to his illustrious homeland and introduce me to the court of the king of the Archeopolitans—doubtless, I thought, privately, to put him in a good humor.

A soon as the company's engineer-topographer had made exact plans of the remains of the important edifices of ancient Paris, preparations were made for departure. In accordance with my protector's proposal, I was lodged in a small compartment of the aerial vessel, which contained food-supplies and some exceedingly complicate scientific instruments. The machine, I was told, had been fitted out at government expense, with all the necessary comforts.

I would gladly communicate to the reader the details I was given on this subject, but unfortunately, everyone wanting to enlighten me at the same time, my memory, like a vase filled too quickly, was unable to retain any of it.

As it was appropriate for me to have a decent outfit, I was made to throw away my hideous cylinder of black felt and my cockchafer-tail suit. Then they draped over my shoulders some sort of mantle of a dazzling parrot-green color, the white being reserved for government antiquaries, doubtless as an allusion to their candid innocence. Afterwards, a sort of bizarrely-formed turban of the same color was fitted around my head.

II. The Bulgers of Archeopolis

After a continuous fight over the deserts of southern France and the Mediterranean, favored by the northerly wind, we descended the flowing day, shortly after dawn, in one of the outlying districts of the immense and noisy city, named Archeopolis, I was informed on the way, because a wandering caravan of antiquaries had founded it six or seven thousand years before.

From certain whisperings of the learned society, I realized that I would be retained in the capacity of a curious beast, in some royal menagerie. Thus, as soon as I set foot on the ground I hastened to decamp and flee at top speed over the macadam of the capital of the civilized world of the year 9957.

As I saw a sufficiently large number of cloaks and turbans similar to mine circulating in the streets, I no longer feared being recognized by my scientists. Nevertheless, for the sake of greater security, I went into a sort of petty barber's shop and had myself shaved, moustache and side-whiskers included, so as to resemble the generally beardless indigenes as much as possible. I paid in 1858 *sous*, which the barber—something of an antiquarian, as everyone there was—accepted with abundant gratitude.

Thanks to that precaution and the national costume in which my paltry frame had been draped, I was able to traverse part of the city without causing the dogs to bark unduly and without the Gallic form of my nose exciting too many sniggers from the rather ugly women that I perceived sitting on broad terraces.

I ended up finding a large edifice in my path decorated with the inscription: ACADEMY OF THE BULGERS. There, I was told, some twenty professors were maintained at the expense of the State. I entered resolutely into a large courtyard bordered by porticoes. On the far side was a façade in a rather grandiose style, surmounted by several domes shining golden in the sunlight.

First, I noticed an astronomical telescope with a very large aperture on a distant platform. It was at least fourteen meters long and was mounted on an exceedingly complicated and bizarrely shaped pedestal. People nearby were referring to it as a marvel. The lenses garnishing the two ends were, they said, so clear and powerfully refractive that the ensemble, perfectly centered, magnified a planet's diameter a million times. Thanks to that giant eye, added a scholar in a canary-yellow cloak, a bloody battle taking place on one of the plains of Mars had been observed the previous month.

I took that story as an old joke, based on the reddish tint of the planet and the belligerent name that it still retained, and said to myself: *It's warmed-over humbug, proof that the antique tradition of the art of the tall tale has been religiously transmitted over the centuries to this brave African nation.*

In a minor courtyard I perceived a transport balloon, somewhat different from the one that had brought me. Someone told me that the ingenious inventor of that machine, whose baroque name escapes me, had attempted a successful trip around the Moon.

"These," someone else added, "are the very simple means that he had employed to travel beyond our atmosphere, to breathe, to combat the extreme cold and to pass without any shock from the Earth's sphere of attraction to that of its satellite: firstly..."

But at that very interesting moment, my narrator disappeared, as if by magic. I was striding rapidly along a gallery, hoping to recover his tracks, resolved to cling on to his cloak until he reached the end of his account, when I found that I had somehow arrived under the cupola of a vast amphitheater, where a short bald man was gesticulating from the height of a pulpit. He was the first individual who had appeared to me without a turban.

I was told that I was in the audience of a lecture by the illustrious and very eloquent Professor of History, Fissbrek de Hardeynagh.

That sublime intelligence had chosen for its lodging an extremely ungraceful ball that resembled, in profile, the body of an orangutan, but what attracted my attention most of all about his person was an enormous bulge protruding from the left of his skull, which was bare at that point. I enquired naively about the manner of infirmity with which he seemed to be afflicted.

I learned, to my amazement, that these sorts of ignoble blisters were the object of profound veneration here. One said of an individual: "He is a Bulger," in the same majestic fashion of which we say: "Monsieur Such-and-such is decorated with the grand sash of the Légion d'honneur."

The ancient system of Dr. Gall—designated, of course, by a new name[17]—had acquired a vogue in Archeopolis of

---

[17] Franz-Josef Gall's system attempting to analyze mental traits and abilities by means of bumps in the skull supposedly

which one can hardly communicate an idea. People there took note of the slightest swelling of the cranium, maintaining it by means of a thousand medical dressings;[18] the hair around it was shaven in order to expose it to the sunlight and facilitate its development. Ominous reliefs were flattened, or even, in certain cases, amputated in infancy. On the contrary, those that prognosticated a definite aptitude for mathematics, poetry, erudition or any fine mental ability were fortified and encouraged. Skulls of the same species were brought together in series, and associations formed of abilities of every sort. Every child who had the good fortune to be born with a clearly-pronounced beneficial protuberance was sure of being well cared-for, of making rapid progress and becoming, before the age of twenty, a model Academician, if not a model Academic.

I was gripped by a keen curiosity regarding the results that this system of classification had produced—the aristocracy of the bulge, as the envious classes of Archeopolis put it. Thus, I immediately forgot the narrator of the excursion to the Moon, in order to open my ears to the sonorous waves that the singular doctor's speech caused to vibrate. At that moment he was readjusting the folds of a large scarlet toga that appeared to be causing him some embarrassment; then he resumed, in a tone laden with pathos:

"Finally, to conclude my comparison between our epoch and ancient times, finally, are we children of Old Africa, we inhabitants of the temperate zone of the globe, not the true elect of Providence? A few thousand years ago, our land, so fortunate today, was still a vast and arid desert of sand, scorched by the fires of the sun, but God displaced the ecliptic in our favor.

---

corresponding to abundances of brain tissue was only belatedly called "phrenology."

[18] There is an untranslatable pun here; *emplâtre* [sticking-plaster] is also employed colloquially to refer to a slap on the head or, in English parlance, "a clip round the ear."

"Today, all the elements that constitute our plant being equilibrated, there are no further examples of those sudden fermentations that once shook cities and turned them upside-down. The seasons and the winds have adopted an almost regular course; thus, no one any longer lacks bread, and human intelligence has taken flight in a manner unknown to the old races, who thought they had attained the limits of civilization.

"We are only subject to a small number of the maladies identified by ancient authors, and we only know the name of the terrible scourge that depopulated the world so many centuries ago: the Asiatic cholera, of which people spoke in terror. Let us mention in passing one of the moral sores of those remote times: the duel, that social scourge, born of pride and a false sense of honor. The duel no longer exists among us. Our tribunals are sufficiently powerfully organized no longer to allow a particular tribunal to exist in the conscience of each individual."

This speech caused me to retreat into myself; I said to myself: *I'm surely dreaming; I'm in the land of chimeras.* Then I finished up convincing myself that I was witnessing a real session, and that the evils of my nineteenth century were nothing but a dream, nothing but a very distant memory.

Here the orator's majestic pronunciations were succeeded by a calmer tone of voice in order for him to add, after a pause, a sort of postscript:

"Such is, gentlemen, a succinct summary, based on the fragments of an ancient chronicle that miraculously escaped the ravages of time, fire and the poor constitution of the paper manufactured in France. Such is, as I say, the revelation of the causes that led, in the latter part of the twenty-first century, to the general decadence of global civilization. The second lecture in the course will be specifically devoted to the mores and customs of the French."

"What!" I exclaimed. "The illustrious professor Fissbrek de Hardeynagh has given an account of the events that led to the fall of our civilization, and I wasn't here! It's enough to make one throw oneself from the top of the Observatory Tower, which is said to be two hundred meters high!"

And in my despair, I was about to climb the one thousand three hundred steps that led to the platform of that tower when a thought stopped me. What if I were to pay a visit to the eloquent professor instead? Perhaps he would satisfy my curiosity briefly—although I strongly suspected that conciseness was not his dominant quality. Onwards!

III. The Decadence of Twenty-First Century Civilization

The illustrious Bulger received me with grave benevolence. I explained the purpose of my visit and my keen regrets. That step appeared to flatter his vanity. I finished by asking him whether, by any chance, the first lecture in his excellent course might have been published.

He contemplated me with an indulgently ironic smile. "Of course—but where do you come from, my dear sir? What! You don't know facts of history that the most worthless of our schoolchildren know thoroughly..."

At that moment, he rang a hand-bell, and a domestic appeared. "Tell little Robinet to come here immediately!"

A frisky brat of five or six with a mischievous expression soon arrived. I was sympathetic enough to be anxious about a red swelling he had on his forehead. *Poor kid!* I thought. *He must have fallen down three flights of stairs!*

It was me who fell from a height when I heard the professor say to him: "Let's see, child. You, who have such a fine relief of memory, recite to this gentleman chapter twenty-six of my *Great Annals of France.* If you get it right, you can have a double ration of jam with dessert, you hear?"

And he became to recite, while shifting his weight from one foot to the other, the following pages:

"By the middle of the twentieth century,[19] the sciences, the arts and industry had attained their apogee in the civilized nations of the globe, which were linked together by railways, electric telegraphs and submarine tunnels. Machines, infinitely multiplied and applied to everything, had very nearly eliminated the employment of human strength. Almost by themselves, they built houses and worked the land, sowing and harvesting, made bread, furniture and clothes, and killed and butchered the animals destined to feed the public. The poorest individual could procure all the objects of basic necessity in return for the light duty of supervising, in shifts, the movements of a few machines placed under the direction of an engineer; no one was unemployed, save voluntarily.

"It was said that it was the return of the Golden Age, but make no mistake: that epoch was the Age of Iron, in moral as well as physical terms. The state of material well-being attained by humankind gave birth to its ruin. It seemed that God wanted to punish humans for having stolen too many fruits from the tree of Science. The multiplication at certain points of the globe of railways and telegraph wires disrupted the normal action of the electricity of the atmosphere. In certain conditions, those immense metallic networks repelled the fertilizing snow of winter and the benevolent storms of summer.

"Previously-unknown maladies afflicted the human species, and the plants and livestock that served to nourish it. In the entrails of the globe, a tidal wave of vague incandescence rumbled, which shook portions of the terrestrial crust that had previously been spared. At the beginning of the twenty-first century, the great capitals of Europe, shaken by volcanic efforts, saw a fraction of their habitations collapse, and about the same time, contact with a comet asphyxiated all the peoples of America.

---

[19] The original text has "twenty-first," but as the story continues with the beginning of the twenty-first century, I have assumed that to be a misprint.

"Religious faith had taken refuge in the depths of a few elite intelligences as if in its ultimate sanctuary, but public worship was a mere matter of form for the majority. Dispossessed of the benefit of manual labor, entire populations lived inactively from day to day, ennui and the cold sentiment of realism in their souls. Everywhere, idleness, having become chronic, had engendered a disgust for life that was translated into thousands of suicides. A fatal inertia of the body and the heart! Among the masses, only brains, and no longer arms, worked; it was a reversal of natural law. Never had a more ardent thirst for the superfluous, the marvelous and unrealizable projects changed the human imagination for the worse. The study of arts, letters and the sciences was no longer the exception but the banal objective of everyone. Everyone thought himself called to a great intellectual role; everyone wanted to be an enchanter, but there was no more enchantment. Printing presses, multiplying everywhere, relentlessly vomited out millions of books at rock-bottom prices. All the evil passions spread their contingent of redoubtable poisons through those vast arteries of social life known as literature.

"Great moral convulsions followed close on the heels of this mortal virus. Reason deserted brains as religion had retired from consciences. Rivalries of love, wealth, commerce, celebrity and political influence degenerated into desperate battles, basely hypocritical, egotistical and perfidious. About 2050, an epidemic madness propagated from individual to individual.

"The civilized nations were then ruled by governments impotent to master the passions in the absence of religious restraint, and composed of strangely complicated mechanisms. Their heterogeneous elements, associated in an artificial manner, constituted a power comparable to powders that fulminate at the slightest agitation; they were monarchic democracies, or, if you prefer, democratic monarchies. It was sufficient, for there to be an explosion, that the monarchic principle turned to extreme tyranny, or that the democratic base degenerated into demagogy. That was the final element that led to the catastrophe. An accusing voice rose up, from no one knew where, to signal the hatred of the masses for the chief engineers who represented financial power, and the aristocratic class.

"Thousands of newspapers made themselves the echo of that fatal voice. Then was realized the ancient apologue of the Limbs and the Stomach. By virtue of the weakness of a fictitious authority and the rapidity of the means of communication, all the peoples rushed toward the same abyss at the same time. A conspiracy was organized that burst forth simultaneously at all points. Everywhere, the engineers were stripped of their wealth or massacred and the machines annihilated, save for those designed for destruction—the only ones that were to survive, to the misfortune of humankind.

"In those days of boundless fury, the châteaux and farms were burned. The fire only spared a fraction of the reserves of seeds, developed by means of ingenious methods, which human intelligence had taken centuries to produce.

"A few ages had attempted in vain to enlighten that blind rage, but what could an atom of reason accomplish in the midst of that general dementia? Soon, necessity removed the blindfold. Attempts were made to re-establish the agricultural machinery, but the agricultural experts had been killed. It was decided that labor would be temporarily confided to human muscles, as in barbaric times; unfortunately, the courage that had been so ardent to destroy weakened in the face of the slow and painful travail that had nourished previous generations.

"The last alimentary resources were squandered by the strongest, as on a raft of shipwreck-victims. Famine ensued, which sowed cadavers; then plague, which multiplied by airborne infection. The earthquakes completed the work of destruction. Only Death brought in a harvest that year.

"A few families succeeded in taking refuge in taking refuge in a remote part of Central Africa. We are the descendants of those families, who miraculously survived the sinking of the immense ship of ancient civilization. We have rediscovered the ingenious inventions of our ancestors, and have added our own to them—but, instructed by the great catastrophe of the twenty-first century, we employ the machines that assist manual labor, and exhibit in or museums, as mere curiosities, those which suppress it."

"Good! Very good! Perfect!" said the professor of ancient history. "Get back to your game of guinguiche;[20] you shall have the promised double ration."

Young Robinet ran off at top speed.

As for me, I thanked the venerable Bulger with reverent insistence, and went to get a little air under a portico.

IV. An Archaeological Conference in the Year 9957

I remained downcast for some time beneath the weight of that lugubrious story, recited by a child. It had impressed me to such an extent that I no longer thought of raising any doubt as to the authenticity of the fats recorded in Monsieur de Hardeynagh's chronicle.

Suddenly, I was distracted from my sad meditations by the conversation of two students, who were talking about a course on French Antiquities. I asked them to tell me where it was taking place.

"A few steps away," was the reply. "If the subject interests you, you couldn't do any better—today there's an extraordinary meeting of the Academy of Antiquarian Bulgers; the most renowned scientists will be speaking at it."

I followed the two young men and installed myself with them on a bench.

While waiting for the opening of the session, I asked a neighbor who was in a communicative mood for information about the great library of Archeopolis, which, I had heard, contained a hundred and twenty-five thousand manuscripts and more than two million printed volumes, as many ancient as modern.

---

[20] This word appears to be improvised, presumably from *guingois* [lopsided].

I learned that that immense deposit of the products of human intelligence had long been classified and so skillfully catalogued in a set of two hundred folio volumes that one could instantly locate any published work on any particular subject. There were thirty categories of books; there was a department head in charge of each one with a proportionate number of fetchers and replacers under his orders. In his exceptional memory were arranged, as in reality on the shelves, all the books in his category. The principal function of that living table of contents was to enlighten people doing research, or simply in search of information.

I began once again to think that I was dreaming.

"From what class," I asked my neighbor, "are the department heads of each category of manuscripts recruited?"

"From among the craniums that have the most pronounced triple bulge of probity, memory and benevolence."

"But isn't that of erudition also required?"

"That's carefully avoided! There was a time when renowned Bulgers were placed in charge of manuscripts. They greeted novice savants with red and pedantic faces; they could not be bothered to disturb themselves for those petty enquirers, and ended up turning them away all the more willingly as they thus reserved the most precious unpublished documentary sources for themselves, their friends and colleagues. Rules then existed that favored the egotistic system in question, but one of our most judicious monarchs, the august Matoupah IX, put an end to that sort of abuse. I'd explain how, if the session were not about to begin."

It was, in fact, opening. I would have like to be able to triple the number of my ears. It began with a partial raising of the curtain, in order to give the numerous laggards time to arrive. Whatever the celebrated professor had said about the displacement of the ecliptic, the climate in Archeopolis was far from temperate; a tropical heat reigned there, and its inhabitants moved with a extreme slowness. In consequence, half a dozen papers submitted to the Academy were read out. I was particularly interested in one that bore the title: *On the occa-*

sions on which the ancient French pronounced the sacred phrase: God bless you! The author concluded, on the thirtieth page that "The exclamation was evidently addressed to individuals who had the whooping cough."

That unexpected resolution made me laugh, but, except for me, the entire audience retained an imperturbable gravity.

Once the petty *hors-d'oeuvres* were out of the way, the true session began. I saw a noble individual come in, clad in a white robe ornamented with ostrich-feathers, whose skull offered two superbly-gleaming protuberances; the more ample was, it was said, that of numerical sagacity. The honorable Bulger was charged with reading the report of the men in the balloon on their excursion to the ruins of Old Paris. That report was so majestically prolix that I shall show mercy to the reader and only cite the last part:

"On the ninth of July, after a difficult march over an uncultivated plain, cluttered with mossy stones and strewn with the debris of windows, slates, and marbles of various hues, we paused on the edge of the Synn—the Seine of the ancient chroniclers—at the place that had once been site of the gardens of the Tuileries, a word that signifies *delights*.[21] It was, as we know, one of the most frequented locations in the immense capital of a thousand gates.

"In a gully full of brushwood, where a snake of an exceptionally dangerous species was hissing, we fund a horse's head in white marble, rather primitive, which has been placed in room number 729 of our National Museum. This fragment was collected a short distance from an ancient highway of great breadth, leading to a town named Vaersall or Versaëlles, an ancient name which, as our honorable colleague Monsieur Hernoïl"—Monsieur Hernoïl took a bow—"has demonstrated, means 'the town to the west', thus called because of its occidental situation in relation to Paris. Everything leads us to

---

[21] A *tuilerie* is actually a tile factory—a label perhaps not entirely appropriate to the palace in question or the gardens that survived it.

believe that the horse's head in question was part of a monument erected in the idle of one of the gardens of the Tuileries to Constable Bonnaparth, who, after the death of Louis XVII, his sovereign, was proclaimed head of state, under the allegorical name of Napoléon, a word of Greek origin signifying 'lion of the forests.'[22] That hero, who died on the island of Corsica, founded a dynasty celebrated in the history of the destiny of France.

"Further away, toward the place where a magnificent basilica stood, covered with silver gilt plaques, known as Saint-Germain-des-Prés, a short distance from the ruin of the Louvre, we exhumed a bronze candelabra still partly gilded, on which were sculpted in relief the three letters I. H. S. One so-called antiquary, drawing from I don't know what apocryphal source, has argued in a pamphlet, which cannot be seriously refuted here, that these three letters, also featured on two antique vases in our museum, originally signified: *Iesus Hominum Salvator*, or simply IHESUS. He adds that, in consequence, monks named Jesuits, taking the same letters as the motto of their order, gave it another meaning: *Iesus Humilis Societas*.

"We shall not enter into more ample detail regarding this singular opinion; to advertise would be to attribute value to it. Our personal research has put us on the right track. In the sixteenth century, under king Henri (the second or third of that name) lived a famous sculptor named Jean Goujon or Gonjou.[23] Now, the heads of the cherubs decorating this candelabrum are certainly attributable to an artful chisel, so we do not hesitate to do honor to that artist, so celebrated in the annals of ancient art. We interpret the monogram thus: JOANNES, the forename of the said Goujon or Gonjou, HENRICI SCULP-

---

[22] Bonnardot adds a Greek tag here, which consists of the Greek *napea* (the name of a wood nymph) and *leon* (lion).

[23] Jean Goujon (1510-c1566) designed the Fontaine des Innocents in the old cemetery and participated in the decoration of the Louvre while it was a palace, some fragments of his work surviving there when it became a museum.

TOR. The cross positioned over the letter H is no embarrassment; it designates that the king in question was very Christian, *rex christianissimus*, as the old chronicles say.[24] I think one would search in vain for a more satisfactory explanation."

I shrugged my shoulders, itching to give vocal support to the oppressed antiquary, but the long and unanimous applause that greeted the conclusion of the learned Bulger did not permit me to raise my voice.

When the enthusiasm had calmed down completely, the orator immediately passed on to another exercise. He had a heavily-oxidized bronze passed around the room, on which the following inscription could be deciphered: GASPARD, BREVETÉ S. G. D. G.[25] I understood immediately where the cylinder came from and what the four initials signified.

I was about to elucidate the question briefly when the savant raised the venerable debris—from the pump of a *clysoir*[26]

---

[24] Henri II was a conspicuously weak king; although not quite as incompetent as Henri III (who did not come to the throne until Goujon was dead) he was dominated by various advisers, latterly his wife Catherine de Medici, who orchestrated the St. Bartholomew's Day massacre after his death, during the intermediate reign of Charles IX.

[25] *Breveté* mean "patented". S.G.D.G.—*Sans garantie de government* [Not guaranteed by the government]—was a precautionary formula added to all French patents of the era in question, to emphasize that the issuing of a patent did not constitute an official guarantee that device in question would actually work.

[26] A *clysoir* was a flexible tube fitted with a cannula, used for introducing liquids into body-cavities; if the author were thinking in terms of enemas he would probably have used the word *clystère* [clyster], so it is more likely that he means to imply a vaginal douche employed for contraceptive purposes. In primitive versions of the device, the liquids were simply poured into an elevated funnel at the far end of the tube, but the mechanically-minded 19th century inevitably produced

of my own time—over his head and addressing the sympathetic members of the audience, who were holding their breath, said:

"We do not know today, gentlemen, exactly what purpose this ancient bronze tube served. Was it part of an astronomical instrument, a musical instrument of a weapon? That is what I hope to clarify shortly in a quarto volume whose first three hundred pages are in press. I shall limit myself here to a very probable supposition with regard to the word BREVETÉ. It is doubtless the name of a family of industrialists well known in the twentieth century or thereabouts, for it can be read on several fragments that we already have in our museum. It is preceded by other forenames such as Grégoire, Crépin, etc.[27] As for the four letters S.G.D.G., I confess that I have spent many sleepless nights searching for their meaning. I hope to succeed, with the collaboration of the honorable Monsieur Hernoïl"—Monsieur Hernoïl took a bow—"in interpreting them in an incontrovertible manner. Thus far, we are inclined to favor the hypothesis that the four letters indicate the birthplace of the Breveté family."

At this point in the speech I could take no more. I got to my feet with the firm intention of enlightening the assembly, even if the president gave orders to throw the indiscreet interrupter out, and was about to launch into my explanation in good faith when a sort of usher, advancing into the middle of the hall, called out in a bass-baritone voice: "Messieurs, it is six o'clock!"

At that sudden exclamation, all the bulging heads stirred and were covered with turbans. More than one honorable col-

---

patented versions fitted with pumps, which were presumably much in demand in busy Parisian brothels.

[27] The name Grégoire, observed on a bronze item in this context, would probably have belonged to the sculptor Jean-Louis Grégoire, that of Crépin to Crépin David, a designed and makes of musical instruments.

league woke up with a start, delighted to have attained the closure of the session and the proximity of dinner-time.

On seeing that entire colony of frogs start hopping, I burst into such crazy laughter that I woke up myself, and found myself in the midst of my nineteenth-century household implements.

Of all that I thought I had heard, only five words had really been pronounced: “Monsieur, it is six o’clock.” At the same instant, the same voice repeated them. It was that of my domestic, who, following orders given the day before, had come to tell me that it was time to get dressed, because I had to set off at eight o’clock on a trip to visit the ruins of Rome.

René du Mesnil de Maricourt: *All the Way! The Commune in 2073*

(1874)

It was at ten o'clock in the morning on the first of November, after reading the newspaper, that I decided to take the big step. At five o'clock in the evening I emptied the fatal cup (pardon me for that old expression, a souvenir of my classical reading). The fact is that I drank from a vulgar tea-cup, slightly chipped, bearing traces of poor gilding. What did I drink? I don't want to give the recipe; people would abuse it.

At six o'clock precisely I lost consciousness, and the last terrestrial sound to strike my ears was that of the dinner bell. I had spent the day writing my testament, thus conceived:

My dear children,

I'm tired of hearing everyone repeat: Good God, where are we going? What does the future have in store for us? Poor France, torn apart by the enemy and by the cruel hands of its own children; poor France, what will become of you?

The future is God's, that's evident, but it's no bad thing to interrogate God about that future, and the surest means of knowing is to witness future events oneself. I want to know what France will become in two hundred years. Well, I shall go to sleep for two hundred years and my curiosity will be satisfied. It's true that I won't be able to reply to the alarmed interrogations of my neighbor, who, as he passes me the paper every morning, asks the eternal question: "Where are we going? What will become us?"

It's necessary to tell you that I have always been profoundly liberal, attached to progressive ideas regarding the emancipation of peoples, but I've encountered so many little snags in the application of these ideas that, to tell the truth,

I'm no longer sure whether I'm red or white. I would certainly have cried "Long live Henri V!" like anyone else, if it had been possible to settle the matter,[28] *just as I cry "Long live the President!"—all the more readily since I have nothing to ask of either of them. Will there be red or white in two hundred years? Is it the future that will be triumphant? Is it the past that will be reborn of its ashes, like an old featherless phoenix? We shall know. You have heard talk of the Indian fakir who can produce artificial lethargy at will. Many scientists deny the fact. No matter! He exists, in spite of the prohibitions of the Académie des Sciences, with the result that I have recovered the fakir's formula and am going to use it on myself in a little while.*

Share out my possessions and act as if I were dead. Behave in such a way that everyone will think me well and truly buried, and keep the most absolute secrecy regarding this adventure. I bid you farewell, for in two hundred years from now you would be two hundred and twenty-five, and since the patriarchs, we have lost the habit of such long lifetimes—but marry, have children and transmit my instructions to them.

I'm going to retire to my little study and go to sleep there; I'll lock myself in. Don't let curiosity or filial love cause you to break down the door to contemplate my cherished and venerated features, bathe my face in tears, etc., etc. All that, by introducing a dose of air in excess of that specified by the formula, would compromise the success of the experiment. My study door must be walled up, masked by wood paneling; the window should likewise be sealed, so that no stranger can

---

[28] Following the collapse of the Second Empire in 1870 and the suppression of the Commune in 1871 the provisional government entered into negotiations with the Comte de Paris, the grandson of Louis-Philippe, who would have ruled as the constitutional monarch Henri V had he not refused to allow the tricolor to remain the flag of France, thus sabotaging the deal and leaving the Third Republic to provide its own head of state.

suppose the existence of the little room, which must be like the bell jar of a vacuum pump. Try to live well, but above all, have children. Let the eldest of the family, at precisely six o'clock in the evening of the first of November 2073, make his entrance through the previously un-walled-up door; let the window be unsealed. Let him present himself without fear, and be ready to answer to me; he will find someone able to talk.

(A few minute details here about the precautions to be taken for the solemn moment.)

Farewell once again, dear children, and may God bless you. Let the descendant charged with awakening me not be too abrupt in his manner, nor hypocritically flattering, for a disagreeable sensation might be dangerous.

Senlis, 1st November 1873
Jean-Nicolas Praquin
Ex-municipal councilor, archeologist and philosopher.

P.S. I have a horror of genealogical trees that remind us of certain aristocratic vanities now drowned in the flood of progress, but take good care of our own families, in order that I may know who my interlocutor is.

P.P.S. Let my dressing-gown be put in pepper, my large boots coated with a thick layer of neat's-foot oil and half a dozen cotton bonnets be preserved, at all costs.

I folded it up, put it in an envelope, sealed it with five large black seals and placed the whole thing in the dining room, very prominently, in order that my family should take cognizance of my intentions; then, as I just said, I locked myself in my study.

That redoubt was very cramped, but I had accumulated many curious and bizarre objects there (the simple mania of an archaeologist and philosopher): a double louis struck under Pharamond; Oceanian swords; Chinese lanterns with grimacing faces; a jar containing a two-head fetus preserved in alcohol; a photograph of a young man whom I had taken into my home and who had never sought to trouble my family; one of an publisher who had got rich without going bankrupt; one of an army supplier reduced to holding his helmet out to passers-by; the portrait of a friend to whom I had lent money and had not turned his back on me—that one I had had painted in oils and on foot; I would have had an equestrian statue made, but didn't have room.

I had even succeeded, by certain very ingenious means, in conserving the tongue of a woman who had not spoken ill of anyone, the modesty of a poet, the generosity of a banker, the conciseness of an advocate, the virginity of the president of an assize court, the utility of a sub-prefect, the services rendered to the public by a postmaster and, finally, a few kind words from a German and an 1812 sausage.

I let a vague, semi-conscious gaze wander over all these things, while a powerful but gentle heaviness gradually paralyzed each of my limbs and a distant buzzing, like the swell of the sea, afflicted my ears. My vision began to blur, and the last object I distinguished clearly was my *mobile* saber[29] hanging on the wall, and I had a slight aftertaste of the potatoes that it had helped me dig up during the winter of the invasion.

That sensation faded away to give way to a dream, and, with my mind focused on the future I was going to investigate, I said to myself: *Is there in the ocean of the political world a man of conviction, honest and disinterested?* And floating on the waves of the ocean thus evoked, I saw a few familiar faces of men of different parties, and a sympathetic face sometimes emerged, alarmed and full of anguish, from the lashing foam. They sank, one after another, while I reached out my hand, seeking to catch them by the hair and save them from the abyss—but my fingers closed on them one by one, and nothing any longer remained in my hand but a wig.

Then the first stroke of six o'clock sounded on the big clock in the hallway, and the dinner bell began to ring. I think

---

[29] i.e., the saber the protagonist had worn while serving in the *garde mobile* of 1870, during the Franco-Prussian War.

that, gripped by a sudden terror, I called out to Joseph, my eldest son—but Joseph could not hear me, because the sound stuck in my throat.

I tried several times, and in an agonizing voice, I succeeded in saying: "Jos..."

1st November 2073, 6 p.m.

"...eph! Joseph!" This time, the word emerged at full volume. Six o' clock was chiming.

"Here I am, Citizen Ancestor," replied a reedy voice—and the door fell in.

I saw, by an electrical light whose source I could not make out, a short, slightly stooped man, whose mahogany-colored beard had a few gray hairs mixed in, wearing large spectacles, dressed in a sort of dull gutta-percha tunic. There was something sickly, surly and yet superb in the expression of his features. He was looking at me attentively, without overmuch curiosity, and seemed to be waiting for me to say something to him. As for me, by a rapid mental effort, I pulled myself together; the entire past appeared to me, and in a calm tone, I asked him: "So you're one of my grandchildren or great grandchildren, and you're named Joseph, like my eldest son?"

"Citizen," the little man replied, in his taut voice—as if the effort were painful—"I should like to believe that I am your relative, but in that regard we cannot affirm anything, because the nation has abolished ancestors, in view of the fact that not everyone can afford such a luxury; to conserve that privilege would contravene the laws of equality."

"But after all, you doubtless bear my family name; you are, I hope, a Praquin, and a good man, as we all are?"

At these words he smiled, and took a visiting card out of a small wallet.

"I called you ancestor," he told me, "because you evidently belong to the old world that our forefathers have overturned, but there are no more family names, and no genealogy, now."

And he held out his card, on which I read:

A". Cressgrowers (Joseph), 225. Citizen.

"And this," he added, "is my companion's card."

A". Cressgrowers (Josephine), 225. Citizeness.

"What diabolical gibberish! Would you care to explain it?"

"Yes, Ancient, but let me get my breath."

At this point, taking a glass-stoppered bottle from his tunic pocket, he raised it to his nose, saying, by way of explanation: "Thanks to the multiplicity of factories, the accumulation of individuals in one place, and the special mode of our constructions, with which I shall soon acquaint you, the supply of breathable air is inadequate, unless we go up in a balloon or on our terraces, so we have oxygen and nitrogen factories, and public reservoirs of compressed air at which everyone can fill his bottle at an fixed price. Don't worry—this air will be sufficient for you for a few hours. Now, this is the significance of our cards:

"The district of Paris in which we live corresponds to the letter A", and Cressoniers indicates the housing-block in which we are lodged; as for Joseph, I will tell you..."

"One moment, my lad. You mentioned Paris, but I know full well that I went to sleep in Senlis, in the département of the Oise, on the ground floor of my house, in a little study cleverly built into the thickness of the wall; that my house was between a courtyard and a garden, facing a little stream called the Nonette. You mustn't tell me tales, you hear, or I'll get annoyed—and I still have solid fists."

"It was thus," my interlocutor went on, "that, in your barbaric times, when brutality replaced logic and force was substituted for the law, you brought your rotten old world to ruin—but as I could asphyxiate you instantaneously before you has raised yourself up by half a centimeter, leave your fists at rest and listen to me."

I was irritated by his tone, which was both conceited and mocking as well as pretentious, all the more so because the French language had undergone a strange metamorphosis during the two centuries I had been asleep. Can you imagine that Parisian jargon, the popular argot that our comedians mimic so hilariously at the Théâtre de Palais-Royal, was the language employed by my interlocutor, with its specific guttural quality supported by gestures of a deplorable triviality? I can but translate his speech into French, in order to be intelligible, while conserving a few of his expressions. It was, therefore, with a certain nervous irritation that I exclaimed:

"Whence comes this familiarity in my regard. Why do you permit yourself to address me as *tu*? None of my children would have dared to do that, and you, you puny wretch, seem to be sneering at me!"

At which abuse he smiled, and in a frankly good-humored tone he replied: "What? And your sister? Old fool! Have you, then, several individualities all to yourself—more than one nose, mouth, pairs of eyes and pairs of ears—so that I should talk to you in the plural, as if you were a whole group of people? That's an error of grammar and common sense, long since abandoned, which is reminiscent of the miserable ages of privilege and capital. Besides, if one of our censors heard me say *vous* to anyone, I'd be subject to a fine of ten thousand francs. Strictly speaking, we may reserve that plural for God"—here he lowered his voice—"since he constitutes, it seems, a whole of several persons, but I've just committed a serious fault in pronouncing that word, which ought never to emerge from our mouths. Now I'll return to the explanation of the cards, but talking tires me out, and we've improved dialogue. Open your eyes and shut up."

He turned his back on me and I saw him maneuvering both hands with an extreme agility.

"You'll see that we have investigated electricity, old man, and studied the nervous fluid, and have been able to make use of their combination."

Immediately, I saw luminous characters surge forth on the wall facing me, which appeared and disappeared like the track of a chemical match in darkness. I read the following:

"You fell asleep in Senlis, facing the Nonette, and you woke up in Paris without having changed location, because Senlis and Paris are now but one.

"Take a large set of compasses and place of one its points at the center of the City, pricking the dorsal spine of Note-Dame; open the other branch as far as Provins; trace the circumference, and you will have a perfectly circular area whose extent is approximately equivalent to that of the old Île-de-France. That great round cheese is now called Paris, or, rather, the Commune.[30]

"Now, cut your cheese by means of a dozen straight lines intersecting at the center, and you will have twenty-four sectors that are distinguished by the letters of the alphabet. A circle, extending as far as the old Saint-Denis circumscribes the first sectors designated by the simple letters mentioned above; a second circle, much more extensive, encloses the continuations of the first quarters, the prolongations of the triangles, and those bear the letter of the alphabet with the sign ". A third circle encloses the series of noted sectors, and so on.

"The advantage of this system is to eliminate any rivalry, since the sectors are perfectly equal. A single glance at my map therefore indicates to a stranger where he needs to look for me in the immense city. But our A" sector is equal in dimension to that of ancient Versailles, and to locate oneself within it requires further subdivisions. The sector is cut into squares by a series of lines drawn at right-angles; each of these squares contains a series of islets or bocks of ten houses, and each house has ten stories; the principal lines isolating the large squares are streets, and the secondary lines merely indicate the drains receiving rainwater. That's one of the reasons

[30] In 1870 Provins was the heart of an agricultural region known for its roses; it is about 80 kilometers from the center of Paris.

why air is so scarce here, and there's even talk of a price-increase at the Main Reservoir."

"What, wretch!" I could not help exclaiming. "You live heaped up in these wells, and that's what you've been able to realize with your ideas of progress, social improvement and the rest! No more air, no more sunlight, no more health, no more life! And we deplored the fate of the workers of Lille and Lyon!"

"That's true! That's true! But it doesn't matter. We have an answer for everything: have a little patience. I'll continue my explanation of the map. You must have understood that Paris, or the Free City, or the Commune, as you wish, is the perfect representation of an immense spider-web cut into twenty-four triangles terminated at the base by the segment of a circle; I have thus expressed myself badly by employing the word 'squares' to indicate our housing blocks; let's retain it for greater clarity of speech, and let's say that a collection of squares constitutes an area that, in our free city of workers, bears the name of a trade union. Now, in the ancient Senlis in which you went to sleep two hundred years ago, there were marshes exploited by cressgrowers; that's why, as a second designation, my card bears the word Cressgrowers. In the same way, we have the areas of Fishermen, Goldsmiths, Advocates, Spadeworkers, Notaries and so on.

"Finally, you want to know why I'm named Joseph? A simple matter of chance. As the family no longer exists, it has been necessary to get rid of family names, and a simple means is employed to label individuals. Here we have recourse neither to the decimal system nor the duodecimal system, nor to the alphabet, but to the old calendar, from which twenty of the most common names—Jean, Jacques, Charles, Joseph, etc. etc.—were extracted, and the Central Council decreed that all the inhabitants of Block II, Section X, will be called Charles or Joseph, in all the houses contained between a particular radius and segment of the circle. As for the number in the sequence, it's that of a person's house and apartment. Thus, when I meet my neighbor, I have only to say to him: "Bonjour, Citizen 226!" What a simplification for police enquiries, if the police still existed!"

I remained pensive for a few moments, without saying a word. Abandoning his system of electric telegraphy and having had recourse once again to his bottle of air, he continued:

"That astonishes you, eh, old man? But that's not all. You wanted to know just now why we live like snakes at the bottom of a well. It's not that bad, though, and I'll tell you about it, briefly. In the era in which you lived as an idle bourgeois, innocently fattening yourself on the sweat of the people, since you had your share of filthy capital and your place in the sun without knowing by what right you had it, a few principles had already been proclaimed which had brought the road traveled thus far to a good end. We—by which I mean our forefathers—put these principles into practice, and brought about a great revolution whose nucleus was Paris.

"After battles, accounts of which would bore you—terrible battles in which our people were crushed like vermin, only to rise again, ever stronger and more numerous, supported by right and justice—and after a number of petty bloodbaths which had the result of annihilating the bourgeoisie, our people remained masters of the terrain conclusively; then people finally understood. The liberated worker has taken over ownership of capital and land, the raw materials of production, and has said to all his brothers in the world: 'Come, poor oppressed individuals, slaves of centuries-old tyranny; come throw yourselves into the arms of liberation.'

"And they came—so many of them, all full of good will and a strong appetite, that it was necessary to appoint quartermasters to prepare accommodations, then organize the work and divide up the capital. We even made an agreement with the other nations, which wanted to continue to live in the darkness of the past, that each one would organize itself as it wished. We were given free rein to apply our ideal of society and government, and were granted free possession of the conquered terrain—which is to say, the great cheese of which I spoke.

"We have accumulated here more than forty million individuals; we had to squeeze together somewhat. In addition to that, land has acquired such value that, even if it were paved over with a triple layer of gold coins, there would not be enough to pay for it. Thus, we cannot amuse ourselves by having promenades, squares and other wasted spaces. What good would they be, anyway, since no one goes out any longer, except on to terraces and in balloon-omnibuses? We have got rid of the ground, and thus used up the surface of the Earth..."

When I remained just as pensive and taciturn, Joseph continued:

"By the coloration of your face and the rapidity of your heartbeat—an extravagant expenditure of air—I can tell in a precise manner what you're thinking; it's not sorcery, merely a physical phenomenon that I would explain to you if I had time. I know what the questions are that you want to ask me, and there are a lot of them. At this moment you're wondering how you come to be both in your old house and one of the modern habitations I've just described to you. Nothing simpler. After having razed, burned and sacked the old Paris, we rebuilt the suburbs and constituted the city of free workers on the plan that you know. Old buildings that could be adapted to the plan were conserved. That's how you came to find yourself sealed in your study like an old toad in its hole."

As if exhausted by this effort, and the sound of his voice weakening, he resumed using the telegraphic system in order to continue:

"Thus, you see that our cards contain the most precise information; with the aid of a few words, a letter and a number, a pigeon-hole can be located instantly. As for the insect that occupies it, he is so similar to his neighbors that individuality, which played such a large role in your world, has, so to speak, been eliminated—to the extent that in seeing me, you see the entire republic."

"That's not funny!" I said.

"Oh yes—jokes were once required to amuse the bourgeoisie! But look, if it were otherwise, what would become of equality? All individuality desires to express itself by climbing over the heads of others. Ours are bowed beneath the yoke of the utilitarian social level."

"And your wife, Citizeness Josephine Cressgrowers A". number…I can't remember it?"

"Number 225; don't make me repeat it again, for an error of name of number might make you end up, when you go out, in the sector of Notaries, Advocates or Bankers, and you wouldn't be able to extricate yourself therefrom. You'll see my companion Josephine for yourself at eight o'clock; she's busy making dinner in the federal kitchen; it's her decad."[31]

"She's making diner herself? And if I understand you right, she's making it for the community. You don't have domestic servants, then?"

"Oh, you poor old man, how you belong to your village and your era. You haven't understood anything about our modern system. I'll get back to more important things. You know that we all live in blocks or islets of ten houses divided into ten floors, which results in a hundred households comprising a man, a woman and a child—no more and no less. Thus, in this block there are three hundred Josephs or Josephines, according to the sex of each individual. Ten blocks constitute a thousand families, or three thousand individuals to feed.

"That responsibility is entrusted to ten women, who are replaced every ten days and who, when the ten days are up, go on to other functions, such as those of clothing manufacturer, launderer, newspaper editor, professor of philosopher, and many others. Only one occupation is forbidden to them, and with good reason—that of advocate. But understand once and for all that there is no longer, strictly speaking, any manual labor. With improved machines activated by heat or electrici-

[31] In the new calendar briefly introduced after the 1789 Revolution, the traditional seven-day week was replaced by a series of ten-day periods, known as *décades*, here translated as decads.

ty, one has only to touch certain switches with one's finger. Thus, forging iron, cutting wood, decorating the façade of a public building, casting a statue and writing a poem are all as easy as playing a tune on a miniature organ; it's only a matter of operating the keys. Having strong arms is, therefore, merely an old expression to us, devoid of meaning, unless it's a matter of the *patriotic capstan*, about which I shall tell you in due course.

"You can see that domestic servants would be unnecessary, an encumbrance, and even if they were to be awarded the title of official citizens, it would be no less shameful for a society founded on equality to conserve such ancient, quasi-feudal customs."

"But in sum, tell me, how is your society of free workers—since that's the name you've adopted—organized?"

"The ultimate foundation, as I've already said several times is *equality*: that is the great principle, and its consequences are these: hereditary property being a monstrous aberration of barbaric centuries in which the strong oppressed the weak, in which one only needed to be well-born in order to sit down at the banquet of the idle rich, has been abolished. Family affections being nothing but disguised egotism, exposing some people to comfort in their households while others find nothing there but beds of thorns, the abolition of the family and the institution of marriage were decreed..."

"Good, good! That's logical—but where do the children come from?"

"No one knows."

"What! No one knows?"

"No. Every citizen must be father to a certain number of little free workers, without his being able to recognize them; none of the children know their parents, and the Commune is the universal mother of all. A short time after your burial, when the great victory took place of labor over capital, liberty in love was proclaimed. Liberty was fine, but equality received rude shocks at every step. Some women had ten lovers, while their neighbors could lower themselves without obtaining the slightest declaration from an old ape; some men transpierced all feminine hearts with their gaze, while all women looked down their noses at their brethren. Add to that a system in which a few reproducers found themselves solely responsible for furnishing the republic, which would have cause some type or aptitude to predominate. It was necessary to renounce all that and submit love to a rational and methodical discipline."

"What sort of discipline?"

"Every citizen, at the age of twenty-one, and every citizeness, at the age of eighteen, is, or ought to be, capable of the work of national repopulation. In consequence, a young man drawn from the adult reservoir, about which I shall speak in due course, is provided with lodging, which is the lot assigned to him, and, by the same token, is provided with a name since the name is attached to the dwelling. The same operation is simultaneously effected in the female reservoir, and, at the same time as shelter, food, work, tools and civil estate, the adult meets the young companion allotted to him at random..."

"With whom he must live..."

"For exactly a year; when the year is up, a round of inspectors or censors arrives, charged with collecting woman and children; the women are distributed to other citizens, year by year, always according to the dictates of a lottery, until they are too old; then they becomes teachers or midwives. As for the children, they are poured into the bosom of Social Maternity. That is as simple as all our institutions, but it seems to require further simplification, and there is talk of applying to national repopulation a certain system of pisciculture that had already been invented in your era. The project is under consideration, and we're awaiting a decree of the Central Council.

"Until that decree is promulgated and printed on our poster-balloons, the children will remain in the Maternity until weaned, and then are confided to the care of united households, which are responsible for them until the age of seven. Then the nation takes them back in order to place them in reservoir no. 1, a period of rough-hewing: writing, reading, telegraphy, rapid calculation, and a few historical and geographical notions. They are then plunged into reservoir no. 2, a period of growth in which they get a general notions of arts and crafts, and finally they are decanted into reservoir no. 3, that of adults, a period of adaptation and improvement in which they are taught all the professions."

"All the professions, you day? What difference is there between a mason and a physician, a wine-maker and an astronomer?"

"None. Equal remuneration; we are adept at everything, to such a extent that a telegram notifies me whether I shall be an advocate for the next decad, a sewer-worker or a censor for the following decad, or whether I shall have to be a representative on the Grand Council while awaiting my turn on the capstan. In a word, we have to do everything—in a mediocre fashion, it's true, but our goal is to attain average proficiency in everything, and. thanks to our numbers, our products are perfect."

"Hmm! I don't quite understand, any more that I understand your capstan. I've often seen sailors devoting themselves to that painful exercise in order to pull up an anchor, but since you practice aerial navigation, you must have got rid of aquatic navigation."

"Not badly reasoned, old chap! We call ourselves that by analogy with, and in memory of, the great national instrument. It must be admitted that coal is scarce, and to obtain it from other nations would require fabulous sums; we have tried hard to dig down into our property as far as the center of the Earth, but it was necessary to call a halt to that in the face of unforeseen difficulties. Ether, chloroform and other substances became rarer, to the extent that we decided that we would become the necessary motor ourselves. Day and night, in each of the twenty-four sectors of the great cheese, thirty thousand men are harnessed to handles, and they push, push, push ahead, while singing the national anthem that reminds us of our emancipation, to the tune of the *Marseillaise.* Now, the collective force produces friction, and from that friction emerges heat, which we direct by means of ingenious apparatus in such a way as to produce clothes, works art or good dinners, like the one to which I invite you, for eight o'clock is about to chime, and the citizeness will not be long."

"Devil take me!" I exclaimed.

"Again, no God and no Devil," said Joseph, imperiously. "I have no desire to pay the fine: ten thousand francs represents a decad's work! These figures might seem excessive to you, but think of the augmentation of productivity, and hence of wages. As we live behind a blockade here, and other nations only accept ready cash, we are forced to have recourse to paper. We even go as far as payment in kind. Thus, I've sometimes received a stuffed crocodile for working at the patriotico-fraternal capstan, and I go to buy breathable air at the local reservoir with an old umbrella. The words you use recall certain primitive superstitions that enchained peoples for too long, and in that regard our laws are explicit."

"So be it! I won't say anything; but I'll make the observation that your capstan reminds me strongly of those Egyptian monuments for which, before the liberation of humankind, the State paid in human sacrifice for..."

"Bonsoir, Citizens! Here I am. I've obtained a double ration from the Federal Council of Josephs for the ancestor, who must be hungry." So saying, Madame Josephine 225 made her entrance. Eight o'clock was chiming.

My study door having been caved in, at simple touch from the citizeness, I saw the wall on which Joseph had exercised his telegraphic talents open up, sliding sideways as if by magic, to reveal a small and very tidy dining-room. On a table were three sets of cutlery and bowls of soup.

The dishes that succeeded one another, seemingly placing themselves before us of their own accord, seemed rather insipid to me, and the portions where measured chemically. As the rapidity of the service astonished me, Joseph murmured, between two mouthfuls: "Improved technology; application of electricity."

At the end of the meal we had beverage of some sort, which reminded me of our old coffee, followed by a vague memory of brandy.

I could not define the exact nature of the items of food and drink; at any rate, after the meal I found myself breathing more easily, quite alert and well, almost cheerful, in spite of the numbness that had weighed upon me since my awakening.

"Electro-chemical phenomena," Joseph whispered in my ear. "Cooking with organic elements reconstituted by science. Galvanization of the stomach..."

The citizeness intrigued me greatly; she had not pronounced two words during the meal and I had been unable to meet her gaze, hidden behind spectacles as massive as those of the citizen, but blue-tinted. His complexion seemed to me to be pale, pasty and unhealthy. She was wearing a kind of waterproof garment, gray in color, like the masculine tunic, but fitted with an enormous hood with advanced edges, like a nun's head-dress, so that her face was lost in its dark depths. One could, however, see a few strands of mahogany-colored hair peppered with white.

I noticed that the citizeness was a trifle stooped, like Joseph, and I wondered whether I might be confronted by an old lady—and yet, a few swift and decisive gestures, and a suggestion of stubbornness in the nostrils made me think that the citizeness might not be as old as she seemed. During the meal she had put a pitcher on her head in order to carry it into the next room, supporting it with both hands like a Greek caryatid; as I saw her disappear she had evoked a rapid vision of youth, beauty and innocence. Beneath the horrible gutta-percha garments I had perceived the curve of hips, the suppleness of a flexible figure; I had thought of those genteel schoolgirls who dress up outrageously to play the roles of grandmothers.

Joseph understood, for, as he had said, the diabolical little man could read my thoughts.

"Ha ha, Ancient!" he said, smiling, "It appears that you were a connoisseur in your day, perhaps an enthusiast, but as I have to leave you alone with the citizeness, be circumspect.

I'm not speaking for myself—I don't have any right to be jealous."

I made a gesture full of dignity and offended decency, and asked Joseph: "Why do you say that you don't have the right to defend your conjugal honor? The woman is your wife and possesses the spousal dignity that we hold precious among us. In a word, she belongs to you."

"You're mistaken," said Joseph, with a certain sadness. "She belongs to the State, to the Commune, if you wish, and the Commune has only lent her to me. In case of any deterioration of accident, I would be responsible for the damage caused to the nation, thus deprived of one of its instruments of repopulation."

"Why is he leaving us, then?" I asked Josephine, when he went out.

"To go drink three cups of a debilitating infusion, read three verses of Klopstock's *Messias* and comment on a chapter of Hegel: the three cups because it has been noticed that his muscles are developing too much and threatening to exceed the limits of the permitted mean; the reading because he has shown signs of a certain vivacity indicative of intellectual tendencies. As the majority here is unintelligent, intellectual tendencies are blunted by friction with German. Would you like to know anything else? Will you soon be finished with your questions? I'd like to interrogate you about the past—but go and see whether the doors are locked. Go on! Look lively!"

She began pirouetting around the table, humming: *I have a restless foot... Oh, the little lambs...*[32]

"Tell me, what did those animals do? Out there, old books of engravings circulate in secret, in which people and animals of the extinct world were seen, but it's forbidden, on the grounds that such things clog up the intellectual wheels. All the same, I'd like to see a lamb or a horse..."

---

[32] The first of these lines comes from a children's dancing song, *Le Pied qui remue*.

Still babbling and hopping around, with a few flicks of the wrist she got rid of her hood, her frightful waterproof garment, threw away her mahogany wig and her blue-tinted spectacles, shook off the dull powder soiling her face and appeared, as I had divined, in the naïve splendor of a dazzling youth.

"Are you an actress, Mademoiselle?" I asked, in bewilderment, feeling quite intimidated by that sudden revelation.

She burst out laughing. "Oh! *Mademoiselle* is superb! *Mademoiselle* is worth its weight in platinum. *Mademoiselle!* You must have come back to our world in order that I should hear that word. But no stupidities, you know, my jewel of an ancestor!"

With that, her dark eyes, shining with murderous mischief, expressed supplication mingled with terror so well that I was overcome by emotion.

"Oh, indeed! It's just that if some censor were to see and hear me, I wouldn't get away with a fine; I'd have to disappear."

"Disappear, poor child! But who are these terrible censors, then, of which I'm always hearing mention?"

"They're no one and everyone. There are no more *sergents de ville* or paid police, as there once were, but half the population is employed in spying on the other, and the slightest infraction of the law leads to the suppression of the guilty party; the Grand Council decided that—to ensure the security of the republic, it's said."

"And what happens to the guilty parties?"

"I don't know. A man vanishes one evening; the next he's replaced by another almost identical, who takes his name, his number, his pigeon-hole, and that's it. Neither seen, nor known, Bonsoir! You made me laugh just now asking me whether I was an actress. Oh no, no more than anything else—and even less, for special aptitudes have been seen in me for music, dance, pantomime, and care has been taken to apply me to cooking and geometry."

"How old are you?"

"We can't know that exactly; something like eighteen or twenty, I suppose."

"And—pardon me if the question is indiscreet—are you already a mother?"

"No, but I will be tomorrow morning. I received notice of it today; an infant will be brought from the Maternity for us—but if it's not healthy I'll refuse it; yes indeed, as we're responsible for the kids, I don't want damaged goods!"

"And you must love someone who is a stranger to you, constraining your sentiments?"

"Love? I don't understand—it's the first time I've heard that; it's doubtless an old word. We don't love anything; we obey the Council; we're entrusted with some brat, told to keep it alive and in good condition; when the general sweep comes around we give the child back and get a receipt in return. After that, another, and so on."

"Do you love Joseph?"

"I don't know; I don't know him; he's like all the others, except that he's young and polite, but, probably out of respect and fear of the law, he's never done anything imprudent, as I have."

"Poor children! Poor children! So this is progress! So that wretched helmet, those spectacles, that wig..."

"Oh well, that's uniformity![33] Has one any right to have a better figure than someone else, more beautiful eyes or more abundant hair? Firstly, the spectacles are compulsory, because by dint of microscopic studies and application, and by dint of living without sunlight, sight is generally weak, and it was decreed one day that, the nation being myopic, it would wear

---

[33] The author inserts a footnote: "Literary probity obliges me to note that I borrowed some grotesque consequences of the egalitarian principle from a humorous article in an English periodical, the *Cornhill Magazine*." The reference is presumably to "A Vision of Communism: A Grotesque" in the September 1873 issue of the *Cornhill*, pp. 300-310; the piece is unsigned but is credited by indices to Bertha Thomas.

spectacles. For us they have to be colored, because it's necessary that no one sees our eyes. As for hair, it's the same principle; in the beginning there were blondes, red-heads brunettes and black-haired people in the Commune; all of that was melted together to obtain a dark mahogany shade, and as a considerable number of citizens were beginning to go gray, the tresses are sprinkled with a few white tints. That's also the reason for the curvature of the dorsal spine that's statutory here. Enough chat of that sort, my Ancient. Tomorrow morning Joseph will be a deputé; he'll show you the city of workers from a balloon, and you'll witness a parliamentary session, after which the Grand Council will deliberate. As for me, I'll re-read my *Theory of Maternity*, for use with the expected little monster. Good night—and above all, don't say anything about what you've seen."

I didn't sleep too badly, and the next morning Joseph woke me up, made me swallow a few hasty mouthfuls, and, preceding me through a number of corridors, led me to the bottom of a sort of funnel, at the top of which, on looking up, I could see a blue circle. It was the sky—the good God's authentic sky. The air, although rarefied, did me good as it filled my chest, and my emotion was so intense that, while following Joseph up the steps of an interminable spiral staircase, I felt tears come into my eyes.

"That's another of the advantages of our Commune system," Joseph said. "It's true that we're deprived of air and sunlight, but where would be the pleasure of enjoying them, if abstention didn't make us appreciate their benefits?"

This time, I could not contain my indignation, and as we were about to reach the terrace and Joseph's upper body emerged entirely into the natural air, I shouted loudly:

"Wretch! Stop pretending! You're twenty years old, your heart beats, you aspire to liberty, light and love—in sum, to that God whom you have expelled from your absurd republic!"

I thought that I would pay dear for that outburst, for he darted a glance at me darker than Clytemnestra's, and we were in a position such that a simple push would have precipitated me to the bottom of the terrible black gulf. That only lasted for a second, though. His face cleared, and it was with a smile of sorts that he held out his hand to help me climb the last few steps. He whispered in my ear: "On your life, not another word until we're 700 meters above the clouds!"

On can easily imagine the general form of the terraces crowning the blocks of ten houses—which is to say, squares about a hundred meters on each side, bordered at the perimeter by a wall sustaining staircases, while vegetable plots ran along the foot of the wall. In the center the orifice of the funnel into which the staircase we had just climbed plunged; and bushes adjacent to the community's chimneys. The uniformity of that glance was unbroken, from one block of ten to the next, save for the occasional tall chimney, like those of our factories. Joseph informed me that they allowed the smoke and vapors of the federal kitchens to escape.

"You see," he added, "that without wasting an inch of ground, we have exhausted the soil, but that our terraces procure a little dessert for the federated. I have no need to tell you that if we have cherries and peaches in midwinter, we owe them to geothermic culture. In sum, the nature of the ground, whether we buy it or make it ourselves, is utterly insignificant, thanks to the prodigies of chemistry."

While speaking, he busied himself detaching the balloon that would transport us to the Assembly. Several others of the same size were anchored along the wall and to the chimneys. It would be difficult for me to describe these vehicles, because they did not resemble anything from our era. They were shaped something like an elongated boat, equipped with four slender wings of vast extent, affecting a sort of resemblance to those of the dragonflies of our rivers.

Without any help from me, and without taking the trouble to explain the mechanism—which I had undoubtedly not understood, for lack of preliminary study—he maneuvered it with activity and precision. When he had sat me down facing him, I found myself transported, without knowing how and without the slightest shock, several hundred meters above the terrace.

"Don't lean over too far, and try not to move. Do you know how very imprudent and talkative you were just now? No one was there; otherwise, in spite of your two hundred and fifty years of existence, you'd have had to forsake your appetite for bread. Oh, if Josephine had too loose a tongue, they wouldn't hesitate to cut it out. You have to take precautions; in our own islet, people know about your scientific resurrection, and people are disposed in your favor, but I can't answer for other sectors. There are still people with an appetite for bourgeois blood, even that of a bourgeois phenomenon, and believe me, the best thing for you to do is to imitate me."

Out of a little cabin under the tiller, like those small boats have, he took a uniform similar to his, including the spectacles and the wig.

"Disguise yourself as best you can with that, make yourself grimy, try to make yourself small and stooped. Not bad. Now we can talk; no one can hear us, unless the crows have been recruited as police spies.

"Well, no, it's true, old chap—we're not happy at all, not at all, and strictly between us, there might well be some hammer-blows in preparation against the president; I don't know whether you might even witness a revolution today."

"What's that? A Revolution! Oh yes, a little revolution to keep your hand in; I see that you haven't forgotten the old tunes. But who is your president?"

"No one, or almost no one; he's a citizen selected by lot. His name and individuality are effaced, since his job consists of counting the votes in the Assembly and transmitting the national will to the Grand Council. To conceal that individuality even better, it has been decided that every president should wear Monsieur Thiers' overcoat, which the Commune has conserved in memory of the services rendered by that great man.[34] If he had not had our forefathers shot or deported, as he did, they would not have attracted to our cause all the sympathy that attaches to persecuted sects. So you'll see his bust in the hall of the Grand Council, with those of the other individuals who, directly or indirectly, precipitated the humanitarian movement: the great despots, Louis XIV, Ali Pasha, Ivan IV, Nero and his consorts, who rendered monarchy odious; the Rousseaus, Babeufs and Proudhons who formulated the doctrine of our ignored grief, our unrecognized rights; the men of action: Amasis the ex-thief, king of Egypt, one of the first to indicate that theft is merely principled rectification, since property-owners were the original thieves;[35] Napoleon III, the counterfeit of his predecessor; Bismarck, one of our most powerful levers…I'm passing over many others, as you'll see.

"The deputés, with their imperative mandates in their pockets, are much less important. Besides, it's the lottery that picks them out, and they only have to express the views of the sector that they represent. With that system, you might think that everything would proceed smoothly, but no, whatever one does; there are still foreign influences, occult but dangerous, that falsify the votes. Thus, there's the big question on today's agenda: ought the entire nation to be bowed down, almost hunchbacked, as if in consequence of excessive labor? Some say yes, others no, and the neighboring nations will certainly be doing their best to make us seem ridiculous; the president himself, old and broken down, would like everyone to resemble him. Hence, discontent among well-built people, who

---

[34] Adolphe Thiers, who took charge of the provisional government after the fall of the Second Empire, had been a liberal and a reformist since the reign of Louis-Philippe, and disappointed many of his supporters by the ruthlessness with which he put an end to the Commune and punished the Communards.

[35] There is no historical warrant for this allegation regarding the pharaoh Amasis II (Amasis I was not of humble origin); the reference presumably relates to Henri Millot's fanciful play *Amasis, ou Une revolution d'autrefois* (1832).

claim to constitute the majority—and as I said, the session will be stormy."

"Well, well! But who are these other nations you mention, and what relationship do you have with them?"

"The map of Europe has been redrawn; it presently consists of three great confederations, to wit: the Slavonic, the German and the Latin. It's to the latter that our city belongs, although it is, so to speak, out of the game, living its own life without concern for races or origins. But commercial necessities put us in contact with the neighbors, and the president receives deputations from all the powers. No one likes entertaining foreigners, whose doctrines might poison the national spirit, and I believe that they feel the same, but it's still necessary that we export the excess of our products, which inundate the Earth, because we manufacture cheaply, and it's also necessary that we obtain raw materials from abroad."

"You never have wars?"

"War!" said Joseph shrugging his shoulders. "But that's the antithesis of democracy. Besides, we've rendered it impossible; consider that, from the height of our balloons, with a few asphyxiating bombs and the resources of electricity, any one of us, at the flick of a switch, could pulverize fifty thousand human beings."

"But haven't the others made the same progress?"

"Indeed, but national secrets are well-guarded and woe to spies! And we're numerous enough for anyone to think twice before troubling us. Anyway, what motive can anyone have for war while we remain within our boundaries and respect the conditions of the European pact?"

"That's true—but the rest of France doesn't adhere to your improved organization of free labor, then?"

"Firstly, France no longer exists, any more than Germany, Italy or Spain. Like us, England minds its own business, trading independently, and lives freely while respecting the liberty of others. As for the former France, it's divided into five or six kingdoms, duchies or republics, according to local taste. Thus, we have a king reigning in the Vendée and part of the Midi, believed to be descended from the ancient Bourbons. A second portion of the Midi is constituted as a Republic, and the third has resuscitated Provençal royalty. In Bretagne, by virtue of archeological research, digging in the tumuli and local archives, a distant cousin of Duc Judicaël[36] has been exhumed and Bretagne has become an independent Duchy again, while a substantial fraction of the North and East recognizes sovereigns of the Orléans branch. There are a great many members of the Bonaparte family; it was decided that they would divide Corsica between them—where, it appears, each of them, at the head of a six-man army, makes war on his neighbors.

"In Spain, of which the Arabs have the impudence to reclaim their share, people get by as best they can. Germany is very nearly what it was before unification, and the Prussians form a small savage population on the shore of the Baltic. In Italy, the work of Victor-Emanuel has been obliterated, but a very embarrassing question arose in consequence: what to do with the Pope, whom even the majority of Romans did not want for a king. A rather ingenious compromise was found; he has his palace in the Vatican, and a few other establishments in other cities, such as Jerusalem and Avignon, but, thanks to the improvement of balloons, he can travel incessantly with his cortege of cardinals and all his staff, floating above nations attached to the Roman Catholic religion. Although he no longer has any land, the spiritual world belongs to him, and by that means, he directs the fractions of his Church scattered over the Earth much more efficaciously..."

While chatting thus, we were rising higher; the balloon's great wings struck the air with incessant rapidity, and we traversed cloud after cloud. Less accustomed than my companion to the rarefaction of the air, I was suffering from it considerably, and was obliged to have recourse to his little bottle.

---

[36] Duc Judicaël of Bretagne was the second person to reign under that title, from 876-888.

"We'll be arriving momentarily. We're near Saint-Denis now."

Indeed, scarcely had he finished speaking than the balloon, gliding obliquely and descending toward the ground, carried us with vertiginous rapidity to the center of ancient Paris, above the Cité, three or four hundred meters from the ground. All the details could be distinguished clearly, as on a relief plan. I was dazzled, and remained mute.

"You find it much changed, eh? Let's stop for a while, and I'll explain what seems to you so extravagant. You'll certainly recognize the location of your capital, but only a fraction of the city survives. We began by demolishing everything, as I told you, and then rebuilding it according to the ideas and needs of modern society. Central Paris is no more than a great plain traversed by the Seine, straightened and channeled. It's in that plain that the nation can set foot on the ground and tread on it. You can see a certain number of great national monuments; I'll point them out to you:

"Firstly, the Cité, where Notre-Dame and the Palais de Justice once stood—which is to say, odious testaments to popular superstition and judicial prevarication—is no more than a vast temple: the temple of free and glorified labor. Inside, it is decorated with three hundred statues or allegorical groups, each representing an industry: the tailor plying his needle, the cook spitting his turkey and the surgeon his patient, etc., etc. Natural grandeur in bronze. It's here that the citizens come, at the renewal of each decad, to honor the only divinities recognized here: labor directed by human intelligence.

"Secondly, higher up, on the site of the Tuileries—a shameful monument to the insolence of kings—raises the Central Maternity, whose function you know.

"Thirdly, to the right and the left, three large circular buildings: the three male Reservoirs facing the three female Reservoirs.

"Fourthly, adjacent to the Maternity, there's the Senate..."

"The Senate?" I exclaimed, in amazement. "You have Senators? But why, then, go to the trouble of overturning an entire social edifice?"

A few rapid wing-beats carried us over the Senatorial palace, where the balloon remained hovering.

"You have only to look and you will understand," said Joseph. "The august individuals are about to go to the Assembly."

And I did, indeed, see a long file of men emerged slowly and majestically, no longer clad in the dirty national tunic but in magnificent purple togas whose hems trailed disdainfully on the ground. A few of them wore the uniforms of generals, and magnificent decorations of all the familiar orders shone on their breasts. I did not understand as yet when, on looking at them more closely, I saw that some were lame or one-armed, others blind, one-eyed or paralyzed, and in the bewildered faces of some, oozing filthy drool, I recognized cretins.

"Now you understand; those are injustices of nature which, with our ideas of equality, we could not tolerate. What could we do? Condemn the nation to adopt all these infirmities? That was unthinkable. Then we thought of indemnifying these poor underprivileged individuals by searching the vanities of the past for means of flattering human self-respect; there is the result.

"Let's pass on to the fifth and last; it's the most important, because it's there that the Assembly sits and the President of the Council resides. That palace occupies, as you can see, almost all of the site of the Champs-Élysées. Let's moor the balloon here, and proceed on foot; while we walk, you might perhaps notice some things of interest."

Although I had been warned in advance, I had some difficulty in suppressing my laughter on seeing a compact crowd of small, stooped, graying men wearing spectacles, so similar to my guide that if I had not taken his arm I would not have been able to recognize him among the others.

"Fear not," said Joseph, with a singular smile, "*kindness* is never wasted"—and in smiling thus, he seemed to want to emphasize his weak pun,[37] whose significance I was about to comprehend. All the balloons, wings folded like grasshoppers at rest, were hooked on to the walls. The very same people who were elbowing one another in order to arrive more rapidly, unceremoniously treading on toes, stood aside respectfully and bowed as the senators went by.

On the site of the former Palais de l'Industrie, an immense crowd was gathered around a monstrous balloon on which one could read, in letters fifteen feet high:

LIBERTY – EQUALITY – FRATERNITY
Hunchbacks Strike!
Live by labor or die in combat!
Long live the Commune!

"There's the stamp of authority—that'll excite you!" said Joseph. "Do you see all these people standing up straight? Let's join them; it's time to confess that I've been conspiring with them for some time, and that I'm one of the leaders of the conspiracy."

And Joseph metamorphosed, as the citizeness had done; he suddenly stood up straight, and his dull, atonal gaze, deprived of expression, became brilliant with malice, revealing an energetic determination.

"Good, my lad!" I said, shaking his hand. "I like you better like this, and I'm entirely ready to slap you on the back. I haven't forgotten the barricades, when, bourgeois or proletariat, we fought for liberty—but here, before fighting, I'd like to know why and for whom."

---

[37] The pun is, indeed, rather weak; the French *bienfait*, here translated as "kindness," although it can also mean "advantage," is a portmanteau term; if its two components are separated, *bien fait* means "well built" or (as I shall shortly translate it, when Joseph's double meaning becomes manifest) "upstanding."

"You're not disgusted, then. Do people who fight ever know those things? They're puppets obedient to strings, but which hands hold and pull those strings one can never know. Personally, I conspire as a matter of taste, for love of it; after several generations of hybridization, I doubtless retain some Bellevillois blood in my veins. Once it was a matter of dethroning a tyrant. The enemies were soldiers, policemen, spies and the whole gang; one took on such and such a minister, or certain deputés, but now..."

"Now you're all ministers, deputés, policemen at the same time—to attack the state is to attack yourselves."

"I don't deny it, but although we no longer have tyrants to demolish, it's still necessary to defend ourselves as best we can against tyranny—and the tyranny is invisible. Being obliged to take on someone, it's the president that we'll overturn, whom we'll crush, although the poor Devil can't do anything and has never thought of tyrannizing anyone. Anyway, there'll be fighting, broken heads, a little diversion from the monotony of existence—isn't that the revolutionary ideal?"

"But you haven't any weapons."

"What do you think our bottles and electrical apparatus are? Do you expect cannon and rifles, as in your barbaric centuries? Less noise, more effect—that's our motto. That's enough for now; you'll see the rest for yourself."

At the end of an immense boulevard the façade of the gigantic Palais National loomed up. The boulevard was bordered by a quadruple rank of shiny green palm-trees.

At that sight, I expressed a certain astonishment, which did not escape Joseph's penetration; replying to my thought, he said: "No, don't think that the globe has warmed up, or that a new inclination of its axis has displaced its latitudes; Africa hasn't been transported to Paris. How can you imagine that, given the price of wood, we could afford such a luxury as trees, even if the soil could support them? Those palm-trees are made of painted zinc, designed for the same usage as certain hollow colonnettes of your time, along the boulevards…at the same time, the object is pleasant to look at. *Utile dulci*[38]—isn't that how your pedants put it?"

Having joined the group of upstanding individuals, we entered an immense hall at the back of which the President was seated, between two men that Joseph identified as the Minister of the Interior and his Private Secretary, both charged, by reason of the President's advanced age and physical debility, with repeating his words to the audience, making use of a giant megaphone.

After a few murmurs in the crowd, negotiations, certain formalities and the reading of reports devoid of interest, a deputé rose to his feet and announced—also with the aid of a megaphone—that he was going to speak on behalf of the deputation of hunchbacks who had gone on strike. (Exclamations to the right.)

The President, combining the functions of Head of State and President of the Assembly, reached slowly and solemnly for his hand-bell, but without his bleak and seemingly petrified face indicating the slightest emotion.

"What self-composure" said someone nearby. "Nothing disturbs him!"

The deputé read the following statement, in the midst of profound silence:

"Citizen President and Citizen Members of the Grand Council, we, the inhabitants of sectors A" through M", regions of hat-makers, physicians, heating engineers, bankers, tax-collectors, etc., etc., in consideration of the fact that neither nature nor age constrains the absolute majority of the nature to maintain a stooped posture;

"That the obligation to feign a slight infirmity is an augmentation of effort without an equivalent augmentation of salary;

---

[38] The concluding words of a line from Horace's *Ars poetica*, which translates approximately as "all approval goes to the man who can combine utility and attractiveness."

"And that, in any case, equality is not significantly diminished by the rectitude of a large number of vertebral columns;

"The inhabitants of the said sectors declare that they refuse to submit to the obligation of slightly curving the spine, unless the Grand Council allows each of them an augmentation of pay of a hundred francs a day.

Followed by signatures, in alphabetical and numerical order."

(Furious clamors to the right. Prolonged applause to the left.)

The Minister leans toward the President, who pronounces a few words in an indistinct voice. The Secretary does likewise.

"Citizens," the Minster then translates, "our President has just said: 'Citizens, it is always with a new pleasure that I see you ready to support the cause of a motion, but refrain from exaggerated zeal, for...'"

The Secretary, addressing the left, continues: "'Citizens, it is with regret that I see you support the cause of insubordination; he who lacks respect for the law...'"

But he is unable to continue. A group of frenzied individuals, leaping on to the platform, surrounds the President and his spokesmen; groans and murmurs are heard, a loud scream, and finally, a singular clink of metal and the sound of a heavy body falling to the floor.

"The President has been assassinated!"

"Every man for himself."

"To arms!"

An indescribable tumult; a debauch, an orgy of vociferations.

The disorder was complete: jostling, stamping feet, electric gleams, menacing bottles, whole rows of men knocked down and trampled underfoot...

Such was the scene in the hall, when a man of Herculean build bounded to the podium, took possession of it, clung to it, and, in spite of the efforts of the Minister and the Secretary, succeeded in holding his position. Tens, twenty, thirty of the bespectacled little men caught hold of his arms and legs, in order to cast him down, but, like a wild boar shaking off a cluster of dogs, he swept them away, throwing them into the auditorium, crushing them against the benches. The ups and downs of the struggle were vaguely visible through the undulations of the crowd.

Finally, having become sole master of the terrain, the stranger appeared in all his glory: a trimmed moustache and a big red beard on his chin, a double breasted coat, a high receding forehead forming a single line with the shape of a backward-tipped hat: a pure-blooded American!

He seethed, stamped and bent the planks of the podium beneath his formidable fists. Seizing a megaphone, he shouted—or, rather, bellowed—loudly enough to drown out all the noise. He was audible all the way to the gates of the Maternity.

"I am Jonathan Nathaniel Simpson, citizen of Massachusetts in the United States of America, and I have come to summon the Free City or Commune, under threat of bodily constraint, to put in my hands without delay the sum of eight hundred thousand dollars..." (Oh! Oh! Listen! Listen!) "...which is owed to me by the aforesaid Commune, as proven by the documents that I shall read to you. So shut up. Parisian vermin!

"This is a receipt from the Minister of the Interior: 'I acknowledge having received, on the first of January 2071 (old style), possessing the authorization of the Grand Council, an automaton representing a President of the Republic, for the use of the Commune, which has been handed over to me by its inventor, Jonathan Nathaniel Simpson of Massachusetts, United States of America, on the condition of his allowing us the sole exploitation of his patent for five years, at the end of which he will be paid:

"'For the construction of the president......$300,000

"'As compensation for the patent...........$100,000

"'The interest on this sum being at the disposal of the aforementioned Simpson for the five years in question.'

"And now, wretches, listen to this: they're my personal bills, verified by your minister, the Secretary and your Central Council:

"June 2072, for having remade for the President a false rib, following a fall from a balloon............$100,000

"July of the same year, for having improved the tone of the voice when addressing the left..............$40,000

"Ditto, for having adjusted the mechanism of the hand that shakes the hand-bell..........................$60,000

"Total...$600,000

"Six hundred thousand dollars due to me, and if you reckon the two hundred thousand-dollars indemnity is exaggerated, when it was necessary for me to repair the President as new, and that my operation might have been publicized...what do you think?"

At that moment, I felt a rather sharp pain in my left leg. Thinking that it was caused by a electric shock, I put my hand to it and encountered the blade of my *mobile* saber, which, by virtue of a random twitch on my part, had just come unhooked from the wall and fallen on to my left leg.

And Joseph—the real Joseph—said to me: "Father, you slept quite badly this evening..."

Alphonse Brown: *The Tell-Tale Insects*
(1889)

I

To hell with science and scientists!

I know that it's customary only to talk about the gentlemen in question with respectful deference and enthusiastic admiration, but I'm breaking with tradition and have no intention of hiding the hatred inspired in me by the pedantry, the conceit and the loquacity that drives them to display, without rhyme or reason, the "vast knowledge" that they've acquired. I curse the telephone, I curse steam power, I curse the telegraph, I curse physics and chemistry. Most of all, I curse entomology!

Yes, a scientist has ruined my life!

Oh, how gladly I would strangle him, how I would laugh at his frightful grimaces while my clenched fingers dig into his neck, hastening to asphyxiate him! I'll never forgive him for the terrors to which I've been subjected, even if he throws himself at my feet and begs forgiveness in the name of his mother.

But what good does it do to get ahead of things and stray into considerations extraneous to the events that have brought me to the office of the examining magistrate? Let it suffice for me to affirm my antipathy toward scientists once more, before beginning my story.

For some years my business had been in jeopardy, and I had exercised every possible ingenuity to hide my true situation. With the tenacity of a gambler counting on a lucky break to recover his money, I hoped that misfortune would stop persecuting me, and that I would end up, by dint of the hard work and energy, method and thrift that I put into everything, redeeming my compromised situation. Alas, all my efforts remained sterile. Like a man stuck in a thick layer of mud, the more I struggled, the further I sank.

To be sure, poverty didn't frighten me, and I knew that I had courage enough to struggle against adversity; but in addition to myself I had my life's companion and my beloved daughter, our dear Hélène.

The merest sentiment of propriety prevents from speaking about my child with all the eulogies that her character and beauty merit. I won't hide it; I was very proud when a friend said to me: "Hélène is a truly delightful young woman."

Whenever we went out together, she leaning on my arm and amusing me with her chatter, jovial and serious at the same time, and me holding my head up like a triumphant Roman, I experienced a naïve impulse of pride on observing how many heads turned as we passed by, and how many eyes—especially those of young men—gave evidence of admiring surprise.

Having reached the age at which the heart speaks, Hélène and the nephew of my neighbor fell in love, and the entire town was soon occupied with their imminent marriage. Now, my neighbor was Juzans—the famous and illustrious Tiburce Juzans, laureate of the Institut, member of several Académies and scientific societies, President of the Phylloxera Commission, Vice-President of the *départementale* Entomological Society, etc.

Tiburce Juzans was—and still is—a perfect specimen of those legendary scientists with parchment-like faces, long graying hair, and a body lost in the folds of a heavy overcoat that had only a distant relationship with soap and the brush. That overcoat—or, rather, that immense frock-coat—was a poem that would have tempted many a naturalist. I'm astonished that Tiburce Juzans never had the idea of exploring the dusty masses and greasy lumps of his own garments. He would certainly have discovered a new world of the infinitely small there, and would have acquired an immortal glory by publishing the results of his research. The renown of Ehrenburg, Pouchet, Pasteur and Dujardin—all those, in fact, who have dedicated themselves to the study of infusoria, flagellates, bacteria and microbes—would have been effaced by comparison with his.

Without exactly being a bad person, Tiburce Juzans was subject to variations of mood that rendered him very taxing and difficult to tolerate. His nephew, Hector Tremont, was well aware of that. Fortunately, nature has created nothing without compensation. The grumpier and sulkier the former was when he emerged from his scientific hobby-horses, the gentler, kinder and nicer the latter became. I could not have wished for a more seductive and accomplished husband for my daughter.

Hector was the entomologist's nephew. Orphaned in infancy, he had been taken in by Tiburce Juzans, who took on the role, in his regard, of a rich bachelor uncle. The nephew received a careful education, and got his teeth into the tree of science, but not very well; by way of compensation, he became an excellent architect. It is not permitted to everyone to go to Corinth—which is to say, to be that surly, prickly, irritable and disagreeable composite known as an intellectual, or a scientist.

One fine summer evening, I received a visit from Tiburce Juzans. Until then, the scientist and I had only had a neighborly relationship. Several times, he had asked me to let him go down into my cellar—a very spacious cellar that received daylight through a large air-vent opening on to the street. He wanted, he claimed, to collect a few insects of a particular species that he had noticed on the threshold of the air-vent, and which must be born, grow and multiply in the darkest corners of beneath a few scattered clods of earth. Naturally, I acceded to that request, which later...but let's not anticipate.

I, triple idiot that I was, said to the scientist: "Don't stint yourself, Monsieur Tiburce; explore the most secret corners of my cellar as much as you like. I'm certain that you won't discover any treasure there."

Treasure! Oh, the entomologist laughed at that, of course. The real treasure, for him, was the larvae, the insects he collected, which he placed carefully in little bottles, and catalogued with Latin or Greek names that were sometimes as long as an Alexandrine of the Decadent school.

To be frank, I must confess that I was expecting Tiburce Juzans' visit. His nephew had told my wife and daughter to expect it, and as I knew its objective, I adopted the rather solemn attitude that befits a future father-in-law.

"My dear Monsieur," my neighbor said to me, right away, "you presumably know what brings me here; there's no need to beat around the bush to explain the purpose of my visit. My nephew is in love with your daughter, your daughter is in love with by nephew; I therefore ask you for the hand of Mademoiselle Hélène on Hector Tremont's behalf."

I lost myself in civilities and murmured the banalities customary in such cases to express how flattered we were, my wife and I, by the honor that was being doing to us.

After questions of sentiment, we broached those of financial interest, and although I am reputedly cunning, I let myself be rolled over—if I might be permitted that expressive terminology—like a conscript. Beneath his apparent straightforwardness, the scientist concealed a strong dose of finesse, and he bargained as well as the most cunning Norman. Then he appealed to my vanity, that eternal enemy of reason, and demonstrated to me by A + B that I was a very good businessman, enjoying a great deal of consideration and great credit, having a well-situated shop and numerous shares in my portfolio—that, in sum, I was a rich man and need not quibble over the figure of the dowry. In brief, I promised 50,000 francs in cash on the day the contract was signed.

Where was I going to find 50,000 francs? I've already said that everything was crumbling around me—and, I'm ashamed to write, in order to maintain my reputation, I gradually had recourse to expedients: expedients unworthy of every businessman concerned for his dignity and his honor. Under vain pretexts, I asked for extensions on my loans, and the renewal of obligations imposed on my funds; I postponed my payments. In a word, I tried to get blood out of stones. All my correspondents complained bitterly about my letters.

What could I do? What would become of me?

Meanwhile, I summoned up all my courage to maintain an impassive expression and not to give any indication of the torments I was undergoing. As my daughter's marriage was not to be celebrated until the end of October, I was still hoping, like a shipwreck victim searching his surroundings for salvation in the form of a plank, that something unexpected might finally come to my aid and permit me to meet the obligation I had so casually taken on.

Between Tiburce Juzans and my family, a relationship was established imprinted with a certain cordiality; the scientist humanized himself to the extent of adopting me as a confidant and acquainting me with the papers that he addressed to the numerous scientific societies that pullulate on French soil. Imagine how interested I was in that! But to ensure my daughter's happiness, I would gladly have been bored; I would have swallowed the entire sequence of *x*s and *y*s with which mathematicians enamel their reasoning, and I would have stuffed my brain with all the barbaric names that are the pride of classification in the natural sciences.

Entomology—there was nothing higher! For Tiburce Juzans, it was the queen of the sciences, the one that prepares the mind for the great conceptions of nature, for the study of pygmies and the infinitely tiny surprises human intelligence with its unexpected marvels, opening previously-unsuspected horizons thereto.

Entomology! (The torturer explained to me that the term is derived from the Greek *entomos*, insect, and *logos*, science.) Was not entomology the most curious part of zoology, which had made the names of Redi, Malpighi, Swammerdsam, Leeuwenhoek, Morian, Réaumur, de Geor, Geoffroy, Latreille, Dejean, de Serres, Blanchard, Léon Dufur, Strauss, Boisduval, Guérin-Meneville, Giard, Rendu and many others that I've forgotten, illustrious?

I also learned that the word "insect" derives from the Latin *insectus*, which means "sectioned" or "divided," by allusion to the rings or segments into which the animal's body seemed to be divided. I learned, too, that the body is split into three parts: the head, the thorax and the abdomen; that the thorax has three sections itself, each having a pair of limbs beneath, and that these are called the prothorax, the mesothorax and the metathorax.

Good God, what names!

No matter; I retained a few scraps of that gibberish, and inserted them sententiously into the conversation when the opportunity presented itself. I didn't talk much, though, remembering sternly that if speech is silver, silence is golden. Tiburce Juzans was radiant, though, and exultant; he rubbed his gnarled hands with childish satisfaction and declared that I had an admirable disposition for learning entomology.

"We'll make something of you," he told me, amiably. "Before they year is out I'll be able to sponsor you with my colleagues and introduce you as an associate member of the local Entomological Society."

I bowed respectfully.

Me, a member of a scientific society! Who would have thought it, when I had previously shown no other ambition than to keep my account-books up to date!

Oh, if Tiburce Juzans had divined the motives that drove me to listen to the rubbish he showered upon me, he would have sent me packing without the slightest hesitation!

I tried to profit from the scientist's benevolent disposition to venture a few timid observations regarding the sum of the dowry, trying to demonstrate that, if money is the sinew of war, it is also the soul of commerce, and that capital invested in my experience, left in the business for a few more years, would bring in a better interest than a vulgar four or five percent—but Tiburce Juzans proved intractable. I had promised 50,000 francs in cash, and 50,000 francs was what I had to deliver, or nothing doing. That Trissotin, that Vadius,[39] dared to compare me to a cockchafer "counting its change." Isn't that what children call the movement that the coleopteran makes when it draws air into its trachea before taking flight?

It was therefore necessary to resign myself to continuing, as in the past, to be an entomologist in spite of myself. Ought I to regret that time, which put my patience so severely to the proof? There is no need, after what I've written, to repeat once again my aversion to science and scientists, but I often had occasion to be surprised, even wonderstruck, by the structure, the behavior, the metamorphoses and the labor of insects, by that world in miniature which reflects, more than one might think, our own passions and our mores.

Are there not insects that live in republics or monarchies? Does one not see some of them building a metropolis, maintaining an army and a police force, exactly like civilized States? Do not oligarchies exist among them reminiscent of ancient patriarchy and Medieval feudalism?

Full of astonishment and admiration, I exclaimed with Linné: "Nature reveals the greatest marvels in the smallest objects.

And with Pliny: "In these beings, so tiny, which appear so trivial, what strength, what reason and what inextricable perfection there is!"

II

Enthusiasm dwindles rapidly when chagrins, disappointments and cares take the trouble to recall you to the sad realities of existence. To think that it was necessary for me to employ dissimulation and strength of character to hide my precarious situation is really quite incredible. I played the en-

---

[39] Trissotin and Vadius are characters in Molière's *Les Femmes savantes* [The Intellectual Women] (1672), pretentious posers adopted by the eponymous ladies, who know no better.

tomologist while sick at heart, and had to seem cheerful while my brain as seething and it seemed to me that my poor head might explode.

"But no one mistrusted me; no one suspected that ruination had come into my house and was slyly lying in wait for me. My colleagues always greeted me with the envious respect that characterizes competitors in the same town; advocates, solicitors and notaries—the whole series of men of law, who have such a profound respect for money—reserved their best handshakes for me, and the president of the commercial tribunal took off his hat to me before I did likewise.

In every existence, however, as Henri Murger wrote, there is a hitch—and my hitch was Aristide Croupart.

Oh, there was no way to deceive him! He saw clearly into my affairs, and I was obliged to buy his discretion with polite gestures—or, rather, abasements—that make me blush with shame when I think of them. I was fortunate when I was not constrained to add to my soft and honeyed words some gratification that the pedant pocketed with a knowing wink. Then again, I guessed, sensed by a sort of intuition that the wretch was an enemy all the more redoubtable because he assumed such humility and retracted his claws. As for me, I detested him, and hated him wholeheartedly. Why? I don't know. Is one master of one's sympathies and antipathies? Love and hate, some philosopher observed, are brothers, like Cain and Abel.

Aristide Croupart belonged to the honorable corporation of bailiffs, and no mortal was ever better equipped to exercise that function, for in place of a heart he probably had a lump of granite, exceedingly dense, solid and hard. If the soul was ugly, the physical appearance had nothing very attractive. A face blotched by the abuse of libations, and adorned by a tubercular nose surmounted a heron-like neck and the limbs of a stork. To be sure, Aristide Croupart did not really belong to the genus of wading birds; malicious gossip claimed that he lived in a holy terror of water, and that, if he ingurgitated very little of it, he put no more on his luminous face. Add to all that an oblique and sly gaze, hesitant gestures, a strangled and shrill voice, and you will have a complete portrait of the individual.

And it was before that marionette that I deployed all the amiability that was within me, that I humiliated myself in order to gain a few days, sometimes only a few hours, when a payment was urgently due. He usually came to see me in the evening, in order to avoid, he said, his visits compromising my situation and my credit. And I dissolved in unctuousness: "Look, it's Monsieur Croupart…what benign wind blows you here? Do me the honor, in a spirit of friendship, of accepting something..."

"With pleasure, my dear Monsieur; everyone knows that your cognac is the finest quality and that your cigars are excellent. To refuse your gracious invitation would be to commit a sacrilege.

And that uncouth lout gorged himself with a calculated slowness, serving himself with a revolting carelessness, emptying half a bottle and snorting like a seal as he blew out the smoke of my cigars. Then he gently let drop the most hypocritical and malevolent insinuations; it was out of pure friendship that he was taking the trouble to disturb himself in order to warn me that a protest for non-payment was imminent and that the bank was about to refuse my signature. I understood, and while the vile rogue twisted the knife in the wound, enjoying my abasement, I let the money fall into the outstretched hand.

One day, Tiburce Juzans and Hector Tremont caught me by surprise just as I was showing Aristide Croupart out, while showing him the most complete deference. The scientist dated an interrogative glance at me, but my aplomb and my casual manner dispelled from his mind the suspicions that seemed to have caught hold of him. I even permitted myself a few jokes. The bailiff smiled and bowed deeply, but I shall never forget the venomous glance he darted at me.

At any rate, entomology implanted itself increasingly in my house, spoiling my home somewhat, of which I was rather jealous. Fortunately, my daughter showed an even greater disposition toward that science than I did, and, either because she wanted to captivate the scientist or because she wanted to please her fiancé, she made quite rapid progress. Tiburce Juzans, moreover, was delighted to find such a docile pupil, and did not spare her either learned dissertations or revealing experiments.

"You imagine, then, Mademoiselle," he said emphatically, "that the origin of insects is mysterious and that no one knows the secret of their birth? The ancients shared that error. For them, these little animals originated spontaneously from pollutions of the soil and the rotting flesh of corpses. The qualities, or rather the instincts, of the tiny creatures derived from the animal whose remains had given them birth.

"Aelian informs us that bees originating in the entrails of a lion are wild, reluctant to work and unmanageable; those born of sheep are idle and devoid of strength; while those which come from the flanks of a bull are valiant, laborious and obedient. Aristotle and Theophrastus fall into the same errors, and their observations always concluded with spontaneous generation. The Middle Ages discovered nothing.

"Finally, an Italian physician, Redi, suggested that the worms swarming in rotten meat, and which give birth to flies, come from eggs deposited by the females. There was a naturalist who took the trouble to observe scrupulously and who, at first glance, discovered one of the most important secrets of nature. Which proves, Mademoiselle, that a great deal of attention is necessary to explain, *ad aperturam libri*,[40] the simplest situations.

Hélène approved, briefly formulated a few judicious reflections and never wearied of listening. Tiburce Juzans repeated Redi's experiments for her benefit. He took pieces of meat, some raw and some cooked, and placed them in uncovered dishes. Soon, a frightful odor polluted the air of the poultry-yard where the dishes had been placed. Need one hide

---

[40] [Like] an open book

the fact that the olfactory nerve was disagreeably impressed? A fine business! Tiburce Juzans sniffed that tainted air with an acrid voluptuousness and paraded his long nose over the jars as if they contained the sweetest and most odorant flowers.

The flesh attracted an incalculable number of flies, whose egg-laying I had the courage to observe. Scarcely forty-eight hours had gone by when innumerable larvae were swarming, wriggling and nourishing themselves in a putrefaction that sickened me. They were maggots, that manna of the line-fisherman. The entomologist did not hesitate to introduce his fingers into the midst of that filthy vermin. Inevitably, he put a handful a handful of larvae into my hand and looked at them almost tenderly.

"Don't you feel the warmth that those little creatures emit?" he said. "That observation was made a long time ago by fanatics of the fishhook."

I did, indeed, experience a sensation of warmth, which astonished me, and which was explained to me by the prodigious activity of nutrition.

"Look," he continued, "admire the strange marvels of these plump white worms, made up of eleven rings that stretch and shrink at the animal's whim, when it withdraws the first three or four segments into one another like a telescope. Although they have no feet, they make quite rapid progress by means of a crawling motion, with the aid of two scaly hooks placed in front of the mouth. Those hooks also serve for alimentation; at rest they're hidden in a sheath. These appendices inform us that we're in the presence of gourmands—let's see if that's correct."

Tiburce Juzans picked up a dish in while a hundred larvae were wriggling.

"Oh yes, my lads," he exclaimed, "we're not mistaken on your account. These worms have no sooner quit the egg than they start to eat. They half-bury themselves in the meat and work their jaws—pardon, their hooks, as if they were dining with Lucullus. They're hearty eaters! They know the most succulent parts and respect the tendinous fibers. During that incessant meal, their body covers itself with a glutinous mucus that softens the flesh and speeds up its decomposition. The quantity of nourishment absorbed is enormous relative to their size, and yet they never excrete any solid wastes. Thus, their growth takes place with an astonishing rapidity, and it has been calculated that fly larvae grow within twenty-four hours to between a hundred and fifty and two hundred times their initial weight.

"In a few days they reach their full development, and then lose the formidable appetite that distinguished them. They take shelter in some dark place, usually in the ground, live in the state of pupas for a variable length of time, according to the season and the temperature, and finally become perfect insects. It's after these curious metamorphoses that the myriads of flies are born that are seen everywhere in summer, principal among which are observed the house-fly, *Musca domestica*, the bluebottle, *Calliphora vomitora*, the greenbottle, *Lucilia caesar*, the flesh-fly, *Sarcophaga vivipara*, the dark green fly, *Musca carnifex*..."[41]

"All this is truly admirable," I hastened to interject, to escape an interminable list, for the terrible entomologist had a prodigious memory.

"I know that," he replied, peevishly, "but your approval shows that you're still ignorant. Does one applaud an actor in the middle of a tirade or a tenor in the middle of a ballad? No, of course not! One waits until they have finished. Word of honor, shopkeepers and all money-handlers are only interested in the fluctuations of commodity prices and the share-certificates tucked away in their strong-boxes. I haven't told you anything yet about the admirable structure of the fly, its

---

[41] Brown uses the taxonomic terminology of his own time, which has been frequently updated since, so some of the Latin names he uses to designate particular families and species are no longer in use. I have retained his versions, but have used English common names rather than translating his French common names, where appropriate.

compound eye composed of hundreds of facets, its feet that permit it to walk on the slipperiest surfaces, or its retractile trunk terminated by two striated lips—and you're stopping me!

"Have I even told you that flies belong to the order of *Diptera*, the family of *Arthericeres*, the subfamily of *Muscidae*, divided into nine sections by Laterille and reduced to three by Macquart, which are the *Creophiles*, the *Anthomyzids* and the *Acalypteres*?"

The entomologist went on like that for a long time, and while telling us many times over that he was coming to a close, spared us no detail and no particularity, inflicting upon us the most complete monograph on the fly that could ever be heard. He also threatened to continue Redi's experiments, or, rather the counter-proof of the repulsive generation that he had forced us to witness. Fortunately, he contented himself with explaining them to us.

"The Italian scientist," he went on, "placed numerous pieces of meat in jars covered with transparent cloth, in order to prevent the flies from depositing their eggs. The air corrupted the flesh, but no larvae developed there. The female flies tried to pass their abdomens through the mesh of the fabric to lay their eggs, but their oft-repeated efforts were always in vain. Redi destroyed the then-current opinion that the corpses of humans and animals are eaten by worms, provided that one takes the precaution of burying them in the ground, even at a shallow depths.

I don't know why that final observation struck me and obsessed me for some time. "What becomes of the cadavers then?" I asked.

"They putrefy, of course, and decompose under the action of chemical agents that the earth contains in great abundance…unless they're embalmed or dried out in order to be transformed into mummies."

"Is the decomposition slow or rapid?"

"That depends on the environment in which the cadaver is placed. Putrefaction is favored by a temperature of between twenty and thirty degrees, moderate humidity and, above all, by oxygen. Insensibly, the matter is subjected to a kind of fermentation, still poorly explained, collapses and dissolves, diminishes in volume by the evaporation of liquids and the emission of gases, among which are usually observed nitrogen, sulfur dioxide, ammonia, hydrogen, carbon dioxide and ammoniac acetate. Afterwards, nothing remains but a fetid residue, a sort of compost mainly made up of miry alkaline salts, a greasy carbonaceous substance, a reddish oil and several phosphates.

"And whether it's a matter of the king of creation, a humble donkey or a dead dog, it's always the same. After a few years, if we assume that the skeleton is completely reduced to dust, it would be a very clever man who, taking a few pinches of the compost of a charnel-house between his fingers, could say whether it had been a man, or an animal. Even Hamlet had difficulty in recognizing the remains of poor Yorick."

"Brrr!" I said, with simulated fear. "That's the case with us!"

"And people are astonished," the scientist continued, "that our system of inhumation gives rise to fevers, epidemics and choleras! Rather than bury corpses more deeply, I'd rather allow them to be devoured by larvae—for, as Macquart says, certain insects seem to be responsible for public health. Such is their activity, their fecundity and the rapid succession of their generations, that Linné was able to say, without overmuch hyperbole, that three flies can consume the cadaver of a horse as rapidly as a lion."

"Putrefaction, inhumation, worms, cadavers!" I cried. "God, how cheerful entomology is!"

I thought that the scientists was about to hit me. He looked at me critically and chided me in this fashion:

"What is there on Earth that is cheerful, Monsieur Businessman? Is it commerce, where the robbers and the robbed, the exploiters and the exploited exercise their ingenuity in deceiving one another? Is it politics? Oh, puppets are numerous in that game, but undertakers are jovial fellows by comparison. I prefer my insects; they fulfill the missions that have been allocated to them down here with an admirable urgency and an absolute devotion...and without making speeches."

The scientist withdrew, furiously, leaving me open-mouthed.

III

It would be overly fastidious to relate everything I learned about entomology, and all the patience I required to tolerate the lessons—or, rather, the scientific tirades—of Tiburce Juzans. I was even less disposed to listen to that eternal chatter because my situation did not improve, in spite of my efforts and continual hard work. The date fixed for the marriage of my daughter to Hector Tremont drew closer, and I didn't have the first sou of the promised fifty thousand francs.

Imagine my anxieties!

In the meantime, my mother-in-law rendered her soul to God. The worthy woman never did me any greater service. Let no one suppose that I mean that final remark ironically. My mother-in-law, an exception to the rule, had loved her son-in-law. After having paid my tribute of regrets, I consoled myself somewhat by thinking that I would gain some time because our mourning would postpone the wedding—and time is money, as the wisdom of nations says, sententiously.

Winter arrived and brought its cortege of dark days, squalls and intense cold. My sadness increased, and my character, ordinarily tranquil and toilsome, underwent a disquieting change. I became finicky, fidgety and misanthropic; trivial things irritated me, and I could not bear the slightest contradiction. Even Aristide Croupart, whom I treated with so much reserve, suffered more than once the effects of my bad humor and was rudely abused. But the strange fellow folded up, yielded, flattened like a bug, allowing the storm to pass, and continued to exploit me shamelessly.

To his misfortune and mine, he arrived one evening in December. The temperature was harsh, the wind blowing in icy blasts, flurries of hail sometimes stinging the faces of the few passers-by that were still to be found in the streets.

My wife and daughter were not there. They had gone to spend a few days with my father-in-law, who lived in a nearby village. I was, therefore, alone, and my temporary isolation rendered me even more irascible. When the bailiff presented himself, I understood at a single glance that he was drunk, and I greeted him rather rudely.

"It's you again, Croupart—tell me what you want, quickly; I don't have time to listen to you."

"Yes, it's me, my dear Monsieur; one would think that you were addressing reproaches to me."

"Enough idle chatter."

"I'm not talkative—that's the least of my faults. Anyway, you know full well that I only talk discreetly. Perhaps my language isn't very flowery; nevertheless you'll listen, if not with pleasure, at least with interest."

I shrugged my shoulders.

"Come on, come on," the triple cretin went on, "don't be annoyed. We'll chat calmly and politely, taking the nice glass of cognac that you're going to offer me—there, on that table."

With a commanding gesture, Croupart indicated that I should serve him. A blast of furious anger rose to my face, but I contained myself. Meanwhile, to create some diversion from the impressions I felt and to reanimate my fire, which was going out, I headed for the cellar in order to fetch a little wood. I grabbed the lamp that was lighting the room and went down. That was intended to show Master Croupart the door, but he didn't seem to understand, and scarcely had I arrived in the cellar than I found him on my heels.

"Come on, Croupart," I said, with concentrated fury, "what do you want? Are you going to leave me in peace—yes or no?"

"Damn it!" the drunkard replied. "You're in a bad mood tonight. Is it the cold that's having this effect?"

I made no reply, and lined up on the ground the three or four logs that I needed to aliment my fire.

"After all," the clown went on, "I know I know full well how to loosen your tongue, my worthy Monsieur…and to soften you up. We need to put an end to the comedy you and I have been playing for such a long time. I'm tired of the way you treat me; it's time the roles were reversed..."

I raised my head sharply, and looked Croupart full in the face, eye to eye, ready to hurl myself upon him to give him a good tongue-lashing if he said another word.

And I saw then a Croupart that I did not know: a sort of drunken Mephistopheles, sniggering at my expression, my anger, the insults ready to pour from my mouth. His pasty face, illuminated by the indecisive lamplight, took on a violet tint; a sardonic smile tightened his thin lips; his right hand was brandishing a sheaf of papers, in the middle of which I quickly made out the IOUs I had signed and the protests ready to be registered.

In a voice that I shall never forget, so acerbic and mordant was it, the bailiff read: "At the request of Messieurs les Regents of the Banque de France, represented by Monsieur the Governor of the aforementioned, the proceedings and diligences of Monsieur the Manager of the Brach at X..., there resident at the Bank premises or his chosen domicile, as relevant, we, Aristide Croupart, bailiff attached to the Civil Tribunal sitting at..."

I recognized the gibberish that characterizes all the more-or-less legal documents of our beautiful land of France, and I shouted violently: "Enough! I'll pay..."

"With what, if you please?" the bailiff went on. "Have you come into an inheritance since yesterday? Have you found a treasure? This time, it's really ruination, ruination without appeal… you'll have to go bust!"

Bust! That's the expression used in the world of business to announce inevitable bankruptcy. A frisson ran through my body, my eyelids swelled with blood, a frightful buzzing whistled in my ears, the veins in my neck and temples bulged: I thought that I was done for and that an attack of apoplexy was about to strike me down.

The prostration into which I was plunged, the mental agony I endured and the despair painted on my face seemed to encourage the bailiff in his evil work. He sniggered more loudly, and his voice took on a hateful tone that chilled me with fear.

"Don't hope to soften me up," he went on, "with your supplications and your promises. For you, I want poverty, shameful poverty. Oh, how I detest you, how I hate you! I've been lying in wait for you for a long time, and my day has finally come. No, no, you won't escape me. I shall hold you panting beneath me, I whom you despise so much, and I shall laugh at your incessant chagrin, your poignant pain. Say an eternal adieu to everything that embellishes your existence. Be dishonored, ruined, withered, and let everyone turn away from your path just as you collapse, weak and desperate. Ah! You want to marry your Hélène to Hector Tremont! Personally, I don't want that, and..."

Until then I had not moved, and swallowed the insults addressed to me, angrily, but when that vile individual pronounced my daughter's name, there was an inexplicable reaction within me. Blinded by fury, I grabbed a log and landed two formidable blows on the bailiff's head.

He fell without uttering a cry, a word or a sigh.

He was dead!

Some sensations are difficult to analyze, so far beyond human nature do they seem, and those I felt after the murder I had just committed were indefinable. My anger did not evaporate suddenly. I imagined that Croupart was simply unconscious, and that he was simulating death in order to frighten me.

"Cease this farce, Croupat," I said. "Get up, return to your office…and let this be a lesson to you. It's never with impunity that you insult an honest man. Get up, Croupart."

The silence that followed my words, pronounced with a residue of bad temper, terrified me. I leaned over the bailiff; his eyes were closed and his mouth was deformed by a frightful rictus. Not a drop of blood was running. Death had probably been determined by a compression of the cerebral matter. Had I not struck him in the fashion that oxen are slaughtered?

Then I was afraid; I felt my hair stand on end and my heart beat as if to break out of my chest.

Picking up the lamp, I went back up the cellar stairs, stumbling, and sat down in the dining-room, for my legs would no longer support me. Then, without knowing exactly what I was doing, I went toward the street and, leaning on the doorpost, I breathed in lungfuls of the icy air agitated by the December wind.

As chance would have it, the clerk of the civil tribunal passed by at that moment. As he was walking precipitately, because of the cold, he did not notice my disturbance, and said: "You must be very warm, my dear friend; if you stand still outside your door for much longer, you'll be found frozen stiff."

"I'm going back in," I replied, unconsciously.

And I went back to sit down by my fire, reflecting that, after all, those brief words exchanged with the clerk created a facile alibi for me to invoke if I were pursued. For—it's necessary that my confession be complete—the first impressions that assailed me related to the consequences of my crime rather than the crime itself. I found a thousand reasons to excuse the fit of anger that had made me a murderer.

"Am I to blame?" I murmured, my head in my hands. "Had I any intention to kill Croupart? Why did he insult and excite me? Why did the wretch mingle my daughter's name with the insolence that he was addressing to me?"

I continued for some time in that tone and I found a good many attenuations to mitigate my crime. I had no right to kill a man, but was the victim really worthy of pity? What was the unfortunate Croupart? A bailiff, a malevolent bailiff who rejoiced in the dread he inspired, the harm that he did. The most terrible stories were told about him; people whispered that he had martyrized his wife and had caused her death. No one held him in esteem. The court used him to inflict the most severe disciplinary penalties because of his drunkenness and habitual bad conduct.

These reflections brought a little calm to my mind. I rapidly realized that suspicion would never be directed against me, if I succeeded in making all traces of my crime disappear. In this extremely cold weather, it was probable that no one had seen Aristide Croupart come into my house, and if he had been seen, that was not sufficient reason for accusing me of killing him. It only remained, therefore, for me to get rid of the body—but that did not seem an easy thing to do.

I went back down to the cellar and locked the interior shutter of the air-vent. My lamp, well covered with a dark shade, only gave out a feeble light within a restricted perimeter; no one, therefore, would interrupt my funereal task.

Come on! Courage!

I ought to declare right away that the sight of the cadaver did not affect me as much as I would have supposed. My nerves, numbed by the succession of violent emotions to which I had been subjected in a short time, left me in a state of languor that muffled my senses.

I thought about digging a hole and burying Croupart in the darkest corner of the cellar, but a few minutes of profound meditation convinced me that it would be madness to employ that overly primitive means. If the slightest suspicion fell upon me, searches would be ordered and it would not take long for the cadaver to be discovered.

What means could be imagined, or invented, to get rid of that large cumbersome body? I thought about burning it, cutting it up, reducing it by the action of acids or quicklime, but, knowing that the slightest clues were sufficient for judges to reconstitute, in every detail, the most mysterious dramas, I always found objections to the execution of the projects I conceived.

Finally, a bright idea occurred to me. I remembered that the walls of the cellar resonated here and there when they were struck, as if there were an empty space. When I had been a child, my grandfather had often amused me by tapping on the wall and making me listen to the particular sound produced by any subterranean excavation. He affirmed that Satan himself responded to appeals that were addressed to him when I wasn't good.

It's claimed that everything in life is of use. That memory saved me. Without losing a minute, I knocked on the wall with a hammer, striking all the stones, listening anxiously to the noise produced by the resonance of my blows. Finally, near an alcove opposite the air-vent, I found what I was looking for. I knocked several times, and a dully sonorous vibration always replied to me. There was no more doubt; there was a void.

There were a few tools in the cellar for the maintenance of the small garden adjacent to my house. I seized a strong crowbar and carefully attacked the stones walling up the hollow. The structure was solid, although cracked could be seen in several places. In less than half an hour I loosened a few stones covering a surface area of about sixty square centimeters. I threw them to the ground and was finally able to penetrate a space partly heaped with rubble but large enough to contain several cadavers.

Armed with the lamp, I explored the excavation minutely, and discovered nothing unusual. Rapidly, I struck the plaster with a few blows of a pick-axe, in order to be able to place Croupart's corpse conveniently.

Suddenly, I stopped, in amazement. My implement had broken one of those large earthenware pots in which French housekeepers keep their provisions of fat. A cascade of gold coins, sparkling and flamboyant, like glowing embers spilled on to the ground at my feet.

Believing that I was the victim of some fantastic hallucination, I rubbed my eyes; I seized handfuls of that gold, which had appeared to me in such unexpected circumstances, and stirred them with the joy of a miser counting his money.

Oh, how far from my thoughts my crime and Croupart's body were at that moment! It was gold, beautiful gold: twenty-franc pieces bearing the effigy of Napoléon I, called the Great, and Louis XV, called the Beloved. A crazy satisfaction invaded my entire being, and I surely felt the exuberant joy that the Count of Monte Cristo—or, rather, Dantès—must have felt when he discovered the immense riches contained in the hiding-place indicated to him by the Abbé Faria.

I collected the gold and wrapped it in a piece of canvas. Was there any more of it? I plied the pick ardently, raked through the mass of rubble—reduced it to dust, one might say—but did not find any more.

Then I seized Croupart's body and passed it through the opening that I had made in the wall. Whether because of the delight procured by the discovery of the body redoubled my strength, or because the nervous excitation to which I was subject freed me from the sensation of the law of gravity, that large body seemed to me to be exceedingly light. I shoved it into the little cellar, covered it with a little rubble, and immediately took measures to return the wall to its original condition. That took an hour. To reestablish the junctions, I mixed a little plaster and introduced it into the interstices with a trowel. In order to erase the evidence of recent work I smeared dust, pulverized earth and ash over the fresh plaster—anything that might give the masonry an appearance of decrepitude.

Satisfied with my work, I counted the treasure I had found so unexpectedly. My fortune amounted to fifty thousand francs. What luck! That was the promised dowry; it was the assurance of my daughter's marriage.

I remembered then, vaguely, a story I had been told when I was very young. It was said that my great-grandfather, being a widower, had been conscripted by the imperial authorities, and that, before joining the army, he had made every effort to hide his liquid assets. The unfortunate man never returned home; a bullet had killed him at Waterloo. My grandfather and my father had not lent overmuch credence to small town gossip. It had required a fateful chain of circumstances to put me in possession of that family inheritance.

IV

Croupart's death did not pass unperceived, but in sum, as he was a rather sorry fellow, no one was overly bothered about him. It was known that he had come to my house, but the prosecutor only interrogated me in the capacity of a witness. The worthy magistrate never thought that I might have been the murderer. One entirely fortuitous circumstance contributed to my reassurance. A cadaver was found in the river, and as it had been in the water for a long time and was greatly disfigured, it was imagined that the bailiff might have drowned himself. There were even some people who thought they recognized him.

I therefore remained alone in the knowledge of my crime…and my remorse. Was it really remorse that I felt? Certainly, I have never trifled with the delicacies of conscience and have always marched through life with my head held high, but the memory of Aristide Croupart did not trouble my nights with hideous nightmares and my mind recovered all its placidity. Did that tranquility come from the treasure I had found—the treasure that would put a end to my preoccupations and worries? It's possible.

Soon afterwards, Helena and Hector Tremont were married. From then on, fortune smiled on me and I succeeded in everything. How could anyone not have confidence in a man who gave his daughter a dowry of fifty thousand francs—fifty thousand francs in weighty and resonant cash? I had more credit than I wanted, and a few well-conducted deals reestablished my compromised fortunes. Chance reversed its direction and kicked the bad luck out of my house.

My happiness overflowing, I was permitted to send the learned Tiburce Juzans to the Devil whenever he harped on about some scientific theory; but as he was now related by marriage, I took a few precautions and persuaded him that my numerous book-keeping occupations prevented me from listening to him.

"Oh, these businessmen!" the scientist exclaimed, raising his arms toward the heavens.

He landed one straight blow, however, that I could not ward off, and which interested me once again in entomology, more than I would have wished. He asked for my authorization to go back down into the cellar to observe the hatching of a few pupae belonging to some genre of insects or other. How could I refuse? It was necessary to yield to the entomologist's desire, for my refusal might have had dire consequences.

Spring was enlivening nature and recalling to life everything that had gone to sleep at winter's approach, so Tiburce Juzans, armed with a powerful magnifying-glass or microscope, went down into the cellar ten times a day and came up full of joy when his observations had permitted him to discover the phases of the metamorphosis he was studying so assiduously.

More than once, the presence of that terrible investigator in my house awakened the memory of Croupart sleeping the eternal slumber in the little cellar into which I had introduced him. It always seemed to me that some unexpected occurrence might put the scientist on the track of my crime. I enquired curiously about the principal causes leading to the prompt destruction of cadavers when they were not buried but enclosed in a hermetically sealed environment.

"They dry out, of course," Tiburce Juzans replied. "The skin becomes parchment-like, sticks to the bones and, after a certain time, nothing more exists than a more-or-less grimacing mummy. If the cadaver were exposed to the air, of course, or were accidentally to come into contact with the air, it would be quite different."

"What would happen then?"

"What happened to the pieces of meat deposited in the grounds when I explained the generation of flies to Madame Tremont. In a few days, it would fall prey to maggots."

"A sepulchral jest," I said, trying to smile.

"Entomology is not what vain people think," the scientist went on, laughing in his turn, "and it teaches many things. I'll wager a hundred to one that you didn't know that it is often a great help to a medical examiner when, by the simple inspection of a cadaver, he is able to establish the time at which death occurred."

"Yes," I replied, keenly impressed. "I didn't know that."

"Indeed," Tiburce Juzans continued. "The problem seems insoluble, and yet it's remarkably simple. Dr. Brouardel was the first to imagine that the remains of certain insects found on a body exposed to the air to a greater or lesser extent might be a sure indication of the time of death. He communicated his idea to a entomologist, Monsieur P. Megnin,[42] and the latter took responsibility for demonstrating the exactitude of that assertion, to the extent that was possible. You're listening, aren't you?"

"Absolutely," I replied, more intrigued than I wanted to appear.

"Monsieur Megnin proceeded methodically, and convinced himself very quickly that the work of the larvae of *Diptera* of the Sarcophagian group, and even those of some coleopterans, like carrion beetles, is not isolated. These larvae, as I've told you before, absorb the liquid humors of bodies, reducing them to a near-skeletal state, then imbibe the fatty acids that are known by the name of corpse-grease. Then they disappear, to be replaced by the larvae of *Dermestes*, which absorb all the remaining fatty material. There are still the tendons and the skin—in sum, al the organic parts that are perfectly desiccated. Then *Anthrenus* and Acarians of the genera *Tyroglyphus* and *Glycyphagus* arrive, which appear in myriads and leave absolutely nothing but the bones, which they cover with their remains and excreta."

"Truly, that's marvelous!" I interjected, to conceal my anxiety.

---

[42] Jean-Pierre Megnin's book *Faune des tombes* [The Fauna of Graves] (1887) was the founding text of forensic entomology; he took his initial inspiration from Paul Brouardel, one of the founding fathers of French forensic medicine.

"Yes, yes, it's marvelous," the scientist continued, delighted to hold forth on his favorite theme. "Henceforth, forensic medicine will be drawn partly from entomology, and murderers will be confounded when they think they can escape punishment for their crimes."

"Has it been proved…?" I stammered.

"Proved? Of course it's been proved. Our hands are full of proof. Thus, in October 1882, the bound cadaver of a nine-year old boy was found in a room in the Gros-Caillou district. The shells of larvae of *Sarcophagus latierus* and *Lucilia cadaverina*—flies that I've often mentioned—represented the remains of the workers of the first year. The shells of larvae of *Dermestes lardarius* and *Anthrenus muscorum* and the corpses of *Tyroglyphus longior* and *siro* represented the residues of the second year. Thus, the death of the child had taken place about two years before.

"On another occasion, the desiccated body of a new-born infant was found at the back of a cupboard. Monsieur Megnin recognized the remains of Sarcophagid *Diptera. Dermestes* were lacking. A few living Acarians were beginning to establish colonies. The death had taken place about a year before. The guilty parties were subsequently arrested, and the facts announced by science thus justified. Are those results not admirable?"

"Yes..."

"Suppose," the loquacious scientist continued, "that Croupart…your remember that Croupart suddenly disappeared? Suppose, as I say, that he died peacefully in some remote spot, or that he was murdered, which is quite probable; well, on inspection of the cadaver I could tell you exactly when he died, within a few days."

Tiburce Juzans left then. One minute more, and I would have fainted like a girl.

Then, to inform myself completely regarding the role of the insects that Tiburce Juzans had named, I studied them, making use of a voluminous treatise on entomology that ornamented my library, and into which I rarely darted a glance. I was fairly well up on the Sarcophaghid and other flies, so I left those aside to get on to the *Dermestes*. One can readily imagine that I wanted something other than a dry list, and when I learned that *Dermestes* belong to the order of *Coleoptera*, the suborder of *Pentameres*, the family of *Clavicornes* and the subfamily of *Dermestidae*, I was by no means satisfied.. I wanted to know about the habits of these devourers of cadavers, in order to know whether Croupart was sheltered from their attacks.

I learned that there are some twenty species spread around all parts of the globe, and that they do not merit their name (from the Greek *dermestes*, red skin) when they are in perfect condition. They are little creatures two or three lignes[43] long, with antennae with eleven joints, of which the last three firm a sort of perfoliate club; the head is globular, small and inclined, the body oval, convex and, rounded underneath, equipped with sparse hair of various colors. They live in flowers, and only the females see out animal matter in which to lay their eggs. The familiar species include skin beetles and larder beetles.

It is the larvae of the latter—whose name explains their action well enough, and which are found in badly-kept butchers' shops—that attack animal matter. They have strong mandibles, short legs. They move slowly and make use as they advance, as a lever, of a tube that terminates their body. Long reddish hairs form a crown around their rings and a tuft at their posterior extremity. For four months they never cease to feed, and even devour one another if they are driven by hunger.

Anthrenus belongs to the same subfamily as *Dermestes*, distinguished from them because they are smaller and because they have solid club-like antennae. The damage done by *Anthrenus museorum* in museums is well-known and the despair of

---

[43] A *ligne* was a measurement used in France prior to the introduction of the metric system; it was equal to a twelfth of a *pouce* (the French inch)—a little under two millimetres.

all naturalist collectors. The larvae penetrate into the exoskeletons of insects and devour everything except the feet and wing-cases. They are very tiny, but make up for their lack of size with a formidable appetite. They shed their skins as they grow, and the last one the shed serves as a shell for pupation.

Carrion beetles, or shield-beetles, thus named because of their large rounded bodies, are Coleopteran, Pentameran insects of the family *Clavicornes* and the subfamily *Silphales*. They attack dead mammals and birds lying in woods and field; they do not bury them but penetrate avidly beneath their skins and soon strip their flesh to the bones. One large black species, *Silpha littoralis*, entertains itself in dead fish thrown up by the waters. Their livery is generally dark, in rapport with their repulsive functions. Their odor is nauseating. The larvae, like the adults, live in the midst of putrefying flesh. They move rapidly and take prompt refuge in cadavers when one tries to seize them.

I knew enough about carrion beetles and abandoned them to start on the study of Acarians, or Acadia. I confess that the scientific name led me astray, but when I found out that it meant mites, ticks and the like I found that I knew more than I thought. Who does not know the cheese-mite, the microscopic insect that one often finds on old bread and dried-up jam? Who has not had to rid a bird-cage of the vermin that pullulates infinitely in the slightest interstices? Well, those are Acarians, imperceptible arachnids that not only attack living creatures but also cadavers, when the Sarcophagids and Dermestidae have finished their repulsive work.

Such were the results of my research, and I declare that I recovered some of my composure when I understood the habits of the terrible insects that Tiburce Juzans had indicated to me as avengers of society and punishers of unknown crime.

V

Everyone is familiar with Beaumarchais' speech about slander, delivered by Bazile in the *Barbier de Seville*:

"Slander, Monsieur? You scarcely know that which you disdain; I've seen the most honest of men close to being crushed by it. Do you think that there is no plain wickedness, no horror, no absurd tale that will not be adopted by the idlers of a great city and believed? And here we have people of some skill! First, a slight rumor, skimming the ground like a swallow before a storm; a *pianissimo* murmur that flies, sowing poisonous seed as it goes; some mouth picks it up and *piano, piano*, slips it cleverly into your ears. The damage is done; it germinates; its creeps; it travels, and *rinforzando*, from mouth to mouth, it goes with diabolical speed; then, suddenly, no one knows how, you see the slander rear up, whistle, swell, visibly increase. It launches forth, takes flight, swirls around, envelops, tears up, drags away, bursts and thunders, and becomes, thanks be to Heaven, a general cry, a public *crescendo*; a universal *chorus* of hatred and proscription. Who the Devil can resist it?"

I passed through all the anxieties to which slander gives rise. Was there not a host of people offended by the recovery of my business and the profits I was making? Had I not awakened some jealousy by the success of my operations and the unexpected good luck that favored me?

A few imprudent words from Tibur Juzans had sufficed to bring small town gossip down on my head.

Summer had succeeded spring and the heat was tropical. The entomologist was exuberant with joy; larvae and pupae were transforming themselves admirably, and he was assembling in my cellar, he claimed, quantities of observations that he intended to submit to the enlightened appreciation of the members of the Académie des Science. To hear him, he was about to transform entomology. Unfortunately for me, however, he noticed an infinite number of flies racing, fluttering and frolicking in the rays of sunlight passing through the air-vent. He recognized, in particular, *Calliphora vomitoria* and *Sarcophaga vivipara*, two species whose larvae are partial to putrefying flesh.

"Word of honor," he said, "the flies are abundant; one might think that there were a cadaver buried in the cellar."

This observation, repeated many times over in front of anyone and everyone, was commented on, transformed, examined and turned over and over, to such an extent that it attracted the attention of a whole society of idlers, hypocritical and envious old women. And the rumor spread, and grew, *rinforzando*, and exploded thunderously!

One morning, all public opinion had me under suspicion. People avoided me, turned away as I passed by, and only greeted me with ill-concealed embarrassment. And the strangest, most baroque, most surprising and most extraordinary suppositions spread like wildfire! Soon, it was whispered that my fortune originated from thefts committed after numerous murders, and that if my cellar were dug up, they would find not only Croupart's cadaver, but those of many strangers to the locality.

I resolved to escape that crescendo, that hateful chorus, by retiring to the country for a while. During a heat-wave, my daughter and her husband were taking refuge in a recently-acquired property about fifteen kilometers from the town. I asked them to provide hospitality for me...and for Tiburce Juzans. Understandably, I did not want to leave behind the incorrigible chatterbox who had unwittingly fed the public malevolence and had bravely declared, without any astonishment, that there was nothing impossible about Croupart's cadaver being buried in my cellar, since the numerous flies escaping through the air-vent testified to the plausibility of the hypothesis.

In the country, however, things were very different. The scientist ferreted everywhere, searched everything, inspected every clump of grass, every clod of earth, every fissure in the bark of every tree—and about the slightest insect he perceived, there were interminable tirades. Really, I was saturated by entomology, and I honestly think that it was my perpetual contact with Tiburce Juzans that gave rise to my insurmountable aversion to science and scientists.

However, I would be lying if I did not confess that certain "lessons" sometimes interested me. I remember one of them, above all, which made a deep impression on my irritated nerves and occupied me sufficiently to make me forget my troubles, my black thoughts and the slanders whose echo still rang in my ears, for a little while.

The heat was oppressive; no cloud veiled the blue sky; the sun was blazing as if to roast anyone imprudent enough to expose himself to its rays. In order to read a book by André Theuriet, the poet of the fields,[44] I sat down in a grove of elms and ash-trees that projected a dense shade on half-scorched ground. The surrounding area was deserted; animals and people alike had abandoned themselves to the enervated languor that unusually high temperature provokes, and were lying down in barns or houses. Only a few swallows were swooping over a cool stream, whose idle waters were streaked by water-insects, which children call whirligig beetles. Nothing could be heard but the shrill cries of field-crickets and the louder stridulations of cicadas. They, of course, were wholehearted in their joy, and making a deafening racket.

Seduced by the coolness to be enjoyed beneath the foliage that was sheltering me, my daughter, her husband and Tiburce Juzans hastened to join me, and installed themselves unceremoniously on the grassy ground. The moment that loquacious entomologist was beside me, it was impossible to read, and I closed my book with a hint of ill humor.

"Ooh, you're taking it badly," he said to me. "It doesn't take much to disturb you and annoy you."

"You're not disturbing me," I hastened to reply. "I wasn't reading any longer; I was listening to the song of the cicadas."

"Ah! The cicadas! *Hemipteran* insects, subsection *Homoptera*, family *Cicadaria*, characterized by antenna with six distinct joints, three small smooth eyes, and transparent veined elytrae. The male has a special organ to either side of the base

---

[44] Probably *Chemin des bois* (1867).

of the abdomen, with the aid of which it produces a loud and monotonous sound. The female has a saw-like auger at the tip of the abdomen, enclosed between two scaly blades; she makes use of it to pierce the wood in which she deposits her eggs. The larvae are white, have six feet and dig into the earth, where they live on plant roots, and..."

"Is there anything drier and more insipid than a list?" I put in, disrespectfully. "Nothing destroys a taste for science like scholars and the pedantic terms they use to lord it over laymen. So, after what you've just said, what do I know about cicadas?"

"Eh? Wretch!" cried the scandalized Tiburce Juzans. "With the sacred scarab, bees, ants, ichneumon-flies and a few other insects, cicadas have a historic past filled with glory. The Greeks celebrated them enviously and delighted in their song. Homer compare the wise old Trojan men seated by the Scaean gates to cicadas, because of the smoothness of their eloquence. In Laconia, a monument was built in honor of their musical talent. Who does not remember the contest of Eunomes and Ariston on the cithara? When one of the strings of the former's instrument broke, a cicada placed itself over it and substituted so well that it helped Eunomes win the victory."

"Which proves," I said, somewhat appeased by the short digression, "that the musical taste of the Greeks was sometimes very singular."

"Be that as it may," the scientist continued, "they put cicadas in little cages to give themselves the pleasure of listening to them. They even regarded their bodies as a delicacy, and Aristotle tells us that they sometimes chose and chewed, for preference, gravid females. In addition, the cicada was a symbol of nobility among the Athenians. Those who claimed descent from an ancient family wore a golden cicada in their hair. Well, Monsieur Bookkeeper, does the insect begin to interest you?"

"Yes," I replied, smiling.

"Why did the Locrians strike the image of a cicada on their coins?" asked Hector Tremont.

"Locris and Rhegium," the entomologist replied, were neighboring towns on the Greek mainland, only separated by a river. Hercules, probably wearied by one of the feats of strength to which he was accustomed, lay down on the ground near Rhegium and tried to sleep—but the cicadas were making so much noise that they prevented the hero from closing his eyes. Hercules began cursing them and obtained an undertaking that they would no longer sing in that vicinity. The cicadas emigrated *en masse* to the Locrian shore, and charmed the inhabitants. Gratefully, the latter put their image on their money."

"Is it true," Hélène asked, "that cicadas don't take any nourishment?"

"They live on the sap of trees that they prick with their rostrum. The worthy La Fontaine gave them a reputation for lack of foresight that they do not deserve, for, before dying in the autumn, they have no need for winter provisions.[45] The ancients imagined that the insects fed on the morning dew, and poetry has accredited that error. There is a charming ode on that subject by Anacreon—you must know it, Hector, being a literate person, and I beg you to recite it for us. It begins thus: "Fortunate cicada, who…which…come on, help me."

"My word, Uncle I don't recall a single word of that ode."

"Perhaps I shall be luckier than you, after a moment's reflection."

And our scientist collected himself, his laced on his forehead, for four or five minutes. Then he got up, shifted his weight from one foot to the other, and, striking the pose of an old dandy addressing a madrigal to Chloris, he recited in a heartfelt fashion:

---

[45] La Fontaine actually adapted his version of the fable of the Ant and the Cicada (usually known in English as "The Ant and the Grasshopper") from Aesop.

"Fortunate cicada, who, in the highest branches of the trees, drinks a little dew, sings like a queen! Your realm is all that you can see in the fields, all that is born in the forests. You are loved by the laborer; no one does you harm, and mortal respect you as the gentle prophet of summer. You are cherished by the Muses, cherished by Phoebus himself, who was given you your harmonious song. Old age does not enfeeble you. O wise little creature, emerged from the bosom of the earth, amorous of song, free of suffering, who has neither blood nor flesh, what do you lack in order to be a god?"

"That's delightful," said Hélène.

"I shall get my revenge with the Latins," her husband added, "and exclaim with Virgil: 'And the whining cicadas shake the bushes with their song!'"

"The fact is," Tiburce Juzans went on, "that the Latins only held cicadas in mediocre esteem. They claimed that their song was raucous, deafening and intolerable. Nevertheless, they affirmed that they rejoiced in the gaiety of mortals, and that the more the latter laughed, amused themselves and sang, the livelier, louder and shriller the stridulations of the cicadas became."

"I've heard it said," Hélène remarked, "that the musical apparatus of cicadas is very curious."

"Indeed, but only the males sing and the females are mute." Then the entomologist added, with the courtesy of a screech-owl: "It's not the same with us; it is, on the contrary, the females who chatter away at random; thus, the Rhodian poet Xenarchus exclaimed: 'Cicadas are fortunate, for their females are deprived of a voice.'"

"Gods!" I murmured. "That such things are said in polite terms!"

The scientist looked at me askance and said, shrugging his shoulders: "*Telum imbelle sine ictu*."[46] Then he continued:

---

[46] A weak shot, devoid of force. The quote is from Virgil's *Aeneid*, where it refers to a dart launched by the aged Priam at Pyrrhus.

"I can't explain the complicated mechanism of the cicada's musical apparatus to you, but I'll show you how they do it. Stay here, don't move, and don't say a word."

Then Tiburce Juzans repeated a curious experiment, attempted for the first time by Solier and his friend Boyer, a pharmacist in Aix.[47] He picked up a little rod, and stealthily drew closer to an ash-tree whose lowest branch was no higher than a man's height.

A cicada was singing at the top of its voice on the branch, warmly caressed by the bright sunlight. The scientist stuck out his lips and whistled in a tremulous manner to imitate the strident sound produced by the insect. The latter, we clearly observed, stopped at first, and seemed to be listening attentively. Stimulated, however, perhaps believing that it was being challenged by a fellow, it resumed its song with a new animation.

Tiburce Juzans never lost sight of it, and seemed intent on hypnotizing it, so wide were his eyelids. He was still whistling, executing a few minor variations, which charmed the cicada, for it came down backwards, stopped, and then came down further, repeating the maneuver until it was at the very tip of the ash-branch.

Then the scientist held out his wand and, to our great astonishment, the cicada stepped on to it and slowly continue its descent. It arrived thus at the hand, and we distinctly perceived the rapid movement of its abdomen, which it alternately drew away from and moved closer to the openings of the sonorous cavities.

Nothing was as simultaneously pleasant and curious as that duel of two virtuosos, so different in size and appearance.

The cicada seemed to be intoxicated by its own melody and the one it heard; its sang and sang with a vibration of its wings, a quivering of its entire being that was scarcely per-

[47] Antoine Solier probably picked this trick up from his fellow entomologist Étienne Boyer de Fonscolombe rather than a pharmacist of the same name.

ceptible, so rapid was it. Wanting to take the experiment further, Tiburce Juzans, still whistling, brought his hand up to the level of his nose.

The cicada understood what was being asked of it, and bravely established itself on the entomologist's nasal appendage.

"Bravo! Bravo!" I cried, carried away by surprise.

But the charm was broken. The cicada flew away into the topmost branches of the ash-tree.

"Well," Tiburce Juzans said to me, "are you satisfied with that lesson, and do you believe that entomology can be an original and amusing science?"

I congratulated the scientist and tickled his self-regard agreeably by comparing him to Orpheus, who also charmed the animals, not whistling, but by singing.

We remained in the country for some three months, and I admit that our studies in the open fields, without reconciling me completely with the science, enabled me to appreciate nature more, while consoling me in my chagrin and soothing the overexcitation of the impressions left by bitter memories.

VI

I had imagined that my prolonged absence would calm that fever of slander that sometimes, if not always, takes possession of the inhabitants of a small town and drives them to exaggerate everything. It was affirmed, however, that my departure proved my guilt. And what did my return prove? Good God, the answer was quite simple: I had come back to deflect suspicion, to deceive Lady Themis. At any rate, public rumor pursued me doggedly, the scandal had built up tremendous momentum and anonymous denunciations were arriving in such quantity at the court that the latter took action, and in order to put an end to it, ordered that my cellar should be searched.

"It's the only means," the prosecutor told me, "of demonstrating the absurdity of the accusations made against you.

In spite of the scrupulous enquiries made by the examining magistrate, I'm happy to tell you that no serious charge has been raised against you."

It was on a fine autumn day that three robust fellows arms with spades and pick-axes turned over the soil in my cellar under the vigilant eye of the commissaire of police, two agents, a gendarme and some junior clerk.

Seemingly impassive, I watched the work, which, I hoped, would dissipate all suspicions and render me the rest of which I was so much in need. When the workmen's tools brushed the wall behind which Croupart lay, and imperceptible torment contracted my features, but they paid no heed to it. They dug and dug, shifting the earth with the urgency of the gravediggers who scandalized Hamlet. On several occasions, they drank a few glasses of wine, and one of them sang an old ballad who sad and languid chorus was appropriate to my situation, and evoked I know not what macabre past.

Finally, the work came to an end. Having dug up a few meters of earth, the spade-workers filled in the last hole and the commissaire of police got ready to leave, offering me his congratulations. I breathed more easily; I was saved!

Suddenly, a shadow fell over the air-vent, and a voice cried: "Oh! Nevertheless, I'm certain that there's a cadaver in your cellar."

Have you ever dreamed that you were falling from an immensely high tower and that, in a few seconds, you would be a bruised, bloodied, misshapen parcel of flesh and bone? One wakes up with a start, forehead covered in cold sweat, panting. I experienced that torture; my heart suddenly ceased beating in my breast and an unaccountable weakness annihilated my courage and will-power,

"Is that true, then?" queried the commissaire, observing the collapse of my self-composure.

I did not have the strength to reply.

But Tiburce Juzans had already come down into the cellar and, without taking any notice of the people surrounding me, and without even looking at me, obedient to his passion, to his mania for checking everything when there was a matter of scientific fact at stake, his eyes followed a few insects on the wall, which were entering and emerging from an almost imperceptible crack that extended all the way to the ceiling. Immediately, I recognized *Silpha*, that devourer of cadavers whose repulsive habits I had studied.

Tiburce Juzans put his finger on the inopportune crack in the wall and cried, triumphantly: "I attest that there is, behind this construction, a cadaver...the cadaver of a human or an animal, I don't know…but there is definitely a cadaver..."

Losing all consciousness of my situation, and the danger to which I was exposing myself, I clenched my fists and howled, furiously: "Wretch! Shut up!"

And I launched myself toward the scientist, in order to strike him, to bite him, perhaps to kill him. The two police agents and the gendarme interposed themselves and held me firmly. Then, everything whirled around me, and for a few minutes I was subjected to the torments of the damned.

The workmen attacked the wall with a kind of frenzy, and every blow of the pick on the stone resounded in my head as if an invisible harpy were hammering my skull. The plaster crumbled, the stones fell, one by one, and the opening giving access to the little cellar appeared to me, gaping frightfully, like one of the mouths of Hell.

Aristide Croupart appeared to me too; I saw him as insolent, malevolent and hateful as on the day of the murder. I even heard his sardonic laughter, mingled with drunken hiccups...

I closed my eyes to escape the terrible vision, but Croupart was still there, in front of me, menacing and terrible, calling all the vengeance of Heaven down upon my head...

"Bring the light," ordered the commissaire.

That simple speech was sufficient to bring me back to sad reality.

"It's true," I stammered. "It's true, I killed Croupart, but I struck him without having any intention of killing him. He insulted me horribly, exasperated me by..."

"Good, good," the commissaire interjected. "You can excuse yourself as you like before the magistrates. As for me, I'm here to make a report and assemble the evidence of the crime."

I maintained the most profound silence, and the workmen introduced themselves into the excavation that served as the bailiff's tomb. Tiburce Juzans finally understood the imprudence he had committed, and seemed devastated. A few dolorous exclamations emerged from his mouth, and proved to me that he bitterly regretted his intemperate speech—but when a question was addressed to him by the gendarme, that majestic representative of authority, his sensitivity immediately vanished, and the scientist reappeared, with his habitual loquacity, his intolerable pedantry and his interminable explanations.

"Yes, Monsieur," I heard him say. "This cadaver confirms the theories of Messieurs Brouardel and Megnin. Take note of the shells left by the Sarcophagid flies, observe the remains of a few *Dermestes* larvae, remark also a few colonies of Acarids that are beginning to attack the extremities of the hands and the feet. Without fear of being mistaken, we can affirm that the cadaver has been sealed up for about a year...

"Science, Monsieur, even when it is preceded by deductions, never leads one astray; I say that boldly, and I shall say it again if..."

The gendarme, bewildered by that flood of words, did not listen to the rest. I fainted in his arms.

What can I add to the lamentable adventure? Happy are the peoples who have no history, Fénélon says, and when I think about all the events that have rendered my existence so bitter and so painful, I can add, sadly: happy also is the man who has no history!

Nevertheless, I await the jury's decision summoned to examine my case calmly. My defender never stops repeating: "Your crime was involuntary, and, after all, it was only a bailiff that you killed. If you're found guilty, you'll benefit considerably from extenuating circumstances!"

Claude Manceau: *A Professional Scruple*

(Georges-Frédéric Espitallier)
(1896)

When the accused was introduced into the assize court, the entire audience experienced an instinctive repulsion, so powerfully did his bestial expression and low-browed skull testify against him.

The crime for which he had to answer was not one of those that permitted pity. He had killed his mother by kicking her to death…or, at least, was accused of so doing—and his previous history was sufficient indication that he was capable of it.

Thus, the public prosecutor had a fine time developing the thunder of his eloquence in a speech as florid as it was melodramatic, in which virulent invective rubbed shoulders with elegiac prosopopeia.[48] The mother—the victim—who was herself, I believe, nothing but a hardened criminal, was aureoled with all the virtues when the advocate general drew her portrait in a somber voice. It is the law of contrasts which demands that the victim is always sympathetic.

In brief it was a good bet that the accused, that scoundrel Jacques Féraut, was guilty; but, to tell the truth, there was nothing as yet to convince someone of his guilt but clues, words and moral indications—and the jurors felt their conviction hesitating, in spite of the fiery quality of the speech.

The prosecution's entire argument hinged on two points. The front of the shirt that Jacques had been wearing on the day

---

[48] Prosopopeia is a manner of speech that represents the supposed words of an absent individual—especially one who is dead.

of the crime was stained with blood, and the bloody imprint of a hand had been left on a door.

Was the blood on the shirt that of the victim? Was the print applied to the wood, like the murderer's sinister signature, that of Jacques' hand.

Everything was there; what point was there is quibbling? The expert was about to give his opinion.

The expert...

When the usher summoned the expert, all gazes turned anxiously toward the side-door. An abrupt silence fell; breath was held—and it was in the midst of that overheated atmosphere, under the crossfire of all those focused gazes, that Dr, Georges Chemin made his entrance into the court.

It was the first time that he had given expert testimony on behalf of the law, and he was very nervous about that debut. At an age when one has ordinarily only just escaped the university benches, the young doctor had already won a veritable scientific notoriety. He had understood that, in the present century, it is necessary to specialize, and had found in forensic medicine a broad path that promised resounding successes. The chemistry of poisons no longer had any secrets from him, and like Raspail,[49] he could easily, if he were asked to do so, have extracted the arsenic from the wood of which the chair was made on which the president of the tribunal was majestically sat.

He was scrupulous too, and convinced...but this was his debut, and his emotion in the face of the apparatus of Justice

---

[49] François-Vincent Raspail (1794-1878), who became as famous for his radical politics as for his chemical and physiological expertise, appeared for the defence in a famous murder trial in 1839, when a man named Louis Mercier was charged with poisoning his mentally-handicapped son with arsenic. The assembled forensic evidence appears to have been contradictory in the extreme, but Raspail's attempts were in vain, and Mercier was convicted.

and under the sentiment of his responsibility was, in truth, entirely comprehensible.

He collected himself swiftly and, wiping the lenses of his pince-nez, which were fogged, he approached the bar, bowed and waited.

The president immediately put him at his ease and asked him to explain to the jurors the results of his expertise. He began, therefore, in a sonorous voice, without looking at the accused.

Everything was, in any case, perfectly clear and precise.

With regard to the handprint, he calls attention to the fact that the hand an individual presents, in the disposition of its ridge-patterns, characteristics unique to its owner. A few bloodstains, formless and coagulated, would not suffice for that identification. They only serve to mark the place where the hand is applied, depositing an invisible layer of sweat, precisely striped with a network corresponding to the ridges. Is it not possible to place a tracing of that network in evidence? That is the whole question. Now, it is easy to make one, by drawing a paintbrush dipped in a clear solution of Indian ink over it; the ink slides over the greasy parts without sticking to them and, by contrast, tints the other parts.

That experiment, the expert has attempted; the image has appeared. It only remained to compare it with the hand of the accused. The proof leaves no doubt; we have the original of the image.

As regards the stains remarked on the linen, that is the infancy of the art, and, in spite of their slightness, their identification was easy; they were not rust, in spite of their appearance; they were blood, and they were the mammalian blood; they were human blood.

"Not true!" cried a hoarse voice. "They were chicken blood."

The expert turned toward the accused, who had inflicted this self-interested lie upon him. Their gazes met, and Georges Chemin shivered at the wretch's ferocious expression. Even so, he turned to the jury and coolly explained his reasoning.

The man's gaze had, however, disturbed him. He was not afraid; it was more a residue of his initial timidity that the loud interruption had reawakened.

The advocate, moreover, had felt the crushing impact that the expert's report had for his client, so he immediately opened fire on this delicate point.

"Oh!" he cried, "a human life is certainly a very small thing, since it is at the mercy of the first young man fresh out of college, provided that he introduces himself under the sacred aegis of science. One dies not hesitate to produce hazardous affirmations when one can shore them up on a few more-or-less well-understood theories and experiments more-or-less well-carried-out. Before the most troubling problems, the young scientists are not anxious, therefore, about the responsibility they are assuming, and when it suffices for them to lift a little finger to strike the head from the shoulders of the accused, they lift that little finger with a glad heart."

The advocate went on for much longer, but out of all his harangue, Georges Chemin only heard the acrimonious words that were more-or-less directly aimed at him.

What! Was his conscience not in good order? Had he not sought the truth in good faith? Had he not explained the matter with all the sincerity of his heart, exactly as it had appeared to him? Was that not his duty, and had he not accomplished it rigorously?

The rest of the hearing went past, for him, as if in a dream, from which he only awoke when judgment was pronounced.

Jacques Féraut was sentenced to death; one could do no less for a parricide, and the verdict was welcomed in the audience by a murmur of approval. But it seemed to Georges Chemin that he was the one who had pronounced the sentence: a condemnation to death. He was the principal architect of it. If he had been less affirmative, if he had shown the slightest doubt, perhaps the accused would have been spared.

What if he were mistaken, as any human might be?

At that moment, he raised his eyes toward the dock where the accused was standing between two gendarmes, and encountered his furious gaze. It was not exactly the gaze of an innocent man, but one is so often mistaken about such things...

Georges Chemin was nailed to the spot, but the crowd drew him toward the exit. He allowed himself to be carried by the flow, his forehead creased; it is hard to tell oneself that one has just obtained one's first death-sentence.

Examining magistrates, defenders and prosecutors become accustomed quite rapidly to the demands of their functions; they are there to put a case; they put the case. Georges Chemin was not accustomed to the demands of his, and anguish gripped him as he thought that a man was about to die because of him.

What if the man were innocent?

He was perhaps the only one to suppose for a single instant that the frightful rogue might be innocent, but by force of mulling over the affair and plucking the strings of his conscience, he had distorted the mechanism of his own common sense.

He wondered whether all his experiments might have been spoiled by error, whether he had taken sufficient precautions—whether he had ensured, in a word, that he had testified to an incontestable truth.

He had never felt such perplexity, such anxiety, and in his laboratory, in order to reassure his alarmed conscience, he repeated his control experiments. Alas, from ten identical operations, he did not obtain absolutely concordant results.

Where then, was the infallibility?

Fortunately the sentence of death had not been conclusive. The penalty could be commuted; it surely would be commuted. There was still hope.

Oh, if only he had been able to intercede personally for his victim! But no, that was impossible; would that not be to confess that he had doubts about the veracity of his own affirmations?

Under that constant and painful preoccupation, he lost sleep. In the rare moments when he dozed off, he was haunted by terrifying hallucinations. He thought he was watching the execution of the unfortunate Féraut.

At daybreak, in a bitter wind, the crowd surrounded the horrible guillotine. Féraut came down, unsteadily. He advanced toward the cold machine; then,, suddenly, a movement of the lever, a flash, a head rolling into the bran in the sinister basket.

And that head turned its eyes, darting a gaze of ferocious hatred at the unfortunate expert who had had it condemned, while its lips opened to murmur words that no one could hear.

That haunting became a veritable persecution for the unfortunate; he suffered fever, delirium, and ended up falling completely ill. He had but one obsession: to assure himself in a peremptory fashion of Féraut's perfect guilt. That was the only means of fully reassuring his conscience.

Oh, if only the condemned man had made a confession! But he refused to do so energetically, perhaps hoping that, in the face of his protestations of innocence, they would be more likely to hesitate over his execution.

How, then, could his secret be extracted from him? He was about to die, and dead men do not speak...except in sentimental novels and melodramas.

How can a decapitated head be made to speak? Is it possible to relight a flame over which the breath of death has passed?

Everything that he knew about physiology returned to his memory; the ancient experiments were scarcely encouraging, and he imagined new ones.

He wanted to have a supreme conversation with the condemned man, at the moment when verity escapes with the soul; he would have it. Yes, he would go to claim the body of the executed man, in the sacred interests of science, and on that freshly-excised head he would attempt the craziest of experiments: he would try to restore it to life momentarily.

But is not death instantaneous? One sees, it is true, the bodies of animals agitating for a long time yet after beheading. Reflex movements, it is said, resulting from the excitation of nervous centers. Who knows?

And he demanded his books, which he read feverishly in his bed.

"What, then is the mechanism of death by decapitation?" said one of them. "How does a individual die, whose head has been abruptly removed, at a single stroke, by a trenchant instrument?"[50]

And the answer is that it produces simultaneously the phenomena of asphyxiation and inhibition. In an animal, it is the asphyxia that predominates. "The convulsive movements that it presents are the convulsions of asphyxia. The blood remaining in the head and the body can no longer be arterialized; then, the sanguine liquid flows rapidly away and leaves the tissues deprived of oxygen and overloaded with carbon dioxide. Those are all the conditions of asphyxia."

But if the trenchant instrument attains the animal's *vital node*—the spinal cord in humans: "Under the influence of the violent shock produced by the blade, and the energetic irritation of the nervous system, there is a suspension, an immediate abolition of the reflex power and automotive power of the nervous centers." No excitation can cause them to react; there is no agony, nor movement, nor convulsions.

But that period of inhibition might only be transitory. If, while it lasts, the blood disappears completely, a return to activity will obviously be impossible; the centers will not reawaken. But if one succeeds in maintaining the sanguine liquid in the vessels until the end of the period of torpor, why should the motor centers not resume their activity? Why should the intelligence, momentarily obscured, not reappear? Why...

---

[50] The author inserts a footnote at this point giving the reference: Paul Loye, *Revue scientifique*, 1888, 2nd series, p.66.

Georges Chemin was young and vigorous, and the strength of his constitution reckoned with his illness. He woke up one day in cheerful sunlight, very weak but free of fever. The sunlight was not sufficient, however, to make him cheerful; gradually, memory returned, and with it, anguishes that caused a feverish frisson to pass over his face.

He retained from his delirium that obsession to interrogate the executed man in a supreme experiment, if the law were to follow its course.

The appeal for mercy was rejected and the execution was imminent. Alas! How could a parricide be pardoned?

In spite of his still-considerable weakness, the young scientist made every effort to ascertain that the body would be surrendered to him after the execution, and without the simulated inhumation that had rendered all previous experiments futile.

At the same time, he made all the necessary arrangements in his laboratory, which was close to the square where the guillotine would be set up.

His favorite pupil asked in vain for the favor of assisted him in his task; by virtue of a eccentricity that might appear inexplicable, the scientist refused all collaboration. He wanted to be alone in confronting the mysteries of that sinister tête-à-tête, especially if some supreme confidence were to result from that macabre colloquy.

The night before the execution, he did not sleep at all. At three o'clock in the morning, in spite of the fever that was making him shiver, he was up and, enveloped in his large operating gown, was striding back and forth in his laboratory, preoccupied, and enervated by the wait.

Finally, a sudden ring of the doorbell made him jump.

When the door was precipitately opened, two men clad in black silently deposited a large basket on the tiled floor, then disappeared as they had come, like shadows.

In haste, Georges Chemin lifted the lid of the basket, and could not prevent himself from shivering at the sight of the bloody head. What! Was it not a simple item of anatomy?

He had to react; and besides, there was not a moment to lose. Everything was ready for the experiment. On the enameled stone table a bizarre apparatus was waiting; at the foot of the table, a poor little dog was sleeping peacefully, an unconscious victim for which death was lying in wait. The operator seized it, tied it up rapidly and plunged his scalpel into its neck, laying bare the arteries. It was a prestigious operation; no practitioner had ever employed greater dexterity and manual skill. Less than a minute had elapsed before the arteries of the unfortunate animal were pumping their blood through slender rubber tubes into the vessels laid bare by the severance of the head of the executed man.

The doctor had recovered his self-composure in the face of professional necessity, and, pressing a rubber bulb gently, extracted the blood of the one in order to replace it in the half-empty arteries of the other.

It was the solemn moment. The doctor, his eyes fixed on that pale face, followed the progress of his experiment. Gradually, a roseate tint brightened the cheeks. A fugitive gleam sprang from the pupils. Yes, perhaps it was the effect of the tension that had tautened his entire being, but the operator thought he saw those atonal pupils become animate, and launch once again that same hate-filled gaze that had blazed in the assize court.

A cold sweat ran down his temples; his breath caught in his throat, while before him, that face convulsed with a quiver of the eyelids, a rictus of the lips.

Breathless and distraught, Georges Chemin leaned toward the man whom he called is victim.

"Speak! Speak!" he cried. "Answer me? Can you understand me?"

It seemed to him that the eyelids lowered.

"I beg you, answer. Were you guilty?"

Was it an illusion? The head oscillated in the pieces of linen sustaining it. One might have thought that it was making a sign of negation, while all its muscles contracted in a frightful grimace.

"Oh, wretch that I am!" moaned the scientist. "He was innocent, and I'm the one who had him condemned!"

And he could not tear his eyes away from those bloodshot eyes, those lips grimacing an insult.

"Alas, alas! He's alive again, and if I detach that tube, it's over; I'll be snatching away forever the shadow of life that I've returned to him. What am I saying? The dog's exhausted. There it is, palpitating and quivering; its blood is no longer flowing. The spark, scarcely reanimated, is about to be extinguished. Féraut! Féraut! He can no longer hear me; hi eyelids are fluttering and closing. He'll die this time, and it's me who has killed him again. Murderer! Murderer! I'm nothing but a murderer! But I want him to live... I'll prolong his existence. It shall not be said, while I live, that I will have let him die!"

Crazed, his eyes haggard, Georges Chemin rolls up his sleeve; on the arm he has laid bare, feverishly, he digs into the flesh, exposing the artery, and sticks the tube of the apparatus to it. And it is his blood, his own blood, that he injects into the stupid head of the murderer.

But as, his two hands being occupied in that task, he can no longer maintain it, that macabre head moves and seems to palpitate in ultimate convulsions. The eyes reopen; the mouth sniggers, mocking the madman who claims to be able to revive a head, a miserable head with no torso, arms, legs, entrails or heart!

The following day, the rumor ran around the town that the savant doctor Georges Chemin had committed suicide. He had been found lying on the floor, his arteries open, next to the operating table where the severed head lay.

Féraut was no longer sniggering.

Georges Bethuys: *Cataclysm*

(Georges-Frédéric Espitallier)
(1896)

That year, the elements seemed completely out of sorts. It's true that people say that every year, which appears to indicate that being out of sorts is the elements' natural state. Which was good luck for Max Eginhard, who, having nothing else to do, thanks to his considerable fortune, had devoted himself to meteorology. When the weather is fine, meteorology is a sinecure, while one throws oneself into it wholeheartedly when atmospheric disturbances are abundant.

The origins of Max Eginhard's considerable fortune were not lost in the night of time, and his intimate friends still remembered the epoch when his maternal grandfather had sold cloth for other reasons than to oblige his friends.

The said grandfather possessed an uncultivated plot of land on the heights of Chaillot; the idea had occurred to him to increase the size of that embryonic property. Who could tell? Wasn't there going to be building in the neighborhood?

"Great cities grow westwards."

He therefore bought land that cost him very little, but remained on his hands, with the result that when he married off his daughter, he gave it to her, in order to get rid of it once and for all.

The son-in-law, who was devoid of flair, found at first that this unproductive terrain was more cumbersome than a bad of loose change, but when the operations commenced that were to culminate in the transformation of the Monceau and Marbeuf districts, he finally perceived his father-in-law's clear-sightedness; the fallow land was an investment for the father of a family. One morning, he woke up as rich as the late Croesus. With the fortune, he became bold, but without acquiring the flair that was definitely not part of his patrimony; he bought vast steppes east of Paris, not doubting that the great city, in letting out its belt, would rapidly transform them into residential housing.

Alas, he forgot that "great cities grow westwards." He died before having seen anything built on his land but a few ragpickers' shacks—tenants not accustomed to paying high rents. Nevertheless, thanks to the immovable properties he owned to the west, his heritage left no cause for complaint.

His heir had been brought up in the comfortable idleness befitting his fortune and had as little flair as his father, with the result that one day, having finished with the partying in which he had indulged more out of snobbery than temperament, he woke up one day to find himself a trifle empty. It was then that he discovered a vocation for meteorology.

It began with rather vague indications. Looking at the sky as he got up in the morning, he said: "Look, it's going to be a fine day," or: "The sky's cloudy; it's going to rain." These observations, judicious as they were, did not exceed, as you can see, the bounds of banality—but, the desire gripping him to know more about them, he stuck his nose into books, put a weathervane on his house and bought barometers of various kinds in order to check them against one another.

He did not fail to attend meetings the many organizations in which the most modest members could, if they had a mind to do it, contribute their little stone to the edifice of science, in the form of notes, contributions and lectures that did not have the solemn and intimidating manner of communications to the Académie des Sciences. And as he generously subsidized scientific enterprises, he very soon won the consideration that attaches to Maecenases.

He was not entirely satisfied, however, being ambitious for the kind of apostolate that consists of instructing one's contemporaries. Not daring to set his sights as high as a chair in the Collège de France, he affiliated himself to the Mutual Admiration Society, the Panphilotechnique, which offered to let him teach geology courses under its auspices.

That was not really his subject, but, all things considered, geology and meteorology are not without points in common; they even provide one another with mutual support. He only had to read up on the former science before teaching it. That is what he did.

Utterly ignorant of everything that it comprised, he possessed the unappreciable advantage, he said, of starting without preconceptions. Received ideas and acquired theories did not exist for him; he would be able to give the science a new impetus, by virtue of his new and profound observations.

His inaugural lesson was a colossal success. Addressing himself to Parisians, he thought that he ought to chose a "very Parisian" subject: the constitution of the Paris basin. The orator renewed that already-old theme by the unexpectedness of his exposition, and gave it the piquant zest of a contemporary manner of speech.

"Messieurs," he said, in substance, "the Paris basin merits that name because it affects the form of one of those household utensils known as bowls. And if, not content to examine the inside of the bowl, we seek to take account of its underside, we observe that the Parisian ground is not just one bowl but a stack of bowls, of increasing dimensions the deeper one goes, because the containing vase has to be larger than the vase contained."

This reason seemed to convince the audience; one young lady, especially, sitting in the front row, did not hide her admiration for the eloquent professor, who continued:

"And that holds good to the enormous thickness—yes, truly enormous—of six hundred meters, where the stack rests on a bed of sand—Gault sand—disposed there for the express purpose of collecting the water filtered by that vast basin, while underneath, a clay mold, forming an impermeable bed, like any respectable clay, retains that water, under pressure, that the artesian wells bring back, in part, to the light of day.

"If, departing from the center of this improbable pile of vessels—I mean Paris—we now follow a radius outwards, it's natural, is it not, that we successively encounter the different layers, each one terminated by a border from which one falls on to the following plate. That change of terrain is clearly marked, especially as one walks eastwards, because, in distant epochs, waters have eroded all the soft or sandy parts partly masking the more ancient formations, as they still cover them in the plains of Beauce and Normandy—with the result that, in advancing toward the Vosges, one encounters a series of crests one after another, some of which form veritable cliffs; and these crests seem to have been placed there so expressly to serve as barriers against floods of invaders that the towns and villages that mark them out almost all bear the names of battles.

"First there is the superb arc of a circle passing through Montereau, Nogent, Sézanne, Epernay and Laon, which limits the tertiary bowl—which is to say, the soil of the Île-de-France itself, well-named, for, as Monsieur de Lapparent[51] says: 'the tertiary massif, eaten away along its border, seems like an island, emerging in abrupt cliffs from the bosom of a vast chalky plain. From time to time, a profound fissure interrupts the cliff and a river flows through it as if through a gully. Thus does the Seine at Moret, the Marne at Epernay, the Vesle and the Aisne outside Reims, the Oise at Chauny, the Brèche at Clermont, the Thévain on the outskirts Beauvais, anticipating the moment when, united in a single flow, the waters of all these rivers quit the tertiary mass between Meulan and Mantes by another defile, the latter less visible because of the rapid rise of the limestone in Normandy.'

"Beneath that tertiary bowl, there is the enormous and thick chalky plateau of Champagne, limited by the arc of Troyes, Brienne, Vitry, Saint-Menehould and Valmy. Then the less accentuated crest of the Argonne, departing from which we encounter the greensand of the Barois, before reaching the

---

[51] Albert Lapparent (1839-1908) helped draw up the geological map of France, which Eginhard is interpreting in a slightly flippant fashion, as well as writing numerous books on the subject.

Jurassic strata of the arc that goes from Chatillon-sur-Seine to Chaumont, Toul and Verdun. Is that all? No, for beyond that is the concentric line from Langres to Montmédy and Mexières, which forms yet another line of defense—the first."

Here the orator thought it appropriate to include a little patriotic couplet pronounced with a tremolo befitting morsels redolent with pathos.

"Oh, Messieurs, as I speak, the diplomats are trying to calm the hot heads of dispute raised once again by the hereditary enemy. Is it not to be feared that the great voice of the canon might suddenly interrupt the conference and overturn protocol? This very day we find ourselves under arms, on the frontier, and, in order to defend the territory of our dear fatherland foot by foot, we shall be able to take advantage of obstacles that Nature herself has been able to design on our soil!"

A murmur of enthusiasm ran through the audience, and an old white-haired gentleman got to his feet to utter an energetic: "Vive la France!" while waving his hat.

It was under the emotion of that vibrant peroration that Monsieur Eginhard bowed to his audience and gathered his papers together.

A few moments later, he went out into the street and headed for home. But at the moment when, getting down from the carriage, he was about to go through the door, two people hurried forward. They were, on the one hand, the young lady who had shown so much enthusiasm at the beginning of the lecture, and, on the other, the old patriot who had so vigorously applauded its conclusion.

"Just one word, Monsieur!" cried the lady.

"I need to talk to you!" shouted the gentleman.

Eginhard was perplexed.

"Madame…Monsieur…the street is doubtless not the most propitious place for conversation, and, if you would like to come up to my study..."

"Monsieur," the old patriot insinuated, as they climbed the stairs, "What I have to say to you will brook no delay, and if Mademoiselle will be kind enough to permit..."

"But no, Monsieur, my confidence is certainly as urgent as yours..."

"Madame...Monsieur, please," the professor interjected. "Gallantry dictates my duty, and since you have only one word to say, Madame, be good enough to come in, while Monsieur will wait for a moment in the drawing-room."

Scarcely had the study door closed than the young woman said, excitedly: "Your lecture was sublime. It has inspired me with such enthusiasm that I have come to ask you: will you marry me?"

It must be admitted that, thus taken by surprise, Monsieur Eginhard could not find a reply before the lady had taken up the thread of her discourse. "Oh, I know! That goes against what is conventionally called propriety in your country. Personally, I'm an American—an American of Spanish origin; I have the blood of Pizarro in my veins, and I'm volcanic, as one says in your country. I'm rich; I love science and travel. A scientist like you needs a wife who understands him and who can also liberate him from the anxieties and material cares that waste his energy; I will be that wife..."

Eginhard was quite nonplused by this unexpected passion, so brutally introduced into his life. He was not immune to flattery, however, and, on raising his eyes, perceived that his interlocutrice was pretty. But still! To have to reply immediately, without having had time to reflect...

"Well," said the other, in a conclusive fashion. "That's settled. I'll go and announce it to my family—and now, you can admit the old gentleman."

She was already opening the door. "Oh! I forgot to tell you my name. Carmencita Calcinata y Constancia. Here's my card."

Eginhard darted a glance at it while she made her exit like a gust of wind.

"Why," he said. "She's one of my tenants in the Marboeuf district."

He did not have time to take the course of his reflections any further, however, for the little old man irrupted into the room. He introduced himself: "Victor de Sourdillon, senior clerk in the Ministry of Foreign Affairs, retired. My occupation has given me a nose for European complications, and after one retires, the instincts of the profession subsist. Well, Monsieur, I've come to tell you, because you appear to me to be the enlightened patriot of whom I've dreamed, that we are dancing on a volcano."

"It's certain, Monsieur..." Eginhard interrupted himself, searching for the name."

"De Sourdillon," the other finished, naming himself again.

"It's certain Monsieur de Sourdillon, that the Parisian basin, without exactly being a volcano, is in a state of perpetual agitation—which is a bad omen for the solidity of our monuments. We are sinking, Monsieur, and Fourier—not the Phalansterian but Fourier the mathematician, less well-known to the general public because he was more sensible—has calculated how many millions of years..."

"Oh, never mind such distant catastrophes. War is at our gates! Have you read yesterday's newspapers? The latest uprising in Armenia has lit the fuse. Germany is taking advantage of it to contest our most sacred rights, and England is ready once again to eat the chestnuts that we have pulled out of the fire. The political barometer is exceedingly low."

"The barometer! That reminds me that I omitted to look at mine today."

While he went over to the instruments, Monsieur de Sourdillon continued: "Well, Monsieur, that situation cannot last. I thought that, in a democratic State, it was the responsibility of every citizen to help, within the measure of his means, to solve the great problems seething on the green carpet of democracy."

"The barometer's going down," said the other, who was doubtless listening distractedly."

"With a few friends, I've founded the Foreign Club,[52] in which we examine questions of foreign politics, with the objective of giving the minister the benefit of our enlightenment: that's first-rate private initiative, and very valuable, for, not having the prejudices of career diplomats, for the most part, we're able to bring new and often unexpected solutions to weighty questions. That is the eminently useful work in which I'm inviting you to collaborate. A man of your competence has a place marked out for him among us..."

Eginhard was following his own train of thought. "The barometer's truly afflicted with St. Vitus' Dance. Look at that crazy curve! What perturbations! I wouldn't be astonished if there were serious changes in the sunspots."

"You ask me: why have you given a foreign name to an association so truly French? To which I reply that, 'club' being an English word, it's entirely natural to attach an epithet of the same provenance to it. Then again, do we, the French, have a short and clear word to express the same idea? Evidently not, and in consequence..."

"The seismographs are also indicating abnormal vibrations of our terrestrial crust..."

"Ah, the seismographs! Oh well—but isn't it strange that the repercussions make themselves felt in the chronic agitation of our colliding nations?"

"That's an eminently philosophical point of view, which does you credit, Monsieur."

"We understand one another marvelously, and I shall hasten to inform my committee that you're accepting the presidency of the Foreign Club."

"But Monsieur..."

"Don't protest; it's settled—and as it's necessary not to restrict ourselves to vain words, I shall publish a pamphlet tomorrow concerning the defense of our frontier, basing my argument on your admirable theories regarding the forms of the terrain. Oh, the tertiary cliff—what a role, what a great

---

[52] "Foreign Club" is rendered in English in the original.

role I shall reserve for it, in accordance with the enormous role it has played in history!"

At that moment, through the open window, they heard the cry of a news-vendor, running and shouting at the top of his voice: "Get *La Patrie*! Latest news! Germans at the frontier! Grave complications in the East! Mass conscription! Get *La Patrie*!"

"Eh? What is he shouting?" said Monsieur de Sourdillon, choked by emotion. "You'll soon see whether my fears were chimerical! I'll go call a meeting of the Club immediately. You'll come—tomorrow, eight o'clock in the morning. Don't miss it!"

He seized his hat and gloves and hurtled away, leaving Monsieur Eginhard bewildered, his head leaning out of the window, while other hawkers were running from all directions, barking their disturbing news—and the passers-by, suddenly gathering, were snatching the papers from their hands.

What a lot of events in so few minutes in the life of the pseudo-intellectual! An engagement on the hoof; affiliation to a Club of amateur diplomats; and war, the threat of war, about to trouble the quietude of his placid egotism!

He tried to go back to work and, sitting down at his desk, took up the notes he had prepared for his second lecture. He read aloud, striving to acquire an oratorical tone.

"Nature loves variety; she has taken care to compose the bowls stacked in our Parisian basin of different materials; and, the better to limit that ancient cradle of our fatherland, she has caused to surge from her loins three enormous supports, made of granite and eruptive rocks: three solid boundaries emerging from the primitive crust, constituting a sort of gigantic basket, into which are fitted the sedimentary layers, whose edges are lifted by the irresistible upward surge.

"Everything rests on the solidity of those supports. If the whim took them, under and energetic interior pressure, to draw closer together, the stack of dishes would be shattered, and towns and villages would fall pell-mell into the cracks, along with their inhabitants.

"Fortunately, such a catastrophe is improbable; I will say more..."

Eginhard interrupted himself to look at his seismograph, which was definitely going crazy.

"Either I'm much mistaken," he said, "or we're going to have an earthquake..."

And, as the barometer no longer appeared to him to be on its best behavior, he added: "…and a cyclone," while the newsvendors were shouting outside, advertising the political storm.

A gust of wind seemed to confirm his prognostications. He got up to close the window, just as his *valet de chambre* came in and presented him with a letter on a tray. It was written on scented paper, in an elongated green-tinted envelope sealed with aventurine.

Eginhard opened it and read these lines, written in a delicate hand, and unsteady orthography:

Mi amigo,

I will not abandon you to the perils of an invasion, siege, famine and bombardment. I shall elope with you, and we will depart for the Argentine Republic, where my flocks graze, tomorrow morning, by the eight o'clock train.

Carmencita.

An elopement and a meeting of the Foreign Club at the same time was too much, and in the absence of the gift of ubiquity...

Desperate to resolve this difficulty appropriately, Eginhard went to bed with a headache.

On getting into bed it seemed to him that the ground gave way beneath him, which he attributed to the nervous state he was in—but he could not mistake for an illusion the whistling of the wind, which was raging, furiously shaking the shutters.

Nevertheless, he got to sleep in the end.

How long was he asleep? He would have been incapable of answering that question when, feeling himself abruptly shaken, prodded and poked, he woke up in the midst of a frightful racket.

Opening his eyes with difficulty, in the dark, it seemed at first to be impossible to take account of what was happening around him.

He was lying on the carpet, his limbs bruised and aching, in the midst of a chaotic mess of colliding furniture and the noise of breaking glass and porcelain.

From the lower floors of the house—doubtless from the entrails of the earth—rose strange rumblings and dull cracking sounds, to which other cracking sounds, more sinister still, replied in the walls, shaking on their foundations...

And the floor was oscillating like the deck of a ship...

The sudden horror of that anguished awakening squeezed the unfortunate professor's throat and paralyzed his screams.

He groped around him, crawling through the debris until he finally bumped into the door.

He stood up, tried to open it, and succeeded in spite of the resistance of the frame, put out of square by the shocks.

Throughout the house, from top to bottom, there were already lugubrious interjections, overlapping calls for help, slamming doors and cries of fright. Then, by the light of candles lit by feel, white shadows moved—people in nightshirts running in panic.

People called for help, and people helped themselves, but, not dead but wounded, they all found themselves standing up and more-or-less intact. The walls had not collapsed, and they thought themselves fortunate to have got away with the fear and the material damage that the nascent daylight permitted them to estimate.

Two further shocks made themselves felt, but the people were battle-hardened, and they were over quickly. Nevertheless, the tenants, fearing that the house might collapse on their heads, felt an urgent need to get out.

Eginhard had gone back into his room and, searching for his scattered clothes, dressed in haste, but he did not want to leave without having consulted his cherished instruments, in order to demand the secret of the abrupt cataclysm. The recording devices were lying around all over the place. He gathered them together. As was only to be expected, the seismographs displayed an enormous smear where the pen had marked crazy oscillations.

As he sought to replace on the table the objects that had been thrown on the floor, the meteorologist noticed his compass, and was suddenly struck by a strange and inexplicable fact. The needle had deviated by an entire quadrant!

There was no doubt about it; he was perfectly familiar with the orientation of the walls of the house, whose windows opened due east and west; the compass was now pointing at one of them. Was it necessary to suppose that the building had suddenly been rotated by ninety degrees? Or had terrestrial magnetism suddenly undergone in implausible metamorphosis?

Eginhard remembered in a timely fashion that in many circumstances, earthquakes have provoked rotatory movements. It seemed that the house really had fallen victim to an effect of that sort. It was a miracle that it had resisted such an effort, which inertia usually transforms into a torsion dislocating the entire edifice.

It was urgently necessary to get out of the tottering building. Instinctively, the professor put his compass in his pocket and went down to the street as quickly as possible. He was not unsurprised to observe that the walls, in spite of a few cracks that rendered the anticipated torsion manifest, had nevertheless remained almost vertical on their foundations; it was, therefore, the foundations themselves that had rotated—and as the house had conserved its position relative to the other houses in the street, the whole street must have been subject to the same movement. Eginhard verified that by taking out his compass and orientating it. His bewilderment knew no bounds, however, when he observed that the angle of deviation was even greater than it had been a short while before. The movement was continuing! Paris was slowly rotating!

A thought suddenly occurred to the scientist...the thought of a landlord. His properties that had been east of Paris the day before were moving northwards. Oh, if the movement could only continue, what value they would acquire!

"Great cities grow westwards!"

He did not have time to take the reflections that were already consoling him for the public misfortune any further. In the street, where people were running around lamenting their fate, coming from opposite directions, Carmencita and Monsieur de Sourdillon appeared, hurtling toward Eginhard.

"Querido!" cried one.

"Dear Master!" exclaimed the other.

And the latter murmured, bad-temperedly, on perceiving the Argentinian: "Oh—that madwoman again!"

"Come quickly," Carmencita continued, breathlessly. "Let's run to the station. I won't stay a moment longer in this Babylon, crushed by divine wrath."

"Our friends are already assembled at the Club," said the other. "I've come to collect you."

"Ah!" Eginhard replied. "In the great peril that threatens France, while the enemy hordes are already at our gates, my place is at the frontier. I'm hastening there! I'm must fly!"

He did, indeed, fly,[53] dragged away by the robust and volcanic foreigner. But Sourdillon would not surrender his prey, and lengthened the stride of his short legs to catch up with the couple.

"You're right—to the frontier! I'll bring the entire Club to the frontier with us!"

Eginhard would dearly have like to climb into a fiacre and obtain a little relief from so much emotion, but the earthquake had cracked all the causeways and overturned the

---

[53] A common, untranslatable pun: *voler* means both to fly and to steal, so Eginhard is not literally flying here, but only being stolen by the passionate Carmencita.

wooden sidewalks, and no carriage was risking traveling in all that chaos. It was therefore necessary to make his decision and go on foot—but they could not agree to a direction. Sourdillon wanted to go to the Gare de l'Est and Carmencita the Gare de l'Ouest.

It was Eginhard, again, who cut to the heart of the question by saying: "What good will that do, since Paris has rotated? The eastbound railway will no longer take us to Le Havre, and the westbound one will surely take us to Bordeaux. All roads lead to Rome...but I'm still not absolutely convinced of that, for if we're on a rotating platform, there must be, at the edge of that inopportune circle, a disjunction of roads, railways, and even rivers—with the result that it would require a hazard that I would qualify as providential if the rotation should stop at the exact moment when the line to Chalon happened to be passing that to Amiens, or for the waters of the Oise to flow into the bed of the Seine. I would be curious, all the same, to know whether the rupture has taken place at the rim of the tertiary bowl, as it would be logical to suppose..."

"In that case," said Carmencita, "in order to satisfy the old gentleman, let's go to the Gare de Lyon; that will be the best way of going northwards; we'll finish up reaching the sea and a steamer that will take us to my homeland. I don't say that there are no earthquakes there, but one never sees cities spinning like tops."

The old gentleman was only semi-satisfied to be thus designated, but he contented himself with this transactional proposition. "Very well," he said. "I'll go fetch the Club members."

Gallantly, Eginhard offered his arm to the Argentinian woman, who set off, swaying on her hips like a launch agitated by the swell and watching her slender feet, only wanting to set them down judiciously in the midst of the confused rubble that had once been the flat surface of a pavement.

At that moment, some bill-posters passed by at a run, their ladders on their shoulders, leaving behind them, displayed on the walls, placards in which the municipal council reassured the public against any panic.

This was their approximate tenor:

Citizens

At the very moment when the enemy is invading our frontiers, and English fleets are menacing our African possessions, and even our Mediterranean coast, a frightful cataclysm has just struck your city.

The authorities owe you the truth; they will hide nothing from you. The terrain that once constituted the Île-de-France, under subterranean forces that it is not possible for us at present to check, and for which the Prefecture of Police will take sole responsibility, has become unstuck and is rotating on its axis. What was north is now south. That, without doubt, will be no bad thing, for, after all, it is only just that everyone should enjoy in turn the advantages and inconvenience of location and orientation. Where the question becomes complicated, however, is the manner in which the edge of this islet accords with the neighboring regions that have remained in place, immobile.

It was inevitable that his readjustment would take place as best it could, and that it would be much like what happens when a clumsy domestic sticks the limbs of a carelessly broken statue back together. The fracture will have dragged Melun away, leaving Fontainebleau immobile in its sands and its forest, breaking the Seine between the two towns; the Marne has been severed between Château-Thierry and Epernay, the Aisne near Craonne, the Oise below the Fère and the rest in accordance.

The railway lines stop, broken at that improbable cut-off point, along with the telegraph lines. Employees are reconnecting the wires in all directions as quickly as possible and at random, but the Paris offices are confounded by the Chinese puzzle posed by the inevitable entanglement resulting from such a reconnection; the distribution tables are now a mosaic devoid of significance.

In sum, Paris is without communications. We resemble shipwreck-victims on a vessel derived of a rudder, and, to complete the analogy, we shall probably run out of water. During the rotation, in fact, our aqueducts have broken, and if they still carry a liquid having all the appearances of water, it is because they have collected it from the lakes in which rivers abruptly cut off from their mouths are accumulating. How can such water be assessed? It is no longer that beverage, as pure as it was hygienic, that we have disputed for so long with the river-dwellers of the Avre and the Loing! Today, they are keeping their water, and we Parisians, after so many sacrifices agreed by your Municipal Councils—drawn on the public purse, of course—we are reduced to drinking an unnamable liquid. The Board of Hygiene, urgently consulted, has unanimously decided that it would be better not to drink it, thus absorbing unknown microbes to which we have not had the leisure to become accustomed in the manner of Mithridates, as happens every summer for the waters of the Seine, surreptitiously introduced into our conduits.

Such is the situation, dear fellow citizens.

But that is not all.

We have received, just now, an alarming phonogram from the observatory, and are delivering it to your appreciation: 'The latitude of Paris is gradually but sensibly increasing.'

"That's horrible! It's terrible!" Eginhard exclaimed, having read it aloud. "And unless the Earth has chosen a new axis of rotation, which science refuses to admit, I don't see what it implies."

He had not finished expressing this remark when more bill-posters stuck up a new poster beside the first. This one was signed by a well-known promoter of the Paris Seaport[54] and was thus conceived:

---

[54] The person the author has in mind is almost certainly J. Émile Labadie, who published *Étude sur Paris-port-de-mer* in

VICTORY

That which the authorities have refused to our legitimate claims, nature has given us gratis: PARIS SEAPORT is a reality, without it costing our shareholders a single sou! All that it required was a simple cataclysm.

While Paris was being shaken by the worrying earthquake that terrified us all last night, the Massif Central of France was subjected to an even more frightful convulsion and was raised up by several hundred meters. The news reached us by means of the optical telegraph that has just been established, in a matter of hours, between the two lips of the fracture that appeared so strangely at the edge of the tertiary basin of Paris.

Lifted up with the central plateau, however, were the sedimentary layers that were spread out at its feet, which now form an immense inclined plane, extending all the way to La Manche. Over the soft clays and marls interposed between these various layers, Paris is gently sliding, along with its suburbs, and in a few hours it will be on the shore of the sea, doubtless destroying the mortal enemies of the great project of PARIS SEAPORT, Rouen and Le Havre, unless those conceited cities have already sunk beneath the waves in the same seesaw motion that elevated the Auvergnat plateau!

Only one thing remains for us to desire: that our vessel will stop in time and not, by virtue of its acquired velocity, fall into the sea—for it is much heavier than water and would

---

1886 and engaged in a long battle with the government regarding the practicality of his plan to render the Seine navigable by oceangoing merchant ships all the way to Paris. He was not alone, however; Prosper Germain's *Paris-port-de-mer* (1912) listed 24 such proposals made since the 18th century. Nor has the idea ever died, a similar proposal was submitted to the President of the Republic as recently as 2009 by Antoine Grumbach.

doubtless sink, in spite of the motto of the city of Paris: fluctuat nec mergitur.[55]

It is Melun that is serving as our prow—Melun, which a fortunate evolution of the basin has carried northwards. The PARIS SEAPORT Company invites all its supporters to go to Melun, in order to be the first to salute the sea. A special train has been organized for ten o'clock in the morning at the Gare de Lyon.

HURRAH!

"Quickly, to the Gare de Lyon!" cried Eginhard, gripped by enthusiasm.

He spotted some porters who had thought of improvising *filanzanes*, in order to transport their fellow citizens like simple Hovas,[56] on the backs of men, through the obstacles of the disrupted streets. Soon, he and his companion were on their way to the Gare de Lyon at the steady trot of these businessmen of a new breed.

One might have thought, in fact, that all Paris had arranged to meet there; the station platforms were crowded with people who were taking the army trains, and Eginhard fell into the arms of Monsieur de Soudillon, who was surrounded by the kindly members of the Foreign Club. They were all shouting as loudly as they could, while waving little tricolor flags: "To the front! To the front!"

An ovation was given to the already-celebrated professor of geology, who nevertheless demurred when asked to make a speech.

---

[55] "Battered by the waves, but unsinking." The city's emblem is a ship, presumably reflecting the fact that the shape of its original site, the Île de la Cité, is somewhat reminiscent of a ship floating on the Seine.

[56] Hovas are natives of Madagascar, where *filanzanes*—light chairs suspended by ropes between two long poles supported on the shoulders of four bearers—were once used as a standard means of transport.

“This is not the time for words, my friends,” he said, “but for actions. At the frontier, we shall find the words that set hearts on fire!”

A formidable pressure transported his entire audience on to the first train to depart; the locomotive whistled, and the train was soon rolling northwards at top speed.

Eginhard was sitting between Carmencita and Sourdillon, who were both intent on serving as deacons to the high priest of science, and both talking at the same time about different things. Pulled in opposite directions by these demanding acolytes, the professor did not know which one to listen to, and clasped his head, which seemed to be about to explode, with feverish hands.

Dominating the tumult of the carriage, Sourdillon was sketching a plan of diplomatic diversion, in which the members of the Foreign Club would be sent forth as sharpshooters to negotiate with the enemy. In the meantime the leader of the band would go to appeal for help to the Pope and the Negus, hoping that the slowness of protocol would permit them to bring the Church’s cannons and the Libya lions to bear before the end of hostilities.

While these words were hammering Eginhard’s right ear, however, the latter was lending his left ear to less transcendent suggestions.

“In my homeland,” murmured the Argentinian woman, we sing this:

Olé!
The storm bursts in the bosom of the earth,
The hurricane roars in my heart,
The volcano vomits lava, and my heart breaks, vomiting its blood!
Who betrays us dies; and we die afterwards!”

Damn it! thought the scientist. *That’s enough to dispel any thought of treason.*

"Our mothers carry daggers in their stockings, and we hide revolvers in our belts, *mio caro*, to reckon with the unfaithful. Oh, let's flee, let's flee to the pampas of my native land!"

The conversation on this theme seemed rather embarrassing for Eginhard, who was doubtless unfamiliar with the practice of replacing the mandolin with a revolver.

Fortunately, they were approaching the terminus; the locomotive slowed down, its brakes screeching, and soon stopped, steaming, beside the platform of Melun station.

"All change!" cried the employees—which was perfectly natural, since the broken track stopped there, to the despair of the troops who were occupying the station, the town and its surroundings. Their mobilization orders had specified that they ought to embark at six o'clock in the morning for Belfort. It was midday; the line no longer existed, and instead of going south-east, the ground itself was taking them northwards. A colonel tackled the stationmaster, complaining that the Network Commission ought to have been able to anticipate the eventuality.

"And in the meantime, the enemy is free to establish themselves on our territory, take out fortifications and advance on Paris. What's going to happen, when they arrive on the Epernay-Craonne-La Fère line, and no longer recognize the valleys through which all invasions take place? They're going to say that our maps are worse than ever! And not to be there to land a blow!"

The promoter of Paris Seaport provided a fortunate diversion by intervening. "Oh, Messieurs, be glad that you're not on the eastern front; isn't it at least as honorable to maintain a garrison in an entrenched camp that's on the move? Spare a thought for the perplexity of the enemy, whose objective has slipped away and vanished! Their cleverly-ripened plan has gone down the river; their preparations were in vain; everything has to be started again, and, confronted by the strangeness of the phenomenon, their strategic science remains indecisive: a momentary hesitation! But that's salvation! Our armies, of which you are only on part, gentlemen, will easily form up in a province on the flank of their line of operations and…but what's that? A pigeon coming down!"

They ran to the bird, under the wing of which appeared a light tube contain dispatches, and while they looked everywhere for an authority to whom the grave responsibility of reading them could be left, everyone began to discuss the thorny question raised by the arrival of the carrier-pigeon.

Certainly, the bird possessed an admirable instinct, and, crossing mountains and oceans, was able to return to its dovecot, without anyone having sufficiently explained, in my opinion, by what mysterious cerebral mechanism it bring that incomprehensible sense of direction into play—but how could it recognize it if, as in the present case, the entire country containing its shelter had started to displace itself on the round ball? Even the cleverest had to admit that they did not know; it was a miracle that the pigeon, evidently bound for Paris, had landed on the Île-de-France in distress.

At the same time, someone wondered exactly where that crazily-drifting ship was. A former naval officer proposed to take a bearing, as if on board. It was necessary to run around all the optician's shops in the town to find a sextant and the mercury to form and artificial horizon to substitute for the marine horizon.

Finally equipped, the former frigate captain stood with his legs apart, as if to resist the swaying of a deck, consulted his chronometer, raised the sextant toward the sun, and...

A frightful clamor stopped him in mid-gesture.

"The sea! The sea!" cried a thousand voices.

Binoculars were immediately aimed. A few kilometers away, a cloud of dust rose up, denouncing the rapid progress of that singular sled, and when the wind dispersed the cloud, the waves were shining in the distance.

At a vertiginous speed, they advanced toward the roaring gulf. Everything was going to fall into it. Only one hope remained, which was that the moving stratum was thicker than the water was deep.

To begin with, on reaching the cliffs that had one sheltered so many charming seaside resorts, which had already disappeared beneath the waters, the enormous calcareous mass cracked as it fell.

There was an immense scream of terror, while a frightful shock knocked people down on top of one another, and buildings collapsed with an indescribable din.

Then, equilibrium was gradually restored, and, the surface of the land not sinking any lower than the level of the water, the gigantic islet continued to slide over the bed of La Manche.

Extreme situations temper the character of individuals. All the emotions that the passengers on that singular raft had experienced in a few hours had hardened them, and, from the moment that they had withstood the initial impact, it seemed that they no longer had any reason to be afraid.

However, as they got nearer to the deepest water, the water-level reached the surface of the ground, invading the lower areas first and forcing the inhabitants—I mean the passengers—to take refuge on higher ground. Soon, though, they had passed the thalweg and as they climbed up the opposite slope, the land gradually emerged again.

Hope was reborn, and Sourdillon tried to profit from it to harangue the club members, while the prefect, to whom the carrier-pigeon had been taken, appeared waving a piece of paper over his head. It was the dispatch.

"Rejoice, Messieurs. Our eastern frontier is no longer under threat. The elevation of our central plateau had as its counterpart the collapse of the Rhineland, which is under water. It's a barrier sufficient against any invasion, for the moment. We no longer have anything to do but march upon the conquest of England."

At the same moment, a new impact shook the ground; the raft had run aground on the English shore, crushing Portsmouth, Brighton and Newhaven and stopping when it ran into the South Downs.

England was no longer a island!

Sourdillon wanted to run ahead, in order to be the first to set foot on British soil, as the Norman conqueror had once done. He took Eginhard by the arm to drag him away, but the latter took out his watch.

"What time," he asked, "is the train to Liverpool, and what day is the liner to America?"

It was Carmencita who replied, and with what an incendiary gaze! "We'll be able to say," she added, "that to go and get married, we haven't taken a banal vehicle."

"Oh, we'll come back," he assured her, "for I haven't forgotten that I own land in Paris that is now west of the city, and 'great cities grow westwards'—it'll be worth a fortune before long. But I don't want to occupy myself any longer with geology, or meteorology—they're too complicated."

C. Paulon: *A Message from the Planet Mars*

(Paul Combes)
(1897)

One evening last summer, I was reading the latest news in *Le Temps* when my eyes were attracted by the following paragraph:

STRANGE LIGHT ON THE PLANET MARS

On Monday evening, Dr. Krueger, the director of the Central Astronomical Bureau of Kiel, telegraphed to all his correspondents: Luminous projection in the southern region of the Martian terminator observed by Javelle, 16.00—Perrotin.

The "terminator" is the penumbral zone separating day and night.[57]

This news was doubly interesting for me. For a long time, the study of astronomy had transported me imaginatively into the marvelous universe that gravitates outside our little

---

[57] Adalbert Krüger did indeed send such a telegram (on 30 July 1894), but it is unclear why *Le Temps* would have obtained the news that way rather than from Henri Perrotin's own press release. Perrotin, the first director of Nice observatory, spent a good deal of time from 1892 onwards searching for bright spots on the surface of Mars, and was by no means shy of seeking publicity for his "discoveries"—or those of his assistant, Stéphane Javelle. Krüger's telegram is, however, cited in John Munro's "A Message from Mars," published in *Cassell's Magazine* in 1895 (which became the first chapter of *A Trip to Venus*, 1897); Paulon—who was obviously able to read English—might have borrowed it from there rather than from a more immediate source.

globe. In the second place, a few years previously, I had attempted, with an old astronomer, an unforgettable experiment in interastral communication.

That extraordinary man, who lived as a recluse in his observatory, had—or believed that he had—opened a correspondence with the inhabitants of the planet Mars, but means of powerful beams of electric light, intermittently interrupted like the signals of the optical telegraph. I had often considered him to be a monomaniac, but who knows? Perhaps he was not so crazy after all.

In spite of myself, I opened my books, searching among the earlier observations for some natural explanation of the strange light.

Finding nothing, I resolved to go out to consult my friend, Professor Gazen, the well-known astronomer, who is particularly renowned for a sequence of splendid spectroscopic research regarding the composition of the sun and other celestial bodies.

The night was perfectly clear; not a single cloud veiled the dark blue immensity. The stars were resplendent in the depths of the sky, like diamonds fallen from the silvery belt of the Milky Way. The constellation of Orion was shining with a remarkable brightness in the eastern sky, and Sirius was sparkling in the south like a living gem.

I searched with my eyes for the planet Mars, and soon picked it out, to the north, like a big red star surrounded by white constellations.

I found Professor Gazen at his observatory, plunged in calculations.

"I'm doubtless disturbing you," I said to him, as we shook hands. "Such a beautiful night must be favorable to your astronomical work."

"You're not disturbing me at all," he replied, cordially. "I'm observing a nebula, but it will remain above the horizon for a long time yet."

"Good! What's this mysterious light on the planet Mars? Have you seen it?"

"I've seen nothing!" he said. "And yet, I observed the planet for a long time last night."

"But...do you believe that some sort of light has really been seen?"

"Oh, certainly. Nice Observatory, of which Monsieur Perrotin is the director, has one off the best telescopes in existence, and Monsieur Javelle is well-known for the care he brings to his observations."

"And how do you explain it?"

"The light is not on the disk of the planet itself," Gazen replied, "so I was inclined at first to attribute it to a small comet. Perhaps, also, it might be due to a Martian aurora borealis, as a contributor to *La Science Illustrée* has suggested, or a range of snowy mountains, or even a brilliant cloud, reflecting the rays of the rising sun."

"And which of these various hypotheses appears to you to be the most plausible?"

"The one that attributes the light to elevated mountain peaks reflecting solar rays."

"Could it not be the nocturnal lighting of a city, or a powerful luminous projection—in a word, a signal?"

"Oh no, my dear chap!" the astronomer exclaimed, with an incredulous smile. "The idea of communication germinated in a few minds a couple of years ago, when Mars was in opposition and close to the Earth. Perhaps you recall the plan that was made to dispose the lighting of Paris in such a way as to attract the attention of the Martians?"

"No…but I think I've mentioned to you the singular experiment that I made some five or six years ago, with an old astronomer who thought he had established optical communication with Mars."

"Yes, indeed, I remember. The poor old fellow was mad. Like the astronomer in *Rasselas*, he had nourished his visionary idea in solitude for so long that he had ended up mistaking for a reality."

"But might there not have been an element of truth in his imagination? Perhaps the 'visionary' was only ahead of his time?"

Gazen shook his head. "Mars, you see," he went on, "is a much more ancient planet than ours. In winter, its polar ice extends to the fortieth degree of latitude, and its climate must be very cold. If human beings have ever lived on its surface, they must have disappeared a long time ago, or be living in the same conditions as Eskimos."

"But might not the climate be ameliorated by continental and oceanic conditions unknown to us? Certainly, in spring, one can see Mars's polar ice-cap extending as far as the fortieth degree of latitude. Nevertheless, when summer begins it starts to diminish, band by the first days of autumn only a few fragments remain. In 1894 those even disappeared entirely."

"The Martian atmosphere is as rarefied as that of the mountains of our globe at a height of eight thousand meters, and a warm-blooded organism like a human could not live there."

"Like a human, yes!" I replied. "But humans are adapted to their environment. We're too inclined to relate everything we observe to those we see every day. How can we claim that the potential of life is limited to what is familiar to us on our own planet?"

"Besides," Gazen continued, without taking any notice of my reflection, "Your old astronomer's project, consisting of making signals by means of powerful luminous jets, was completely impracticable. No artificial light exists capable of reaching Mars. Think about the immense distance that separates the two planets, and the two absorbent atmospheres to be traversed. The man was mad!"

"I read the other day that there's an electric searchlight in America that can be perceived a hundred and fifty miles away, through the lowest regions of our atmosphere. Such a light, appropriately directed, could be seen from the planet Mars, and there's no reason to suppose that the Martians haven't invented one even more powerful."

"And if they had," said Gazen, laughing, "the idea that they've had of sending us signals just at the moment that it's possible for us to reply, is simply stupefying."

"I don't see anything extraordinary in the coincidence. Two minds often have the same idea at the same time. Why not those of two different planets, if the propitious moment has arrived? Certainly, there's only one unique Mind that inspires the entire universe. Besides, the Martians might have been sending us signals from time to time for centuries, without our having perceived them. Perhaps, at this very moment, we're losing precious time, while they're striving to attract our attention. Would you care to look?"

"Yes, if it'll give you pleasure. But I doubt that we'll see the slightest luminous projection, human or otherwise."

"At least we'll see the surface of Mars, and that already constitutes an admirable spectacle. It seems to me that the contemplation of celestial bodies through a good telescope ought to be part of a complete liberal education, by the same entitlement as a voyage around the world. And yet, although people who wander around the Earth in search of new locations, with great difficulty and at great expense, are numerous, those who think about the sublime spectacle of the heavens that one can contemplate without leaving home are rare. Gazing at those distant worlds has the power to elevate and purify our souls, like a sacred hymn, a noble painting or the verses of great poets. It always has a good effect."

Silently, Professor Gazen turned his large refractor telescope in the direction of Mars, and observed the planet attentively through the large tube for a few minutes.

"Is there no light?" I asked.

"None," he replied, shaking his head. "See for yourself."

I took his place at the ocular, and could not help shivering on seeing the copper-tinted little star that I had seen half an hour before become seemingly much closer, transformed into a vast globe. It resembled a lunar crescent, for a considerable part of its disk was illuminated by the sun.

A white patch indicated the location of one of its poles, and the rest of the visible surface was divided into alternating red-tinted and green-tinted regions. Fascinated by the spectacle of that living world, full of light and pursuing its perpetual course through the unfathomable ether, I forgot my question, and a religious emotion filled my entire being, as under the dome of a vast cathedral.

"Well? What are you doing?"

That voice recalled me to myself, and I began a minute inspection of the dark fringe of the terminator, trying to discover the slightest ray of light there—but in vain.

"I can't see any luminous projection—but what a magnificent spectacle in the telescope!"

"It certainly is!" the professor agreed. "Although it's not always easy to observe the planet Mars, we know it better than the other planets, and at least as well as the moon. Its topographical features have been drawn with care, like those of the moon, and have been given the names of famous astronomers."

"Including you, I hope."

"No, I don't have that honor. It's true that I know someone, an enthusiastic amateur astronomer, who has baptized a quantity of plains and mountains on the moon with the names of his friends and acquaintances, including mine: the Durand crater, the Dubois gulf, Martin bay and so on—but I regret to say that the scientific authorities have refused to sanction that nomenclature."

"I presume that the bright patch in the southern hemisphere is one of the polar ice-caps," I said, my eyes still fixed on the planet.

"Yes," the professor replied, "and one can see them very distinctly advancing in winter and retreating in summer. The reddish-yellow areas are probably continents with ocher-colored soil, and not, as some have thought, vegetation of the same hue. The greenish-gray areas might be seas and lakes. If so, land and water are more equally distributed on Mars than on Earth—a circumstance that would tend to equalize climates—but another, most ingenious hypothesis has recently been formulated by the American Percival Lowell, who has devoted himself very particularly to the study of Mars, and who has recently published a most remarkable book on the planet."[58]

Keenly interested by this introduction, I quit the ocular momentarily in order to listen to the professor.

"On the third of June 1894, which corresponds to May the first in the Martian calendar, Lowell measured the austral polar cap, which extended to the fifty-fifth degree of latitude or thereabouts and was in the process of melting; hundreds of square kilometers were disappearing every day. Now, wherever the loss of the bright white surface was occurring, a dark band appeared, probably produced by the initial fusion of the polar ice. That band followed the retreat of the polar ice, diminishing in breadth with the dimensions of the cap. By the following August there was no more than a scarcely-perceptible fine line around the portions of the ice cap that still remained. Finally, on the thirteenth of October, when the snow had entirely disappeared, the place that it had finally occupied with its border became unrecognizable, and took on a yellow color.

"This having been established by telescopic observation, what can that dark border be if not water? It has the color of it, it follows the melting of the ice-cap step by step, and it disappears with it. Monsieur Lowell concluded that water, very rare on the surface of Mars, only exists in a liquid state thanks to the melting of the polar ice. The American astronomer linked that hypothesis to an explanation of Schiaparelli's famous channels, of which you have certainly heard mention."

"Oh, certainly—the network of regular lines, some of which reach as far as 4,000 to 4,800 kilometers in length, but whose average length is about 2,400 kilometers."

"Well, Monsieur Lowell is of the opinion that that system of lines, so straight and symmetrical, radiating from par-

---

[58] *Mars* (1895)—the first of Lowell's three books on the planet that became his abiding obsession.

ticular points, the manner in which they put certain points in communication with others toward which other lines converge in their turn, can only result from artificial endeavor. According to him, the lines correspond to the routes of canals dug with the aim of bringing fertility over long distances to areas deprived of humidity."

"Does he have proof?"

"This is what he claims as proof. Two facts are incontestable, since they can be verified telescopically: that the channels are visible in certain seasons, and that in others—always the same ones—they vanish; which is not a consequence of increased distance, because it's when Mars is closest to us that certain channels are not visible, while they become visible when the planet is further away. Nor can one explain the disappearance of the channels by the hypothesis of clouds or fogs that hide them from our view, because, at the same time, the terminal line of the dark regions is as clearly delineated as when the channels are perfectly visible. The channels thus become visible, augmenting or diminishing, for reasons unique to them.

"Although their appearance is temporary, however, their location never varies. Moreover, patient observation shows that, when they are invisible, they become perceptible gradually. One sees them, as it were, increase and decrease in determined seasons. That visible development follows the melting of the polar ice, and it is noticeable that no channel becomes visible until the melting of the ice has made visible progress. Those closest to the polar cap appear first; they become increasingly distinct thereafter, and take on a darker color over time.

"The explanation that presents itself most naturally to the mind is that there must be a flow of water from the pole to the equator; but that is insufficient. In fact, it is necessary to wait a few months for the channels to become visible at the equator; it should not take that much time for the water to arrive there. Besides, in order to be perceptible, it is necessary that the channels be at least a degree in width, which might seem enormous for artificial canals.

"Thus, Monsieur Lowell attributes the observed appearances to the vegetation that develops along the banks of the channels some time after the irrigation of the soil by the water they have brought, which explains the phenomenon of their progressive appearance and the changes they undergo.

"The change in the appearance of the channels consists, not in their seeming broader but in their becoming increasingly dark, and consequentially distinct. If there were high mountains on the Martian surface, they would interfere with the straightness of the channels, but observation informs us that the planet is relatively uniform. The channels are visible in reddish regions as well as well as greenish ones, because they develop or augment the vegetation there with the moisture they bring. They are, therefore, irrigation canals, which, at their meeting-points, give rise to veritable oases.

"From all of the preceding arguments, Monsieur Lowell concludes that, water having become scarce on the planet Mars, the most important problem for the inhabitants must be procuring it. What increases the probability of an intelligent cause for the channels is that double ones can be perceived—which is to say, forming two parallel lines along their entire course; no designer could trace more perfect parallel lines. Their separation varies between four and a half and six degrees, and the vegetation of each, developed along its length, appears to be about a degree in breadth.

"In this hypothesis, the vast red-tinted areas must be vast arid plains or deserts; the systematic patches formerly considered to be lakes must be regions of vegetation, true oases that form, as their changes in color and dimension demonstrate, at points where several canals intersect."

"But in that case," I exclaimed, "the Martians, capable of constructing such a vast irrigation system, have means of action at their disposal that are unknown to us. Their science is more advanced than ours, no doubt about it."

"Don't be too hasty in your conclusions," said Gazen, smiling. "All that is only a hypothesis—very ingenious, I admit, but still, a hypothesis. The natural environment of the Martian surface differs significantly from ours, and the appearances it presents cannot all be explained according to our terrestrial views. Let's make suppositions and try to verify them, but let's not affirm anything."

While he was speaking, mentally overexcited in spite of myself by Lowell's hypothesis, I had resumed my place at the telescope.

Was it an illusion of my imagination? Was it a reality? My attention was suddenly caught by an extremely bright luminous point that appeared on the dark side of the terminator south of the equator.

"Oh!" I cried, involuntarily. "There's the light!"

"Really?" Gazen replied, in a tone that mingled surprise and doubt. "Are you quite sure?"

"Entirely. There's a very distinct light in one of the reddish areas."

"Let me see!" he said, excitedly.

I surrendered my place to him.

"It's true!" he declared, after a moment's observation. "I assume the light has been hidden from until now by a cloud."

Taking turns, we continued silently observing the strange light.

"That can't be the light that Javelle perceived," Gazen said, finally. "It's in the region named Hellas."

"To make signals," I murmured, returning to my obsession, "the Martians would probably have to employ a whole system of lights. Since they have a network of canals, there's no reason why they shouldn't have a telegraphic network, to coordinate their attempts at different points of the planet."

The professor took his place at the ocular again, and I waited for the result of his observations with keen interest.

"Is as stable as possible," he said.

"That stability is cause for reflection," I said. "If it were variable, it would be more readily interpretable as a signal."

"But there's no indication that the signal is necessarily destined for the inhabitants of the Earth," Gazen said, with mocking seriousness. "It might be a floating lighthouse, or a nocturnal message for the autumnal maneuvers of the Martians, who are undoubtedly exceedingly bellicose."

"Seriously what do you think it is?"

"I confess that it's a mystery to me," he replied, becoming profoundly thoughtful. Then, as if struck by a sudden thought, he added: "I'd be astonished if the spectroscope didn't offer us some enlightenment in that regard."

While he was setting up the instrument, I returned to the telescope and observed the enigmatic light once again, which stood out almost in the center of the disk.

Gazen fixed a magnificent spectroscope to the telescope, which he used for his research on nebulas, and recommenced his observations.

"Truly," he exclaimed, getting up from his seat and advancing toward me "that's the most remarkable thing I've ever seen in my long career as a spectroscopist!"

"What is it?" I asked, looking into the spectroscope in my turn, in which I could distinguish a few feeble streaks of colored light standing out against a black background.

"You know that we can take account of the nature of a substance in the incandescent state by decomposing the light it emits in the prism of a spectroscope. Well, those bright and variously colored lines that you perceive constitute the spectrum of a luminous gas."

"Really! And that gives you some indication regarding the origin of the light we've perceived?"

"It might be electric—an aurora, for example. It might be a volcanic eruption, or a lake of fire similar to the Kilauea crater, the famous volcano in the Sandwich Islands. To tell the truth, I have no idea. Let me see if I can identify the bright lines of the spectrum."

I surrendered the spectroscope to him, and when he had looked attentively he exclaimed: "By Heaven! That's extraordinary! The spectrum has changed. Eureka! I recognize it now.

It's the spectrum of thallium. I'd recognize that splendid green line among a thousand."

"Thallium!" I cried, marveling in my turn.

"Yes," Gazen replied, excitedly. "Make a note of the observation, and also the time. You'll find a notebook for that express purpose on my desk."

I did as I was asked, and awaited further observations. The silence was so profound that that I could clearly hear the ticking of my watch, set before me on the desk.

After a few minutes, the professor exclaimed: "It's changed again—make another note."

"What is it now?"

"Sodium. Those two yellow bands can't be confused with any other."

A profound silence reigned, as before.

"Another change!" cried the professor, extremely excited. "I can now see a double blue line. What can that be? I believe it's iridium."

Another long pause followed that indication.

"They've disappeared!" murmured Gazen. "A red line and a yellow line have taken their place. That's lithium. Hold on! Everything's gone black."

"What's happening?"

"Everything has disappeared." As he spoke, he detached the spectroscope from the telescope and observed the planet anxiously.

"The light's no longer there," he added, after a minute or so. "Perhaps another cloud is passing above it. Well, we'll wait. In the meantime, let's examine the situation. It seems that we have some reason to be satisfied with tonight's work. What do you think?" It was with a triumphant expression that he stopped in front of me.

"I believe it's a signal!" I said, with conviction.

"Why?"

"Why else would the changes be so regular? I've measured the duration of each spectrum, and I've found that each one lasts for about five minutes before another takes its place."

The professor remained silent and pensive. I continued: "Isn't it from the light that reaches us from them that we've acquired all our knowledge relative to the constitution of celestial bodies? A ray from the most distant star brings with it a secret message for anyone who can read it" Well, the Martians will naturally have had recourse to the same means of communication, as being the simplest and the most practicable. By producing a powerful light they can hope that our attention will be attracted to their planet, and in making it produce characteristic spectra, easily recognizable and modified at regular intervals, they can distinguish their light from any other, and show us that it has an intelligent origin."

"And in consequence?"

"And in consequence, we know that the Martians have a civilization at least as highly developed as our own. To my mind, that's a great discovery—the greatest since the world has existed."

"But it's of little use, to us as well as the Martians."

"From that point of view, a great many of our discoveries, especially in astronomy, are very little use. Suppose you find the chemical composition of the nebula you were in the process of studying...will it reduce the price of bread? No—but it will interest us and inform us. If the Martians can tell us how Mars is constituted, and we can do the same with regard to the Earth, that will certainly be a mutual service rendered to one another by the two planets."

"But the communication can't go any further."

"I'm not so sure of that."

"My dear friend! How can we, on Earth, understand what the Martians say, and how can they understand what we say? We have no common language."

"That's true—but chemical compounds have certain well-defined properties, don't they?"

"Yes. Each one even possesses some particularity that distinguishes it clearly from all the others. For example, those which resemble one another in color or hardness differ in weight."

"Precisely. Well, can't we employ their spectra to designate precisely those particular qualities—*to express an idea?* In a word, can't the Marians talk to us via spectragrams?"

"I see where you're coming from," said Professor Gazen. "And now that I think about it, all the spectra we've observed this evening belong to the group of alkaline metals and alkaline earths, which have very characteristic properties."

"First of all, I suppose the Martians only wanted to attract our attention with a striking spectrum."

"Lithium is the metal we've discovered most recently."

"Good! We can get from that the idea of enlightenment."

"Sodium," the professor continued, "is a metal that has such an affinity for oxygen that it burns in water. Manganese, which belongs to the same group as iron, is so hard that its scratches glass, and like iron, it's magnetic. Copper is red..."

"Signals relating to colors can be taken directly from spectra."

"Mercury, or quicksilver, is liquid at ordinary temperatures, and can give us the idea of *movement, animation*, or even of *life*."

"Having obtained certain fundamental ideas," I continued, "by combining them, we would arrive at conceptions other than the original ones. We could establish an entire ideographic language by signs—the signs being the luminous spectra of different chemical substances. Numbers can be transmitted by simple occultations of light. Then, spectra can enable us to pass by means of an easy slope to equivalent signals: long and short flashes variously combined, similarly obtained by luminous occultations. With such a code, our communication would become indefinite, and would no longer present any difficulty."

"If the Martians are as advanced as you would like to believe, we'd have a great deal to learn from them."

"I hope that we could, and I'm sure that the world could, at least, obtain superior enlightenment on certain points."

"In any case," said the professor, darting another glance at the telescope, "we'll pursue our observations assiduously."

Then he added: "For the moment, the Martian philosophers don't seem to want to take their experiments any further. And as the nebula is still there, I'll work on it for a while before finishing for the day. If tomorrow is a fine night, come to see me again. We'll continue our observations—but believe me, it's best not to say anything about them."

As I went back home, I contemplated the rutilant planet gain, as I had done when I came—but very different sentiments were stirring in my heart. The distance and isolation that separated me from it seemed to have disappeared I the meantime, and is stead of a cold and alien star, I saw a familiar world, a friendly planet, a companion of the Earth in the eternal solitude of the universe.

In my dreams, I found myself transported to the very surface of Mars, where an army of scientists was maneuvering a gigantic reflector with the aid of marvelous machines, projecting fantastic beams of light toward the Earth.

When morning came, I ran to buy the interesting book by Percival Lowell that Professor Gazen had told me about, and until the evening I remained immersed in reading it. Everything confirmed my ideas regarding the Martians.

The planet Mars is older than the Earth. Life must have appeared there much sooner, and, in consequence, have been evolving for a longer period of time. If the canals of Mars are the work of animate beings, the latter must be presently endowed with an intelligence more refined than ours, and perhaps our railways, telegraphs, telephones and economic systems were surpassed there a long time ago. To have been able to establish an irrigation system that embraces the entire planet, they must have a social situation in which political parties no longer tear one another apart and different nations regulate their affairs other than by the right of the strongest.

As for the sudden and ephemeral beams of light that have been observed departing from the place where the polar ice-cap has lost its dazzling whiteness, Percival Lowell believes that it is a mistake to attribute them to signals sent by the inhabitants of Mars. According to him, they are easily explained by the eastward reflection of fragments of glaciers that remain attached to mountain slopes, produced at the moment when the planet's rotation gives those slopes the appropriate angle—like those luminous beams that sometimes dazzle us when the window-panes of some house send the rays of the setting sun back to our eyes.

But the luminous spectra?

That is what Percival Lowell has neither seen nor explained, and what I expect to succeed in elucidating with the aid of Professor Gazen.

Unfortunately for our plans, the sky was cloudy the following day, and it has remained more or less unfavorable since then for the observation of Mars. Given these circumstances, and in the hope that some other astronomer, in a more limpid climate, might be able to continue this research. Professor Gazen and I thought it best to publish our discovery without further delay.

C. Paulon: *The Blue Laboratory*

(Paul Combes)
(1898)

Miss Madeline Rennick was an orphan, who no longer had any close relatives, and who made her living in London—with some difficulty—giving private lessons. So, when Dr. Chance, an English-born naturalized Russian living in St. Petersburg, offered her a hundred pounds sterling a year to provide an education for his two daughters, she resolved to accept the situation without a minute's hesitation.

She said goodbye to her friends, and packed her trunk. She took with her, among other things, a small revolver with a silver handle, and fifty bullets.

She arrived in St, Petersburg without any mishap. Dr. Chance was waiting for her at the station. He was a rather handsome man, but myopic, having passed fifty.

He greeted the governess with cold politeness, gave instructions for her luggage, and took her directly to his residence on the Ligovsky Canal. There, the young woman was received by Madame Chance, a woman who seemed to be, in every respect, the opposite of her husband. She was half-Russian and half-German by birth, conducted herself in a manner full of curiosity, and was also as uncongenial as possible.

Miss Madeline's two pupils were pretty girls, though. The older was tall and had her father's dark eyes; she had a beautiful frank expression; her name was Olga. The younger was shorter, with sharp features; she was called Maroussa. Both spoke English quite well, and the warmth of their welcome made the governess forget their mother's indifference.

It was about a month after her arrival in St. Petersburg when Maroussa said to her one afternoon: "You must find it terribly dreary here?"

"Not at all," the governess replied. "I've wanted to see Russia for a long time."

"You know, of course, that our father in English, He's been living in Russia since the age of thirty. He's a great scientist. How your eyes shine, Miss Madeline! Is it because science interests you?"

"I took a course in science at Girton," the young Englishwoman replied—and she returned her attention to the Russian novel that she was reading.

At that moment, a coldly polite voice spoke almost in her ear. She looked up, and to her great astonishment saw that Dr. Chance, who never—or hardly ever—favored the female gatherings of his family with his presence, had come into the room.

"Did I hear correctly?" he said. "Is it possible that a young lady like you is interested in scientific matters?"

"I like science immensely," Miss Madeline replied.

"It gives me great pleasure to learn that. The fact is that I came expressly to ask you to do me a favor. At times, I experience an intolerable pain in the right eye. If I make use of it, on such occasions, the agony becomes worse. I'm suffering that torture today. Would you come downstairs and act as my secretary for a few moments?"

"Certainly—I'd like that."

Immediately, Dr. Chance headed for the door, beckoning Miss Madeline to follow him. Two minutes later, she found herself in his study. It was a vast room, whose walls were garnished with shelves laden with books from floor to ceiling, only interrupted by a large window that let in an abundant light, and a door leading to some mysterious room situated beyond.

"My laboratory!" said the doctor, seeing the young woman's gaze stray in that direction. "Someday, I'll have the pleasure of showing it to you. Now will you please write to my dictation?"

"Yes. In shorthand?"

"Certainly—that's capital! I beg you to give me your closest attention; the article I'm going to dictate to you has to be in the post to England this evening. It's due to appear in the *Science Gazette*. Since you're interested in such things, I'll tell you what its subject is. Miss Rennick, I've discovered a method of photographing thought!"

The governess was gripped by astonishment at this confidence. The doctor perceived her amazement; his eyes shone as if emitting sparks.

"You don't believe me," he said, "and in that, you're like the majority of the public to whom I've made appeal. I'll doubtless be held in derision in England…but let's wait until the end. I can prove what I'm saying, but not yet…not yet... Are you ready?"

"I'm all ears," Miss Madeline replied.

The doctor's face brightened; he sat down on his sofa and began to dictate, while the governess rapidly noted down his every word. An hour later, he stopped.

"That's all!" he said. "Now would you like to transcribe in clear, in your best handwriting, everything that I've just dictated. When the young woman nodded, he added: "Accept, if you please, these ten roubles, for the pleasure and the collaboration you've given me. Not a word of protest! I'm still in your debt." He fixed Miss Madeline with a long and profound stare, and departed slowly.

It took the young woman more than two hours to transcribe the sentences that had flowed so easily from the doctor's lips. When the task was finished, she went back up to the drawing-room.

When she went in, Olga and Maroussa ran to her. "Tell us what happened!" the demanded.

"But I've nothing to tell you."

"Impossible! You've been gone for five hours."

"Yes, and during that time, your father dictated a piece of work to me, which I took down in shorthand. Then I transcribed it I clear, and I left it on his desk."

"Please Miss," said Olga, "tell us what the subject of our father's article was."

"I'm not at liberty to do that, Olga."

Olga and Maroussa looked at one another. Then Olga took the governess's hand. "Listen," she murmured, "we have something to tell you. Later, you'll often go into the laboratories..."

"Is there more than one, then?"

"Yes. Now, please pay attention. You understand that our father will ask you to help him often. He'll probably also ask you to assist him in his experiments in chemistry. But our father has another laboratory, which you haven't yet seen: the blue laboratory, about which we need to talk to you. We have a secret, Maroussa and I, which relates directly to that laboratory. It weighs upon us, sometimes heavily."

While she was speaking, Olga shivered, and Maroussa's face became very pale. "Will you hear us out?" she added.

"Certainly—and I promise to respect your secret."

"Then I'll tell you everything, as briefly as possible.

"About two months ago, a few gentlemen came to dine with us. They were Germans, and they were very learned. One of them is called Dr. Schopenhauer; he's a great scientist. When the wine was on the table, they began to talk about something that made my father angry. Soon, they all began quarreling. It was amusing to listen to them. They went red, and our father went pale.

"Our father said: 'I can prove what I'm saying.' I'm sure that they'd forgotten everything, even our existence. Suddenly, our father got up and said: 'Come with me, gentlemen. I'm in a position to make my thesis absolutely clear.'

"They all went out of the dining room then, and went into the doctor's study. Our mother said that she had a headache, and retired to her boudoir, but Maroussa and I were very excited, and we slipped into the study after the scientists. None of them had stayed in the first room. They had gone into the laboratory, whose door you've already seen. At the far end, a door was open, leading to a long corridor. The scientists and our father, absorbed by their preoccupations, went into it. Maroussa and I followed them.

"Our father took a key out of his pocket and opened a door in the wall. We found ourselves on the threshold of another laboratory, two or three times as large as the one we'd just left. In one of the corners, there was an extraordinary dome of some sort, projecting from under the floor. Maroussa and I noticed it as soon as we went into the room. Fearing that we'd be sent away, we slipped behind a big screen and waited there, while our father and the scientists talked to one another about their secrets.

"Suddenly, Maroussa, who has always had a mischievous streak, suggested that we stay there, in order to examine the place at our ease when our father and the Germans had gone. I don't know why I agreed to carry out that bold plan, for our father, when he left, would certainly lock us in—but we completely forgot that detail. After a short time, he appeared to have given the gentlemen satisfaction, and they all left the laboratory as rapidly as they had come. Our father switched off the electric light and we found ourselves in the dark.

"We heard the sound of footsteps drawing away along the corridor. We stood up, full of gaiety and mischief, and I said to Maroussa: 'Now let's switch the light back on!'"

Overcome by a sudden emotion, Olga fell silent. She continued in a hesitant voice: "We hadn't taken two steps into the room when—oh, Miss Madeline! What do you think happened? We heard a knocking sound that resonated as if it came from a floor situated beneath our feet. It came from the direction of the strange dome I told you about. A desperate voice shouted, three times: 'Help! Help! Help!'

"We were terrified, and all our bravado vanished. Maroussa fell to the ground and I uttered the sharpest screech that a human throat can produce. It was so piecing that our father heard it. The knocking ceased, and we heard our father's footsteps coming back.

"When he opened the door, Maroussa was on the floor, groaning, pointing her finger at the dome. She was too frightened to be able to talk, but I cried: 'There's someone shut in there, under that dome in the corner. I distinctly heard someone knocking, and then a voice shouted *Help!* three times!'"

"'Crazy!' said our father. 'There's nothing in there. Come here this instant.'

"He shoved us out of the laboratory, locked the door, and ordered us to go back to our mother. We told her everything, but she also said that it was crazy, and seemed very angry. She didn't even try to console Maroussa, who was crying—I'm the one who had to comfort my sister...

"But that night, Miss Madeline, we heard that cry again in our dreams, and it's haunted us ever since. Miss Madeline, if you help our father, he'll certainly take you to the blue laboratory. If he ever does, I beg you, look and listen, and tell us—oh, tell us!—whether you can also hear that terrible, distressing voice!"

Olga fell silent; her face was white, and her forehead was covered with beads of sweat.

Miss Madeline promised to shed some light on what had just been revealed to her, and indeed, from that time on, it seemed to her that she had an important mission to fulfill. There had been something in Olga's physiognomy while she told her story that rendered the governess absolutely certain that her pupil was telling the truth. The young Englishwoman therefore resolved to be prudent and vigilant, to act cautiously, and, if possible, to discover the secret of the blue laboratory.

To that end, she rendered herself agreeable and useful to Dr. Chance. Many times, when his eyes made him suffer, the scientist had recourse to her secretarial skills, and on each of those occasions he gave her ten roubles for her trouble. During these conversations, however—and Miss Madeline often remained with the doctor for quite a long time—she never could never penetrate his confidence to any extent at all. Never, even for a minute, did he lift the veil that hid his true character from every gaze—except once; and the story of that incident is the principal object of this narrative.

From the viewpoint of an ordinary observer, Dr. Chance was a man of good, even refined manners, but cold. From time to time, in truth, one could see his eyes shine as if they were quartz crystals from which a sudden shock had drawn sparks. From time to time, too, his gaze became anxious and his lips taut, while moisture pealed on his forehead, when an experiment in which Miss Madeline assisted him promised to present an exceptional interest.

Eventually, one afternoon, he had to do some very important work in the blue laboratory. He asked the governess to assist him, and asked her to follow him.

It was, with no fear of contradiction, a very well-organized laboratory. Three of the walls were garnished with shelves supporting all kinds of apparatus: Bunsen burners, porcelain bowls, balances, microscopes, bottles, jars, mortars, flasks—in a word, everything necessary for carrying out the rituals of chemistry.

In one corner, in conformity with young Olga's description, there was a strange dome, between one meter and one meter fifty tall, covered with a black cloth reminiscent of a cloak.

That was the first time that Miss Madeline had worked with the doctor in the blue laboratory, but after that afternoon, she returned there with him on many occasions, and became quite familiar with the room.

Finally, one day, the scientist was obliged to leave the young woman alone in the laboratory for a few minutes. Miss Madeline was, by nature, full of courage; she did not waste a moment in taking advantage of the unexpected opportunity. As soon as the doctor left the room she bounded to the mysterious dome and, lifting the black veil, she saw that it was covering a glazed frame doubtless communicating with a room situated below. She tapped the glass forcefully with her finger.

The effect was instantaneous. Miss Madeline immediately perceived a somber face looking up at her from below, and observed that between her and the apparition there was a second interior partition made of thicker glass. The face, expressing terrible suffering, was haggard, thin and pale; the young woman had never seen such a facial expression.

Each as astonished as the other, they were contemplating one another in silence when, the sound of the doctor's footsteps having become audible, a trembling hand rose up as if to implore help, and the vision vanished into the darkness.

Miss Madeline drew the black veil down over the dome and returned rapidly to her work. Dr. Chance was myopic; he came in, trying to identify the contents of two phials he was holding in his hand.

"Tell me," he asked, "what is this substance?" Then, looking at the young woman suspiciously, he added: "How pale you are! Are you ill?"

"I have a slight headache," she replied, "but I'll be all right in a moment."

"Would you like to postpone the work? I don't want to damage your health?"

"I can continue," the governess replied, suppressing her emotion by means of a effort of will.

The shock had passed; having experienced a moment of dread, she felt more at ease. In sum, her suspicions had become realities; her pupils really had heard that cry of distress. There was someone locked in a somber prison beneath the blue laboratory—God alone knew with what terrible objective.

Miss Madeline's duty was as clear as daylight.

"Dr. Chance," she said, when the most important part of the work was complete. "What is the purpose of that singular dome in the corner of the room?"

The scientist, who had his back turned to the governess at that moment, replied: "I warn you that you mustn't ask me questions. There's nothing in this room that does not have its utility, but if you become curious and start spying, I won't need your services for long."

"As you please! But you Englishwomen aren't in the habit of spying!"

"I believe that you're honest," said Dr. Chance, approaching her and looking her full in the face. "Well, in this case I'll have pleasure satisfying your curiosity. The dome is part of an apparatus by means of which I make a vacuum. Now, no doubt, you're as knowledgeable as you were before."

"I'm no wiser."

The doctor smiled sardonically. "I've finished my experiment," he said. "We can go."

Miss Madeline went straight to her room and locked herself in. She did not want to be disturbed by her pupils until she had formulated a complete plan of action.

She sat down and thought.

No danger could now deflect her from the enterprise on which she was decided. The miserable victim of Dr. Chance's cruelty would be rescued, even if she had to sacrifice her own life—but she reckoned that her only chance of success was to deceive the scientist's vigilance with regard to his prisoner.

Having determined a plan of action, Miss Madeline resolved to proceed immediately with its execution. That same evening, she dressed for dinner, selecting her best clothes. She had an old black velvet dress that had belonged to her grandmother. The velvet was superb, but the cut was old-fashioned. That old-fashioned appearance would doubtless add to the young Englishwoman's charms in the doctor's eyes; on seeing it, he would recall one of the beauties that had pleased him when he was young. To accompany it, she pinned a beautiful piece of lace around her neck, cleverly and gracefully folded, arranged her hair very high on her head and powdered it abundantly.

Naturally, she had hair as black as ink, white skin, pink cheeks and dark eyes and eyebrows. The effect of the powdered hair immediately removed the appearance of a conventional young woman of our own day, and gave her a resemblance to one of those ancient portraits that men admire so much.

When she came into the drawing-room, Olga and Maroussa ran to embrace her, with cries of admiration.

"How beautiful you are, Miss Madeline!" they cried. "But why are you dressed like that?"

"I had a whim to put this costume on," she said. "It belonged to my grandmother."

"But why have you powdered your hair?"

"Because it harmonizes better with the costume."

"You look charming. I wonder what mother will say."

When Madame Chance appeared, she looked at the governess with a certain astonishment, but did not say anything.

At dinner, Miss Madeline perceived that Dr. Chance observed her picturesque costume with an intrigued gaze, immediately followed by a nod of approval. "You remind me of someone," he said, after a moment's silence. He turned to his wife. "My dear, of whom does Miss Rennick remind you?"

Madame Chance looked at the young woman with a curious and unsympathetic expression. "Miss Rennick is a little like the portrait of Marie Antoinette just before she was guillotined," she remarked.

"That's true!" the doctor replied, nodding his head. "There's certainly a resemblance."

Miss Madeline, firmly determined to seduce him, moved her chair a little closer to his and they began to chat. She talked much more brilliantly than she had done until then; the scientist listened with surprise. She soon saw how the conversation pleased him, and took advantage of it to provoke his confidences.

He began to tell stories of his youth, of the era when his fat German wife had not yet appeared on the horizon of his existence. He also described his conquests of those long-gone days, and laughed merrily at his own exploits.

The conversation had taken place in English, and Madame Chance was evidently unable to follow the doctor's brilliant remarks and the young woman's piquant replies. After having watched her with increasing astonishment, she sighed softly, lay back in her chair and closed her eyes.

The two girls were chatting together without having the slightest suspicion of anything.

"Can we go to the drawing-room?" Madame Chance finally asked.

"You can, my dear," the doctor replied, swiftly, "and the fact is that you had better do so, you and the children. As for Miss Rennick, she has to do some work for me this evening. Didn't I tell you so, Miss Rennick? Will you be kind enough to follow me to my study? If you finish your work quickly, I'll do something for you. I can tell from your behavior that you're devoured by curiosity. Yes, don't try to deny it. I'll satisfy you. You can ask me to reveal one of my secrets this evening. Whatever you ask me, I'll do my best to please you. I'm in a particularly good mood this evening."

"Miss Rennick seems tired," said Madame Chance. "Don't keep her downstairs too long, Alexander. Come on, children!"

The girls smiled at the governess, gave her a slight nod of the head, and followed their mother, while Miss Madeline accompanied the doctor to his study.

When they were alone, he looked her full in the face. "I repeat to you what I've already said," he began. "You're full of curiosity. That which doomed your mother Eve will be your ruin too. This evening, I see in your eyes and ardent desire to get my secrets out of me—but let me ask you a question. What can a young woman like you have to do with science?"

"I love science," she replied. "I revere it; secrets are precious. But what can I do for you, Dr. Chance?"

"You talk in a very reasonable fashion, Miss Rennick. Yes, I have need of your services. Come with me to the blue laboratory."

He went ahead, opened the door in the wall, flicked the switch of the electric light, and they were inside the somber room, with its dark human secret. Dr. Chance crossed the room and began to examine a few microbial cultures very carefully.

"In fact," he said, "this experiment is not sufficiently advanced to tell us anything new this evening. I won't have need of your assistance until tomorrow…now, what can I do for you?"

"You can keep your promise and reveal your secret to me," Miss Madeline replied.

"Certainly—what would you like to know?"

"Do you remember the first day I helped you?"

"Very well."

"I wrote out some work for you that day. The subject was the photography of thought. You promised your English readers that, in a month or six weeks, you would be in a position to prove your assertions. That time has elapsed. Prove to me that you were telling the truth. Show me how you photograph thought."

Dr. Chance stared at her for a moment. Then his face contracted, his lips parted, displaying his bright teeth, and his eyes flashed. He put out his hand and placed it on the young woman's shoulder. "Are you ready?" he demanded. "Do you know what you're asking? I can reveal that secret to you. I'd willingly reveal it to you, if I thought you were capable of hearing it."

"I can hear anything," she said, drawing herself up to her full height. "At present, I'm entirely given over to my curiosity. I'm not afraid. Is your secret frightening, then? Is it a terrible thing to photograph thought?"

"The ways and means by which these secrets are enveloped by nature are full of terror," he replied, slowly. "But you have asked me for them, you shall know them…on one condition."

"What?"

"That you wait until tomorrow evening."

She was about to reply when a domestic appeared on the threshold of the laboratory, presenting the card of a visitor.

Dr. Chance darted a glance at it and said to Miss Madeline: "Dr. Schopenhauer is asking for me. He needs to tell me something important. I'll return in a few moments."

The governess remained alone. She could scarcely believe her senses. She was alone in the blue laboratory. An opportunity so unexpected must surely be providential. She launched herself toward the dome like an arrow. She took off the veil and leaned over it, trying to pierce the darkness that extended beyond it with her gaze. She could not see anything, however. She tapped the glass with her finger; that awoke no sound, not the slightest response. Had the victim been imprisoned in an even more profound cell, then?

Undiscouraged, Miss Madeline rapped again. This time, the result of her effort was a feeble, distant and terrible groan. Anxiously, in spite of the risk that she was running of being heard by Dr. Chance, she shouted: "If there's someone there, speak!"

A feeble and hoarse voice replied from the depths of the earth, as if it were yielding up its last sigh: "I'm an Englishman, unjustly imprisoned!" There was a long pause; then these words arrived, more feeble still: "Put to the torture!" Another silence; then the voice resumed: "In the shadow of death. Help! Save me!"

"You'll be liberated in twenty-four hours!" Miss Madeline relied. "I swear it, in God's name!"

She took action immediately, boldly, following the inspiration of the moment. She ran to the door, took out the key, and with a block of paraffin wax she carefully took an imprint. Then she replaced the key in the lock, and put the paraffin wax bearing the imprint into her pocket. Having done that, she marched back and forth across the laboratory, trembling violently, trying to regain her self-possession.

The doctor did not come back, but Miss Madeline did not want to remain in the blue laboratory any longer. She put out the electric light, locked the door, took out the key, went along the long corridor and knocked on the door of the other laboratory. The doctor opened it immediately. She gave him the key without looking at him, and went up to her room rapidly.

That was a frightful night for her. She was not afraid for herself, but every thought in her mind was feverishly orientated toward a single object. She wanted to rescue the martyrized Englishman, even at the risk of her life.

Before morning, the young woman had firmly resolved to take two steps: the first, to obtain a second key to the laboratory; the second, to go to see the English consul. She did not know the consul's name, but she knew that he had a responsibility to protect English subjects. Dr. Chance was a naturalized Russian, but the prisoner was an Englishman. She wanted to appeal to her homeland to obtain his deliverance.

Having calmed her overexcitement with these plans, Miss Madeline dressed as she usually did and devoted herself to her usual occupations all morning. All her splendor of the previous evening was gone, and she had become once again the simple and placid English governess.

At half past midday lunch brought the whole family to the table. Dr. Chance made himself particularly agreeable, and Miss Madeline noticed that he was watching her surreptitiously. For a moment she feared that he might suspect something; then, judging that to be impossible, she tried to remain calm.

Toward the end of lunch, and just as she was about to get up from the table, the doctor placed his hand on the young woman's and said: "I'm worried that you're so pale. Do you have a headache?

"Yes."

"Oh, Miss Rennick, your emotions are getting the better of you. That headache is due to nervous excitation."

"I don't have any reason to be nervous," she relied.

"Forgive me! You do have a reason. Do you remember what I promised to reveal to you this evening?"

She looked him in the eyes and replied: "I remember."

"I regret to disappoint you, but an unexpected business matter obliges me to leave St. Petersburg. I'll be gone for about two days."

"But my dear Alexander," his wife said, "I didn't know anything about this."

"I was about to tell you. The essential thing, for now, is that I can't fulfill a promise made to Miss Rennick. See how downcast she is; her passion for science increases the more she satisfies it. Miss Rennick, I must leave this evening at eight o'clock, and I won't return until Saturday. I need you today for almost all of the afternoon. Would you please join me in my study at about half past two?"

The governess promised, and left the dining room with her two pupils. It was the time usually devoted to lessons, but it was important, not to say essential, to Miss Madeline's plans that she be able to take advantage of the time—the precious time, for it as half past one, and only an hour remained at her disposal.

As soon as she was alone with her pupils she closed the door and looked them in the face. "Listen to me," she said. "I have something very important to do. I can trust you, but only up to a point; besides, I don't have time to tell you anything."

"Oh, Miss, Miss!" exclaimed Olga. "Have you discovered something?"

"Yes, but I can't breathe a word of it at this moment. You can help me to do more."

"I'd be delighted," said Maroussa, beginning to leap about.

"Oh, calm down, Maroussa! It's a matter of life and death. It's now half past one; in an hour I have to be in your father's study; in that interval, I have a lot to do. I need to see a locksmith and get a key made. I'll ask him to have it ready this afternoon, and I beg you to go and collect it when you go out later. Don't let anyone know about it; do it all in secret and bring me the key, carefully."

"Our nurse will go with us," said Olga. "We'll give her the slip easily. Which locksmith are you going to?"

Miss Madeline gave them the name of a shop she had noticed in a street nearby; then, not having a moment to lose, while her two pupils retied to their room, she wrote the following letter to the English consul:

Chance house, Ligovsky Prospekt.
Dear sir,

I implore your immediate assistance. I have discovered that an Englishman is being detained in a subterranean cell in this house, and tortured. I am a young Englishwoman, resident there as governess. I have resolved to go to this Englishman's aid, but I can do nothing without you. Dr. Chance is leaving St. Petersburg tonight at eight o'clock. At nine o'clock, I shall be in the large laboratory overlooking the garden, known by the name of the blue laboratory. I shall give a domestic instructions to take you there, if you are willing to come to my aid. In the name of God, don't fail in this, for the case is urgent. The Englishman and I are exposed to great danger. I request your assistance for two English subjects.

Your devoted servant,

Madeline Rennick.

Having written this letter, the governess put it in her pocket, dressed in haste and went out without being perceived. Madame Chance was taking a nap while Miss Madeline was supposed to be occupied with her pupils.

On her way to the consulate, the young woman stopped at the locksmith's and gave him instructions to make a key according to the imprint in the wax, asking that it should be ready in two or three hours, so that Miss Chance could come to collect it between five and six o'clock.

From there she ran to the consulate, handed over the letter, asking that it be transmitted immediately, and got back in time to be in Dr. Chance's study at half past two. The latter asked her to perform several urgent tasks immediately, and, at ten to eight, departed as he had said that he would.

Olga handed the key, which she and her sister had gone to fetch, to the governess in secret. The latter asked a domestic, putting three roubles in his hand, to bring the Englishman who would doubtless present himself at about nine o'clock to the blue laboratory.

At eight twenty-five, Miss Madeline took the key, armed herself with her revolver, and went down to the laboratory, which she opened without difficulty. She was less emotional than she had expected. She switched on the electric light and looked for the entrance to the subterranean cell. It was a trapdoor equipped with a ring, fitted into the laboratory floor.

The governess lifted up the trapdoor easily, and saw six or seven stone steps descending into the darkness. There was an electric switch on the wall; she pressed it, and a little incandescent bulb illuminated a large subterranean vault, whose extremity disappeared into the darkness, and from which a feeble plaint came.

The young woman headed in that direction and perceived a man, tightly tied up, lying on the ground. His face was cadaverous; he could not move. His lips were moving without emitting the slightest sound. Only his eyes spoke.

Miss Madeline fell to her knees and said to him: "I told you that would rescue you. Here I am! Have for fear. Your bonds will soon be broken and you'll be free."

The unfortunate shook his head sadly. As the Englishwoman was astonished by that gesture, she felt a hand touching her shoulder.

The consul already! It must be nine o'clock.

Miss Madeline turned round. Dr. Chance was standing calmly behind her, not manifesting the slightest surprise.

"Miss Rennick," he said, "I will now keep the promise I made to you yesterday to reveal my secret.

"It is by means of the man you see at your feet that I have succeeded in photographing thought. He was once my secretary. I perceived that he had a weak character. I hypnotized him; he became the slave of my will, and I was able, by experimenting on him, to discover marvelous secrets. What is the torture of a man in comparison with such results?

"Now, listen! When I first left you alone in the blue laboratory, unsuspectingly, I perceived as soon as I returned, by your agitation, that you had discovered something. That was the reason why I left you alone again—for Dr. Schopenhauer's visit was purely imaginary. I heard your cry, I saw you take the imprint of the key, and I foresaw everything that was about to happen. Well, the secret you were burning to know, I shall tell you.

"It is a scientific fact, well known in physiology, that in the darkness, the retina of some animals secretes a pigment named *visual purple*. If, for example, a frog in killed in darkness and its eye, after death, receives the image of an object in the light, that image will be reproduced on the retina, and can be fixed with an alum solution. In addition to that, I first observed that by fixing my own gaze on an object for some time, and then looking at a photographic plate in a dark room, the object that I had seen was reproduced on the plate after development. Are you following me?"

Madeline could only nod her head.

"I'll continue, then. Which gave me to suppose that thought itself could thus be photographed. Subjective intellectual impressions produce molecular changes in the cells of the brain; why could those changes too not decompose visual purple and give a distinct image on a negative exposed to its influence for a sufficient time? I carried out an experiment and found that such is, in fact, the case. In dreams, especially, that impression takes on a striking clarity. Has any more fascinating problem ever absorbed a scientist? Look at my victim! Ought he not to congratulate himself for suffering in such a great cause?

"Every night, I raise his eyelids with special apparatus, and while he sleeps, his eyes remain open, projecting their rays into the darkness for hours, on to a sensitive plate, where they inscribe his dreams.

"By employing products such as cocaine and opium, I give him particular dreams.

"That's my secret! Anyway, during the day, I'm grateful. I feed my patient well. He can't die...but it's quite possible that he'll go mad, because of the suffering his nervous system undergoes. Would you like to see one of the developed photographs?"

Miss Madeline uttered a scream of horror. "Not one more word! You're a demon with a human face."

"Women are hypersensitive," said Dr. Chance. "Remember that you wanted to know. Remember that I warned you that the secret could not be stolen from me without terror, nor without horror. I hoped that you would rise above that horror. I was mistaken! But now that you know my secret, you can't leave here, and as you have an excessive imagination, I shall experiment on you. You'll be an excellent subject."

"No! Rather kill me!" cried the young woman, falling to her knees.

"That's what I propose to do," said the doctor.

He took her hand, forced her to stand up, and led her gently—she no longer had any consciousness of herself—under the dome of glass, which he closed around her by means of a similarly glazed sliding panel. She remained there alone.

Almost immediately, the sound of powerful pistons was heard, functioning within the chambers of a pump, and Miss Madeline sensed the air around her becoming rarefied. She was indeed, as the doctor had previously told her, under the bell-jar of a vacuum pump.

Her chest constricted, she fell to the ground, and perceived through the glass roof the laughing face of the diabolical scientist.

Just as she was about to lose consciousness, she thought of her revolver, and still had the strength to seize it and fire into the air. Then she fainted, while the dome shattered noisily.

When she came round, the young Englishwoman found herself safe in the English consulate.

She learned that the consul, having arrived on time, had had Dr. Chance arrested. His victim, having been rescued and taken to the hospital, was gradually recovering from his suffering.

The Russian newspapers made such a fuss about the scandalous adventure, horrified by the scientific aberration of Dr. Chance and praising Miss Madeline's courage, that the latter, irritated by the celebrity, returned to England, swearing that she would never set foot in St. Petersburg again.

Emma-Adèle Lacerte: ***Nemoville***

(1917)

To the delicate poet and exquisite friend
Gaëtane de Montreuil, this book is dedicated.[59]

PREFACE

The stories of Jules Verne having once populated my young imagination, I have tried to make that great narrator of voyages and adventures live again by publishing this book.

It is in memory of *Vingt mille lieues sous les mers* and *L'Île mystérieuse*, to which it is a sequel, that I have entitled my book *Nemoville*, in honor of Captain Nemo, the inventor and proprietor of the *Nautilus*. The *Nautilus* will be found again in my story; I have retrieved it from the abyss for a while. Those whom the great submarine have interested before will doubtless be glad to hear mention of it again.

I recommend my book only to those who like adventure stories, but I do not doubt that those who prefer sentimental ones will follow the two heroes, Gaetane and Roger, with interest.

---

[59] Gaëtane de Montreuil was the pseudonym of the journalist and poet Georgina Bélanger (1867-1951).

1. Abbé Bernard

It was eight o'clock in the evening on the twenty-eighth of October 1875. The weather was magnificent, although slightly cool.

In the pathways of a garden, which still contained a few belated flowers, a priest was walking, while reciting his rosary devotedly. The priest in question might have been forty or perhaps forty-five years old. His intelligent and handsome face was still young, although white hairs were mingled with his blond tresses.

The priest was Abbé Bernard. His poor health did not permit him to carry out any holy ministry, and he was visiting one of his friends, a parish priest. Abbé Bernard was doubtless ever ready to hasten to the bedside of someone who was dying, and although he was supposed to be resting completely, that did not mean that he was inactive.

The garden in which Abbé Bernard was walking on that October evening belonged to the presbytery and was situated on the edge of the ocean. The Atlantic waves came to break within the very confines of the garden. The abbé loved to contemplate the immensity, which led him to meditate on the grandeur and power of the Creator. For him, nothing was more impressive than the ocean, because for him, nothing spoke more loudly of God. The sea had always exercised a powerful attraction on Abbé Bernard; he sometimes said that if he had not had a priestly vocation, he would not have chosen any other profession than that of mariner...but the Lord's voice had made itself heard, and he had not resisted its call.

Slightly fatigued by his walk, Abbé Bernard sat down on a garden bench, in an attitude of profound meditation. The waves came to die at his feet, and their lapping seemed to be the echo of a hymn of adoration, which rose up from his poetic and pious soul.

Suddenly, the priest started at the sound of a voice nearby, which said: "Is it Abbé Bernard to whom I have the honor of speaking?"

The abbé turned his head and saw a man dressed like a mariner leaning against the bench on which he was sitting. The priest had not heard him approach.

"Yes, my friend. What can I do for you?"

"Would you come with me, Monsieur l'Abbé? I want to take you to a dying man. Come quickly, please."

"I'll come with you. I'll run to the presbytery, collect the things I need, and I'll be with you momentarily."

The abbé went into the presbytery and went to the library. The priest who was his host was not there. Hastily, Abbé Bernard scribbled a few words to inform him of the reason for his absence; then he took a warm overcoat and a few light objects that he might need, and left.

When he arrived in the garden he saw the sailor, who seemed to be waiting for him impatiently.

"We're going by water, Monsieur l'Abbé," he said, abruptly.

The priest sat down on the bench of a strangely-formed yacht, and they set off. Complete silence reigned on board; nothing could be heard but the sound of the yacht's engine. Abbé Bernard did try to ask the mariner a few questions, but the latter probably did not hear him, as he made no reply.

After an hour or thereabouts of that silent navigation, on a very calm sea, the mariner left his engine, came over to the priest, and said to him, in a very polite tone: "I regret, Monsieur l'Abbé, that it will be necessary for you to consent to wearing a blindfold."

"Why the mystery?" replied the abbé. "I refuse."

"It's necessary," his companion repeated, without any rudeness. "I give you my word that no harm will come to you." And without giving the priest time to reply, he threw a tarpaulin sack over his head, which he tied up tightly.

The abbé did not even try to defend himself. No one could mean to harm a man who had done nothing but good all his life. Besides, he was not strong enough to struggle against the robust matelot.

Abbé Bernard thought that he heard a strange noise, as if the waves were opening up to swallow the yacht, but he told himself that it was a trick of the imagination, for the navigation continued rapidly and calmly.

It continued for another hour at least, and then he felt the vessel come to a sudden stop. He heard the sound of voices and footsteps, and then a hand gripped his own.

Someone said, still without any rudeness: "Come with me, Monsieur l'Abbé."

They took a few steps—perhaps fifty—and then the priest felt his blindfold being removed.

He saw that he was in a room brightly-lit by electricity, in the middle of which, on an extremely tidy bed, a dying man was lying.

2. A Shipwreck

Two years before the events recorded in the previous chapter, a small steamboat was struggling against the waves of the Pacific Ocean. That sea does not always justify its name, and on that day—the fourth of June 1873—it presented a terrible aspect. The steamboat was fighting, and fighting bravely, but the wind blowing from the west was causing it to pitch fearfully. The boat was shipping water, which constrained those who were not members of the crew to take refuge in their cabins or the saloon.

On the stern of the boat, its name could be seen, inscribed in large black letters on the white-painted wood: *Queen of the Waves*. She belonged to a San Francisco company.

The passengers, who were not very numerous—fifty in all—were emigrants, but not emigrants of lowly origin devoid of knowledge and education. They included a few lawyers, two physicians, engineers and mechanics. Fortune had not smiled upon them; they were merely in search of a more favorable country of residence.

The steamboat continued its frightful pitching. Suddenly, an enormous mass of water invaded the decks of the *Queen of the Waves*, putting out the fires and causing muffled explosions.

There was a danger of panic, because the steamboat, whose tiller was having hardly any effect in that torment, could not stay afloat. The *Queen of the Waves* was nothing but a wreck, swaying from port to starboard. The passengers felt that they were doomed.

And there was no land in sight! The mariners' telescopes searched the horizon in vain. There was nothing to be seen—nothing at all. It was a terrible situation! The lamentations of the women and their desperate screams mingled with the noises of the tempest. All hope of salvation seemed lost.

At about three o'clock in the afternoon, however, the man on watch shouted, resoundingly: "Land! Land! Ahead and to starboard!"

The deck of the *Queen of the Waves* was immediately covered by passengers. About five miles away, they were able to discern some kind of promontory. Was it *terra firma*? Was it merely an island? But that hardly mattered: continent or island, it was salvation—if they could reach it.

The man at the helm redoubled his efforts.

The boat was no more than a mile from land when it hit a reef. Immediately, the *Queen of the Waves* heeled over on to her side, and they realized that she could not right herself again. The passengers were all men of intelligence and courage, though. They helped the sailors get the lifeboats—of which there were only four—afloat. Risking their lives a hundred times over, the passengers were provided with the means to save themselves.

Unfortunately, the last lifeboat, containing the captain and the crewmen, came too close to a submerged rock, made contact with it, and was seen to sink beneath the seething ocean waves.

That was a great misfortune, for, even if they succeeded in freeing the steamboat, how could they put to sea again without a captain and sailors?

Alas, they could not take time out to mourn the loss of the crew; it was necessary to take care of more urgent matters, as quickly as possible. Some of the shipwreck victims devoted themselves to those tasks; they made several trips to the grounded vessel, bringing back provisions, blankets, weapons and so on.

It was as well that they did, for two hours later, the *Queen of the Waves* broke up against the reef; soon, nothing remained of her but floating debris on the furious sea.

3. A Strange Land

At what point on the Earth's surface were they? Without instruments, they could not take a bearing. The only certain thing was that they were on land somewhere in the Pacific; it was necessary to be content with that information, for the moment.

That land, off the shore of which the *Queen of the Waves* had been wrecked, was strange. There were fallen trees and profound excavations everywhere. In certain places, one might have thought that the granite that formed the basis of the ground had been opened up and split in two by some cataclysm. Evidently, there had been an earthquake there, not very long ago; the most capable of the castaways estimated the interval at two or three years at the most.

There was not a living creature to be seen, human or animal. Had the place ever been inhabited? Nothing supported that supposition.

For the moment, the castaways were obliged to give their attention to a more imperious preoccupation: that of fortifying themselves with a little nourishment and getting some rest—for they were all, as can be imagined, exhausted by fatigue. Without even taking the trouble to light a fire, they improvised a meal of cold conserves, then rolled themselves up in blankets and went to sleep, entrusting the job of guarding the camp to the dog Turko, who belonged to a young engineer by the name of Roger de Ville.

The next day, the storm had calmed down. The sun was shining, and its warm radiance put a little hope into the hearts of the castaways. When they had had breakfast—this time allowing themselves the luxury of hot coffee—they decided to undertake an expedition of discovery.

It was important to know the nature of the land on which they found themselves. Was it an island or the continent? All the castaways tried to convince themselves that the latter hypothesis might be correct, for if they were on the continent it would be easy enough to reach its habitable regions. If, on the other hand, they were on an unknown island...

They did not even want to dwell on that possibility; it was too terrifying.

In any case, the poor castaways put their trust in Providence, which had not abandoned them, and would surely come to their aid.

Two young men, Roger de Ville and Paul Lamontagne, offered to go on the expedition. They wanted to go up to the summit of a mountain some seven or eight hundred feet high, which loomed up majestically not far away. From the top of that mountain they would either be able to see the land extending as far as the eye could see, or the sea surrounding them in a circle that the castaways had little hope of crossing.

Roger and Paul left, therefore, at about nine o'clock in the morning. They took food supplies, two traveling-blankets, two carbines, a sturdy rope and a powerful marine telescope. It was decided that Turko would remain in the camp, but when the dog saw his master leaving, it was impossible to hold him back. Deep down, Roger was not displeased to be taking him along; he did not like to be separated from the faithful animal for long.

There was no lack of wishes of *bon voyage* for the expeditionaries, and the others followed them with their eyes for as long as they were in view.

It is not my intention to give you long and minute details of that excursion, and all the difficulties that the travelers encountered on the way. Try, if you can, to give yourselves an idea of what a walk of that sort might have been like, in an unknown country interrupted by ravines and rendered almost impracticable by a thousand natural hazards. It was not until dusk was approaching that Roger and Paul reached the top of the mountain.

They could not have chosen a better observatory, and both of them, in turn, scanned the horizon with the marine telescope. Then they looked at one another, and said, almost simultaneously, with a note of discouragement in their voices: "It's an island."

"A volcanic island," Roger added.

"May God protect us!" Paul replied.

The two friends went back down to the valley and continued on their way, searching for a suitable place to spend the night. They remained silent now, not daring to communicate to one another the somber thoughts that were assailing them. What horrible news they would have to take back to their companions the next day!

Both of them were thinking: *How can we get away from here?*

They might perhaps be able to build a raft, but how could they steer it? They did not know where in the ocean the *Queen of the Waves* had run aground, having drifted helplessly at sea for so long.

Soon, Roger and Paul stopped, having reached the shore of the sea. It was there that they decided to spend the night. The place was ideal in its savage beauty, with its cliffs plunging steeply into the waves, its profound caves and its immense blocks of superimposed granite, which only seemed to require a push from some giant hand to topple into the seething water.

No vestige of vegetation was visible there, however, and by virtue of indications that could not deceive Roger's expert eyes, the two young men understood that the location had been recently visited by an earthquake—and observation that was scarcely cheerful or encouraging, in the circumstances.

The ocean, on the other hand, presented a peculiarity that could not fail to interest the two friends in spite of the anguish of the moment. The water was so clear that the gaze could plunge into it to a considerable depth; when the waves calmed down, they could even make out the sea-bed and perceive fish swimming below the surface.

The young men were so tired, though, that they did not waste time in vain commentaries. They wrapped themselves in their blankets and fell into a profound sleep.

4. A Great Discovery

Roger and Paul lingered over their breakfast the following morning. They chatted to one another, trying to frame escape plans, whose futility they sensed. They had the conviction that the castaways of the *Queen of the Waves* were condemned to certain death on the rocky desert isle. Life had not treated them like spoiled children before that day, alas, but they liked their harsh stepmother all the same, and promised themselves, with all the energy of their twenty years, to find a means of escaping the horrible fate that was lying in wait for them.

Before returning to the camp, they wanted to carry out a further exploration of the sea shore. In spite of the tragic thoughts preying on their minds, they were subject to the attractive charm of that grandiose and terrible nature.

The limpidity of the water as so extraordinary that they thought they were victims of an illusion. Suddenly, Roger put his hand on Paul's arm, and said: "Look—what a monster!"

With his finger he pointed out a form that was indeed monstrous, which was motionless in the sea, scarcely ten feet beneath the surface.

"It's neither a whale nor a shark," said Paul. "There are none of that size."

As he spoke, he threw a lump of rock into the water a few feet away from the monster—but the latter remained motionless.

"That's strange," said Roger. "I've a mind to dive in and take a closer look."

"Think twice about that," Paul replied, "You'd be going to certain death—the monster could swallow you in a single gulp."

"I'd like to know what I'm looking it, though," Roger went on, in a determined tone. "I'll tie the rope around my waist and simply dive in. The water's so clear that you can follow my every movement; if you see that I'm in trouble, haul on the rope, and that will be that."

In spite of Paul's remonstrations, Roger did what he had said, and soon let himself slide into the sea. He did not stay there long. Having kicked the monster once, he returned to the surface.

"Haul in the rope" he shouted. "Haul away!" Then, when he had returned to his friend's side, he continued, in a voice trembling with emotion: "I didn't risk my life in vain, my friend—I've just made a great discovery. That monster you see there, immobile, is…you'll never guess what it is!"

"I'm not in the mood right now to try to solve riddles," Paul relied, gravely. "You'd do better to tell me right away what the bizarre thing is to which you seem to be attributing such great importance."

"Well, it's the *Nautilus*. The *Nautilus*!"

"The *Nautilus*!" Paul repeated, now as excited as his friend. "The submarine whose extraordinary adventures amused and intrigued our imagination to such an extent when we were children? Are you sure of what you're saying, Roger?"

"It's the *Nautilus*, I tell you. I saw its name inscribed on the stern, along with the motto *Mobilis in mobile.*[60] Now I

---

[60] The motto inscribed on the *Nautilus* translates as "mobile in a mobile element."

remember the tale told by a certain Cyrus Smith, in which he described the death of Captain Nemo and the sinking of his submarine on the coast of an unknown island in the Pacific, a couple of years ago."

"Yes, yes!" Paul exclaimed. "I remember too—in which case, the *Nautilus* is a tomb, since it carries the mortal remains of its owner, Captain Nemo, within it. What use can the discovery be to us, anyway? If we're destined to perish in this rocky desert, we can't even make it known to the world."

"I can't resign myself to dying here as easily as that, and our discovery might just help us to escape this dangerous island. If we can refloat the Nautilus we can use it to sail away. What's the point of your being a mechanic if I have to suggest ideas like that to you—which are, it seems to me, right up your alley?"

"Extravagant ideas have never been my province," Paul replied smiling, "but in the situation we're in, the enterprise in worth trying, and I'm certain that all the castaways of the *Queen of the Waves* will think the same. You can count on everyone's good will to bring your bold project to a successful conclusion."

"Let's go tell the others about our discovery, then—they'll be waiting for us back there."

They left at a brisker pace. Now that hope had returned to them, they felt ready to make plans for the future again.

Roger, who had a romantic imagination that sometimes seemed extravagant to his placid friend, suddenly said: "You can't imagine how this staggering discovery has excited me. When I read the story of the *Nautilus* I dreamed about living in a submarine city, with a small and selected population; the land, with all its miseries, seemed to me too paltry a domain." He became increasingly excited, and added: "A submarine city would be ideal!"

"I think you're out of your mind," his companion told him, unable to share his enthusiasm for the domain of fish, "but if you can promise the future inhabitants of your city to rid them of some of the tiresome afflictions one finds on land,

I think that half the world's population would be glad to go with you."

"I'm not joking," Roger continued. "My dream is extravagant, I know, but it's not unrealizable, and she shall see. It wouldn't be so difficult to construct other submarines, and we could link them together by corridor-tubes, detachable at will. If one of the submarines needed to returned to the surface, it would only have to detach itself from the others. If the entire city occasionally had the whim to make an expedition to the home of the land-dwellers, one would only have to detach all the tubes, and every inhabitant of the city could make the journey along with his house."

"My word, that would be quite something," said Paul, half-won over by his friend's project.

At that moment, Turko started leaping about and licking his master's hand, as he always did when he was happy.

"Look," said Roger. "Turko approves of my project. That must be a good omen."

"Are you really thinking of imparting that extravagance to the castaways of the *Queen of the Waves*?" Paul asked, with a serious expression. "They'll certainly think you've gone mad."

"People can think what they like," Roger replied, "But I'm holding on to the realization of my dream, and I won't let go of it. I'll go to live underwater on my own, if no one wants to go with me, but I'll go regardless."

"No, you won't go alone, for I'll go with you—that's understood. Fundamentally, you know, I wouldn't be displeased to hollow out that niche away from the land, which has thus far refused me everything of which my ambition has dreamed: glory, wealth, love..."

"We won't be on this island long enough to build submarines," Roger continued, as if he had not been interrupted by his friend's pleasantries, "since we'll have to leave this volcanic region, where it wouldn't be a good idea to stay for too long."

The two friends continued on their way in silence.

Their return was greeted with demonstrations of joy by the other castaways, who listened with a great deal of interest to the story of the marvelous discovery. They all knew the story of the *Nautilus* and Captain Nemo, and to Paul's great astonishment, when Roger, without any considerable preamble, proposed his plan or an underwater city, it did not encounter the opposition he had feared. A few people raised feeble objections, but others, numbered among those who had suffered a great deal from the wickedness of the people of the land, manifested a veritable enthusiasm for the young engineer's original idea. One slightly older man of taciturn appearance, named Richard, even offered to advance the funds necessary for the realization of the extraordinary project.

It was decided to refloat the *Nautilus* immediately, and they set to work the following day.

5. Morte Morieris[61]

We left Abbé Bernard at the bedside of a dying man.

At first, the priest thought that he was alone with the moribund, but soon he perceived a young man sitting by the bed.

The latter got up and bowed to the priest. "Monsieur l'Abbé Bernard, no doubt?" he asked. On receiving an affirmative nod, he continued: "I'm Doctor Desmarais and this man is my patient. I haven't been able to save his life, alas,. He's going to die."

"It's God's prerogative to give life or take it away," the priest replied. Then he approached the bed.

The invalid seemed to be asleep. The abbé placed his hand on the dying man's forehead, and the latter opened his eyes. He seemed both surprised and relieved to see the priest,

---

[61] These words are extracted from a Latin version of what God says to Adam in *Genesis* after discovering his sin; an approximate literal translation is "dying, you will die," but the King James Bible puts it so much better: "Dust thou art, and to dust thou shalt return."

who made a gesture to the physician instructing him to leave the room. Then he sat down next to the sick man, offering him soothing words of encouragement and consolation.

"I've a great deal to tell you," the dying man murmured, "and time is running out!"

"Speak," said the priest. "Then I'll give you absolution from your sins and administer the last sacraments of the church."

"Father," the sick man went on, "I have only loved one person in my life: my daughter Marcelle. For her, in order to see her rich and happy, I was prepared to go as far as crime..."

A fit of coughing interrupted the confession. The invalid went so pale that the priest thought that he was about to render his last sigh, but he soon recovered his voice, which continued, weakening all the while:

"One evening—it was fourteen years ago—one of my friends, Jean Demers, arrived at my home. He had just lost his wife, whom he adored, and he believed that he too was afflicted by an incurable illness; he left a few hours later in order to spend the little time remaining him on earth in the country of his birth, where he no longer had any relatives.

"Before going to die there, he wanted to entrust his daughter to me. She was the same age as mine, six years old. He made me promise to bring her up in accordance with her fortune, which as considerable, and gave me a well-stuffed portfolio.

"I promised everything he wished. Then, when he went away, having hugged his daughter, I counted the assets without paying any heed to the child, who was weeping and calling for her father..." The dying man sighed. "I need to hurry," he said, "for I sense that I'm fading fast…I established, therefore, that the portfolio's contents were worth nearly half a million…and for me, who had just lost my petty fortune in misguided speculations, the temptation was too strong…I gave in to it.

"No one had seen the child enter my home. I decided to make her disappear, before anyone suspected her existence in the house…and her fortune would be my daughter's...

"I told the little girl that I was going to take her back to her father, and I walked toward the docks; she followed me without any resistance. A ship was about to leave. I handed the child over to the captain of the vessel—a man with shifty eyes—and gave him five hundred dollars. The boat sailed that same night, and my friend's daughter belonged henceforth to Captain Laurent.

"All went well for me for several years, but two years ago, I received a letter from my old friend Jean Demers! He had been cured, and informed me that he was coming back. Alarmed by the news, I decided to flee the just wrath of the man I had betrayed, and took passage on the *Queen of the Waves*, which was wrecked on the coast of an unknown island.

"Afterwards, I decided to hide myself away, with my daughter, in this city where no one would ever think to come to look for me, under the false name I had taken. Henceforth, I bore the name Richard."

"My brother," the priest asked, "is it under the secrecy of the confessional that you are telling me these things, or do you want me to repair the evil that you have done, if that is possible?"

"Oh, repair it! Repair the evil!" the dying man croaked.

"Then tell me what became of the child."

"I don't know, alas," the dying man barely breathed. "I don't know..."

"Tell me her name," said the priest, leaning over to put his ear close to lips of the dying man, who seemed exhausted.

"Her name…her name…is..."

He did not finish. Death had closed his eyes forever.

Hastily, the priest pronounced the words of pardon, then closed the dead man's yes and called for Doctor Desmarais. The promptitude with which the latter responded to the abbé's summons caused the latter to suppose that he had not been far away—but the priest was too thoroughly honest to suspect that anyone might have been eavesdropping on the confidences of a dying man.

Doctor Desmarais was, however, one of those men who keep their eyes lowered—and people who cannot look others in the face generally have something to hide.

Soon, light footsteps were heard in the corridor. The door of the room where the dead many lay opened, and a young woman about twenty years old came in. This was Marcelle. She fell upon her father's body and began moaning like a little child.

"Father, Father, my dear Father..." Turning abruptly to the priest, she begged him: "Oh, tell me he isn't dead!"

The abbé replied with words of consolation, talking to her about resignation and the will of God. Marcelle finally understood that all hope was gone, and surrendered to a crisis of grim despair, which ended up causing her to collapse. She fell to the floor, inanimate.

The physician immediately knocked on the door of a neighboring room, and an old maidservant appeared.

"Mademoiselle Marcelle is in need of your care," the doctor said, simply, without paying any more heed to the young woman. He added: "Monsieur Richard is dead."

The old maidservant made a desolate gesture, leaned over the young woman without looking at the dead man, lifted her up in her robust arms and carried her out of the funereal room.

"Now," the priest said to the doctor, "one final prayer for the man who has just rendered his soul to God, and I'll return home."

As he finished his prayer, the same old maidservant reappeared and gave him a piece of paper, folded and sealed.

The abbé opened it, and read:

The governor of the city requests Abbé Bernard to be kind enough to follow the guide who brought him. The governor has important things to communicate, and a proposition to make to him.

The abbé could not suppress a start of surprise.

What could the governor have to say that's so urgent? he wondered. Asking himself this question, he followed his guide.

6. The Governor

Following his guide, Abbé Bernard went through long exterior corridors, all lit by electricity. The journey went on for fifteen minutes, at the most; then the guide knocked on a door and a manservant came to answer it.

"Please follow me, Monsieur l'Abbé," said the manservant.

The priest went into a splendid room. He sat down in an armchair and waited. Perceiving a magnificent organ at the far end of the room, he got up and went over to it, and started to play. He played Gounod's prayer,[62] and put his soul so thoroughly into his work that he did not hear a young man come in, who paused in the doorway of the room to listen.

Eventually, the abbé turned round and noticed the newcomer, who said: "Permit me to congratulate you, Monsieur l'Abbé; I've heard Gounod's prayer many times, but never have I found it so beautiful."

"I love music," the priest replied, "and I was unable to resist the temptation of trying out this instrument while waiting for the governor. I hope he won't be long in coming, for I'm in a hurry to get back home."

The young man bowed, and said: "I'm the governor of this city, and my name is Roger de Ville."

The abbé manifested considerable surprise, but he smiled. "Excuse me. I assumed that the governor must be an old man—or, at least, a man somewhat older than you."

Roger de Ville smiled in his turn. "I'm only twenty-four, Monsieur l'Abbé, but I was elected by acclamation. All the inhabitants of this city, with one exception, were happy to

---

[62] The music that Charles Gounod provided for the singing of the *Pater noster*.

confide such an important responsibility to me." And Roger began laughing, with the insouciance of his youth.

"Monsieur le Gouverneur, would you be kind enough to tell me immediately what you have to communicate to me; I'm in a hurry to get home. But permit me to tell you that you have strange ways of doing things in this city…I was virtually abducted, my eyes blindfolded. Such conduct does not have my approval, as you can hardly doubt, Monsieur le Gouverneur."

"I regret that we've been forced to act as we have done, but it was necessary and you won't be annoyed any longer when I've told you what it is that I have to say to you. To begin with, I ought to tell you about the origins of this city; it's only two years old."

"I'm listening," said the priest.

Then Roger de Ville told the story of the wreck of the *Queen of the Waves* and the discovery of the *Nautilus*.

"Since childhood," he added, "I'd dreamed on living in a submarine city, and my dream has been realized. To be sure, we haven't adopted Captain Nemo's system—we make excursions on to land whenever we please—but we prefer life under the sea, which is good to us. I'll show you our city tomorrow, Monsieur l'Abbé, and I'm certain that it will interest you."

Abbé Bernard was so surprised—or so wonderstruck—by what he had heard that he was unable to reply for a few moments.

"What you've just told me is truly marvelous, if not magical, and I congratulate you on having been able to realize such an extraordinary dream," he said, laughing. "Many people who have more modest ambitions are still unable to satisfy them; you're a fortunate mortal, Monsieur le Gouverneur—but I wonder what you can possibly want from me, and what I could add to your wellbeing."

"Well, yes, Monsieur l'Abbé, you could add to the well-being of all the inhabitants of Nemoville, by agreeing to become the city's curé. Will you accept that position?"

The priest hesitated; he had listened to Roger's story with interest, but he was far from expecting such a proposal. Initially, it seemed to him to be unacceptable, and he shook his head as a sign of refusal.

"I haven't told you, of course, the reason that led me to make you the offer—which is that all the inhabitants of Nemoville belong to the Roman Catholic faith, and you'll have no lack of things to do here. Children have been born in the city since its foundation, who haven't yet been baptized, and if you had refused to come here this evening, Monsieur Richard would have died without receiving the consolations of religion."

This explanation of the facts succeeded in convincing the abbé, who did not want to shirk a duty that seemed to him to have been mapped out by Providence. He gave in immediately and held his hand out to the governor, saying: "I accept, Monsieur le Gouverneur, since I shall be able to work here for the glory of God."

"Thank you," the governor replied. "You won't regret it—I give you my guarantee. You will, therefore be the curé of Nemoville from now on." He opened a door that opened into the reception-room. "This will be your room. Tomorrow, I'll show you around the city. In the meantime, I'll wish you good night."

They went their separate ways, both satisfied.

7. Nemoville

The governor was waiting for the curé at the door of his room the following morning. After enquiring as to his health, he accompanied him to the dining-room, where Paul Lamontagne was already present, whistling cheerfully as he waited for his friend, beside a cage in which a magnificent canary was executing its savant trills.

Roger introduced his friend to the curé, who immediately remarked, while smiling: "Everyone seems very cheerful here, including the canary, who seems no less happy for residing in the domain of fish."

"Good humor is contagious here," Paul replied. Laughing wholeheartedly, he added: "That's due to the fact there are no usurers in Nemoville."

The new curé could not help laughing at that sally, and replied that some of Nemoville's inhabitants had doubtless run into those dangerous bipeds on land, and could not have found any better way of escaping them than to bury themselves under water.

Breakfast was prolonged, which was very pleasant—Nemoville did not often have the advantage of a new guest—and the curé delighted Roger and Paul as much by his wit as his generosity, of which he soon gave evidence.

For his part, the abbé immediately felt captivated by the young mean's sterling cheerfulness. He learned, in the course of the conversation, that Paul was the governor's secretary, and congratulated him on that account.

It was Roger who replied: "He ought to have been the governor, for Paul risked his life twenty times over during the refloating of the *Nautilus*."

"I did my share of the work, that's all—and I can claim no great merit for it, after all, since it was a matter of saving myself along with everyone else."

Roger tried to protest, but Paul changed the subject. Addressing the curé, he said: "You're going to visit Nemoville this morning, and make the acquaintance of your parishioners. I'm certain that they'll all be glad to see you."

"I see that you've named your city after Captain Nemo."

"We owed him that," Roger replied, "since we took his ship—for which, it's true, he had no further use."

"While for us," Paul put in, "it was a different matter. Without the *Nautilus*, we'd have been condemned to perish on a deserted volcanic island. We gave the captain a funeral worthy of his tastes and exploits, and utilized the vessel to escape the dangerous region into which our shipwreck had thrown us."

"You had every right to do so," the priest said, smiling. "Now, Monsieur le Gouverneur, I'm at your disposal."

"Let's go," said Roger, getting to his feet.

Nemoville was about a thousand meters square; the submarines were linked together by exterior corridors. Everyone had his own submarine; the corridors were the city's streets.

No one was a prisoner in Nemoville; every submarine could be easily detached from the external corridors and could rise to the surface of the sea under its own power, at will.

Sometimes, the entire city rose to the surface of the sea to renew its supplies of air—and it was a very strange spectacle to see that artificial island surging out of the water. It could move around freely, changing its situation, drawing near to a coast or plunging to the bed of the ocean deeps.

Oh, the people of Nemoville were very fortunate!

The governor's residence was at one of the city's extremities. The other residences were grouped together, as in the streets of a veritable city.

Accompanied by Paul and Roger, Abbé Bernard made a tour of his new parish, and was welcomed everywhere by demonstrations of the most enthusiastic joy. Mothers held out their children to him, in order for him to bless them; sick people felt relieved by his words of consolation and counsels of resignation.

Monsieur Richard's daughter, Marcelle, wept silently on seeing him, for he was due to preside over her father's funeral in a few hours' time. The priest spoke to her softly about resignation and the will of God.

When he left Marcelle, he was guided to a small dwelling some distance from the others. They knocked at the door, and a domestic came to open it.

"How is Monsieur Duflot this morning?" asked Roger.

"Not too bad, Monsieur le Gouverneur," the domestic replied. "Monsieur is very anxious to meet our curé."

In a richly-furnished room, a man was lying on a chaise-longue. He might have been fifty. Monsieur Duflot was not one of the castaways of the *Queen of the Waves*.

One day, when Roger and Paul were visiting the land, they had seen a man sitting on a rock, who was examining the Nautilus attentively. As the travelers were about to re-embark, the man came up to them and said; "Is it true that there's a submarine city where one can live in peace, far from the conventions of society, far from all the stupidity and falseness that flourishes on land?"

"Yes, Monsieur, that city exists, and we live in it," Roger and Paul replied. "Would you like to join us?"

"I'd like nothing better than to go with you right now. I've lost all those I loved; I've been betrayed by those who pretended to love me. Now I'm alone, and want to live far from land—whether in the sky or under water, it's all the same to me. I just want to get away from the land, where I've suffered too much."

"Come with us," said the two friends, without further ado. "Come, Monsieur."

"My name is Duflot," the stranger replied.

"A name to cherish," Paul riposted. "A name entirely appropriate to a city beneath the sea. My name is Lamontagne—don't you think it a trifle ill-fitting, for someone living in a submarine?"

"This man is doubtless your servant?" Roger asked, pointing to an individual standing beside Monsieur Duflot. "There's room for him too."

And that was how Monsieur Duflot had become an inhabitant of Nemoville.

The curé spent some time in Monsieur Duflot's home, and promised to come back soon when he left.

They returned to the governor's house, where lunch was served. There was only one submarine that they had not visited. It was in the center of the city and seemed to be as large as the *Nautilus*, but, as neither Roger nor Paul had suggested that they visit it, the priest dared not make the request.

Abbé Bernard was very glad that he had agreed to become the city's curé.

8. A Wreck

Monsieur Richard's funeral having taken place, Marcelle seemed inconsolable—or, like the daughter of Rachel, did not want to be consoled.[63] Only one inhabitant of Nemoville had access to her, and that was Doctor Desmarais. Marcelle and the doctor were supposed to be engaged to be married, but better informed people said that the young woman seemed to fear the physician rather that loving him. Since her father's death, it was said that she was subject to the influence of his personality, which was scarcely compassionate; someone even insinuated that Monsieur Richard's daughter felt a greater affection for the governor, because she occasionally blushed with pleasure on seeing him.

All of that was only rumor, though, and Roger only seemed to show Marcelle the ordinary courtesy of a well brought-up young man. The gossip faded away of its own accord.

Curé Bernard had been in Nemoville for two days when Roger suggested that they undertake a little fishing-trip on the surface of the sea. The curé agreed with pleasure, and all three of them left, for Paul was in the party too; he was rarely apart from Roger.

The fishing was truly miraculous, and Paul maintained that the curé had bought them good luck. When they had a considerable provision of fish of all sorts, they returned to the submarine city.

Turko, the governor's dog, had accompanied his master, as usual. Now, Turko was a good and docile dog, very popular in Nemoville; it was so well-established that Turko never barked without good reason that a howl from the faithful dog

---

[63] In fact, the Biblical Rachel—the mother of Joseph—had no daughter; it was Rachel herself who was said not to want consolation in a passage from St. Mathew's gospel, which refers to her (symbolically) weeping for her children following Herod's massacre of the innocents.

was a certain indication to his master that something extraordinary was happening. Roger and Paul were therefore rather surprised, on their return from the miraculous fishing-trip, to see the dog stand up on the side of the boat and utter a prolonged howl.

"There's something extraordinary," said Roger, immediately.

"Indeed," Paul replied. "Turko's not accustomed to having lugubrious whims."

And they both set about examining the sea attentively.

"Might it be that wreck over there that's causing Turko to howl?" asked Paul, pointing to a vague form floating some distance away.

"Let's go see," said Roger. Speaking to the curé, he added "I always take Turko's warnings seriously, for he's given me a thousand proofs of his keen sense of smell."

They steered the boat toward the wreck, and were soon able to observe that it was a launch that was drifting at the whim of the waves, rudderless.

"An empty launch," said Paul. "Let's tow it back to Nemoville."

"At the moment when the fishing-boat came alongside the launch, however, they perceived, to their surprise, that it was not empty. A woman was lying inside it, motionless. She seemed to be dead, but when they bent down over her they could see that she was still breathing.

They made haste to transport the shipwreck-victim to Nemoville, and went to Marcelle's residence, where the priest suggested that the sick woman be left. Doctor Desmarais was summoned, who gave effective care to the young woman—for she was young, and very beautiful.

The shipwreck victim soon recovered consciousness, and as she could not appropriately be accommodated in the *Nautilus*, Roger asked Marcelle to look after her—which the latter immediately agreed to do. Blushing with pleasure, Marcelle replied that she would be happy to render that service—and she was telling the truth, for she thought that the governor could not fail to take an interest in the woman he had saved from death, and that he would come to see her when the opportunity arose. The young woman's generosity doubtless lost some of its merit in the light of that self-interested thought, but who could blame her, knowing the sentiment that was in her heart?

The stranger was deposited on a bed and abandoned to the care of the old maidservant, while Marcelle went back to the drawing-room, where Roger was awaiting the doctor's verdict before leaving.

He asked Marcelle for permission to come back to see how the invalid was. "Mademoiselle Marcelle," he said, "Will you permit me to come back to obtain news of your protégée?"

It was the first time that he had addressed her by her first name, and that poor girl thought she could see that as an augury of a sentiment responsive to the secret flame in her own soul. Poor Marcelle!

Unconscious of the emotion he had just caused, Roger waited for a reply, which they young woman articulated in a tremulous voice—and Paul, who was present, was the only one who divined the orphan's secret.

"Poor girl!" he murmured, very softly.

9. Gaetane

Marcelle and Gaetane offered strangely contrasting styles of beauty, and that evening, on seeing them both in the little drawing-room of the submarine, it would have been difficult to say which of them was the more beautiful: the blonde Marcelle, with her profusion of golden hair and her lily-and-rose complexion punctuated by her large blue eyes; or the brunette Gaetane, whose dark tresses framed a very pale, symmetrical face, which seemed to brighten her profound brown eyes.

For the first time, a week having gone by since the events that we have recounted, the two young women were spending the evening together in the drawing-room.

"Your reproaches make me feel bad," said the soft and musical voice of the stranger, "but while I feel very grateful to the man who saved my life, I can't help feeling a genuine malaise when he looks at me or speaks to me. I don't hate him, no matter what you say—that would be an ingratitude of which I'm incapable, but he frightens me, really and truly."

"Doctor Desmarais frightens you! But he's extremely generous to you."

The reader will already have understood from this little dialogue that Marcelle had tried to give Gaetane the impression that the doctor had saved her life. To deceive herself, Marcelle told herself that the doctor really had saved her life, since she had barely been breathing when the governor had confided her to his care.

The day before, the physician has spent some time with the young women, and had shown himself particularly amiable with Gaetane. He had surprised her slightly by asking her, in the course of the conversation: "Was your father in the navy, Mademoiselle?"

She had replied that her adoptive father was indeed Captain Laurent, and that had appeared to interest the physician so keenly that she had asked him spontaneously: "Did you know him, Doctor?"

The doctor had said, hurriedly: "No, no—it's a simple coincidence of names that led me to ask the question."

He said goodbye almost immediately thereafter, but as he was leaving he made a sign to Marcelle, who followed him. They spoke together for some time, and when the physician went he said to the young woman: "Don't forget that everything depends on you, Marcelle; I promise you that you'll be the governor's wife within three years if you follow my advice, and I'll marry Captain Laurent's daughter. In serving my interests you'll also be serving your own."

Marcelle made a resigned gesture, and when she went back in, her red eyes revealed that she had been crying.

She had scarcely taken her place beside Gaetane again when the old maidservant came in, carrying the governor's card on a tray. Marcelle blushed so violently that her companion asked her what was wrong.

"It's the governor of Nemoville asking to be admitted," said Marcelle, adding: "He often calls." Lowering her eyes, as if she were afraid that Gaetane might detect the lie, she went on; "I hope he'll like you...because of me."

"I understand," her companion said, with a mischievous smile. "He's your fiancé."

Marcelle did not correct her; she pretended that she had not heard, and rose to her feet to go to meet Roger as he came in. She introduced Gaetane, for whom the young man's eyes had seemed to be searching as soon as he crossed the threshold, and all three sat down and spent an hour together, chatting gaily.

Gaetane, who had recovered all the freshness of her youth, was truly dazzling with beauty, while Roger gazed at her, blushing and slightly timid.

"I hope you're bored in Nemoville, Mademoiselle?"

"Oh no!" she replied. "It's very nice here; I feel safe with Marcelle."

"I don't want Gaetane to leave me," Marcelle added. "I've been so lonely, since my father died." As she said that she looked at Roger, searching his eyes for a flame she did not see. He was listening to her while looking at her companion.

When Roger went back to the *Nautilus*, he was distracted and preoccupied—which was not usual for him. As he went in he met Paul, and told him where he had been.

"I'd already guessed by your expression," the other said to him. "An expression I'd never seen before that pretty shipwreck-victim arrived in Nemoville."

"What do you mean?" asked Roger, stopping in front of his friend.

"I mean that you're in love, and that I've known since the first day. That's all."

10. A Glance at Nemoville and its Inhabitants

Two months have gone by. Anyone casting a glance at Nemoville would have envied the lot of its inhabitants. Not all the Nemovillians were happy, though—the governor, to begin with, who had lost much of his insouciance and good humor. He had not made much progress with regard to Gaetane; on the contrary, she seemed colder and more reserved than ever toward him. One day he had tried to kiss her hand; she had withdrawn it indignantly, and said to him, angrily: "How dare you!" Then she had left the room before he could ask for an explanation of her strange conduct. Since then she had avoided him ostentatiously.

On the other hand, it was no secret in Nemoville that Doctor Desmarais was very assiduous toward the young stranger; he was often seen heading for Marcelle's dwelling, but everyone knew that it was no longer Mademoiselle Richard that he was thinking about.

One day, when Doctor Desmarais was with Gaetane, he had got down on his knees and made a declaration of love so unexpected that she was nonplussed. As she made as if to get to her feet and escape from the doctor's protestations, the door to the drawing-room had opened and Marcelle came in, accompanied by Roger, who stood there dumbfounded by the sight of the romantic spectacle offered by Gaetane and the physician.

"I'll talk to you in my boudoir," Marcelle had said, laughing. "It would be a pity to disturb such a sweet tête-à-tête."

Roger had replied, coldly, that he had only come to obtain news of the ladies, and that he had urgent business—and he had departed without saying a word to Gaetane, which had made her very unhappy. He had not been aback to Marcelle's abode since.

As for Marcelle, she seemed to be increasingly under the dominion of Doctor Desmarais, and the latter seemed more active and craftier than ever.

Paul Lamontagne also had fits of sadness of which he alone knew the secret.

Abbé Bernard witnessed his friends' sadness, but he kept silent, not daring to provoke confidences that were not offered freely.

11. The Mysterious Submarine

It was Christmas Eve. It was exactly two months since Abbé Bernard had accepted the position of curé of Nemoville. For some time he had been very busy. Since his arrival in the submarine city, the curé had taken it upon himself to organize a chapel in which he would be able to say mass every morning. A submarine that had been abandoned by a family whose members had preferred to return to the surface had been put at his disposal. It was not very comfortable there, especially on Sundays, for the inhabitants of Nemoville liked to attend mass, and some of them were obliged to hear the divine office from the corridor.

On that twenty-fourth of December the abbé was very busy, because he had been asked to celebrate midnight mass and he wanted to give that mass as much solemnity as the location permitted.

At about ten o'clock, Roger said to the abbé: "Would you care to take a little walk with Paul and me?"

The curé accepted, and Roger led him toward the city center.

Everyone in Nemoville seemed to be cheerful that evening. People were strolling around the corridor-streets, all lit by electricity.

They went into a submarine that the priest had not yet visited. The priest was not curious, but the mystery of that submarine, in which no one appeared to be resident, had sometimes intrigued him.

"Go in first, Monsieur l'Abbé," Roger said to him—and the cure, having gone into the interior of the submarine, uttered an exclamation of surprise and joy. "How beautiful it is!" he said. "It's magnificent."

"It's Nemoville's Christmas present to its curé," the governor replied. "Do you like your church, Monsieur l'Abbé?"

The abbé wept with joy. The sound of footsteps became audible in the corridors; it was the Nemovillians, who were coming to present their homage to their curé, and Roger, on behalf of everyone, offered the priest the submarine church.

"We've all worked on it," he explained. "Some carved the statues, others drew up the plans, and even the children did their bit, collecting the seashells that decorate the main altar on the shore."

The abbé was visibly moved; he could only repeat: "Thank you, thank you, my good friends!"

It was a very strange spectacle, the scene that unfolded that Christmas Eve beneath the ocean waves. The great transatlantic liners passing some distance overhead did not contain a more joyful and carefree crowd.

Roger gave the signal for everyone to return home, requesting that they all come back when the bell sounded for midnight mass.

Abbé Bernard and Roger were the last to leave the church. They headed for the Nautilus, where the abbé felt the need to rest after so much excitement.

12. Midnight Mass

At a quarter to midnight the church bell of Nemoville made itself heard. Immediately, the streets filled up with all the inhabitants, who headed for the church. No one wanted to miss the first midnight mass. Soon, all the residences, with the exception of those which contained sick people, were empty.

The organ from the *Nautilus* had been transported to the church, and a fine mass was in preparation, for there was no lack of musicians in Nemoville. When the governor and his secretary had taken their placed in the emblazoned benches that had been prepared for them, a skillful hand played the first chords of a Christmas carol. At that moment, the chapel door opened, and Monsieur Duflot appeared, in a wheelchair pushed by this faithful domestic. Roger went to meet him and installed him next to his seat.

A soft and vibrant voice then intoned the first words of the ever-beautiful song *Minuit, Chrétiens.* On hearing that voice, the governor shivered and his neighbor placed his hand on his heart as if to stop it beating. That voice was Gaetane's. When the pious song had ended, Monsieur Duflot leaned close to Roger's ear and asked him: "Who was that singing?"

"It's Mademoiselle Laurent," the governor replied.

The two men did not speak again for as long as the mass lasted, but when they came out of the chapel Monsieur Duflot picked up the conversation where he had left it.

"That young woman has a truly angelic voice, don't you think, Monsieur le Gouverneur?"

"Angelic indeed," Roger replied. He added: "That young woman's entire personality has something ethereal, almost supernatural, about it. Nothing about her seems to resemble other women. You'll observe that, Monsieur Duflot, when you get to know her. To make use of an old cliché, she seems to be an angel astray on the earth."

"When an angel descends to earth," Monsieur Duflot went on, smiling, "it's generally to make some mortal happy." He looked at Roger slyly.

Roger smiled, and replied: "Or unhappy."

Monsieur Duflot did not reply, but thought he had divined that Roger was already in love, and without hope.

When the first chords of the old carol *Il est né le Divin Enfant* had sounded it had been Paul's turn to feel moved by the singer's voice, for he had recognized that of Jeanne, the daughter of Doctor de Chantal, with whom he was in love.

After the mass, all the people mentioned in this chapter, except for the two young women, Gaetane and Jeanne, gathered at the governor's house. The curé was also among the guests.

Contrary to his habit, Monsieur Duflot had accepted the invitation to dine in company, which he did not generally do. Monsieur Duflot was not a cheerful guest, but he had the kindness to keep his incurable sadness to himself, and as he had traveled a great deal he was very interested to hear conversation. He was not one of those who seemed to have seen everything through a magnifying glass and take their listeners for simpletons; he spoke when he was asked a question and was able to remain silent when appropriate.

"Monsieur le Curé," Monsieur Duflot asked, all of a sudden, "does that young woman who sung *Minuit, Chrétiens* so well have relatives in Nemoville?"

"Mademoiselle Durand is an orphan," the priest replied.

"Durand? Isn't her name Laurent?"

"Indeed," Roger replied. "Her name is Gaetane Laurent."

"Gaetane! Her name is Gaetane?" queried Monsieur Duflot, interestedly.

And the abbé said, almost at the same time: "Laurent? Her name is Laurent? Are you quite certain, Roger?"

"Absolutely certain," Roger replied, "since she told me herself. She's the daughter of Captain Laurent."

The curé was preoccupied throughout the rest of the dinner, and although he tried to seem cheerful, Monsieur Duflot was distracted and thoughtful.

At about five o'clock in the morning, the guests retired and went to get a little sleep.

13. Gaetane Looks for Employment

Christmas had been over for two days and Nemoville had resumed its customary appearance. Abbé Bernard, for one reason or another, had not seen Gaetane again. The young woman eventually anticipated of the priest's desire to have a conversation with her about her family.

On the twenty-seventh of December, when the abbé went into the sacristy, he saw the young woman waiting for him.

"I'm glad to see you," the curé said, smiling, "because I wanted to talk to you—but first, tell me what brought you here."

"I've been in Nemoville for two months now," Gaetane replied, timidly. "Two months of idleness—but I don't like idleness, and I've come to ask you whether you can help me to find some sort of employment. Marcelle is very good, and I know that she'll be disappointed to see me go, but I have to. I wouldn't make the sacrifice of separating myself from her without good reasons, because I like her very much, for all the kindness she's show me since I've been here."

"You're doing the right thing, my child; idleness is bad for you. I'll try to find you some employment immediately."

"Thank you," said Gaetane, effusively, getting up to leave.

"I thought that your name was Durand," the priest said to her, retaining her momentarily. He added: "It's Roger who corrected me yesterday evening."

At Roger's name, the young woman blushed violently, and the priest noticed it.

Good, good! he thought. *Love has made a victim of that candid child.*

"The name Laurent is that of my adoptive father," Gaetane said. "I didn't know any other family—although I was five or six years old when Captain Laurent adopted me, and I have vague memories of my childhood before then. I remember having seen my mother on her death-bed, and look—I can't forget her features, for here's her image, which I wear next to my heart."

As she said this she showed the priest a little locket, which contained a miniature of a woman: a young and beautiful woman, who was smiling.

"I also remember that my father took me with him on a journey. After that, I only remember the time I spent with my adoptive parents: Captain Laurent, a coarse man who always spoke to me harshly, and his wife, a poor creature who trembled before him but who was good to me. That poor woman did everything she could for me; she was the one who taught me to read and write, and everything she knew. I was sixteen when I lost her, and I mourned her sincerely, or I'd lost the only friend I had then."

"Poor child!" murmured the priest.

"Captain Laurent didn't make life too hard for me, though, until the tenth of October last. Pierre Laurent, his son, arrived aboard the ship that had become my home since my adoption by the captain. I scarcely knew Pierre, for his father had sent him to a distant boarding-school at the age of ten, and he had only come aboard occasionally.

"I hadn't seen him since the death of his mother. He had never inspired any great sympathy in me, because he was cruel and stupid, but on seeing the young man again, fat, common, and arrogant, I found him veritably repulsive. Unfortunately, he was smitten with me, and asked me to marry him. As you have doubtless guessed, I refused. Without paying any heed to my refusal, however, he and his father fixed our marriage date, and told me that I had to comply. They had chosen the twenty-fourth of October.

"I won't tell you the story of all that I had to suffer under Captain Laurent's roof after Pierre's arrival. On the twenty-third, the eve of the date fixed for our marriage, Pierre assembled his friends to 'bury his bachelor life,' as he put it. In my cabin I heard the songs and remarks of those wretches, and I could, so to speak, follow the phases of their drunkenness—for that 'burial' was no ordinary party, I assure you.

"At about two o'clock in the morning, I heard no more and I concluded that they were all drunk and asleep. I left my cabin on tiptoe, and went as far as the door of the ward-room. I listened, and opened the door slightly. I was not mistaken. Pierre and his guests were sleeping off the wine, some lying on the table, others underneath it, a few on the floor or in armchairs. I decided not to miss the chance of salvation that was offered to me. I ran on to the deck and jumped into the lifeboat that was in tow behind the ship, and fled as fast as I could row.

"For two days my launch floated on the ocean; the hope of encountering a rescue vessel gave me courage. In the end, though, my strength failed me; the oars fell from my hands and my launch became a wreck. I lay down in the bottom, no longer having the strength to support myself, and awaited death without regret...

"I fainted from weakness and fatigue, and I don't know how long my boat drifted before being picked up by Doctor Desmarais, who saved my life."

"Doctor Desmarais!" said the priest, surprised. "Who told you that it was Doctor Desmarais who saved your life?"

"It was Marcelle!" Gaetane replied, surprised in her turn by the abbé's question.

"Mademoiselle Marcelle is ill-informed, from what I can see," the priest went on. "I witnessed your rescue, my child, and I know full well that Doctor Desmarais was not there." The priest smiled. "But what does it matter—the essential thing is the good fortune of our being saved."

For Gaetane, however, it was very important that it was not the doctor who had rendered her that service. She experienced a kind of relief at the thought of owing nothing to that man, toward whom she had a secret antipathy—for which she had reproached herself as ingratitude since Marcelle had told her that he was the one who had saved her life.

"Who was it, then, who plucked me from the waves?" she asked, anxiously and hesitantly.

"It was the governor himself, my child," the priest replied. "We were coming back from a fishing trip—Roger, Paul and I—when we perceived your launch. We thought at first that it was empty, but we'd decided to tow it back to the *Nautilus* anyway, and it was only when we were close enough to hitch it up that we saw that there was a shipwreck-victim aboard."

Gaetane had difficulty hiding her emotion on learning that it was Roger who had saved her life. She left the sacristy less unhappy than she had been when she came in.

14. The Chantal Hospital

Doctor Desmarais was not the only physician in Nemoville. Doctor de Chantal, although he was not in practice, also soothed human suffering. His age and his infirmity prevented him from going, as he once had, to the homes of invalids, but people still came to consult him, for he had retained the confidence of his patients.

Doctor de Chantal was a specialist in surgery, and he had made his residence into a hospital. His daughter Jeanne assisted him in his charitable work.

If we have barely mentioned Jeanne de Chantal before now, it is not because she does not merit more scrupulous attention. On the contrary, the discreet role that she was content to play in Nemoville, between her father and his patients, had not prevented her hand being sought in marriage several times already by the most eligible bachelors in the city. Jeanne did not seem to be in any hurry to leave her father, however—or perhaps she had not yet met the candidate of her choice.

For Doctor de Chantal, his daughter's conduct was no mystery; he knew that she was in love with Paul, the governor's secretary, and he fully approved of her choice, which matched his own, for the doctor loved Paul like a son and he knew that he would not be able o find a better husband for his child.

Doctor de Chantal's hospital had become insufficient for the number of invalids. Paul suggested that he take over the former chapel and convert it into a hospital. There was only one corridor separating that submarine chapel from the physician's dwelling. It seemed to be a good idea, and it was immediately adopted. A few days later, Doctor de Chantal was the happiest man in Nemoville when he was able to hang a placard on the door of the former chapel on which one could read, in capital letters: CHANTAL HOSPITAL.

With its hospital, its church and its numerous submarine residences, Nemoville now had the appearance of a genuine city. Roger was delighted with that; it seemed him that he had realized the unrealizable.

Every day brought some happy occurrence in the mysterious city, but the greatest of all, without any doubt, was the marriage of Paul and Jeanne de Chantal, which was to be the first one to be celebrated in the submarine city. Roger wanted it to be a celebration worthy of the amity that bound him to his friend. The whole city came up to the surface for the occasion, and the submarines were decorated with flags as if to announced Paul's happiness to the heavens. They spent three days in the sun; then the city dived beneath the waves again.

Curé Bernard took great deal of interest in the Chantal hospital; he spent an hour there every day in the company of Jeanne and the doctor—and it was during one of his visits that he suggested that the doctor take Gaetane into his service. The proposition was accepted with enthusiasm on the physician's part as well as Jeanne's, who was delighted with the idea of having a companion of her own age alongside her. She wanted Gaetane to move in with her that same evening.

There were, in consequence, no two happier people in Nemoville that day than the curé and his protégée.

15. A Social Gathering in Nemoville

The marriage of Paul and Jeanne was celebrated with as much pomp as the conditions of life in a submarine city permitted. The little church was decked out with flags; there was a banquet at the governor's residence, and there was dancing in the evening to the sounds of an orchestra.

Marcelle, who had been invited to the wedding, and had hardly been disposed to refuse, wanted to have the first dance with the governor. She considered that honor to be her due. Gaetane, who had avoided meeting Roger for some time, had not, however, been able to dispense with attending Jeanne's marriage and the celebrations that would be its consequences. She was therefore present at the ball. As soon as the orchestra started playing, Doctor Desmarais went to bow to her and beg her to great him the dance in question.

She made an excuse. "I can't dance," she said.

"Come anyway," the physician persisted. "It will increase my pleasure to give you your first lessons."

"Excuse me," she said, "but I'm obliged to refuse you that pleasure."

The physician bit his lip in chagrin, and went to ask Marcelle to dance with him—but Marcelle, who had Roger in her sights, replied that she was taken.

Marcelle felt her heat beat faster when she saw Roger got up and come toward her; she had already prepared a smile that she believed to be irresistible, but the governor bowed to her without pausing and headed toward Gaetane, to whom he spoke—and Marcelle felt tears of range come into her eyes when she perceived Doctor Desmarais, who as watching her from a short distance away.

She saw Gaetane reply to Roger with a negative gesture, and the latter take the young woman's hand with an insistent gesture. Then she saw them, a moment later, face to face with Paul and Jeanne.

There was a suffocating warmth in the ward-room of the *Nautilus*. After the dance, Roger proposed to Jeanne that they should seek to refresh themselves by taking a walk in the corridor-tubes that formed Nemoville's streets. She accepted. He took her to the Chantal dwelling, which had been transformed into a greenhouse for the occasion. It was difficult to conserve the idea of being under water on seeing the profusion of plants that had been disposed within that submarine dwelling; one might just as well have been in an Oriental garden

Roger's first words were to compliment his companion.

"One can't dance badly, with such a good conductor," Gaetane replied, simply.

"It wasn't without apprehension that I solicited the favor of the first dance from you, for I saw you refuse Doctor Desmarais," Roger said, having decided not to miss the opportunity to find out whether there was anything to the rumors circulating in Nemoville with regard to Gaetane and the doctor.

"I'm scarcely disposed to grant the smallest favor to that man," the young woman replied.

"But what about the story that's going round Nemoville that you're engaged to the doctor?"

"Well, Monsieur le Gouverneur, if that story is going round the city, it only proves that people in Nemoville are very badly informed. I was led to believe that it was him who saved my life, and out of gratitude, I tolerated his presence and tried to overcome the instinctive and inexplicable repulsion he inspires in me. That, undoubtedly, is what the people of Nemoville misinterpreted." She added: "I have no sympathy for Doctor Desmarais, and I hope that he has no interest in me."

"It would be necessary not to know you, Mademoiselle, in order not to be interested in you," Roger said, gallantly.

Gaetane smiled at the compliment, and replied: "I thought that flattery only dwelt on land. The young woman rose to her feet. "But let's go back to the ballroom—your fiancée must be worried by your absence, Monsieur le Gouverneur."

"My fiancée!" said Roger, surprised. "Who is this fiancée you are telling me about, whom I have not chosen?" Laughing, he added: "I thought that the governor of Nemoville was at liberty to offer his hand and his heart to the wife of his choice."

"And the wife of your choice isn't Marcelle, Monsieur le Gouverneur?"

"The wife of my choice, Gaetane," said Roger, calling the young woman by her Christian name for the first time, "from the first day I saw her, is you. Would you like to be my wife?"

Gaetane was so surprised and so emotional that she was unable to answer.

He took her in his arms, and in a very faint whisper, she replied: "Yes."

"Ah! I suspected that it would end up like this," said a joyful voice close at hand. It was that of Abbé Bernard.

"Will you bless our engagement?" Roger asked him.

"Gladly," the priest replied. "When will the wedding be?"

"In a month's time?" said Roger, interrogating his fiancée with his gaze.

"In a month's time," she replied.

The newly-engaged couple and the curé went out of the greenhouse together and headed toward the ward-room.

When they turned into a lateral corridor a man came out of the shadows, raised his fist in the direction of the fiancés and murmured through clenched teeth: "In a month's time...we'll see about that."

The man who had spoken was Doctor Desmarais.

16. The Portrait

The curé of Nemoville had no presbytery as yet; he was still living in Roger's abode. The *Nautilus* was so large and so comfortably fitted out that there was room for several people there without them getting in one another's way. In any case, the priest was in no hurry to get away from Roger, for whom he had a great affection, and the long conversations they had together were a distraction that both men appreciated.

Roger had put a part of the *Nautilus* at the curé's disposal, and the ward-room served them as a common room. One morning when the priest was alone there, plunged in serious reflections, someone knocked on the door. It was a domestic, who had brought a letter from Monsieur Duflot. It read as follows:

Monsieur le Curé, I have been confined to my room for two days, and as I have a great desire to see you, I beg you to do me the favor of coming to my home as soon as you can.

The curé, who had nothing urgent to do at that moment, decided to answer Monsieur Duflot's invitation immediately.

"It's very good of you to reply to my invitation so soon," Monsieur Duflot said to him, on seeing him. "I was bored, and I took the liberty of asking you to give me a little of your time."

The two men started chatting about the city's news—for there are current events even in Nemoville, news of which is transmitted from one submarine to another as it is transmitted from one house or street to the next in a terrestrial city.

"Great preparations are being made for the governor's marriage," the abbé said. "Paul left for the land this morning; he won't be back until tomorrow."

"She's making a fine marriage, that young stranger," Monsieur Duflot said, "not to mention that Roger is the most good-hearted man I know. If I had a daughter, I'd want that young man for a son-in-law." Monsieur Duflot's voice trembled as he added the final words.

The abbé was about to make some observation when he noticed the portrait of a young and smiling woman hanging over the bed. He moved closer and looked attentively at the charming face, which immediately reminded him of the one he had seen in Gaetane's locket.

"That portrait is of my wife," said Monsieur Duflot, who had followed the priest's gaze. "My poor Gaetane, so soon removed from my tenderness."

"Your wife's name was Gaetane?" the priest queried, struck by the resemblance and the coincidence of names. "Permit me to ask a question, Monsieur Duflot: is not the name of Duflot a veil to hide your identity? Tell me, is your name not Jean Demers?"

"How do you know that?" cried Monsieur Duflot. "Who told you who I am?"

"The man who told me is no longer alive, and you must pardon him," the curé began. "Here, he bore the name Richard, but he did not have time to tell me his real name; death sealed his lips before he was able to tell me the truth."

The priest then told him about his meeting with Gaetane, and the resemblance between the two miniatures.

"I can no longer have any doubt," said Monsieur Duflot, excited and tremulous. "That young woman is my Gaetane; I understand the emotion that gripped me when I heard her sing during the midnight mass. It was the voice of blood that spoke within me. She has her mother's voice. You've seen her, Monsieur le Curé—does she resemble her mother? Does she resemble this portrait?"

"Yes, she has the same delicacy in her features and the same softness of expression; this image might be that of the young woman, in a few years' time."

"How impatient I am to see her—when shall I have the pleasure?"

"In half an hour," the priest replied, getting to his feet. "I'll go look for her right away."

"How good you are, Monsieur le Curé."

17. The Catastrophe

It was the eve of the day fixed for the wedding of Gaetane and Roger. The young woman was no longer living in the home of Doctor de Chantal; she had moved into her father's dwelling on the same day that she had found him again, and no longer left him except to spend a few hours at the hospital when her services were required.

Monsieur Demers—who had resumed his real name since his daughter had been restored to him—seemed ten years younger. He had decided to take up residence with the young couple immediately after the marriage. In the meantime, Gaetane scarcely left her father's side, she felt so happy at no longer being without a family.

For once, fortune seemed to be smiling on all the inhabitants of Nemoville.

Monsieur Demers had got out of bed and as comfortably installed in an armchair. Gaetane was beside him, along with Doctor Desmarais, who seemed not to be despairing, in spite of the events that were impending. The somber individual had become more sullen as the date of the wedding approached; sometimes, however, he wore an enigmatic smile and even pronounced words that would have seemed to bode ill if anyone had listened to them.

At five o'clock in the evening someone knocked on the door, which was immediately opened, and Jeanne Lamontagne came in without ceremony. She bowed to Monsieur Demers, embraced Gaetane and said a cold *bonjour* to the doctor.

"I've come to steal Gaetane from you, Monsieur Demers," she said. "Paul has gone ashore and won't be back until tomorrow, my father's spending the night at the hospital, and I'll be condemned to spend all the time alone if you refuse me Gaetane's company."

"It's understood, then," Monsieur Demers replied. "My daughter will spend the time with you."

"I'll be back early," Gaetane added, looking at her father.

Soon, the two young women left together, after having embraced Monsieur Demers, who watched them leave with a sight sadness.

Doctor Desmarais took his leave in his turn. A malevolent smile curled his lips. In the corridor, he shook his fist in the direction in which the two women had gone.

"The bells of Nemoville will ring in two days, but not to announce a marriage; they'll sound a knell, my disdainful pretty." The physician's face was horrible at that moment, and if the person to whom the threat was addressed had been able to see it, she would have trembled.

Gaetane and Jeanne went to the hospital, where they stayed with Doctor de Chantal until nine o'clock, and then went back to their dwelling. At about eleven o'clock, they went to bed.

At midnight, all Nemoville seemed to be asleep.

It was at that moment that a shadow surged forth in the corridor that linked Doctor de Chantal's dwelling to the hospital, and made its way into the submarine where they two young women were asleep.

That sinister shadow was Doctor Desmarais. He remained in the engine-room for a quarter of an hour, and emerged murmuring; "Monsieur le Gouverneur, your beautiful fiancée now belongs to death."

That evening, Roger and he priest had stayed up late. They had been making plans for the future. It was scarcely an hour since they had parted and they were both in bed in their rooms when, all of a sudden, Turko—who slept in his master's bedroom—started howling lamentably. Roger, waking up with a start, tried in vain to impose silence on him; the dog persisted in moaning, as he very rarely did, and only when something tragic was happening.

Roger got up and made a tour of the *Nautilus*, but seeing nothing abnormal, he called to the animal and made him lie down by threatening him.

The following morning, at about six o'clock, Roger was woken up again by hurried knocking on his door.

"Quickly, quickly, Monsieur le Gouverneur!" someone shouted outside. "There's been an accident."

Roger opened his door, and found himself in the presence of two men, who were carrying the unconscious Doctor de Chantal.

"We found the doctor in the corridor. He seemed to be dead."

Doctor gave the physician some care, however; he soon opened his eyes again and seemed very surprised to find himself aboard the *Nautilus*.

"My daughter! My daughter!" he said, immediately.

"What's the matter?" Roger asked. "Where's Madame Lamontagne?"

"Alas! Alas!" moaned the poor father.

He explained that, after the two women had left him the previous day, he had stayed at the hospital, but when he tried to return home in the morning, he had been unable to open the door of the corridor that linked the two submarines. Looking through the porthole, he had then observed, to his horror, that the other submarine as no longer there.

Roger tried to reassure the poor father by telling him that if the submarine had been detached from the corridor, it could not be far away, its engine not being activated. "Let's depart immediately, and we'll soon catch up with it."

The physician did not appear to be as confident. Three submarines set off in search of the two women, but all the searches, whether on the surface of the sea or beneath the waves, were unsuccessful.

Roger, the curé and Monsieur Demers, who had taken part in the searches, returned to the *Nautilus* discouraged. They decided to wait for Paul's return to take further measures and organize searches on a larger scale.

The suffering of the two fathers and the fiancé is easily imaginable. They were no longer speaking to one another—what could they say?—but none of them thought of hiding his tears.

18. Paul Lamontagne's Return

Paul Lamontagne had completed his mission ashore and came back to the submarine city with a joyful heart. He had seemed to be away from his beloved Jeanne a long time, and he was anxious to see her again. He was looking forward to laughing with her about the presentiment she had had, before his departure. She had wept when he left, and that had made him regret not taking her with him, but he knew that Doctor de Chantal relied upon his daughter to help him care for his patients, and the young couple had made the sacrifice of their first separation—which was, in any case, only to last for a matter of hours.

Paul was singing happily, at the top of his voice:

Sail, frail cockleshell
Over the blue waves
Take me back to one
Who can make me happy.
Sail, sail, frail cockleshell
Sail over the blue waves

Sail, frail cockleshell,
Over the blue waves.
The sea is calm and lovely,
The sun radiant.
Sail, sail, frail cockleshell
Sail over the blue waves

Sail, frail cockleshell
Over the blue waves.
Faithful beside the hearth
Soft-eyed Jeanne awaits me.
Sail, sail, frail cockleshell
Sail over the blue waves.[64]

Shall I go straight home? he asked himself. *Or shall I go see Roger?*

He decided on the latter, and headed for the *Nautilus*.

Nemoville offered a truly singular appearance, floating as it was beneath the surface, and Paul could not help noticing that, although he was used to the spectacle.

"But we're happy here," he murmured, by way of conclusion to his thought, "and our little submarine kingdom is worth as much as all the domains of the land."

---

[64] My poetic talents were unequal to the task of reproducing the rhyme-scheme and eccentric scansion of this song without distorting the meaning of the words out of all recognition, so I have been content to translate the meaning of each line literally.

Paul reached the *Nautilus* as went in without having himself announced. To begin with, he only saw Roger, whom he greeted joyfully—then his eyes made a tour of the ward-room, and he perceived the curé and Doctor de Chantal, who were looking at him with sad expressions that struck him hard.

"What's happening?" he asked. "Why these distressed expressions? One would think that some disaster had occurred."

"A disaster has indeed occurred," the curé replied. "Be brave, Paul! In any case, all hope is not lost—we'll find them."

"In Heaven's name, explain yourself. What's happened?"

Roger told him about the accident that had separated the two submarines used by Doctor de Chantal."

"Jeanne!" was all that Paul said, as if all his grief were contained in that beloved name.

"Let's get under way immediately. Let's separate and search the ocean in every direction. We must find them, at all costs."

All the submersible launches set off immediately on the hunt, after having been provided with food-supplies for several days. The curé, not wishing to abandon those who were remaining behind, blessed the travelers and said: "May God guide you to them."

19. A Terrible Awakening

Having stayed up rather late, Gaetane and Jeanne did not take long to go to sleep. Gaetane had retaken possession of the bedroom she had occupied when she was living in the physician's house, which everyone continued to call "Gaetane's room."

At about two o'clock in the morning the young woman woke up with a start; she had just dreamed that Roger had been in danger, and that she had tried to save him without being able to do so.

What a dream! she said to herself, and tried to go back to sleep. Then she felt the trepidation of the vessel, which told her that it was moving. She was astonished by that singularity. Why had she and her friend not been warned that Nemoville was going to change location tonight?

Slightly anxious, she got up and checked the time on her watch. It was only two o'clock in the morning. The inhabitants of Nemoville had not started traveling in this unexpected fashion since Gaetane had been living among them, but she was unfamiliar with the habits of the Nemovillians. She looked out of one of the submarine's portholes, and was able to ascertain that he vessel was indeed moving.

What does it matter, she said to herself, *whether we're stationary or in motion, since those who love us are with us?* Gaetane had not yet realized that disaster had overtaken them.

She heard Jenna calling from the next room: "The boat's moving, Gaetane—did you know that we were due to move tonight?"

"No," she replied. "Is it usual for the people of Nemoville to change location unexpectedly, like this?"

"No," said Jeanne, "and that worries me. It seems to me that something extraordinary is happening. Let's get up right away and go see what my father has to say."

They got up and got dressed. As they went to open the door to the corridor linking the two submarines they instinctively looked through the porthole in the door and saw, to their horror, instead of the line of the corridor, always lit by electricity, the sea washing over the thick glass of their narrow window.

They uttered simultaneous screams; they had just realized what had happened. The submarine was alone on its sinister voyage.

"If we'd opened that door we'd be dead!" Jeanne exclaimed, making sure that the door was solidly bolted and proof against the pressure of the waves.

"Heaven protected us," said Gaetane. "If you'd opened the door, the water would have rushed into the submarine and that would have been the end of us."

"We need to go up to the surface," Jeanne said, immediately. "But how do we operate an engine with which neither one of us is familiar?"

They both began courageously to study the engine. Alas, the task was hard, and the poor women were in a state of mind that made it seem harder still. Finally, they had the satisfaction of seeing the submarine rise up and part the waters, and they saw the sky. They were then in less danger, and were able to scan the horizon in search of some vessel that might come to their aid.

It was, however, in vain that they searched the horizon for hours on end; the sea seemed to be deserted in this region—and the submarine continued to cut through the waves rapidly, carrying the poor women further away from those whom they loved.

20. Desperate Hours

"Gaetane," said Jeanne, "we mustn't forget to keep our strength up; we'll probably need it for a long time yet. Let's get some food."

"I can't think about anything else but our peril," her companion replied, "but I'll follow your advice, Jeanne; you're more courageous than me, I can see—you're not allowing yourself to get depressed. Alas, shall we ever see those that we love again?" And Gaetane dissolved in tears.

"Don't despair, my friend," her companion said. "It's certain that Paul and Roger will do everything possible to find us. They must already be searching for us—and perhaps they're not very far away—who knows? Let's take turns to watch the sea, in order not to miss any chance of salvation. While one of us rests, the other will keep watch, until we've been picked up by a rescue vessel or found by our friends."

Jeanne began her watch first; she insisted that her companion go and get a little rest—and Gaetane, worn out by emotion and fatigue, eventually went to sleep: a benevolent slumber that brought a measure of forgetfulness and a restoration of strength.

That day was terribly long for the two women; interrogating the sea with their anxious eyes, they saw nothing appear on the waves that might offer them even the illusion of salvation.

Jeanne, who had continued her watch until dusk, saw that the sky was blackening and that the waves were becoming more menacing; she understood that a storm was brewing. She was alarmed by that, because it greatly increased the all-too-evident danger they were in. The boat pitched and rolled, like a wreck.

It was time to wake Gaetane for her to take her turn on sentry duty, but Jeanne hesitated to tear her away from benevolent sleep. She waited another hour; the storm continued to build.

Finally, Gaetane awoke of her own accord, at the sound of thunder and the dull roar of the waves shaking the submarine. She came to join her friend, reproaching her mildly for letting her sleep for too long; then Jeanne went to lie down in her turn. She was literally exhausted by fatigue and anxiety.

Gaetane sat next to her in order to keep watch, for she felt so nervous that she would not have been able to remain alone some distance away.

The night that she spent was difficult, to say the least; as was understandable, the blackest thoughts assailed her mind. She had lost all hope of seeing those she loved again, and she expected to feel the submarine break up on some rock just beneath the surface of the water. Only one thing seemed certain to her, and that was that she and her friend were irredeemably lost.

Toward morning, the tempest became so frightful that nothing in the submarine remained in place any longer; the crockery was smashed, the furniture fell over, and the disaster inside the boat combined its horror with that outside.

Jeanne woke up. All day the tempest raged; the young women were obliged to tie themselves to their beds in order not to roll on to the floor. The submarine sometimes seemed to climb mountains and then slide into an abyss, but it kept moving; the wretch who had wanted to send Jeanne and Gaetane to their doom had prepared his vengeance well.

At about four o'clock in the morning, the two women experienced a terrible shock. It seemed to them that the submarine had just crashed into a rock. The vessel remained stationary for a moment; the poor women went to look out of one of the portholes and saw that the submarine had, in fact, touched a rock.

Thinking that it was the end of everything for them, they waited in silence for death to take them. They were soon able to observe, however, that the submarine was moving again; they risked going outside and perceived that the storm was easing.

It died down as swiftly as it had begun. Two hours later, the ocean was calm and the sky clear. Gaetane and Jeanne wanted to take stock of their situation, and, frightful as their distress was, they began to hope again.

They thought that Paul and Roger would not take long to find them, even though they had little doubt that they had traveled many leagues. They almost forgot their suffering in thinking about the anguish that their loved ones must be experiencing.

Alas, they had not yet realized the full extent of a new danger that was threatening them: the submarine, holed, was slowly filling with water. They noticed it because of the noise of the water filtering through a narrow fissure. Courageously, they set about baling out the water, but their combined efforts were no match for the sea, which seemed to be gradually swallowing the submarine. It slowly sank, while continuing its deathward course, more slowly now.

Suddenly, Gaetane called to Jeanne and said: "Look at those albatrosses. Isn't that a sign that we're not far from land?"

"God willing," said Jeanne, unenthusiastically, for discouragement was overtaking her—which was not astonishing, after so much suffering.

Gaetane's anticipation was realized, however. Soon, the two friends perceived land, and the boat seemed, miraculously, to be heading that way. A few minutes later, it ran aground without a shock, as if fatigued. The water had invaded the engine-room.

21. A Bandit's End

The day after the tragic departure of Jeanne and Gaetane and Paul and Roger's departure in search of them, Abbé Bernard was very surprised to hear noises and shouting in Nemoville's streets, which were ordinarily so peaceful. He hastened to discover the cause of the anomaly, and found a man who was holding another by the collar, who was shouting as he tried to strangle his antagonist.

"He's the one who did it, and he won't get away with it—I saw him coming out of Doctor de Chantal's house at about midnight," the man replied to those who asked him the reason for his conduct.

The priest tried to calm the fury of the man who had appointed himself the avenger of the two women whom everyone in Nemoville was mourning, and convinced him that only the governor had the right to punish the accused as he merited. The latter was none other than Doctor Desmarais.

Given the assurance of the man, who swore that he had seen the doctor emerge from the submarine where the two women were, at an hour when everyone was supposed to be at home, according to the city's regulations, the curé decided to have the physician imprisoned and hidden from sight. He had never had a profound sympathy for the man, whose attitude, brazen and sly at the same time, he had never liked. Doctor

Desmarais had always seemed to him to be a sort of living enigma, and he told himself that perhaps the man's innate wickedness had reacted against the open and frank souls of Gaetane and Roger, with whose instinctive repulsion for the physician he was familiar.

Confronted by the shouts of the crowd and the intervention of the curé, the doctor, sensing that he was doomed, reacted audaciously and folded his arms. With a cynical laugh, he said: "Well, yes, I'm the one who detached the submarine, having started up the engine." He was unable to say any more, because the crowd rushed at him and the cure, and almost tore him from the hands of his captors.

Roger and Paul were away for a week. They came back more desperate than they had been when they left; the searches had been fruitless. Gaetane and her companion seemed to be irredeemably lost.

As soon as the governor arrived, the curé told him about the doctor's arrest, and the circumstances that had motivated it.

"The wretch will be punished as he deserves," said Roger, coldly. "This very evening, he'll be taken ashore, where he'll pay the penalty for his crime."

"Ah!" said Paul. "The wretch doesn't deserve to see the sun again; have a rope tied around his neck, Roger, and drown him like a mad dog."

"No," Roger replied, "We'll give him a trial on shore, and his judges will decide his fate."

That same evening, the governor and his secretary, and a few men from Nemoville chosen from among the most important, went to the submarine in which the physician had been imprisoned. He was to be transported in one of the submersible launches that they used for traveling when they did not want to displace the city's submarines. The wretch's hands and feet were tied and Roger had him thrown into the launch that he was piloting with Paul.

Occupied with maneuvering, the two friends paid no heed to the prisoner, thinking that it was impossible for him to escape—but the sound of a body falling into the sea soon attracted their attention. Turning round, they saw, to their chagrin, that the wretch had succeeded in freeing himself from his bonds and had jumped overboard. They saw him swimming, some distance away.

He did not get far, though, for one of the men in the launch following the governor's boat had seen the prisoner's ploy and, immediately steering toward him, knocked him unconscious with an oar. The wretch sank, and did not reappear. The mission of the administrators of justice was therefore concluded.

They returned to Nemoville and told Abbé Bernard what had happened. He contented himself with murmuring: "May God have pity on his soul."

Nemoville resumed its customary appearance for a little while, but no one could forget the two beloved women who had been stolen from the affection of the husband and the fiancé, and Roger and Paul could not help thinking that their happiness was gone forever. They resolved to devote a considerable part of their time to searching for Gaetane and Jeanne, so long as they had no proof of the futility of their search.

One morning, after making preparations for a long absence and entrusting the direction of Nemoville to Abbé Bernard, they set off in quest of their two beloveds.

22. The Lost Rock

We left Gaetane and Jeanne at the moment when their submarine came to rest, slowly filling up with water. The two women were desperate; this time, it was no more than a matter of a few minutes before they saw death envelop them with its cold mantle.

The waves were still rocking he vessel; they lifted it up one moment, and then seemed to be playing cruelly with the wreck before dragging it down to the sea bed. Suddenly, a wave more forceful and furious than the others carried the submarine backwards, and with a single thrust, threw it on to the rock, which was only a short distance away. For the two women that was salvation.

The submarine clung to the rock, which had just completed opening it up, and remained motionless. The two women hastened to disembark on to the stony shore, and observed that they were on a flat rock of meager extent, on which no vegetation was visible. A short distance away, however, there was an island, which seemed to be linked to the rock on which they were standing by a chain of submerged rocks. The top of a reef could be seen emerging periodically, and the water seething in other places enabled the deduction that there were other reefs just below the water level, all heading in the direction of the island on which verdure was perceptible, presently gilded by the setting sun.

They brought a few blankets out of the submarine, and a few more things they needed to maintain their strength, and, exhausted by fatigue, they lay down to sleep. Needless to say, that sleep was not populated with beautiful dreams; it is, alas, the consequence of misfortune to leave traces in the mind that even that great healer sleep cannot efface.

The next day, the two women busied themselves with finding a way to get to the island, which appeared to them to be more habitable than the desert rock on which they found themselves. At a certain time of day, they observed that the chain of rocks linking the isle to the reef where their submarine had run aground was almost entirely exposed.

They ventured forth courageously on to the slippery boulders, sometimes being waist-deep in water, and succeeded in reaching the island. They explored it briefly and then came back to the submarine, which was still wedged on the reef. They took out of it everything they could: provisions, furniture, linen, blankets, and risking slipping into the sea with their burdens a thousand times over, they transported all of it to the island.

A few hours later, the water covered the chain of rocks again, and the submarine, wrenched from the reef by the tide, sank beneath the waves. The two women watched it being slowly swallowed up, and, on seeing it disappear thus, they felt that a last link was being broken. For them, it was a dear witness of their past happiness that was disappearing forever.

23. Albatross Island

In the middle of the island where the castaways had now established themselves there was a small mountain, at the foot of which was a deep cave. Gaetane and Jeanne decided to make their abode there. They transported everything they had taken from the submarine and set about organizing their new life. They had little enthusiasm for that work of installation, alas, for they knew that the cave would henceforth be the tomb of their illusions, while they awaited the one in which their flesh would lie.

That first day passed rather quickly, in spite of the anguish that was tearing their hearts. Exhausted by fatigue, they went to sleep and did not wake up until morning. The sun extended a gilded ray into the heat of the cave, and that appeared to them to be a good omen.

"Who knows?" Gaetane said to Jeanne. "Perhaps this island isn't as far from Nemoville as we think. Anyway, it's certain that Roger and Paul won't easily abandon the hope of finding us. This fine sunlight puts hopeful thoughts back into the soul."

Jeanne was not as optimistic, but she did not wish to discourage her companion and replied: "You're right; we must never despair, for then we'd have no reason for living."

A veritable cloud of albatrosses had just landed on the island. The birds seemed to be at home, and, looking at the two women curiously, they came very close to them and accepted the crumbs that were thrown to them unceremoniously.

"If this island doesn't have a name yet," said Gaetane, "it ought to be called Albatross Island."

"That's the name we'll give it," Jeanne replied, "and the rock where we landed could be named Deliverance Rock."

"And what about the cave?" Gaetane asked, again. "Why not Nemo Cave, in memory of our dear Nemoville?"

"And what about the mountain?" asked Jeanne in her turn.

"What do you think of Mount Bernard?" Gaetane replied.

"Oh yes—it will bring us luck, it seems to me, to give it the good abbé's name" Jeanne replied, enthusiastically.

"Now let's move in," said the two young women, as one. "Let's take advantage of the sun that is lavishing its light on us today, and put all our effects safely away in the cave before nightfall."

First they made a fire of wood on the strand, and prepared their breakfast. To see them thus occupied, one might have mistaken them for tourists on a pleasure trip, for in spite of their profound sadness, they often laughed at one another's ineptitude; it is the privilege of youth to laugh sometimes, in the midst of tears.

"Let's proceed in the manner of Robinson Crusoe," said Gaetane. "Let's make a list of our effects and then classify them. Let's designate a place for everything and put everything in the place assigned for it."

Fortunately, they had a large quantity of provisions; they had been careful to take all those that were in the submarine, and Doctor de Chantal's abode was always well-supplied in that regard.

They had left items that were too heavy for them to transport in the submarine. Gaetane's wardrobe was reduced to what she was wearing, but Jeanne's was well-furnished and the two friends were the same size, so that detail was not troublesome. In any case, they were not at all concerned with elegance for the moment; as you can imagine, our heroines had too many serious matters to think about.

The cave formed three irregular chambers, of which the young women resolved to make the best use possible. By common accord, without even discussing the matter, they set about embellishing their rustic domain with everything they had at their disposal. They both had an innate liking for comfort and elegance, and even in the midst of their distress, they took care to give their primitive dwelling a hint of femininity and god taste.

The largest room was converted into a kitchen-dining-room. The crockery, silverware and appropriate furniture they had saved were placed there. The beds were placed in another. In the third, they stored the provisions and all the things of which they had no immediate need.

When the installation was terminated, Nemo Cave was quite pretty, and if its residents had been able to entertain any hopeful thoughts they would have been happy, for they lacked neither comfort nor liberty—but they were far from those they loved, and thought that they would never see them again.

24. The Flag of Nemoville

The castaways had already been on Albatross Island for some days when they ventured into regions distant from the grotto for the first time. That morning, the sunlight was so beautiful that they felt less sad and more courageous. They therefore decided to explore, in order to take account of the extent of the island, and perhaps also in the vague hope of finding indications that the place had previously been visited by human beings. They set off, carrying provisions for the whole day, determined not to come back until they had made a tour of the island and scaled the mountain.

They followed the shore for about a mile; then it was necessary to climb the hill, which presented a slope that was almost sheer. The mountain had no other vegetation than stunted trees, which seemed scorched by the sun; even grass was sparse there; in the main, there was nothing but arid rock.

Having made that observation, the two voyagers rejoiced in having abundant provisions in their cave, for they realized that they would not have been able to count on that ingrate soil for their nourishment.

As every cloud has its silver lining, however, the poor women told themselves that at least that circumstance meant that they were not in danger from wild beasts, which might have invaded the island if it had been able to nourish them.

"Poor Paul!" Jean sighed, nevertheless. "Shall I ever see him again?"

"Dear Roger!" said Gaetane, in her turn, echoing Jeanne.

"Let's plant the flag of Nemoville over the cave, in order to guide our return," Jeanne suggested.

This plan was immediately carried out. It was not done without difficulty, but they succeeded in it. They planted it in a fissure in the rock and fixed it there solidly by means of earth and stones. The flag of Nemoville was blue—the color of the waves. A water-lily was painted in one corner, surrounded by the inscription: *Mobilis in mobile.* As you can see, the Nemovillians had adopted Captain Nemo's motto.

Now, Gaetane and Jeanne said to themselves, *if a ship passes within sight of the island, its crew can't fail to see our flag and come to our rescue.*

The two women tried to take life philosophically, by maintaining the hope of seeing their loved ones again. It seemed to them to be impossible that they should die like this, in the bloom of youth, on a desert rock. That gave them courage, and they tried to make their sojourn in the grotto, and everything surrounding it, as pleasant as possible.

They extended fishing-nets from Deliverance Rock, and by that means they were able to vary their menu and eke out the provisions they had taken from the submarine. In the uncertain circumstances in which they found themselves, the strictest economy was a wise course of action that they were careful not to neglect. Their only prodigality was to throw the crumbs from their table to the albatrosses, which still came faithfully to land around the two women when they sat down on the shore to take their meals, as they did whenever the temperature permitted.

For several days, however, these winged friends had not come in such large numbers, and that saddened Gaetane and

Jeanne, who feared seeing the island's only visitors, which were a pleasant distraction for them, desert it entirely. They had become used to seeing the snow-white birds fluttering around them, begging politely for food, which they eventually took directly from the two friends' hands, and they were amused by the sight of the albatrosses quarreling over the crumbs they threw to them.

One morning, Gaetane and Jeanne went down to the beach, as was their custom, to prepare their breakfast there. While Jeanne went to check the nets they had extended from Deliverance Rock, Gaetane lit a fire and made coffee. When that was done she went back into the cave, put her ear to the wall and listened momentarily.

She went pale and murmured: "There's no doubt about it, alas. We're on a volcano, and a catastrophe is imminent."

Jeanne came back, dragging the nets full of appetizing fish. They set about preparing a few of them for their meal, and were obliged to defend their catch against the albatrosses, which did not seem disposed to stand on ceremony, and were already preparing to serve themselves a generous portion of the net itself, which it was necessary to put away safely in the cave.

The boldness of their friends amused Jeanne and Gaetane momentarily, and permitted them to set aside their sadness and secret apprehension, which they had not yet dared to communicate to one another. The breakfast was cheerful, the young women trying to deceive one another with regard to the terrible truth that each of them had discovered—for Jeanne had also known for several days what the island on which they were living was.

25. Mount Bernard

It was the tenth of May. Jeanne, busy preparing breakfast on the beach, no longer resembled the Jeanne was saw a few days earlier, hiding her anxiety in order not to alarm her friend, and trying to seem cheerful while she was mortally afraid. Today, Jeanne could no longer hide her anguish, for the anguish was visible in her drawn features and extreme pallor, as well as in her nervousness, which she could not control.

Gaetane came to join her; she also bore the marks of the days of secret terror she had endured, in her face and behavior. The two friends seemed to be afraid to look at one another; even so, they exchanged a cordial *bonjour* and manifested the same amity.

That morning their appetites were also lacking; they nibbled their food, often darting covert anxious glances toward Mount Bernard.

Suddenly, a dull rumbling reached the ears of the two women.

"I knew it," they said to one another, replying to the mute interrogation of their eyes. "We can't stay in the cave any longer. What shall we do?"

"It wasn't a vain indication that our albatrosses fled the island a few days ago," said Gaetane. "The volcano is about to erupt. What are we going to do?"

"We could transport a few effects to Deliverance Rock and establish ourselves there for the night, in order not to be caught by surprise while we sleep by the eruption of Mount Bernard."

"You're right, I think," Gaetane replied. "It seems to be preparing new misfortunes for us."

They did as they had said, and it was as well that they did, for the following night, while they were asleep, wrapped up in their blankets, on the bare rock, they were woken up by the sound of the volcano in all its fury.

Hot lava overflowed all the way to the beach, and a gigantic flame climbed into the sky, illuminating it like a vast firework. The spectacle was magnificent and terrible. It lasted all night.

The next day, everything resumed its usual appearance, but two days later, there was a terrible earthquake. The entire island shook, and seemed to totter, as if it were about to sink into the ocean.

26. *The Return*

Roger and Paul were on their way back to Nemoville. Their search had been fruitless, and they had felt a need to see their friends again, from whom they had been separated for a long time.

They had scoured the Atlantic, going from north to south, without finding any trace of the submarine containing Gaetane and Jeanne.

One night, when they were sailing on the surface, they passed a large volcanic island that was in eruption. The spectacle attracted the two friends, who drew closer to the island. They stayed all night, contemplating that gigantic illumination; then, the following day, when everything seemed to have returned to normal, they had the bold idea of exploring the shores of the mysterious island, in order to see whether it might be inhabited.

They approached it, with the intention of landing if that were possible. As they were looking for a place where they might safely anchor the submarine, Roger raised his eyes and, perceiving the flag flying over the cave—which the lava had not reached—thought he was seeing things.

"Paul! Paul!" he shouted. "Look at that flag! Who can have planted it there, if not Gaetane and Jeanne!"

"Our beloveds have surely been living on this volcanic island," Paul replied. "May Heaven grant that we haven't arrived too late to save them."

Prey to joy and dread at the same time, the two friends disembarked on to the beach and started exploring in all directions. They started shouting: "Gaetane! Jeanne!"—but the two women could not hear them, and as the submarine had not landed within sight of Deliverance Rock, they could not see the objects of their search.

The two men went into the cave, and thus found evident proof that the women for whom they were searching had been living there. They experienced a moment of veritable discouragement, for they thought they were also seeing proof that they had perished in trying to escape, and had been swallowed alive by the molten lava.

Who could describe the grief of those two men, confronted by the certainty of such a terrible disaster!

They let themselves fall on to the beach and wept, as one mourns the collapse of one's happiness at twenty years of age.

The worthy dog Turko, who had accompanied his master, began manifesting signs of joy to which Roger and Paul paid no attention, given the state of mind they were in. Turko stretched his legs and danced on the shore, uttering little barks of joy. He came back to his masters and went into the cave, from which he soon emerged again, leaping with joy and clutching a handkerchief that had belonged to Gaetane in his teeth. He came to deposit it at Roger's feet.

The latter put his hand on the dog's head, stroked him and said: "Good dog!"

Finally, the two friends got ready to return to their boat—but the dog did not seem to want to go with them. He stopped on the shore, barking obstinately—and when Roger called to him to come aboard, the animal fled toward the chain of rocks leading to Deliverance Rock.

At that moment, the tide was high, and only the summits of the reefs could be seen, which looked like isolated snags that it was impossible to cross.

The dog's antics ended up troubling the travelers. "What can Turko's behavior signify?" Roger asked. "The poor women, frightened by the danger, might perhaps have fled in that direction, and it's their trail that Turko is scenting—but if so, they must certainly have drowned."

"Let's make a tour of the rock," Paul suggested.

They climbed back into their boat and made a tour of the rock, sticking as close to land as prudence permitted.

27. A Jackal

On Deliverance Rock, Jeanne and Gaetane had spent an emotional night, which had ended up exhausting their strength and their courage. While Roger and Paul were searching for them on the island, they were lying down on the rock to rest, after having taken a little nourishment. They did not hear the sound of the boat, nor the words of the two men manning it. They had finally gone to sleep, acquiring the slumber that they had not been able to attain in the frightful anguish of the night. But for the animal's sense of smell, salvation would have passed them by without them suspecting it.

It was impossible to land on the rock because of the numerous snags that surrounded it like an insurmountable girdle. Paul and Roger explored the rock with a marine telescope, but could not see the two women, who were lying in a declivity. They went around the reef without suspecting that the objects of their search were within two hundred meters of their rescuers.

Understandably, however, Paul and Roger were unable to decide to leave the place where they were certain that the women they were searching for had been living.

"Let's go back to the island," Roger proposed. "We'll spend a few days here, if we must, and we won't go away until we're certain that Gaetane and Jeanne are dead."

So they returned to the island, and, having made the boat safe for the day, they disembarked and made preparations to stay there for an indeterminate time. Turko seemed happier than he had ever been since the departure of the two women, whom he had been accustomed to follow and chase through the narrow corridors that served as Nemoville's streets.

On touching land, the dog returned to the cave and took the path that led to the chain of rocks again. The two friends, who were watching him, said to themselves: *It's obvious that they must have run away in that direction.*

With a common accord, they decided to wait on the island and to see whether the sea might bring back the cadavers.

In the meantime, they decided to make another tour of the island, and even took temerity as far as to approach the mountain, which was still hot. Finally, convinced of the futility of their search, they came back to the beach and lay down in the sunlight to rest.

The tide went out; soon, the tips of the reef were uncovered. Turko seemed to have been waiting for that moment; he did not even wait for the water to withdraw completely. Suddenly lifting his nose in the air, he uttered a joyful howl, and started swimming. Roger and Paul, who had fallen asleep, were soon on their feet, following the dog with their eyes. The latter was swimming with confidence, battling the forceful waves, which were drawing him away from the rock and seemed to want to swallow him up. He disappeared momentarily inside one monstrous wave, which seemed to be dragging him down to the sea-bed.

"Turko's doomed," said Riger, regretfully. "But what did he scent in that direction?"

From the place where they were standing, Paul and his friend could not see Turko land on the far side of the rock, but the dog was safe. The animal was so exhausted by the struggle he had sustained against the waves, however, and so bruised by the asperities of the reef, that he uttered a long plaintive howl and let himself fall on to the rock. For a few moments, he whimpered, incapable of moving.

Jeanne and Gaetane heard that plaint. Frightened by the idea that some dangerous animal was on the rock where they had sought refuge, they began to tremble. There was no possibility at that moment of getting back to the island—of which, in any case, they were terribly frightened after the events of the night. The sea was still covering the rocks that were the only route by which they might escape the dangerous location.

This time, they told themselves, it was death that was lying in wait for them, and they commended themselves to God, who had willed their ordeals.

28. Waiting

After the departure of the dog, which they regarded as a further misfortune, Paul and Roger no longer knew what to do. Inaction weighed heavily upon them, but there was nothing they could do but wait for the sea to send them the cadavers of the women they loved—and while they were despairing, the sea retreated and uncovered the refs that separated them from Jeanne and Gaetane.

After waiting for some time, they heard howling coming from the rock where they had been unable to land.

"Turko's safe!" said Roger, joyfully. "But since the faithful animal hasn't come back, he must be injured. His plaintive howling says as much. I'm going to see where he is."

Paul protested, but in vain. Roger headed for the chain of rocks and observed that it was possible to cross over on foot—not without considerable risk, to be sure, but he cared little about risking his life now that the woman who had been all its charm no longer existed.

He set out toward the chain of rocks, with water up to his armpits. Paul set out after him, and after a terrible battle against the waves, they were able to land on the larger islet. Turko got to his feet, one of which could no longer support him, and welcomed his master with joyful barking. Sticking his nose in the air he started uttering little cries again, punctuated by the caresses he lavished on his master, trying to drag him in the direction of the two women, who had been rendered more dead than alive by the sound of that barking, which they took for that of a jackal or some other predatory animal.

Roger paused to bandage Turko's paw, and in the meantime, Paul explored the rocky plateau. On seeing him take that direction, the dog manifested such signs of joy that Roger commented on it to his friend. Paul had just reached the summit of the islet, silhouetted against the sky like a statue of hope.

At that moment, Jeanne turned in that direction and saw her husband standing on the rocky pedestal, scarcely two hundred paces away. She uttered a piercing cry of "Paul!" and started running toward him.

Paul heard her, and saw her too. He went to meet her, and the next moment, the two spouses fell into one another's arms.

Gaetane had followed her friend, and Roger, who had heard Jeanne's cry and recognized her voice, also came running. He received Gaetane in his arms.

They waited for the tide to go out completely before returning to the island, which was the only means of getting back to the submarine, still safely anchored in an inlet. In the meantime, needless to say, the four individuals exhibited no lack of verve and gaiety. They never stopped talking about the anguished thoughts that had assailed them during their cruel separation, which they had thought irreparable.

As soon as the state of the tide permitted it, they went back to the island, without neglecting to carry Turko, who certainly merited that service after the one he had rendered, by virtue of his sense of smell and his courage.

They did not want to wait until the following day to leave that dangerous locale. They embarked immediately, and set off for Nemoville.

They arrived two days later. Roger was surprised to find the city floating on the surface, which as not usual—but the mystery as explained immediately, after the compliments of welcome had been exchanged and the Nemovillians' joy had been unleashed at the sight of the two women, who had been thought to be lost forever. Nemoville was in a dangerous condition; it needed major repairs, and the curé had judged it prudent, while awaiting the governor's return, to take the city up to the surface.

The next day, Roger's first concern was to visit all the submarines comprising the city and to take stock of their condition. Accompanied by Paul, he was able to ascertain that the city needed to be almost completely rebuilt. The two friends conferred, then decided to convene a meeting of Nemoville's principal inhabitants.

That evening , everyone met in the governor's residence. He explained the situation and asked the members of the audience whether they wanted to continue life beneath the sea or whether they would prefer to resume their existence on land, in the sunlight.

Roger awaited his friend's decision anxiously. After some discussion, in which reasons for and against were advanced, the majority of the inhabitants decided to return to the land.

Roger hid the sadness that decision caused him, because he saw that Gaetane—who, like all the other women of Nemoville, was present at the meeting—seemed pleased by this prospect.

Roger made the decision to celebrate his marriage aboard the *Nautilus* and then scuttle the submarine, along with the entire city.

The next day, he left with Paul and came back a few days later, borne by a steamship that stopped close to the *Nautilus*.

The submarine had been decorated for the wedding celebration; the interior resembled a greenhouse, and the flag of the city had been hoisted.

Abbé Bernard blessed the marriage in the ward-room of the *Nautilus*; then all the inhabitants of Nemoville embarked on the steamer, and from the ship's deck, they witnessed a strange and magnificent spectacle. By means of a mechanism prepared by Paul, a trapdoor opened in the bottom of each submarine, and, engulfed by the water, Nemoville sank slowly beneath the waves.

When the ocean had closed over the city, Gaetane looked at her husband and saw that he had tears in his eyes.

"Are you crying?" she said, in surprise.

"It's the end of a dream," he replied, "but I shall live in another, more durable and sweeter, with you."

"And I shall no longer be jealous of Nemoville."

A few moment later, the steamship got under way, bearing the inhabitants of the sunken city to their new destinies.

29. In which the characters of interest are seen again

Four years have passed since the solemn and moving moment in which Roger saw the city in which he had lived several chapters of his life sink into the depths, on his orders.

A young woman is walking on a terrace on a beautiful summer evening. She often looks toward the road, and seems to be impatient to see someone appear for whom she is waiting.

A three-year-old child is beside her, and suddenly cries: "There's Papa and Monsieur l'Abbé."

Indeed, two men are getting out of a carriage at the garden gate; one is Roger and the other the former curé of Nemoville.

As one can see, the friendship has survived the sunken city, and in coming back to land, Roger did not want to separate himself from all the inhabitants of the submarine city.

Having embraced his wife and son, Roger says to Gaetane: "Jeanne and Paul are following us; they'll be here in a few minutes."

These words prove that Roger and Paul have remained good friends. They are also good neighbors; their properties are adjacent, and the abbé goes from one to another like an older brother; he plays the role of godfather for Gaetane's son and Jeanne's daughter.

Pierre Mille: *Three Hundred Years Hence*
(1922)

Henny was not very sure what the rusty bar or iron or steel was that Pousse, the blacksmith, had just thrown on to his charcoal fire. It had strange ringlets on either side running from top to bottom. Gripping a piece of the bar, already red hot, in strong pincers, one of Pousse's sons turned it over and over in front of the cutter. Standing beside the antique patched leather bellows, his younger brother stimulated the fire.

Pousse's wife came in with a bucket of water. She was almost as tall and strong as her husband. Her breasts hung loose in a sort of hempen sack, her only garment. She had sabots on her feet.

"That's good," said the blacksmith. "Put it down here."

He breathed out and picked up his hammer, but then set it down again. "It's large nails you want, is it?" he asked Henny. "What for?"

"Yes, big ones," the young man replied. "For the partition in the stable, between the cattle and the pigs. It's rotten—the pigs get through and disperse the cows' straw. Big nails, like this one..." He held up some long pointed objects with four faces, almost as completely oxidized as the steel bar.

"Those were made back in the day, by machine," said the smith. "They only worked like that—by machine—the ancients. Things like that aren't forged any more, now. They're from way back…hundreds and hundreds of years. How many? Who can tell? It was my father's grandfather who learned to be a smith again, on his own, here…where did you find them, the things you're showing me? In the roof of that old building—the church, as they call it?"

"I've been there, but there's nothing left. Nothing at all—except the big roof-beams."

"Yes, the rest's gone. It's all been taken away, so many different people have been there. And it's the same with those big houses—the so-called châteaux. You know the one at Toué? I went there the other day, with one of our crews. We took the last stones. They'll serve to reinforce the town walls, to the west. They aren't strong enough."

"I know. That's where They got in, last year."

"As I remember better than you, thanks to these," said the smith, pointing to his twisted leg and then, with another gesture, to a minuscule circular blue scar on his shoulder.

"And They killed my son!" said the woman. "Oh, if we only had guns. *They* have them!"

"There are a few left," said Henny, "but what about powder? And even if we had powder, the rifles only take cartridges made of copper, or some other metal in thin sheets. Where can we find that?"

"I could take care of that well enough," the smith affirmed. "It's the powder, as you say, that's lacking. *They* have it!"

"Not much," said Henny. "Not many guns, either—because it needs heaps of things to make guns: coal, iron, steel, complicated machines, and workshops for all that..."

"They have them, though!"

"Yes. Milot, who lived with them because he wanted to work in their laboratories, but whom they wanted to kill, and came to hide here, says that it's always like that, that it's one of the laws of humanity. He says that he read in a very old book, written in ancient French, that all industries, since the beginning of the world, for clothing, houses, means of transport, have gone from heights to depths, that they had periods of decadence after periods of perfection. The arts too..."

"The arts?" the smith repeated, not understanding. It was a word that had lost all significance or him.

"All the arts and all the industries," Henny went on, "except the making of weapons. People always continued to make weapons, always inventing them, always improving them, ever since the first man. That never stopped."

"I can understand that," said the smith. "It's not like that for us, but the Others! The only means they have of eating is to take by force what we Fieldfolk produce to eat ourselves. It seems that everyone knew how to read before. Me, naturally, I don't know—but you ought to read that book to us in the winter evenings, when you come to our house with your Jène."

"I've never read it myself. I don't have it. I told you that it was Milot who told me these things. If I had it, it wouldn't do any good, since it's written in an ancient language. You wouldn't understand...any more than we understand the people who are three days' march away."

They were speaking a disfigured French, from which certain consonants were beginning to disappear, or had already disappeared, and in which vowels were transposed. Three centuries before, Henny had been pronounced Henri, and Jène had been Jeanne. Cheuzi had been Chousy, near Compiègne. And they did not know that some of the words they pronounced—those signifying the meat produced by cattle, sheep and poultry, and also those relating to war and fortifications—were Russian or even Chinese words, deformed.[65]

All of that was too difficult for the smith's slow and uncultivated mind to comprehend. He returned to the nails.

---

[65] With the exception of proper names, Mille does not attempt to display an "eye-dialect" demonstrating the changes to which he refers, so his story—the dialogue as well as the narrative—is a kind of translation. He was undoubtedly aware of the oft-quoted observation that, following the Norman conquest of England, the names given to cuts of meat in English were derived from the French (beef, mutton, pork) because it was the aristocrats who ate meat, while the names give to the animals, raised by the conquered population on their behalf, were derived from the Anglo-Saxon (ox, sheep, pig). He does not, however, attempt to synthesize the new Russian- or Chinese-derives terms that his fallen Frenchmen use to describe items that no longer "belong" to them, thus undermining his argument somewhat.

"Well then," he said, "these you've bought me—where did you find them?"

"At home. In a wing of the house that's falling into ruin. I'm demolishing it bit by bit, and putting aside anything that might be useful."

"Yes, everyone does that. But what happens when there's nothing left to demolish? People haven't seen the end of their troubles. What will our children do?"

"Your grandfather already asked himself that question, and we're still going. Whatever happens, humans live on; they adapt in order to live, free to get thinner, like plants in poor ground."

"That's true," the smith agreed, simply. "Better to live poorly than die."

At that moment, his eldest daughter came in, carefully carrying two large earthenware pots.

"You've come from the potter's? You were there a long time. Were you watching the pots turn?"

"Not just that, for sure," she said, calmly. At eighteen, more powerful than beautiful, well set on her solid hips, with a cheerful expression, she was rounded by pregnancy.

"You're right," the smith concluded. "As long as the young ones continue to make love, the world will go on."

Passing their scorched hands over their leather aprons, his two sons approved, laughing heartily.

"We make even more children so it's said. The old ones say so."

"It's probable," Henny replied. "We no longer work the land as in the old days, with machines; we can no longer get what we lack from elsewhere, and have to produce everything ourselves, so we need more children. Then again, They kill them...and more of them die without being killed: there are no more doctors."

"Yes there are" said the smith. "There's old mother Jette. She knows about healing."

"Before," Henny affirmed, "there were doctors."

The smith shrugged his shoulders; he was better adapted than Henny, in whom the miserable shreds of culture and tradition he had received from his family sometimes inspired an ardent regret for the long-gone days that were becoming legendary.

The man who was striking his anvil, his face illuminated by white flashes of superheated metal, remained placid. He was a man without memories; he found his way of life tolerable, having known no other. From the bucket into which he had thrown them, still red hot, he took out a few dozen roughly-hammered nails, their heads flattened with a final blow of the hammer, somewhat similar to those that had once been found driven into the walls of Roman ruins or the most ancient Christian churches, but even more primitive in appearance. His were the produce of an industry that had begun again, hesitantly; the others of an art that many generations had been able to transmit.

Henny put them in the satchel he wore at his side. "What do you want for them?"

"Do you have any eggs?"

"Yes—Jène looks after the coop very well. The hens are laying."

"Four dozens nails makes four dozen eggs."

"You don't give your work away!"

"Do you think it's easy to get iron? You have to go a long way along the track nowadays—it's a long time since that was taken. It's run out..."

Henny recognized then the provenance of the rusted metal bar, with it's strange ringlets running from top to bottom, which the smith had just cut in order to obtain the raw material for his work; it was from a railway track. Such was the mine from which the surrounding country had supplied itself for three hundred years.

In the beginning, the local inhabitants had destroyed the tracks out of prudence, to prevent the Enemy—the people they called the Town-Stealers—from making use of it to reach them. Now, it was a long time since the locomotives had even been heaps of scrap iron; they had been taken apart piece by piece. One of them had been wrecked a few leagues away. The memory had lingered because the villages had fought a battle over the copper tubing.

Copper! An almost-irreplaceable metal for making the stills in which alcohol was brewed. Cheuzi had come out ahead, and it was his competence in repairing the apparatus that had made the smith one of the most important men in the neighborhood. The community—one might almost say the tribe—of Cheuzi was richer in consequence; the surrounding villages, which had no stills, bartered wheat, livestock and animal-hides tanned by oak-ash and bark in exchange for the precious alcohol—for alcohol was almost all that remained of civilization!

Sometimes, to procure it, they went as far as trading their ploughs: ploughs that had reverted to the swing-ploughs of the earliest times, which were all that the smith could forge—so he denounced the poor quality of his tools and his rivals' lack of skill. The result of that was that some of the artisans of the people who had fallen back into barbarity still retained, by virtue of the shadow of competition, a certain desire to work well, a reside of patient ingenuity.

To get back to his house, Henny went along the fortifications. All the villages were fortified now, in a rudimentary fashion, but which rendered them capable of resisting an assault by horsemen without firearms—which was, fortunately, more often the case than not.

These villages, which had diminished in number, were also more populous than before; the smaller ones, less capable of resisting attacks, by virtue of their situation, had been abandoned. That was why Cheuzi, which had only had five hundred inhabitants in the days of civilization, now had more than fifteen hundred. At the confluence of two rivers, the course of which protected it from the north-west to the north-east, only open to the south, it had become a small town gathered and heaped up within its boundaries, no more extensive in surface area than before, composed of narrow and tortuous streets with houses of two or three stories—but behind each one of them, so far as was possible, an interior courtyard was reserved for animals, agricultural implements and stored crops.

A few houses from the old times survived, especially those that had been built before the era of the Great Scourge, going back to the seventeenth or eighteenth centuries, but the economical constructions of later eras had collapsed. New ones had been built in their stead, which the very incapability of the builders had rendered more massive. They had plain wooden shutters, pierced with opening to let the light through, with no glass windows—for these peasants could no longer obtain glass, considering even fragments of it as a precious substance that served for ornamentation. Eventually, it had become customary to replace stairways with retractable ladders, so as to oppose assaults more effectively and take refuge on the uppermost floor, where foodstuffs were stored and as much as was feasible of the crops they produced.

Henny stopped in at the house of his nearest neighbor, Pafot. He needed a hand to repair his pig-pen. The custom of benevolent mutual aid had been gradually introduced, by necessity, among the Fieldfolk; save for a few indispensable artisans—smiths, weavers, potters—there were no more tradesmen; everyone obtained his nourishment by working the land. That was a further encouragement to fathers of families to increase the number of their children, to profit from their arms. Then again, it was necessary to supply the weavers with hemp or wool, ready spun, and to ferry clay to the potters. The division of labor is a city thing. It has never been established in rural areas in any era, and since the great crisis it had entirely disappeared.

Pafot, who would once have been called Parfond, told Henny that he was bringing in his hay, but that he would send him a "prisoner" the following day. That name was given to a category of inhabitants that had effectively become the community's slaves: captives taken in the battles that the village was often obliged to fight. They were employed in work of general interest, or hired out to individual Fieldfolk. A considerable number of them were Russian, German or even Chinese, but if by chance—which happened fairly frequently—a daughter of Cheuzi accorded them her favors, the children they engendered were born free, as the concept of true slavery had disappeared from custom.

That was one of the rare traditions that the Fieldfolk had retained, unsuspectingly, from the forever-abolished era in which it had been deemed that no man should, in any circumstances, become the property of another. Gradually, however, these alliances were modifying the type of the race, and simultaneously hastening the deformation of the language. It was not uncommon now for Cheuzis to have canthused eyes, prominent cheekbones and more-or-less triangular faces. This evolution had been accentuated after the sack of Cheuzi two generations before, when the village had been taken by the Town-Stealers; many men had then been killed and almost all the women raped by the revolutionaries' Chinese mercenaries.

Singularly enough, however, these people of a new race continued to call themselves French; the idea that the country—a country whose limits and configuration they did not know—was theirs, and only theirs, stuck in their minds, obscure but profound and ineradicable.

They were the people of France.

After visiting Pafot, Henny went back to his own house. The door, made of roughly-but solidly-assembled thick planks sealed with heavy crossbeams was secured by night, or in case of necessity, by a strong wooden bar, and closed by day by a knotted cord. There were no longer any locks; that was contrivance too skilled even for the proud smith.

Henny undid the knot.

The dwelling must once have been a fairly large residence, consisting of two adjacent buildings run together. One of them, in ruins, no longer bore more than the framework of its roof; the other had been maintained, repaired by Henny's ancestors and by himself, to the meager extent of the means art their disposal. As elsewhere in the village, the glazed windows had been replaced with plain wooden shutters. The majority of the interior doors were missing.

In winter, it was much more difficult to heat the edifice than the houses of a different sort that the Fieldfolk had learned to construct, in which large chimney-hoods accommodated massive heaps of firewood; these hearths of the civilized era, designed for a different combustible material or only maintained or appearances' sake—for traces of a central heating system had been found in the cellars—could only put out a feeble warmth.

Several hundred years before, it had been possible to find, in the rural regions of France, ancient châteaux fallen into ruins and transformed into farms: where once there had been tapestries and furniture testifying to a concern for elegance, frivolity and beauty, revealing in the carved relief of wood, the gilt of old frames and the evocation of painted figures, one no longer saw anything but harnesses hanging on the walls, onions drying in a corner, a crude table, long and stout, devoted as much to the concerns of cooking as eating, and coarse chairs and benches. Henny's house was like that. He experienced no shame in consequence, having never seen anything else, living as everyone else around him lived.

"Jène! Jène!" he shouted.

No reply. At first, he did not feel any anxiety. Cheuzi was not under threat at present. He knew that his wife was healthy, happy and cheerful.

She's still with her chickens, he thought, *or even in the stables*.

The hens greeted him with the round and disdainful gaze that they reserve for humans, and the unpredictable gait that always takes them to the place one is convinced they ought not to go. In the stable, the cows, lying in their straw, raised their heads momentarily, then continued ruminating; it was only the master, a human of whom it as unnecessary to be afraid. That observation sufficed them. But Henny did not see Jène anywhere, not even the ancient flower-garden, where only vegetables grew now.

He went back into the house, and went up the rickety stairway to the first floor. Then anguish gripped his heart.

"Jène!"

He breathed again. From above, stifled by the bundles of hay that filled the grain-loft, from further away than the grain-loft itself, from a garret into which he could not remember every having gone since childhood, a voice replied.

"Is that you, Henny? Wait—I'm coming!"

Very young, still almost a child, Jène climbed over the bales heaped up to the ceiling unhurriedly, moving both slowly and surely, like a true peasant, as of habit.

"My little Jène! You frightened me! I couldn't find you..."

He told himself that he had had no reason to be alarmed, and reproached himself. The people of the present era lived in perpetual expectation of the worst, knowing from experience that the next minute could never be free of peril—but all those around him were hardened to it. As Père Pousse, the smith, had said, it was sufficient to be alive. People only escaped one danger to confront another!

Well, that was the very condition of life, as wild animals—those hunted by humans and beasts of prey alike—must doubtless conceive it. From the first moment to the last, there was always the threat of imminent death—and yet they adapted to that incessant horror; their palpitations ceased abruptly with the cause that gave birth to them; they played, they made love.

Henny's sensitivity, however, was keener; almost alone, perhaps by virtue of an atavistic return, he knew the poignant sentiment that his distant ancestors had experienced: apprehension—futile, even pernicious apprehension, the inhibitor of the instinctive reflexes of defense and conservation. Henny was frightened, like a man of old, a lover of old: his little Jène!

The people of the civilized era had not known the power of such symbioses. What had then united a male with his mistress, with a woman, was pleasure, and sometimes—increasingly rarely—children, but everyone had continued to live a separate, independent existence. For Jène and Henny too there was pleasure and desire, but they also had the imperious injunction of the land from which they obtained their nourishment. It demanded, in order to allow itself to become fecund, a man and his wife, laborer and housekeeper, incessantly attentive to the cares of the stable and the poultry-coop, economical and also prudent with what virile arms brought in.

"What were you doing, Jène? I looked for you everywhere. The idea that you might be up there...what's that you're hiding?"

She had just come to a halt, radiant with a singular joy that he could not recall having read in her features for years. Subjected to hard and monotonous labor, the daughters of the Fieldfolk became serious very young. The period of their adolescence scarcely inspired a sort of animal coquetry in them, that of their initiation into the pleasure of transports in which there was more excitement than gaiety. The Fieldfolk, it is true, had recovered a taste for singing that their ancestors had lost, but their emotional songs—even those into which they tried to put some joy—were merely passionate, and they did not usually dance in pairs, but in groups from which a single male or female dancer would occasionally detach themselves.

Jène, one of the region's rare blondes, appeared slender but solid. Her mind had its reason, her blood its violence; she was both impetuous and logical. A long time before, the difficulty of obtaining sufficiently thin steel needles—stout ones were still made, in raw iron, hammered and then sharpened on a whetstone—had caused women to renounced tailored clothing. Jène's chemise, in hempen fabric, was merely a sort of sack with sleeves, open to allow her bronzed and vigorous neck to pass through. Her skirt, made of a pale russet wool—the natural color of the sheep's fleece, because it was becoming increasingly difficult to obtain dyes for coloring, was composed of two unstitched pieces that overlapped one another slightly on the left side. Her feet were bare, like Henny's and almost all Fieldfolk in summer, unless they wore sabots to work in the fields. In winter, they wrapped strips of woolen cloth around their sabots.

With her rounded, sunburned perfectly-shaped arms, Jène was hiding something behind her in a triumphant, ecstatic manner.

"What is it?" Henny asked. "Come on, show me!"

At that moment, penetrated by the contagion of the playfulness discovered in her entire attitude—he felt as young as she was. He was, indeed, only a few years older. But Jène persisted in hiding the object she as clutching so jealously from his view.

"Guess!" she said to him. "You told me that there was nothing in that room at the back of the grain-loft—me, I have a better memory! I thought I remembered having seen some kind of box there when I was very small—and suddenly, as if in a dream, I saw, I was sure, absolutely sure, that the thing, under its layers of dust, was leather! Leather, you understand? Hard leather, such as is no longer made, tanned as no one any longer knows how to tan!

"I went up into the room. The box was closed by an iron catch, not a knotted cord. It must be old, then—very old. But the catch was all eaten away by rust; I broke it with a single blow of a wooden mallet. And it was full of things, inside! Dresses—can you imagine? So light! What were they made of? Clouds with gold, pink, the green of trees, the blue of the sky. Yes, clouds! They fell into dust when I tried to unfold them—but at the bottom, in a pretty case that had protected it, there was this! Look, Henny, look!"

They had come back downstairs, and were in the large hallway at the bottom of the steps. With a seemingly amorous gesture, Jène opened what she called the "case" to display two small high-heeled dancing-shoes in silvery white satin spangled with gold, with rhinestone rosettes.

"How shiny they are! How they shine! And they can be even shinier!"

She rubbed a few soapwort leaves between her hands, plunged them into water, rubbed the rosettes with them, and then rinsed them with impure water. The stones, resuscitated, emitted little gleams, reflected in her eyes.

There is an incantation in certain things. Suddenly rediscovering a sentiment of devotion, a need to pay homage to the feminine grace that had vanished generations before, Henny, clad in his coarse woolen cloak, went down on one knee and made as if to put the frail objects on the bare feet of his wife, who was standing in front of him, enthusiastically, as if she were already dancing.

"You're mad, Henny, mad! And silly! Oh, silly! On my bare feet, dressed as I am! That can't be—they weren't made for that, I'm sure of it. You'll see."

He witnessed the miracle of coquetry that surged forth, the sumptuous coquetry of olden days. Jène went to search in a heavy chest, made of slats of oak assembled with difficulty, for her most beautiful, finest roll of hempen cloth, measured as much as necessary with her eyes and arms, and detached the piece with a decisive gesture.

"You'll see," she repeated. "You'll see! What a pity it's too small!"

The women of the era collected fragments of glass preciously. An intact window-pane was a treasure for which people might trade an ox; it was the rarest gift that a lover could give his mistress. By placing beneath the pane a fragment of zinc, also recovered from the rubble, one obtained a mirror with unsteady, wretched reflections. Jène possessed one of those mirrors; she had always been very proud of it. Today, however, she mourned its insufficiency.

An instant more, and she was naked, in all the charm of her youth, the ardor of the blood that flowed in her veins, and a neat, strong grace that rose from her round knees up her long thighs to her polished abdomen, which rounded in the shape of a lyre to the pink tips of her breasts: vigorous, healthy, made for desire and possession.

On another occasion she would have been proud of that charm, but she was no longer thinking about it; she was no longer thinking that she might be beautiful in the nude; she was only nude in order to dress herself. A woman does not give herself to her costume; she learns to give herself, much later, when she has savored the appetites she arouses.

Over the curve of her hips, and her forward-leaning torso Jène unrolled the beige cloth—that poor, humble fabric. Its folds had to accompany the form of her body—an instinctive science informed her of that—held by only one or two of the bone clasps that had taken the place of pins. She found the right placement: a knot over her right shoulder, the left breast uncovered, the other disappeared beneath the surge of candid folds.

She reflected, biting her lip. "No," she said, "that's not right yet..."

She found a means to lower the cloth at the back, quite low between the two shoulders, drawing it forwards half way to the two firm, round globes. Turning continually around the imperfect and insufficient mirror, she became impatient at never being able to see herself in full.

"You're beautiful!" the wonderstruck Henny affirmed. "You're very beautiful, I assure you. How strange that is! I didn't think you could be so beautiful!"

She combed her hair with a boxwood comb that Henny has fashioned with his own hands one winter evening at the smith's house, meditated again, and secured it over her forehead with a double string of red berries.

"Now," she said. "Now!"

"The little shoes, the lovely shoes!" Henny proposed, intoxicated.

"On my bare feet? You don't have any idea…no, wait!"

Taking the finest strips with which she bound her ankles over her sabots on icy and snowy days, she wrapped them around her legs, all the way to the knees, slightly interlaced. Their hue fused with the hem of the sort of stola that her feminine genius had just reinvented. Then, sitting down like a queen, she said: "You can put the shoes on me now!"

He knelt down for the second time.

"How small they are! How small they seem! Will you be able to walk in them? It's impossible...unbelievable!"

She took a few hesitant steps, embarrassed by the high heels, which disconcerted her, then recovered her self-confidence, bowed, walked and danced, drunk with joy, as if her young head was in the clouds.

"Aren't I beautiful!"

She repeated: "Beautiful! Beautiful! Beautiful!" She chanted the word, the incantatory power of which she felt emanating from her entire body And, by virtue of a contrast that he felt bitterly, rendered gauche, humiliated to the point of anger in his woolen cloak and the woolen undercoat that she had knitted with her own hands, Henny felt ugly, dirty, coarse, inferior to her, at the very moment that he felt a furious desire to carry her away, to take her, to have her all to himself, underneath him, without any longer seeing her but conserving nevertheless in his eyes the image of that tall, slender woman, splendid, as he had never seen her before.

He only had to take one step, though, make a gesture; she fell into his arms. She had understood, at the same time as the exasperation of his senses, his timidity; she experienced, in consequence, an immense satisfaction, stronger and more delightful than the strongest and most delightful ecstasy, for which, however, she was prepared. She was not taken, this time; she gave herself. That was a new, unknown sensation for Jène, the revelation of the power that womankind had once possessed, which exited her to the point of frenzy.

Suddenly, though, as he was about to become her master again, the master who takes, tears, violates, she pushed him away with her extended arms, and cried: "Henny! Henny!"

"What?" he said, interrupted but brutal.

"Henny, they must have existed—those things, all those things? The time of joy and beauty, the time when women were beautiful, as I've just tried to make myself beautiful?

And that, my costume, was only a semblance, a lie that would have made them laugh if they were to come back... Henny, Henny, what was there in those times, and why does it no longer exist?"

Thus it was that the great revolt began among the Field-folk, which shook the power of the Town-Stealers.

José Moselli: *The Eternal Voyage; or, The Prospectors of Space*

(1923)

I

Sitting at a table made of planks supported by two trestles, Professor Daniel Vorels, round-shouldered, with long graying hair, was checking his calculations once again. It was a long job.

Although it was only January, in the heart of winter, there was no fire in the grate. No shutters of the windows; not even curtains. No carpet on the worn and disjointed tiles. Everything in the room reeked of misery, the most complete deprivation.

The wallpaper was reduced to damp tatters, exposing the damp-soaked plaster to view. The ceiling had several yawning cracks. No furniture, except for that table and the staved-in wicker chair serving a scientist as a seat.

Against the walls, badly-planed wooden shelves were bending under the weight of enormous folio volumes and badly-stitched pamphlets.

Through the dirty, cracked windows, patched in places by strips of paper, the black sky, dotted with stars, could be made out, as if veiled by a fog.

Further away, the calm and shining sea.

Professor Daniel Vorels' house—or, rather, hovel—was situated on one of the hills that overlooked Nice from the north-west: a peasant's hut with crumbling walls.

Many years before, Daniel Vorels had owned a château in the region, with hundreds of hectares of land, and a numerous staff.

The land, the château and the fortune had all melted away. Daniel Vorels, physicist and astronomer, had commissioned telescopes built to his own design, incessantly modified, destroyed and replaced. He had imagined increasingly complicated instruments. He had sent long papers to various scientific societies throughout the world—merely to end up ruining himself and having himself treated as a madman and a maniac.

His two daughters had died of consumption and poverty. Presently, his wife was dying in the kitchen—a kitchen that also served as a bedroom.

Daniel Vorels had reserved one of the two rooms for himself—the one in which he was in the process of checking his calculations. He loved his wife, his life's companion, but he preferred science to her.

The coughs and moans of the unfortunate woman broke the silence of the night intermittently and Daniel Vorels, disturbed in his meditations, made a movement of ferocious impatience: the impatience of the scientist for everything that is not science.

Abruptly, he got to his feet. His ravaged features, emaciated and hollowed out by deep wrinkles, stretched. His blue eyes shone with a pure and candid joy. His thin, colorless lips parted in a smile that uncovered the few yellow stumps that served him as teeth.

He brandished the crumpled pieced of paper covered with equations that he held in his fleshless and parchment-like hand.

"And it took sixty-eight years!" he murmured, in a discouraged tone. "If only..."

A louder choking sound resonated, drowning out his voice.

"Charlotte!" he exclaimed, bounding toward the door separating the two rooms.

He opened it and went into a little kitchen with smoky walls, in a corner of which a thin straw mattress was placed on the floor. On that meager bed, an old woman wrapped in two worn and frayed cotton blankets was coughing violently. A coarse tallow candle, set on the ground, illuminated her features—and the somersaults of the flame made fantastic shadows dance on that face, already marked by death.

The unfortunate woman was raised up on her elbows. Only her dark eyes were alive in her pale face. "Daniel!" she breathed, in a hoarse voice, while her fingernails raked the covers.

"Charlotte, my darling!" the old man cried, brandishing his piece of paper. "We're going to be richer than Croesus...untold wealth that will make our fortune! I've redone my calculations! Do you hear? It's really radium. The spectral analysis proves it. And the other invention is quite ready. Yesterday, I dispatched a lump of lead. Took off like a balloon! You hear? A month to construct the apparatus! Six days for the voyage, and we'll come back with a kilogram of radium. Count up what that will bring, at a hundred thousand francs a gram...and that's assuming less than half the market price. A hundred million! Do you hear? I'll set aside half for your cousins. That leaves us fifty million. We can buy back the château, the land. You'll be cared for, happy. And people will finally realize that I was right. Tomorrow, I'll...oh!"

In his mental excitement, Daniel Vorels had ceased looking at his wife.

His eyes suddenly lowered toward her, and he saw that she had fallen backwards, inert, her eyes vitreous, her jaw distended—dead. While the companion of her existence was taking flight into new dreams, the old woman had left him forever.

"Charlotte!" cried the scientist, falling to his knees on the flagstones. "Charlotte! Listen!"

He grabbed his wife's bony hands, and reality abruptly imposed itself upon him. Charlotte Vorels was dead. Two tears sprang from his reddened eyelids, burned by late nights and insomnia.

Gently, piously, he folded the old woman's hands over her breast, kissed her forehead tenderly, and got to his feet.

"Everything has its price," he murmured. "It's fate that decided that I should experience the greatest grief of my existence today, at the same time as my greatest joy. Poor Charlotte!"

II

Nine o'clock in the morning had just sounded at Nice Cathedral. In spite of the winter chill, bright sunlight gilded the city.

An automobile—the latest model, all varnish and nickel—stopped in front of the William Olson Bank in the Avenue de Verdun.

William Olson, a fat bald man with yellow side-whiskers, green eyes bordered by flaccid bags, ruddy cheeks and a square jaw, leapt lightly on to the sidewalk, which he crossed in three strides.

Greeted by the doorman, he went across the great hall, where a few clients were already waiting, and plunged into his office. Having taken off his overcoat, he installed himself behind the vast mahogany desk and pulled the heap of papers constituting his mail toward him.

William Olson had principles. He wanted to see everything, read everything; he annotated the most unimportant letters and nothing left his bank without him applying his own signature to it.

Armed with a silver-bladed paper-knife, he began to open the letters piled in front of him. Almost immediately, however, the sound of voices and footsteps reached him through the padded door. He frowned, and pressed the ivory button of an electric bell fitted to his desk.

The door opened; a red-faced uniformed employee appeared. "Monsieur le Directeur," he began, "there's a sort of madman who..."

He did not finish. A tall, bare-headed old man sent him spinning against the desk, to which he had to cling on to prevent himself from falling.

"Madman! Me?" muttered the intruder, whose eyes were shining like hot coals. "That's the last straw! Yes, Olson, it's me. I have great news to tell you, and this imbecile tries to stop me getting to you. If you knew..."

William Olson was calm now. "That's all right," he said to the employee—who, having recovered his composure, was looking at him. "You can go."

The man withdrew, more alarmed than ever.

"And now, Monsieur Vorels, what do you want?" the banker demanded, in a tone that was not very welcoming. "You know what I said to you. I'm sticking to it!"

"I haven't come to ask you for anything," Daniel Vorels assured him, sitting down casually in one of the comfortable leather armchairs facing the desk. "I've simply come to tell you that Madame Vorels, your cousin, died the day before yesterday, in the morning, and that I buried her yesterday evening."

Olson frowned. "Died of poverty, eh? By your fault."

"Perhaps. I haven't come here to find out how you feel about me. Madame Vorels died of consumption. I tell you that in case you want to know the exact cause of your cousin's death."

The banker made a gesture, simultaneously evasive and interrogative. His expression was clearly asking the question: "What do you want with me, then?"

Daniel Vorels understood perfectly.

"I've come to make you a business proposal," he explained. "Don't look so disgusted. Hear me out. I'll be brief. I've come to you because you know me and, if you accept, the matter can be settled more rapidly. If you don't, I'll go to see other capitalists.

"Here it is: my research, which I've been pursuing for more than forty years, have permitted me to determine the composition of the Sun and the Moon, thanks to the spectroscope. I've invented a new spectroscope of a sensitivity and precision compared to which Fraunhofer's spectroscope is a child's toy. I've thus been able to determine that the surface of the Moon is strewn with rare metals, including rubidium and thallium—which also exist, as you know, in the sun. Only one of those metals remained an enigma to me, because of the nature of the luminous rays it emits. The discovery of radium, and the spectral analysis of emitted by that metal, has proved to me that the unknown metal that exists on the surface of the Moon is none other than radium...

"There is a formidable deposit there, in a pure state. According to my calculations, there must be hundreds of tons, located in one of the protuberances—or craters, if you prefer—in the Sea of Clouds. The crater is designated by astronomers by the name of Ptolemy.

"Can you see the extraordinary speculation that one might make by going out there to fetch a kilogram or two of that radium?"

"I can see that you're mad, Monsieur Vorels, and that you're causing me to waste my time, which is precious," said William Olson, tranquilly. "Let's leave it at that, if you please." He reached for the button of the electric bell.

"Precious as your time might be, you will, I suppose, allow me to finish?" the scientist replied, in the same tone. "I am mad, but not mad enough to talk about a deposit of radium on the Moon if I didn't know a means of getting there easily. For that, it's necessary to spend a hundred thousand francs, in all. And I'll prove it to you.

"Are you familiar with the effect of light on selenium? Light has the property of attracting that metal, a property primarily utilized by toymakers to make little, extremely light windmills turn, the sails of which are coated with a selenium-based compound.

"I have discovered a metal—or, rather, an element—that possesses the property of being attracted to light like iron to a magnet. That metal exists in a colloidal state in certain plants—heliotropes, for example—and that is what explains why they invariably turn toward the sun. I won't enter into further explanations because you wouldn't understand. I've brought a little of my product with me. I'll coat any object whatsoever, of your own choice, and you'll see what will happen. Would you like to hand me that paperweight?"

Daniel Vorels pointed to the base of a nickel-plated shell set on the banker's desk. Without saying a word, Olson nodded his head.

"Close the shutters, please," the scientist ordered.

William Olson as so completely nonplussed that he obeyed, mechanically. The room was lunged into obscurity.

Thanks to the feeble light filtering through the slats of the shutters, the banker was able to see Daniel Vorels take a lead flask from his pocket, which he uncorked, and whose contents he poured over the paperweight. The object in question immediately emitted a phosphorescent glow so intense that the office was lit up by it, as if by an arc-lamp.

Vorels placed the object on the external windowsill.

"Open up," he said. "And watch carefully!"

William Olson, excite in spite of his Anglo-Saxon phlegm, looked at the paperweight and saw it quiver, as if agitated by tremors. The banker lifted up the sash-window and opened the shutters.

He heard a whistling sound, as the paperweight, with the velocity of a stone launched by a slingshot, passed before his eyes and rose toward the ether, in the direction of the sun. Within an instant, it had disappeared.

"Am I mad?" Daniel Vorels demanded.

"No, no!" murmured William Olson, looking at the scientist with a hint of fear.

"Thank you. Well, if you don't think I'm mad, perhaps we can make a deal. Radium is undoubtedly the only remedy against cancer and numerous skin diseases. It's worth nearly two hundred thousand francs a gram. We'll lower that price to ten thousand francs, and we'll bring back ten kilograms—ten thousand grams—from the moon! That's a hundred million francs. Half for you, the other half for me. I'll distribute it to scientists myself...to scientists who aren't members of Academies, to researchers...to madmen...that's my business.

"I'll give you the plans of the apparatus I've designed for going to the Moon. According to my calculations, it will take three days to get there, and a little less to come back. The apparatus consists of two concentric spheres; between them is a few thousand liters of glycerine, in which the interior sphere bathes. That glycerine will serve as a shock-absorber for the landing on Earth…and also on the Moon.[66]

"Two hermetically sealed doors, connected by a conduit, will permit entry to the apparatus and exit therefrom. One of the two men forming the crew of the machine will collect the radium, which exists in the state of a powder, and fill two lead bottles with it. That man will be equipped with a diving suit of my design, which will permit him to move while conserving his equilibrium in spite of the difference between the effects of gravity on the Earth and the Moon. He'll be able to breathe by means of a cylinder of compressed air.

"The handling of the apparatus and its steering will be..."

Daniel Vorels interrupted himself. The door of the banker's office opened to give passage to a tall young man, apparently about twenty-six years old—a veritable athlete, with his square shoulders, his enormous biceps and his jutting jaw.

"Hi, Pop!" he said, in a lazy voice, while negligently smoothing out a crease in his nut-brown waistcoat. "Hi, Mr. Vorels. I heard some of what you were saying about your little deal. You know, I'd quite like to go to the Moon. Ha ha! Usually, it's bankers who do moonlight flits; now, it'll be their sons. And you'll cut me a slice of the cake, eh, Pop? Two or three little millions!"

Having pronounced these words in a vulgar drawl, Tom Olson let himself fall heavily into an armchair, whose springs groaned beneath him.

---

[66] Moselli indulges in wordplay here, as more than one French writer of speculative fiction did, apparently spontaneously, improvising the term *alunissage* by analogy with *atterrisage* [landing], but I cannot retain it in English.

Without responding, Daniel Vorels looked the newcomer up and down. The latter presented the most perfect specimen of a playboy: cynicism, thirst for enjoyment and brutality mingled amiably in his clean-shaven face.

The scientist shrugged his shoulders. "It makes no difference to me," he said, without bringing up the indiscretion committed by Tom Olson. "But if you come in on the deal, you have to promise to follow the instructions you're given scrupulously. The success of the enterprise, and your life itself, will depend on it."

"Oh, me, I'll take any risk—won't I, Pop?" the young man assured him.

"Let Monsieur Vorels speak," said the banker, considering his son with pride and affection.

"I've finished," the scientist declared. "The two spheres will be made of nickel-plated steel. Inside, electric lighting, provisions for ten days, a machine-gun for defense, in the unlikely event that the Moon is inhabited and the natives want to attack us. A sidereal compass, of my own invention, for navigation. And for steering apparatus, exterior segments permitting the mathematical regulation of the exposure of the surface coated with my product to luminous rays.

"Thanks to a little table I've drawn up, which will be fixed next to the controls, no error can be made. I've calculated the weight of the machine at different stages of the journey, while it's submissive to the attraction of the Earth and then that of the Moon. The velocity will be such that the journey there and back can be completed in less than a week, in the absence of any untoward incident. The specific gravity of the apparatus, with its crew and its provisions, will be slightly less than that of sea-water, so that it will float if it happens to land in the ocean. According to my calculations, though, it will land in India, slightly to the north of the island of Ceylon, and, as the landing will take place in broad daylight in the tropical zone, the Sun's rays should be sufficiently luminous to cancel out the effects of weight, which will permit a landing as gentle as possible. So..."

"I'm going, right, Pop?" Tom Olson, put in.

"You're mad," the banker complained, shrugging his shoulders violently. "Let us talk!"

"But since Mr. Vorels says that there's no danger..."

"Leave us in peace! We'll see! According to what you've just said, Monsieur Vorels, it seems to me that the affair is viable. The conditions suggested by you seem reasonable. But before signing, I'll ask you for permission to have your plans and calculations examined by an expert: Professor Joachim Goats of the University of Cambridge, is in Nice at present. He...."

"I'm sure of myself!" Vorels cut in.

"I don't doubt that—but business is business, and I'm risking my money. Besides, you're not risking anything. I'll give you a receipt for all your plans and calculations..."

"It's just that I don't have duplicates, and if they were lot, my entire life's work would be annihilated!" Vorels protested.

"I'll promise, on the receipt, to pay you ten million francs if a single one of the items you've given me is lost. Your papers won't leave my office and will be locked in my safe. Go and fetch them, then, and come back. We'll draw up a contract today. I'll telephone Professor Goats. He's at the Imperial Palace."

Daniel Vorels got to his feet. He looked at the banker and his son, with an imperceptible hesitation. The idea that his work would be submitted to the criticism of one of the official scientists that he detested was extremely disagreeable to him, but a rapid reflection convinced him of the uselessness of any protest. Any businessman he approached would want to be sure, before making a deal, of the efficacy of his calculations and his formulas.

"Agreed," he said. "I'll be here this afternoon."

He shook hands with the father and son and went out.

William Olson and his son exchanged smiles. The banker's was slightly cynical.

"Tall stories, eh, Pop?" Tom sniggered.

"No—it's serious. He carried out an experiment in front of me that…but it will be a pity if that madman benefits from the affair..."

"Sure! But you'll let me go up there, won't you, Pop? It'll set me up."

"That depends on what Goats says. I have every confidence in him. If there's no danger, you can go; otherwise, we'll send some poor hero. Remember that you're all I have, my boy. Come on—give me a hug!"

"You, know, Pop, I was going…I came to ask you for a few sous. I got cleaned out last night in Monte Carlo—a run of bad luck. Five hundred louis should suffice,"

William Olson suppressed a slight grimace, which concluded with a smile in which pride and affection were mingled. "You're a naughty boy, Tom," was all that he murmured.

III

At three o'clock that afternoon, Daniel Vorels returned to the bank. Orders had been given. He had no obstacles to overcome this time in order to get to William Olson.

"Do you have the papers?" the banker asked, as soon as the clerk had closed the door behind Vorels.

"Yes—all of them. The spectral analyses of the lunar region where the radium is; analyses made at different times, always identical; the experiments carried out with the aid of siderite..."

"Siderite?"

"Yes—the product attracted by light. These experiments prove that siderite is sensitive to the action of any light source. That produced by the Moon will suffice, if it's utilized according to my indications. Here, finally, are the plans and schematics for the apparatus that will permit the Moon to be reached in three days. I've determine the exact mass of the machine, including the crew and equipment, the coefficients of resistance of the metal, and the mechanism permitting the external screens to be maneuvered. And here are the blueprints of my sidereal compass, permitting navigation in space without any calculation, taking account of the simultaneous motion of the Earth and the Moon. I've also brought the plans and description of my protective suit. You shall see."

Having emptied a stout, scarred and frayed moleskin document-case on to the desk, taking out the various files that he had placed in front of the banker, whose contents he had identified, the scientist said: "That's all. Nothing missing."

"Thank you," said William Olson. "If you care to remind me once again of the numbers of the files, with the list of items that they contain, I'll write them down. That will permit me to give you a detailed receipt, in which your intentions will be minutely described; that way, you won't have any surprise to fear. I like to do things correctly. I'll sign and date it. You won't need to come back for three days—just long enough to allow Professor Goats to examine your formulas rapidly. If, as I'm convinced, they're viable, I'll pay you a hundred thousand francs by way of an advance and give you *carte blanche* to begin the construction of the apparatus. Is that all right?"

"Yes—except that I want it stipulated that I will take part in the expedition. I'm ready to die, but I'm curious to see for myself whether certain hypotheses I've formulated concerning the nature of the lunar soil are correct, and..."

"You want to make the voyage?" the banker exclaimed.

"Yes. I'm absolutely set on it. You can choose the second voyager—that's a matter of indifference to me."

"But…you're old! Oh, I believe that you're in good health and likely to live for a long time, but, after all…if you had a heart attack or a stroke…fell ill…at your age, anything is possible. You understand?"

"Yes, but what does it matter? Thanks to the explanations I shall give you, and the tables attached to the interior of the machine, my companion would still be able to carry out the necessary maneuvers, which are quite simple and easy. I shall merely be a passenger, so to speak."

William Olson gave a slight shrug. "As you wish!" he agreed. "Now, let's get started. Would you care to dictate to me, and go swiftly—I'm used to taking rapid notes."

Daniel Vorels bowed. Methodically, with careful gestures, he brought out his schematics, plans and formulas one after another, omitting nothing, specifying the nature of each document. There were a great many!

It was after five o'clock in the evening, and the banker had switched on the electric light some time before, when the inventory was finally concluded. William Olson read it back, collating each item, finished his list and signed it.

"We're in accord!" he concluded. "Now I'll give you a document in which all our conditions will be set out; fifty per cent each of the products of the expedition, whatever they might be. All expenses my exclusive responsibility, up to a hundred thousand francs. That's all right?"

"Yes, and the absolute right for me to make the voyage," the scientist insisted.

"Naturally," said Olson, smiling.

He drew up the receipt, signed it, added the bank's stamp, and pinned the list of papers to it. "There!" he said. "Do you need any money now?"

"No, thank you. I still have thirty francs. That's more than I need for three days." With these words, Daniel Vorels shook the banker's hand and went out. William Olson followed him with a cynical gaze.

An hour later, the old scientist had returned to his hovel. Although it was dark, he did not light any source of illumination. He did not have any, having burned his last candle to maintain a vigil over his wife's body. He had nothing to eat. It was pride that had made him tell the banker that he had money. He did not have a centime.

He let himself fall on to the mattress that had served as Charlotte's death-bed and, with his eyes half-closed, sank into a long reverie. In spite of his impatience to see his life's work take on substance, he waited for the third day to return to the bank.

Finally, the longed-for moment arrived.

"Monsieur William Olson is away!" the clerk replied, looking him up and down scornfully.

"But he told me that...he...he's expecting me!" the unfortunate man stammered, unable to believe his ears. "He must have given instructions."

"He hasn't left anything. And you'd better clear the floor, old man! That's all you can do!" the clerk advised, charitably.

Daniel Vorels stiffened. "Oh, but this is shameful. It's a mistake! I'm Daniel Vorels, and I agreed with..."

The door of the antechamber of the room where this scene was taking place opened abruptly, and Tom Olson appeared, frowning, his eyes hostile, an ominous snigger twisting his clean-shaven lips.

"What's all this noise?" he demanded, pretending not to see Vorels.

"It's...this man, who wants to see Monsieur le Directeur, even though I've told him that Monsieur le Directeur is away!"

"Well, my man, you'll have to go—my father isn't here," said Tom Olson, simply.

The old scientist started in protest. "What! But, Tom—don't you recognize me? I'm Daniel Vorels, who...who..."

"Daniel Vorels? Don't know him. You'll have to write to my father—he'll reply if there's any need."

"But...but...I came here three days ago—you know that very well, Tom. You were here, and..."

"Are you mad, friend? Go on, get out—or I'll teach you to come and play the fool in a respectable place of business! Simon! Throw this pilgrim out for me, and in future, don't let this kind of vagabond in, all right?"

Stupefied and indignant, Daniel Vorels could make no reply. The employee, profiting from his distress, seized him by the shoulders and shoved him brutally out into the street.

Overwhelmed, Daniel Vorels remained motionless for a few seconds, open-mouthed, his tall thin body quivering.

Eventually, he calmed down. Already, passers-by were staring at him. He understood that he was being taken for a madman, and succeeded in getting control of himself.

"Fortunately, I have the papers," he murmured. "I won't allow myself to be robbed like this."

Forgetting his fatigue and his weakness, he headed for his miserable dwelling. He reached it, lifted up the mattress under which he had hide the portfolio containing the inventory of the papers handed over to the banker and the draft of the contract signed by the latter.

The portfolio was empty.

As if struck by lightning, Daniel Vorels collapsed on to the mattress.

He had been robbed. All his hopes, the fruit of his entire life's work, the results for which he had ruined his family, caused the death of his children and his wife, had been wiped out.

IV

For nearly five months, the newspapers had been taking about nothing but Joachim Goats' lunar expedition. First, short articles had appeared announcing that Dr. Joachim Goats of the University of Cambridge had invented a marvelous machine that, thanks to the utilization of light, had succeeded in conclusively vanquishing the laws of gravity.

Naturally, innumerable letters had come to the professor from the four corners of the world; he had limited himself to replying that he deplored the indiscretion, that the information was true but that his discovery had not yet been perfected.

A few weeks had passed. Then Joachim Goats had announced that the work was complete, and that, thanks to the generosity of an English Maecenas, he was about to utilize his discovery to construct an apparatus designed to explore the Moon.

That news had been greeted with unanimous incredulity. Joachim Goats' colleagues had assured him that the idea was an unrealizable chimera; others had quietly insinuated that Joachim Goats, by dint of looking at the stars, must have lost contact with material reality—in brief, that he must be a trifle deranged…or, to put it another way, mad.

Interviews had appeared ridiculing Joachim Goats' project; jokes were made about the scientist in music hall revues; actresses had made entire audiences laugh at the expense of the man who wanted to go to the Moon. Songwriters got mixed up in it.

In brief, no one had taken the scientist seriously, some because they were jealous of him, others out of ignorance, the great majority, as usual, by virtue of snobbery.

People do not like novelties or innovations. Now, it was accepted that it was impossible to go to the Moon. Thus, anyone who talked about doing so was a lunatic. If America had not been discovered and Christopher Columbus came back in the twentieth century, he would have had great difficulty finding the money to equip his vessels. Some people would have made fun of him, others would have taken him for a mere swindler.

Joachim Goats, however, let people say what they wished. He did not even deign to protest.

The newspapers had tried to make him reveal the name of his generous Maecenas—that innocent fool, it was whispered—but in vain.

And the weeks had passed. Joachim Goats had disappeared.

He had simply gone to the north of Scotland. There, on a high mountain in the county of Sutherland, a minuscule construction-yard had been set up, not far from Loch Shin. Thirty specialists carefully chosen from the principal nations of the world—particularly Germany, England and the United States—had been put to work: engineers, physicists, mechanics and electricians. A few steelworkers helped them to construct the mysterious apparatus designed by Daniel Vorels.

While this work was being carried out under the direction of Joachim Goats, building the two concentric spheres separated by a layer of glycerine, an expedition comprising twenty botanists had been traveling though equatorial Africa gathering supplies of certain plants described by Daniel Vorels, the sap of which, distilled by special procedures and added to colloidal metals, would form the mysterious siderite that was so sensitive to light.

Joachim Goats had personally supervised the distillation of these plants, and had thus manufactured a supply of siderite adequate to coat the external sphere of the lunar apparatus completely. Experiments he had carried out had proved, without any possible doubt, the Daniel Vorels' formulas were sound. Several objects, coated with siderite by Goats, had risen up and disappeared into the sky, toward the Sun or toward the Moon.

And the weeks had gone by.

One morning, William Olson, who had stayed in Nice, had received a coded telegram, which he had been expecting for some time. The apparatus was ready. In five days' time, the Moon would be in the most favorable position, relative to the Earth, for the success of the adventurous voyage.

William Olson had taken the express, and within forty-eight hours had arrived in Inverness, from which he had traveled to Ben Kilbreck.

The same day, the newspapers, not merely of the United Kingdom but of the entire world, published the following note, eloquent in its laconism:

Sir William Olson and Professor Joachim Goats announce that, within forty-eight hours, at five o'clock in the morning on the day after tomorrow, the apparatus invented by Joachim Goats and financed by William Olson will leave the Earth for a short voyage to study the surface of the Moon. It will be piloted by Joachim Goats in person, assisted by the well-known sportsman Tom Olson, the son of William Olson. The point of departure is situated on Ben Kilbreck, near Helmsdale in the county of Sutherland.

That was all, but it was enough.

From everywhere in Europe, thousands of curiosity-seekers, skeptics and envious individuals, raced toward the north of Scotland. Trains, boats and automobiles converged on the county of Sutherland. Special trains had to be put on. Traffic was jammed on several of the major roads of Great Britain. Hundreds of aircraft, chartered at fabulous prices, plowed through the skies. There were seven accidents on the railway, dozens of people crushed by automobiles and two airplane collisions.

Journalists flocked to Ben Kilbreck in hundreds—and the stories sent by the first reporters to arrive in Scotland increased the curiosity of the entire world.

Scientists—the very ones who had ridiculed Joachim Goats' invention—let it be known that, after all, nothing was impossible for human beings, and that, personally, they would not be astonished…that they had always predicted…that science had limitless possibilities...

In sum, the individuals in question gave evidence of a prudent opportunism.

One last detail: numerous tradesmen installed themselves on the slopes of Ben Kilbreck, erecting tents and setting up benches and tables, and posting prices: ten pounds sterling per night to sleep in a hammock, three pounds for breakfast, six for lunch!

Commerce never surrenders its entitlements.

V

The departure of the *Britannia*—as William Olson, a patriot above all else, had baptized the machine—was to take place at five o'clock in the morning, which was two hours after sunrise, for it was the middle of summer, and the nights are very short at that time of year in the north of Scotland.

Needless to say, the hundreds of curiosity-seekers gathered for the occasion had not slept at all that night.

On the slopes of the surrounding mountains, in the valleys, amid the heather and the gorse, the ground disappeared under a veritable human sea that spread out, with currents like those of the ocean, and as just as noisy. At intervals, there were automobiles, like little islets, whose owners were perched on their roofs. Cries, howls, murmurs and appeals, including whistle-blasts, formed a confused rumor like that of surf.

On the vast rocky esplanade forming the top of Ben Kilbreck, platforms had been set up. They were plastered with Britannic flags and formed three sides of a square, facing north, west and south respectively. The direction of the Orient had been left free, because that was the one in which the *Britannia* would be taking off. The apparatus was standing in the center of the square, maintained in equilibrium by a light wooden framework. At its summit, the circular hatchway was visible that would permit the voyagers in space to take their places inside.

A kind of carapace, formed by mobile segments around a common axis, made of pieces of black-painted canvas, covered the sphere. By maneuvering thee segments from inside the machine, a greater or lesser extent of the sphere's surface could be exposed to the light, which thus permitted its velocity and direction to be regulated.

A light bamboo ladder was leaning against the apparatus. At the foot of the ladder a group of five individuals had gathered: William Olson, his son Tom, Professor Joachim Goats, and two gentlemen in black suits: the Under-Secretary of State for Aeronautics, Sir Archibald Munro, and the Minister of War, General Lord Algernon Kimball. They were talking in low voices, seemingly impassive. From time to time, Joachim Goats, a stout clean-shaven man in gold-rimmed spectacles, consulted his chronometer.

Tom Olson was radiant. He had had difficulty obtaining his father's permission to undertake the adventurous voyage, and had ended up overcoming the banker's resistance by force of insistence, and also by remarking that, in order to harvest the radium, it was better, for reasons of prudence, that a member of the Olson family should be present. It is necessary to expect anything. Joachim Goats was an honest man, to be sure, but it was better to make sure that he would be obliged to be. William Olson allowed himself to be convinced.

Tom, clad in a warm aviation-costume, affected a detached air, although he was rather anxious; he was thinking about the perils of the voyage and wondering whether he would come back. It would not have taken much insistence for him to renounce his part in it. He darted clandestine glances at the pale sky into which he was about to plunge.

William Olson was even more anxious that he was. Bandit as he was, the banker knew no pity or scruple, but he had one weakness: his son. He loved him with a savage affection, and would have set fire to the world in order to boil him an egg. At present, he was bitterly regretting having authorized him to go, but everything was settled. The ministers were there; the entire world knew that Tom Olson was about to launch into the ether. It was impossible to back out.

The Minister of War exchanged glances with Professor Joachim Goats. A few more minutes...

In spite of his sixty years, Lord Algernon Kimball slowly climbed up on a small podium draped with the Union Jack. Silence fell instantaneously.

In a curt and harsh voice, General Kimball delivered a eulogy to British science, British courage and British generosity:

"Not only have the English explored and colonized the world," he said, "but now they are going to explore the Moon. This apparatus has been invented by an English scientist, and constructed by English engineers with English capital. It is crewed by Englishmen!

"I have no commentary to add. England, which has always been the foremost of the civilized nations, will be the first to explore interplanetary space. Thanks to the generosity of William Olson and the science of Joachim Goats, new possibilities will be opened up for our industrialists, our unemployed, our emigrants and our businessmen.

"The future of England is opening up, more brilliantly than ever. Either the Moon is inhabited, which will allow us to trade with it, or it is deserted, in which case we shall colonize it, like Australia.

"Ladies and Gentlemen, I have the great honor to have been charged by His Gracious Majesty to announce to William Olson his elevation to the dignity of Companion of the Order of the Bath, and to Professor Goats his elevation to a baronetcy! Ladies and Gentlemen, three cheers in honor of Old England, and its intrepid voyagers!"

A tempest of cheers burst forth, and lasted for several minutes, prolonged by surrounding echoes. William Olson had paled slightly. His appointment to the Order of the Bath put a lid on his life's ambition. He was ennobled—him! And he was about to make millions! Everything was smiling on him.

The memory of Daniel Vorels imposed itself upon his mind for half a second. "Imbecile!" he thought, with all sincerity.

But Joachim Goats looked at his chronometer one last time. The moment of departure...

An energetic handshake, an accolade, and the professor slowly climbed the steps of the bamboo ladder leaning against the apparatus.

"Goodbye, Pop!" murmured a voice, rendered anxious by the thought of the perils that its owner was about to run.

"God protect you. Son!" said the banker, forcing himself to remain calm. Look after yourself—no imprudence! Listen to the professor! I've given him my recommendations. You will pay attention, won't you? And come back safely. You...see you soon, Tom! See you soon!"

People watched them in respectful silence. They drew apart.

Tom Olson marched to the ladder. He turned round to look at his father one last time, and climbed up with the tread of a condemned man mounting the scaffold. One last glance at the blue sky and the Scottish mountains, and Tom Olson disappeared inside the sphere.

The ladder was removed. A slight grating sound within the reigning silence; from inside the machine, the voyagers were closing the hatch. The metal lid descended.

A long minute went by.

Several of the segments covering the sphere slid over one another, uncovering a smooth, polished surface that seemed incandescent. There was a sort of hoarse whistling sound; the sphere pivoted slightly in its wooden cradle, and shot away into the blue, as if drawn by a formidable invisible magnet.

It remained visible for a few seconds, climbing with vertiginous rapidity. It dwindled, and finally disappeared.

It was only then that the cheers resounded again.

VI

After a few hours rest in Inverness, William Olson had departed for Nice, where he spent the entire year.

"Someone telephoned several times today for Monsieur le Directeur," his secretary told him. as soon as he returned to the bank, "but the person in question didn't want to leave his name."

"No matter!" said Olson. For the moment, his bank was a matter of indifference to him. He had but one thought: the *Britannia*, which would bring him back his son, ad a few kilograms of radium…worth millions...

He installed himself behind his vast desk and started opening his mail, but without taking any interest in the task. He had scarcely opened half a dozen letters when the telephone set in front of him rang.

He put the receiver to his ear—and went pale. He had recognized the voice of Daniel Vorels.

"Hello? Is that really Monsieur William Olson with whom I'm in communication? Don't hang up. This will interest you.

"As I had counted on piloting the apparatus whose plans you stole from me myself. I didn't mention to you that the coating of siderite can only last for four days at the most—

which is to say, enough to reach the Moon. I intended to take a supply with me, in order to replace the coating once I had arrived on the Moon's surface.

"Naturally, Professor Goats hasn't thought of that—which will ensure that the *Britannia* cannot and will not return. As for the formula for siderite, it no longer exists. Prudently, you and Professor Goats, that thief, didn't want to have any copies made…and I've joined your school.

"I've been to Scotland. I introduced myself into your camp, and I succeeded in stealing the formula of siderite, which I destroyed. As the product was already prepared, you had no more need of the papers. They no longer exist. That cost me the few sous I got from the sale of my miserable hovel. I'm avenged..."

Haggard and open-mouthed, William Olson heard the metallic click indicating that his interlocutor had hung up.

He remained motionless for a few seconds, listening, as if he were expecting further explanations.

Suddenly, the blood rushed to his brain; he uttered a howl like a wild beast, and collapsed on his desk, felled by apoplexy.

The *Britannia* never came back.

No more was ever heard of Daniel Vorels.

William Olson is still alive, a resident in a lunatic asylum.

José Moselli: *The Planetary Messenger*
(1924)

Muffled in thick furs from top to toe, Ottar Wallens, the geologist, and Olaf Densmold, the astronomer, advanced slowly over the ice-field.

Fifty meters ahead of them, the sled guided by Lobyak, an Alaskan Indian, was gliding over the white plain. Then there was the wilderness: frozen snow, blocks of ice, grey sky, devoid of reflections. Not a breath of air, but a temperature of twenty-eight degrees below zero.

The three men—the geologist, the astronomer and the native—had left their ship, the three-master *Sirius*, eleven days before, which had brought them from Bergen as far as Wilkes Land. The *Sirius* had advanced as far as the seventieth parallel before being stopped by the ice-sheet.

The expedition's objective was not, strictly speaking, to reach the South Pole, but to get as close to it as possible and to complete the observations of Amundsen and Shackleton, from the meteorological, astronomical and geological viewpoint. As the *Sirius* could go no further, the two leaders of the expedition had decided to advance across the ice-sheet.

In addition to numerous scientific instruments, including a small wireless telegraph apparatus, they were carrying provisions of all kinds for six weeks, light and improved camping equipment and weapons all securely stowed on a sled pulled by twelve Alaskan dogs steered by Kobyak, a gigantic Redskin hired in Nome in western Alaska.

Ottar Wallens, the geologist, was about forty-two years old. He was a strong fellow, slightly round-shouldered, with a round face and a snub nose supporting a pair of spectacles with horn frames. He was brusque, and quick to lose his temper. A member of the Royal Academy of Christiania and numerous scientific societies, he had published several works on the composition of the polar continents, which made him an authority.

His companion, Olaf Densmold, had just turned fifty-one. He was thin and bony, with a face like the prow of a ship furnished with little round eyes, dark and piercing. Taciturn by nature, he remained mute for entire days. His notable work on the satellites of Jupiter had caused a considerable stir; he was cited as one of the foremost living mathematicians.

In the course of the long crossing undertaken by the *Sirius* between Bergen and Wilkes Land, which had taken more than two months, the scientists, who were already acquainted, had become friends—or, rather, got used to one another. Both, at any rate, were equally interested in the success of the expedition that bore their name...and now, side by side, they were advancing over the bleak ice-sheet.

They did not say much. Since their departure they had had time to tell one another everything, about their past, their projects, their ambitions and their disappointments, and there were no incidents to discuss.

It was the end of September, the Antarctic spring. A pale sun appeared for a few hours every day.

Olaf Densmold made a few astronomical observations of no great interest; then they set off again. March, camp, meal, sleep—life was monotonous.

Kobyak was as taciturn as Densmold; if he talked, it was to his dogs, to encourage or threaten them. The crack of his whip's thong constituted the bulk of his speech.

The sled had already left behind the region attained by previous explorers. It was now advancing into the unknown—an unknown as bleak as it was monotonous. No plants. No trees. Nothing. The ice. In places, it was a uniform plain; further away, gigantic blocks in extraordinary, tormented forms: perfect cubes, veritable frozen waves, dunes, pyramids, the whole cut by precipices, cliffs with neat edges, as if carved by a machine. Some of these precipices were several meters wide; it was necessary to go around them. Their depth varied between ten and a hundred meters. Gurgling sounds sometimes rose up from them, revealing the labor of melt-water. Elsewhere the ice gave way under the weight of the explorers, who had to devote all their attention to following the tracks of the sled closely—for the dogs' instinct did not deceive them.

That day, they had already been on the move for four hours, and they appeared to be making satisfactory progress, not very tiring. The stillness of the air rendered the cold quite tolerable, and the surface of the ice was sufficiently smooth.

For a few moments, however, Kobyak, who usually marched head down, raised his face toward the pale sky, turning is head from right to left, like someone sniffing the wind.

"He has an odd expression, the guide," Ottar Wallens suddenly muttered to his companion.

By way of response, Densmold shrugged his shoulders fatalistically, as if too indicate that Kobyak's countenance was of no importance to him.

"The barometer's high, though," Wallens went on. "I don't think any storm's threatening us."

A further shrug from Densmold.

At that exact moment, Kobyak heard a kind of whistling, which stopped the dogs in their tracks—and the Indian, turning round, waited for the two scientists to catch up with him. Which they did.

"Well?" demanded Wallens, curtly.

"Camp," said Kobyak. "Shelter. Big storm. Big storm coming. Not good."

Without saying a word, the two Norwegians approached the sled and consulted the barometer that was attached to it. It indicated SET FAIR—but the alcohol, in its glass tube, was lowering with terrifying rapidity.

It was definitely necessary to camp.

The three men busied themselves with that.

Within a few minutes, the dogs were unhitched and tied up, the sled placed in a hollow in the ground. Then, with the aid of their knives, the explorers carved blocks of ice, with which they built a sort of conical hut that would serve them as a shelter.

Meanwhile, the sky had darkened somewhat. The dogs, which had just finished their ration of smoked salmon, distributed by Kobyak, were growling dully.

In the hut, the alcohol stove had been lit. A kettle set on top was singing softly.

Suddenly, the storm burst with unexpected violence. Within a few seconds, swirls of thick snow were falling from the blackened sky, while the sinister howling of the dogs mingled with the whistling of the squalls.

The hut, well constructed, did not budge.

A long hour went by. Their meal concluded, the three men had lit their pipes and were smoking in silence.

Kobyak suddenly got up. In response to Wallens' mute interrogation, he pointed to the hole, hollowed out at ground level, that had permitted the explorers to enter the ice-hut; the snow had blocked it completely.

It was necessary to clear the opening; if not, they would be asphyxiated before very long. The Indian had understood that before the scientists.

Armed with his snow-knife, he slowly cleared a path through the icy wall. In a few minutes, he had dug a kind of tunnel into which he disappeared.

Enveloped in their thick sleeping-bags, Ottar Wallens and Olaf Densmold lay side by side, having not exchanged a single word. They could not do anything except wait.

The formidable growl of the tempest reached their ears, no longer muffled but distinct, very close.

Amid the whistling gusts, frightful detonations resounded, drowning out the barking of the miserable dogs, which were howling desperately.

"Kobyak must have cleared the opening completely," said Wallens. The tumult of the storm blotted out his voice.

An icy blast, penetrating through the hole into which the Indian had disappeared, caused the flame of the stove to flicker. A brief but very obvious quiver shook the hut—and the detonations ceased.

The dogs barked more loudly.

A few minutes went by. Kobyak did not reappear.

The two scientists were still mute. They assumed that the Indian must be working to clear the entrance to the hut within a wide perimeter, in order not to be obliged to do it again.

But an hour went by, then two...

Otto Wallens saw that Densmold was asleep. He was snoring. The geologist consulted his watch and saw that it had stopped. He felt his throat gripped by a strange anguish, so violent that he turned to his companion and shook him awake.

"Well?" demanded Densmold, sitting up and frowning.

"It's been more than three hours since Kobyak went out, and he hasn't come back."

"Three hours?"

"At least. My watch has stopped."

Instinctively, Densmold took out his own. "So has mine," he observed, astonished. At eleven minutes past two."

"Eleven minutes past two—mine too!" said Wallens sliding out of his sleeping-bag as quickly as he could.

The stove, almost out of fuel, was no longer producing anything but a flame without warmth.

Ottar Wallens shivered, and drank a few sips of the stewed tea contained in the saucepan suspended over the stove. Then, having taken an electric torch that had been set on a box, he moved to the barometer.

He started in alarm. The column of alcohol seething in the glass tube was moving up and down, marking 800, 750 and 700 millimeters within a minute.

"Come and look at this, Densmold!" he exclaimed, in a tone of voice that caused the astronomer to think, momentarily, that he was mad.

When the latter, too, had seen the strange agitation of the alcohol, he was transfixed by amazement. "Phenomenon…telluric…aurora…astonishing!" he murmured.

"We need to find out what happened to Kobyak," Wallens observed.

The astronomer made no reply. Plunged as he was in profound reflection.

Without insisting, Wallens slid into the tunnel hollowed out by the Indian through the wall of ice. Crawling on his hands and knees, he went around an abrupt bend to his left and emerged, two meters further on, beneath columns of fine but densely-aggregated snowflakes that the squalls were whirling around diabolically.

The darkness was complete, but toward the southeast—an approximate direction—Ottar Wallens thought he could make out a diffuse glow with a greenish tint, which seemed to be coming from the ground.

Was it an illusion? A mirage? Some new phenomenon of refraction? Head bowed beneath the violence of the wind, the geologist wondered.

The thought of Kobyak wrenched him from his hypotheses. At the top of his voice, he called out to the Indian. He did not see anything move, and heard nothing.

The dogs were no longer barking. Only one noise persisted: the formidable whistling of the wind.

"Kobyak! Kobyak!"

Nothing.

Ottar Wallens' disquiet gradually turned to anxiety—an anxiety close to terror, all the more so because he felt himself gripped by a bizarre feeling of sickness. It seemed to him that a powerful vibration was agitating the ground beneath his feet and the air he was breathing.

He stiffened himself, and called out again—with no more success.

In the darkness, he headed toward the sled, which formed an enormous white mound a few paces from the hut. He soon reached it. As he passed close to the dogs, he heard a few feeble whimpers, which reassured him slightly.

Stopping beside the sled, he renewed his appeals; they were as vain as the others.

The vibrations he could feel were becoming increasingly intense. It seemed to him, now, that a veritable tremor was agitating his body, the ground and the snow.

I'm going mad! he thought.

Having closed his eyes, he opened them again, and saw nothing abnormal—except for that greenish light toward the south-east, which seemed to emanate from the ground itself.

"Kobyak! Kobyak!" he shouted, again. Only the gusts of wind replied. The dogs had fallen silent.

Suddenly, Ottar Wallens was afraid—a terrible, panicky fear; the fear of going mad in the snow-veiled darkness.

It seemed to him that frightful perils were lying in wait for him. He summoned up all his self-composure, and slowly made his way back to the hut.

Not without difficulty, he found the opening, which the snow was already beginning to obstruct. He unblocked it, and, sliding into the conduit, cleared a path all the way to the interior of the hut.

Sitting on a box, with is elbows on his knees, Olaf Densmold was looking at something that he was holding in his hand.

"Kobyak hasn't come back?" asked the geologist, stupidly, although he could see perfectly well that his colleague was alone in the hut.

"No," said Densmold, curtly, raising his head. "But my compass is completely crazy. The needle is no longer pointing in any direction. It's pointing toward the ground, as if we were on top of the magnetic pole."

"Yes, yes..." Wallens murmured, preoccupied.

"What? Are you trying to say something?"

"Um…no…but I felt an odd vibration just now, and I saw…something green…a green glow, close by..."

"Ah!"

"Yes…not far from the sled," Wallens specified.

"And Kobyak?" asked Densmold, after a moment's silence.

"No trace. I called several times. I went as far as the sled. I went past the dogs. He's not there."

"Fallen in the snow, no doubt, and been covered over," Densmold muttered. "That compass worries me…after the barometer…which is increasingly unsteady. Strange!"

"And our stopped watches. You didn't feel that vibration? It was as if I were drunk, just now."

"Perhaps," the astronomer murmured. "I can't be sure..."

The wind must have lost strength, for its roaring could scarcely be heard.

Ottar Wallens sat down next to the stove. "Best to wait for daylight," he concluded. "It won't be long."

Densmold remained mute. He continued staring at the large compass he was holding in his hand. "I wonder what it means!" he murmured, eventually. "One might think that the compass were displacing alternately to either side of the magnetic equator. Look, Wallens! The needle…it sometimes points east, sometimes west. Curious!"

"Curious," the geologist repeated. "But…Kobyak? Do you think he's dead?"

Making no reply, Densmold gave a slight shrug.

Ottar Wallens shivered. "It's cold," he murmured. "If Kobyak's dead, we'll be in a difficult situation…with regard to the sled…and the dogs to look after."

"The compass worries me more. How are we going to steer?"

"We have reserve compasses..."

"Which must be as crazy as this one..."

"The stars..."

"Oh, we can take direction from them—but what if it's foggy? Anyway, perhaps the phenomenon is only temporary. It would be interesting to know the cause and write it up!"

"Let's wait for daylight," Wallens concluded. "It won't be long." So saying, the geologist got into his sleeping-bag and tried to go to sleep, without succeeding.

Densmold, still sitting on the box, continued staring at his compass. Wallens saw him suddenly get down on to his knees, introduce himself into the tunnel connecting the hut to the outside and disappear. He came back less than ten minutes later.

"It's daylight," he muttered. "I've found Kobyak."

"You...where is he?"

"Dead. Eaten by the dogs. I killed two of the beasts, trying to make them let go of his remains. I got carried away. It was a mistake. Come and see. The storm's over."

Alarmed, and still prey to a dull anxiety. Ottar Wallens slid out of his sleeping-bad, readjusted his fur garments, and went out behind the astronomer.

Outside, there was absolute calm. Nothing any longer recalled the formidable nocturnal storm. A lugubrious grayish-yellow daylight illuminated the ice-field. In a few strides, the two men were beside the dogs. On the ground, amid the blood-stained snow, the shapeless remains of Kobyak were visible. The digs, sitting motionless on their haunches, ears pricked, eyes bloodshot and muzzles panting, seemed anxious. They did not budge when they saw the scientists approaching.

"The...the *thing*! Did you see it?" Wallens demanded, extending his arm toward the south-east. He had just remembered the greenish light that he had seen during the night.

It had disappeared.

Olaf Densmold turned round. He was still holding his compass. "The thing?" he repeated. "Yes! It repels the compass needle! Come on!"

Leaving the dogs behind, the two men went around the white mound formed by the snow-covered sled and, guided by the magnetized needle, advanced at a rapid pace. They covered about a kilometer without discovering anything.

The "thing," whatever it was, was further away than they had thought.

They were beginning to doubt its existence when, having climbed a rise in the icy surface, they made out a cavity a few meters away, with the approximate form of a funnel about fifteen meters in diameter, and double that in depth.

They drew nearer to it. Having reached the edge, they recoiled, dazzled. At the bottom of the cavity lay something that looked like an enormous emerald: a polyhedral emerald with multiple facets, about seven meters in diameter. The facets, hexagonal in shape, appeared to be a little less than ten centimeters in diameter. A diffuse greenish light sprang forth from them.

Olaf Densmold shook his head and looked at his companion, who looked back at him.

At the risk of sliding into the icy funnel, they both moved a little closer to the rim. Wallens almost overbalanced; the astronomer only just had time to hold him back. A fragment of ice, dislodged by Wallens' boot, rolled into the funnel and collided with the polyhedral emerald.

A kind of hum was heard, increasing in pitch, becoming a dry whistle, which gradually intensified, modulating a series of very soft but very intense sounds one by one.

In the meantime the polyhedron changed shape.

Unable to believe their eyes, the two scientists watched the facets disappear, the walls of the *thing* becoming as smooth as those of a block of crystal, and the thing itself took on the form of a perfect sphere—a sphere of emerald!

"I'm going mad!" said Ottar Wallens, rubbing his eyes.

"*I'm going mad!*" repeated an echo from the depths of the funnel.

"Shut up," muttered Densmold, who was staring with wide open eyes, his lips pinched.

Slowly, the sphere was changing shape.

It became a cone, a cube, and then, successively, a rectangular parallelepiped, a pyramid and a cylinder: the principal figures of three-dimensional geometry.

The sounds continued to emerge. They were chromatic scales of an infinite softness, with short or long-drawn-out notes.

As motionless as statues of stupor, the two scientists watched without finding a word to say.

Suddenly, the sounds ceased. The *thing* resumed the form of a polyhedron—the one it had had originally—with glittering facets.

"Either we're crazy, or we have before us the most marvelous thing that has ever existed," said Ottar Wallens. "The men who have invented this, and who..."

"*They aren't human!*"

"They aren't human?"

"No! This…apparatus can't have been transported here. It must weigh several tons, and..."

"Oh!" Wallens exclaimed. "You think it's come…from another planet?"

"I think so. It's apparently made of a substance that doesn't exist on Earth, a magnetic metal—my compass is the proof of that—which is as malleable as mercury. That's what permits it to change shape. It doesn't flow, doubtless being attracted toward the center of the thing by apparatus we know nothing about. Magnetic or gyroscopic? And the *thing*'s inhabited. The…people inside wanted to prove their science to us by setting the principal figures of geometry before our eyes..."

"Anything's possible," Ottar Wallens admitted, who was gradually recovering from his stupor. "Although there's no reason to believe that the inhabitants of other planets make use of the same geometry as us. Henri Poincaré has demonstrated that Euclidean geometry is the most appropriate, but he also proved that others exist!"

"I know. But you're not unaware that the other planets are spherical, like the Earth…that they're composed of the same elements as our globe. Why not think that science on other planets has followed the same path as on ours?"

"We need to go down into the funnel and enter into communication with these people," Wallens murmured. "They must have means at their disposal that we don't know. It was them who, just now, reproduced my voice when I said that I was going mad. They must be able to hear us. Oh, Densmold, we've made a discovery that's a thousand, a million times more important than that of a pole! Just think that we're going to be the first humans to communicate with our brethren of other planets, and..."

"Are you sure that they're beings like us, Wallens?" the astronomer cut in, staring at his colleague.

Wallens felt a slight shiver. "I think so!" he said.

"If they are, it's necessary to be very wary, my dear chap! Man is a wolf to man! What if they intend to murder us?"

"They've come as ambassadors, and aren't stupid enough to massacre the first creatures they see! And we should be honored to be the people who welcome them..."

"Gently, Wallens! These beings, whatever they are, have come to explore the Earth. How can they know, on seeing us, that we're humans—which is to say, that we're the most civilized, and the only rational, beings on the planet? Suppose that they themselves have the form of dogs? They might think that dogs were the kings of the Earth, and that we're..."

"My dear Densmold, the best way of finding out is to go and see!" Wallens observed. "You're wasting time."

"Let's go," said the astronomer, briefly.

The sides of the funnel, carpeted with a thick layer of snow, were fairly easy to descend, all things considered.

Lying on their bellies, the two men let themselves slide over the white surface, slowing themselves down with their hands and knees. Within a few seconds they were at the bottom, their feet touching the surface of the *thing*.

They got to their feet, and realized almost immediately that the polyhedron was giving off a mild heat that had melted the ice around it, and was continuing to melt it. Thus, the *thing* was slowly descending, while hollowing out in the mass of the ice what mariners call a "bed."

Olaf Densmold knelt down beside the polyhedron and took off his gloves. With his bare hands, he felt one of the facets. The surface was as soft and smooth as the finest satin. A soft warmth emanated from it.

"Oh!" exclaimed Wallens, who was still standing up, looking into the polyhedron. "There's someone…I saw…a silhouette, like that of a human…a biped. They're human…it was a man, Densmold. I had..."

A brief whistle-blast rang out, followed by eight more.

Instinctively, the two scientists stepped back. They had felt the *thing* vibrate beneath them. Backed up against the ice, they saw the polyhedron resume a spherical form.

In its upper part a cap about seventy centimeters in diameter rose up, pushed by four rounded stalks. The lid stopped a little more than a meter above the sphere. Through the opening, an unimaginable being appeared.

It bore some resemblance to a human of short stature, but not a man possessed of true skin and bone. A sort of sheath, made of a gray substance reminiscent of lead, was molded to its torso and limbs. Of facial features, there were none to be seen. Instead of eyes, large goggles garnished with faceted lenses. Nose and mouth hidden beneath a mask bristling with hairs seemingly made of red gold. Hemispheres of gray metal, about half the size of an orange, covered the ears. The sheath enveloped the feet and hands, which—like the rest of the body—seemed to be coated with a thin layer of lead.

The extraordinary creature stood upright and leaned on the emerald lid, with slow, awkward, maladroit, almost grotesque gestures, and remained there for a few seconds, considering the two scientists—who, for their part, never took their eyes off it.

The being was undoubtedly reassured, for it walked slowly toward them. One might have thought that the soles of its feet were fitted with suckers, like the feet of flies, for it did not slip once on the uniform and sloping surface of the sphere.

"It's a Martian!" said Ottar Wallens.

"Or a Venusian," observed Densmold.

Whatever it was, the being came to meet them.

Having arrived in front of them, it extended its arm, touched them, and palpated them. They shuddered; the strange individual's hands were veritably scorching. On contact with them, the scientists felt a bizarre sensation of wellbeing and lightness. One might have thought that the hands were producing a beneficent current that gave strength and vigor.

Turning round, the being bent down, and drew several geometrical figures on the funnel's wall of ice—simple ones first, then more complicated ones: helices, ellipses and sinusoidal curves. Finally, it stopped and waited.

With the aid of his ice-axe, Olaf Densmold traced in his turn other figures of transcendent geometry.

The being must have understood their meaning very well; it immediately demonstrated relationships by means of the new symbols. And, doubtless content to have thus entered into communication with the two Terrans, it made a sign for them to follow it, climbed the side of its strange apparatus and disappeared inside.

Ottar Wallens and Olaf Densmold, with increasing alarm, observed that the surface of the sphere was now becoming uneven—which permitted them to climb up it relatively easily.

The astronomer introduced himself into the opening first. He fell about four meters on to an elastic floor, which deadened his fall, and was immediately joined by Wallens.

The two men saw that they were in a spherical compartment about four meters in diameter, whose walls produced a greenish phosphorescent light—the same shade that Wallens had perceived the night before. By means of gestures, the bizarre being drew the attention of its guests to a motionless globe floating like a balloon, equidistant from the floor and the ceiling. It was made of a shiny black substance somewhat reminiscent of agate, and measured less than a meter in diameter.

The being touched it. Luminous dots appeared on its surface, irregularly disposed.

"Oh!" Densmold exclaimed, in a strangled voice. "But that's a map of the sky…seen…seen from Mercury!"

"From Mercury?"

"Yes, from the planet nearest to the Sun, which completes its orbit in twenty-eight days, and where the ambient temperature must be frightful! Look—there's the Sun…and then, on the other side, Venus, Earth, Mars... Marvelous! Satellites unknown to us... Oh!"

The luminous dots had abruptly disappeared. The entire sphere was suddenly nothing but a block of light.

Shadows appeared on it.

Gradually, the two scientists recognized the terrestrial continents: the two Americas, the Old World, Australia...

But a kind of fog erased everything, and, as if they were stationed at the ocular of a colossal telescope, the two men saw passing before them plains, oceans and cities—cities whose houses appeared, one after another, in their natural dimensions.

"New York!" said Densmold, who had traveled a great deal. "Can you see Long Island? The Singer Building? Ah! There's a tropical island…an archipelago…doubtless the Bermudas..."

Europe… London...

Everything disappeared. The black sphere lit up inside again.

Breathlessly, Densmold and his companion made out a planet where everything was red, covered by banks of clouds.

"Mars! That's Mars!" Densmold explained.

Was it Mars? Who could say? Strange cities appeared, complicated architectures, among which were beings resembling humans equipped with crabs' pincers and protruding eyes, circulating and jumping about, accompanied by other nightmare creatures.

And again, the sphere went black.

Not far away, a kind of large funnel made of gray material, filled with a liquid that resembled molten gold, as suspended above a tripod. The strange being took the knife that Densmold was carrying in his belt and threw it into the funnel.

The wooden handle disappeared immediately, as if eaten away by an acid. The steel blade bubbled, lost its form, became a sort of sponge, and changed color.

The being took the metal fragment out of the vat and handed it to the astronomer.

"Oh! But...it's silver!" exclaimed Densmold, after examining it.

Ottar Wallens took it from his hands and ascertained, with no possible doubt, that the steel blade had been changed into a silvery mineral.

The metal fragment having been handed back to the extraordinary being, it was successively transformed into lead, gold, platinum...

"The unity of matter! They've mastered the unity of matter!" murmured Densmold, almost wild-eyed.

But the being took his hands and made him touch two balls, reminiscent of diamonds, embedded in the wall.

Immediately, the astronomer felt his fatigue disappear. Blood flowed to his brain. Everything seemed clear to him, natural and ordered. It seemed to him that he was now capable of solving the most transcendental problems.

Ottar Wallens, having touched the two balls felt the same impression of physical contentment in his turn.

They had not yet seen everything.

By means of an invisible mechanism, the uncanny creature caused a trapdoor framed in the floor to rise up. Through the opening, the two scientists made out pistons, crank-shafts and complicated cog-wheels.

"It's all broken in there!" Wallens suddenly exclaimed, leaning over the hole. "That's why he had to land!"

The geologist straightened up. He felt rejuvenated. He had recovered the vigor he had had at twenty. A large smile had spread across his sullen face, and the austere and taciturn Densmold was in the same state of mind.

With its hand, the being showed the scientists a box set on the floor. It pressed lightly on one of its corners, and a dull hum became audible.

By means of gestures, the being tried to explain something that must have been very important. Densmold and Wallens racked their brains, looking at one another, but they did not understand—no, they did not understand.

Tirelessly, the being repeated its demonstration, its explanation.

A gentle music resounded, in different keys, divided into three parts, its chords as marvelous as any terrestrial musician had ever contrived.

The ball on which the map of the sky, terrestrial cities and those of another planet had appeared lit up. Fleshless faces appeared, their skulls scarcely covered by thin parchment-like pellicle, with toothless mouths and piercing little round eyes like balls of emerald. Those eyes were gazing with curiosity and anguish; the features vibrated, grimacing.

They were doubtless inhabitants of Venus or Mercury, who could see their fellow—the one they had sent to Earth and for whom they could do nothing—by means of the mysterious sphere.

Ottar Wallens and Olaf Densmold, their hearts gripped by anxiety of a dolorous sympathy, saw the being turn back to them and, doubtless, stare at them through its thick goggles. They thought they saw the lenses of the goggles dulled by a slight mist.

"He's weeping!" murmured Wallens.

The agate ball became black again.

For ten seconds or so, the scientists and their host remained motionless. The green light emanating from the walls enveloped them with a livid halo that gave them a phantasmal appearance.

The being continued to stare at the two men.

Finally, it seemed to come to a decision, and leaned over the box that had produced the extraordinary music and few minutes earlier. Crackling vibrations were coming from it, separated by silences. These vibrations were sometimes brief and sometimes prolonged. Each series differed from the preceding one, as much by its sonorous intensity as the rapidity with which the sounds were emitted.

"Those vibrations," Densmold murmured, listening to them, "doubtless represent the relationship of things—of everything. The world is nothing but an ensemble of vibrations, Wallens, as you know; the slowest are sonorous, then luminous. Sound, light and matter are merely vibrations differing only in intensity. Those we can hear—I sense it—represent all the states of matter: solid, liquid, gaseous, sonorous, luminous, electrical. The great secret is in front of us and this man…this being…knows it. Look!"

Shadows appeared on the black ball. A dazzling violet light appeared.

"Luminous vibrations," murmured the astronomer.

A sort of hemispherical gong appeared in silhouette; the two scientists saw it vibrate, while the sonorous waves emitted by the box resounded more slowly...

There was no mistake about it; the mysterious being was trying to communicate the different wavelengths of luminous and sonorous waves to the humans. It was doubtless watching their faces for the effect of his demonstration. But did it understand human expressions? Who could ever know?

It suddenly stopped its fantastic experiment and, as if seized by a new idea, bent down. Through the trapdoor opened in the floor it pointed out to its guests the displaced cogwheels and the bent crank-shafts of the mysterious mechanism that they had already seen.

"The engine that permitted this machine to get here has broken down," Wallens murmured, shaking his head, "and the poor Mercurian—if he is a Mercurian—takes us for miserable savages from whom he can't get any sense. Our science is nothing by comparison with his. We need to take him back to the *Sirius*, and then come to fetch his apparatus…or, at least, to take it apart.

"Enclosed in this hull are the solutions to the principal scientific problems that have been studied since the world began. If we can succeed in understanding the Mercurian and making ourselves understood, human science might gain ten centuries. Think that this being is familiar with vision at a distance, through the ether, that he can communicate with other planets that he..."

"Yes, but if he dies, or we die, all that is lost," Densmold interjected.

A faint whistle was heard.

The being, who was standing under the opening of the sphere, rose up slowly, vertically, as if drawn by a balloon. Beneath him, the two men thought they could make out a shadow—the shadow of a cylinder on which he was standing.

Having reached the rim of the opening, the being climbed on to it, awkwardly, and disappeared outside. His arms showed through the hole and made the two men understand that they should place themselves under the opening, as he had done.

Wallens, whose mind was a little quicker than his companion's, was the first to divine what was being asked of him. He immediately felt himself lifted up, as if by the floor of a elevator—and yet his feet were not resting on anything visible.

Having climbed over the rim of the opening, he stood upright on the sphere beside the mysterious being. Densmold joined him shortly afterwards.

With its extended arm, the being immediately indicated the four cardinal points. It pointed to the Sun, around which its hand described a kind of orbit. Then, still moving awkwardly, it descended from the sphere and stepped on to the bottom of the funnel of ice, the slope of which it began to climb.

The two scientists followed it without saying a word, wondering what it intended to do.

The being reached the surface of the ice-field and stood up. Densmold and Wallens saw it suddenly shiver and recoil, in the grip of a terrible fear.

Two of the dogs forming part of the sled-team had just appeared.

"Get back, filthy beasts!" growled Densmold.

Too late! The two dogs, in unison, had leapt at the being's throat. It closed its hands upon them.

A whistling sound drowned out the barking of the dogs; a puff of green smoke sprang forth, and the group—the being and the dogs—collapsed on the ice, as if thunderstruck.

Rooted to the spot, the two scientists watched. They no longer understood, no longer knew...

The dogs already had vitreous eyes. They were quite dead…but what about the mysterious being?

Densmold was the first to recover. He went to the inert body of the extraordinary individual and touched its arm. A feeble shock, like that produced by an electric current, made him jump.

He stepped back, livid.

The being still did not move.

"But…it's *burning*!" Wallens exclaimed, hoarsely.

It was true. A mist was rising from the body lying on the ice.

The two scientists, who thought that they were going mad, saw the sheath of grey metal curl up, open and burst, revealing red parchment-like skin; they heard crackling: the ear-covers, the goggles and the mask melted under the action of a heat whose source remained invisible. And around the body, the ice liquefied, forming little rivulets of muddy water that congealed again a few meters further away under the effect of the rigorous ambient temperature. The hair of the two dogs turned red, mingling its characteristic odor with the acrid and metallic scent emitted by the cadaver of the nameless being.

In less than five minutes, it was all over. Nothing more remained on the ice but the bodies of the two dogs, half-consumed by fire, and a few blackened strands similar to tin-plate debris.

"I'm wondering if I might be mad," said Wallens, gravely.

"We aren't mad," Densmold affirmed. "But we might yet go mad, irrespective of all this. We have to set a course and make a forced march back to the *Sirius*. We can get there in ten days..."

"What about the compass?"

"Oh—yes! Well, if we can't make use of our compasses, we'll use the wireless telegraph to call for help, giving them our position."

"That might be better."

Without saying any more, the two men headed back to the sled. In the hours that followed they cleared away the thick layer of snow that had covered it—a rude and thankless task; the intense cold had hardened the snow, and made it difficult to scrape away.

Finally, the sled was free. The scientists reached the wireless telegraph apparatus.

With pausing for a moment's rest, without even eating anything, they set up the collapsible antenna they had brought, made of tubes of duralumin that slid into one another, and stabilized it by means of stays.

It was dark—a pale and foggy night—by the time they had finished. They rapidly heated up a little tea and pemmican in the hut where they had spent the preceding night, swallowed it all and went back to work, by the light of little electric torches.

All the efforts they had just made were in vain. Olaf Densmold realized that the apparatus was no longer working. The accumulators were flat. Guaranteed accumulators, tested extensively before their departure! It was impossible to send any message at all.

"Nothing to be done!" murmured the astronomer, having re-examined the accumulators. "The *thing* must have caused our accumulators to lose their charge. We have no option but to go back to the *Sirius*."

Ottar Wallens made no reply. He looked at his colleague, and they both understood. They were thinking about the crazed compasses. It would be necessary to navigate by the stars. If it had not been for the fog, that might have been possible, albeit difficult—but for want of precision in their calculations, the two men risked wandering for a long time on the ice before rejoining their ship—and their provisions would not last forever.

"We'll get our bearings as often as possible," Densmold declared. "We'll rectify our direction as many times as necessary, but we'll get there. It's the destiny of humankind that we're holding in our hands!"

"Yes," the geologist murmured, "that's true..."

They distributed a ration of smoked salmon to the dogs, checked their ropes—for only the two dogs that had perished with the being had escaped—and went back into their ice-hut.

All night long they talked, feeling neither cold nor fatigue; the marvelous possibilities opened to science by the extraordinary apparatus fallen from the sky kept their minds occupied. Innumerable problems, biological, astronomical and geological, were about to be elucidated. Mathematics would make progress. They would know what electricity was, what matter was, what life itself was!

And while human beings still existed on Earth, or even on the neighboring planets, the names of Ottar Wallens and Olaf Densmold would never die! What glory! A superhuman glory, above all others!

At daybreak, the two men rapidly swallowed a little tea and dried powdered eggs. They went out. The weather was good.

The two scientists, not without a certain awkwardness, repacked the equipment of the camp. They loaded it on to the sled, to which they hitched the dogs. And headed northwards, toward the *Sirius*.

They soon realized that they were not going as fast as they had hoped. The dogs, reduced in number by four, and instinctively divining the inexperience of their guides, only went forward slowly, stopping whenever they liked and only starting off again when they wanted to.

All the compasses remained crazy, and it was necessary to navigate by means of the sun.

At midday, Densmold called a halt and took a bearing. He calculated that the sled had drawn thirteen kilometers nearer to the *Sirius*. Only half a stage! More than four hundred kilometers remained to be traversed before reaching the ship—four hundred kilometers in a straight line, which meant more than six hundred in reality.

"We'll have to ration ourselves," Wallens declared.

"Yes."

The two men ate, and set off again, still as slowly.

They covered twelve stages: less than a hundred kilometers, for several times, enveloped by the fog, the explorers went astray and lost ground.

The compasses were no longer crazy now—they were no longer functioning at all, the needles having lost their magnetic properties due to some unknown cause.

But the supplies might last two months with careful rationing...

Alas, one night, while the two exhausted scientists were asleep, the dogs, having detached their insecurely-fixed ropes, had a feast. Pemmican, flour, smoked salmon, dried eggs—they spoiled what they did not devour.

When they awoke, Densmold and his companion saw the disaster at first glance. The dogs had fled, and of their provisions, nothing to speak of remained.

"It was you who tied up the dogs yesterday!" Densmold remarked, fixing is colleague with a cold stare.

"I tied them up solidly—I don't know what's happened!" the geologist protested, in all good faith.

"Let's gather up what can be saved," said Densmold, without persisting. "It's not much, but we couldn't carry any more, and the sled's too heavy for us to think of taking it."

What remained? Enough for them to live on half-rations for a week, perhaps, and then...

Without saying a word, the two men collected the debris of every sort that was scattered over the ice.

The appetite of the big dogs of Alaska is formidable. The beasts had not left much.

In an hour, they had finished.

The scientists, bent beneath the weight of their sleeping-bags and their meager provisions, set off over the interminable ice-field.

Wallens was carrying the stove and the supply of alcohol, Densmold had taken charged of the sextant, the chronometer and the books necessary to calculate a bearing.

Fortunately, the weather was good.

Six stages were crossed.

The food supplies diminished rapidly. In order to be able to march, the unfortunates had to eat.

No more fog. They were now advancing in the right direction.

"No more than 101 kilometers," Densmold declared, one day, having taken a bearing. "The ice is flat here; we can do that in three days..."

"Yes, but we only have a pound of pemmican left."

That day, the two men each ate fifty grams of food, and made one final cup of tea with the last of their alcohol.

Densmold, although he was the older, still had some strength, but Wallens seemed reduced to the utmost limit of weakness. They decided to rest for a few hours before setting out again.

With empty stomachs, and their temples beating anemically, they lay down side by side in their sleeping-bags.

Toward the middle of the night, Wallens, who was not asleep, caught sight of his companion slip out of his sleeping-bag, stick the little bag containing the last of the pemmican in his belt, roll up his pack and put it on his shoulders.

He understood. Densmold, who had reproached him several times for slowness, was about to abandon him, in order to travel more rapidly and keep for himself the scraps of provisions that constituted their last resource.

"Densmold!" he called out, involuntarily.

The astronomer turned round. "Oh, you're awake," he said, coldly. "Well, yes, I'm leaving you. We'll both perish if I wait for you, that that won't do anyone any good. I'm going to try to reach the *Sirius* by a forced march. Someone will come to look for you. *Au revoir!*"

"Densmold! You can't do that! You can't abandon me..."

"I can," declared the astronomer, who had paused. "It's my duty. Science before all! You'll slow me down. If I stayed with you, we'd both perish. Adieu!"

And he drew away at a rapid pace.

Ottar Wallens groped at his belt. In spite of his weakness, he had kept an automatic pistol, in order to make use of it if some prey appeared. He armed it, raised his hand, took aim and pressed the trigger.

A detonation. A scream.

His skull shattered, Olaf Densmold collapsed on the ice, and did not move again.

Exactly two weeks later, the little expedition sent out by the Sirius in search of the two scientists who had not come back discovered Olaf Densmold's corpse lying on the ice, with a bullet in his head.

And Ottar Wallens? Had he died of hunger? Of cold? Had he been swallowed by a crevasse, in a snowstorm? He was never found.

And somewhere, toward the austral pole, the nameless engine, come from who knows where, continues, under the action of its weight—if it is subject thereto—to sink into the ice, taking with it the secrets for which humans have been searching for hundreds of millennia, and will find…when?

SF & FANTASY

Henri Allorge. *The Great Cataclysm*
Guy d'Armen. *Doc Ardan: The City of Gold and Lepers*
G.-J. Arnaud. *The Ice Company*
Cyprien Bérard. *The Vampire Lord Ruthwen*
Aloysius Bertrand. *Gaspard de la Nuit*
Richard Bessière. *The Gardens of the Apocalypse*
Albert Bleunard. *Ever Smaller*
Félix Bodin. *The Novel of the Future*
Alphonse Brown. *City of Glass*
André Caroff. *The Terror of Madame Atomos; Miss Atomos; The Return of Madame Atomos; The Mistake of Madame Atomos*
Félicien Champsaur. *The Human Arrow*
Didier de Chousy. *Ignis*
Captain Danrit. *Undersea Odyssey*
C. I. Defontenay. *Star (Psi Cassiopeia)*
Charles Derennes. *The People of the Pole*
Georges Dodds (anthologist). *The Missing Link*
Harry Dickson. *The Heir of Dracula*
Jules Dornay. *Lord Ruthven Begins*
Alfred Driou. *The Adventures of a Parisian Aeronaut*
Sâr Dubnotal *vs. Jack the Ripper*
Alexandre Dumas. *The Return of Lord Ruthven*
Renée Dunan. *Baal*
J.-C. Dunyach. *The Night Orchid; The Thieves of Silence*
Henri Duvernois. *The Man Who Found Himself*
Achille Eyraud. *Voyage to Venus*
Henri Falk. *The Age of Lead*
Paul Féval. *Anne of the Isles; Knightshade; Revenants; Vampire City; The Vampire Countess; The Wandering Jew's Daughter*
Paul Féval, *fils. Felifax, the Tiger-Man*
Charles de Fieux. *Lamékis*
Arnould Galopin. *Doctor Omega*; *Doctor Omega & The Shadowmen*
G.L. Gick. *Harry Dickson and the Werewolf of Rutherford Grange*
Nathalie Henneberg. *The Green Gods*
V. Hugo, P. Foucher & P. Meurice. *The Hunchback of Notre-Dame*
Michel Jeury. *Chronolysis*
Octave Joncquel & Théo Varlet. *The Martian Epic*
Gustave Kahn. *The Tale of Gold and Silence*

Gérard Klein. *The Mote in Time's Eye*
Jean de La Hire. *Enter the Nyctalope; The Nyctalope on Mars; The Nyctalope vs. Lucifer; The Nyctalope Steps In*
Etienne-Léon de Lamothe-Langon. *The Virgin Vampire*
André Laurie. *Spiridon*
Gabriel de Lautrec. *The Vengeance of the Oval Portrait*
Georges Le Faure & Henri de Graffigny. *The Extraordinary Adventures of a Russian Scientist Across the Solar System* (2 vols.)
Gustave Le Rouge. *The Vampires of Mars*
Jules Lermina. *Mysteryville; Panic in Paris; To-Ho and the Gold Destroyers; The Secret of Zippelius*
Jean-Marc & Randy Lofficier. *Edgar Allan Poe on Mars; The Katrina Protocol; Pacifica; Robonocchio; Tales of the Shadowmen 1-8*
Xavier Mauméjean. *The League of Heroes*
José Moselli. *Illa's End*
John-Antoine Nau. *Enemy Force*
Marie Nizet. *Captain Vampire*
C. Nodier, A. Beraud & Toussaint-Merle. *Frankenstein*
Henri de Parville. *An Inhabitant of the Planet Mars*
Gaston de Pawlowski. *Journey to the Land of the 4th Dimension*
Georges Pellerin. *The World in 2000 Years*
J. Polidori, C. Nodier, E. Scribe. *Lord Ruthven the Vampire*
P.-A. Ponson du Terrail. *The Vampire and the Devil's Son*
Maurice Renard. *The Blue Peril; Doctor Lerne; The Doctored Man; A Man Among the Microbes; The Master of Light*
Jean Richepin. *The Wing*
Albert Robida. *The Adventures of Saturnin Farandoul; The Clock of the Centuries; Chalet in the Sky*
J.-H. Rosny Aîné. *Helgvor of the Blue River; The Givreuse Enigma; The Mysterious Force; The Navigators of Space; Vamireh; The World of the Variants; The Young Vampire*
Marcel Rouff. *Journey to the Inverted World*
Han Ryner. *The Superhumans*
Brian Stableford. *The New Faust at the Tragicomique;The Empire of the Necromancers (The Shadow of Frankenstein; Frankenstein and the Vampire Countess; Frankenstein in London); Sherlock Holmes & The Vampires of Eternity; The Stones of Camelot; The Wayward Muse.* (anthologist) *The Germans on Venus; News from the Moon; The Supreme Progress; The World Above the World; Nemoville*
Jacques Spitz. *The Eye of Purgatory*
Kurt Steiner. *Ortog*

Eugène Thébault. *Radio-Terror*
C.-F. Tiphaigne de La Roche. *Amilec*
Théo Varlet. *The Xenobiotic Invasion*
Paul Vibert. *The Mysterious Fluid*
Villiers de l'Isle-Adam. *The Scaffold; The Vampire Soul*
Philippe Ward. *Artahe*
Philippe Ward & Sylvie Miller. *The Song of Montségur*

MYSTERIES & THRILLERS

M. Allain & P. Souvestre. *The Daughter of Fantômas*
A. Anicet-Bourgeois, Lucien Dabril. *Rocambole*
A. Bisson & G. Livet. *Nick Carter vs. Fantômas*
V. Darlay & H. de Gorsse. *Lupin vs. Holmes: The Stage Play*
Paul Féval. *Gentlemen of the Night; John Devil; The Black Coats ('Salem Street; The Invisible Weapon; The Parisian Jungle; The Companions of the Treasure; Heart of Steel; The Cadet Gang; The Sword-Swallower)*
Emile Gaboriau. *Monsieur Lecoq*
Steve Leadley. *Sherlock Holmes: The Circle of Blood*
Maurice Leblanc. *Arsène Lupin vs. Countess Cagliostro; Lupin vs. Holmes (The Blonde Phantom; The Hollow Needle)*
Gaston Leroux. *Chéri-Bibi; The Phantom of the Opera; Rouletabille & the Mystery of the Yellow Room*
William Patrick Maynard. *The Terror of Fu Manchu*
Frank J. Morlock. *Sherlock Holmes: The Grand Horizontals; Sherlock Holmes vs Jack the Ripper*
P. de Wattyne & Y. Walter. *Sherlock Holmes vs. Fantômas*
David White. *Fantômas in America*

SCREENPLAYS

Mike Baron. *The Iron Triangle*
Emma Bull & Will Shetterly. *Nightspeeder; War for the Oaks*
Gerry Conway & Roy Thomas. *Doc Dynamo*
Steve Englehart. *Majorca*
James Hudnall. *The Devastator*
Jean-Marc & Randy Lofficier. *Royal Flush*
J.-M. & R. Lofficier & Marc Agapit. *Despair*
Andrew Paquette. *Peripheral Vision*
R. Thomas, J. Hendler & L. Sprague de Camp. *Rivers of Time*

www.ingramcontent.com/pod-product-compliance
Lightning Source LLC
Chambersburg PA
CBHW060422030726
47495CB00003B/687